What People Ar

Dirk Strasser's Conquist
and Previous Titles

Dirk Strasser's novel *Conquist* with its deep characters and historic odyssey is an enchanting story splashed with darkness and light.
Eugen Bacon, World Fantasy Award finalist and award-winning author of *Danged Black Thing*, *Mage of Fools* and *Chasing Whispers*

Strasser is a master ... It is a joy to behold Dirk's impressive oeuvre finally getting the notice it so justly deserves: I won't be able to call him an unsung hero for very much longer. Enjoy and behold what the fuss is all about. Now turn the goddamn page and watch the show! It's Dirk Strasser time.
Jack Dann, Nebula and World Fantasy Award winner

Strasser tells a riveting odyssey of conquest, magic, and redemption that fans of historical fantasy will devour.
Gabriel Robertson, *Aurealis*

Praise for *The Books of Ascension*
Dirk Strasser's *Zenith* ... is on my list of all-time worldwide Top Ten fantasy novels ... It does what all good quest novels do and does it better than almost any of them—that is, it creates wonders.
Richard Harland, multi award-winning fantasy author of *Worldshaker*

I read the last two hundred pages in a single sitting ... *Zenith* deserves to sell as many copies as all the other best-selling quest fantasy novels which fill our bookstores, if only because it does what they do as well as (if not better than) they do it. *Zenith* is enjoyable, entertaining and, in the end, a satisfying read. What more can I ask for?
Eidolon

Apart from *Lord of the Rings* and *Game of Thrones*, the other fantasy series I've really enjoyed include *The Books of Ascension* trilogy by Dirk Strasser ... there will be a song called "Mountain of Sorrows" based on this series on the next Elvenpath album *Pieces of Fate*.
Till Oberbossel, lead guitarist and songwriter for German power metal band Elvenpath

These books have shown me why I appreciate and love fantasy so much. All of the parts of this trilogy blend so effortlessly ... This series is one that fantasy fans will adore and fly through. If you haven't discovered Dirk Strasser's *The Books of Ascension* series, do yourself a favor and pick them up. You'll not be disappointed.
Pretty Little Pages

The world sucked me in like some Stargate with its action sequences, the political maneuvering and interactions between the characters.
Keiko Mushi, *Fantasy Books That You Might Not Have Heard Of*

With great writing, characters who go through such steady development readers can easily follow along on their journey, and an epic, engaging world, Dirk Strasser has weaved an intriguing fantasy series that is a must-read for all fans of epic fantasy.
I Heart Reading

When I finished this last book in the trilogy, I was sad to leave Atreu's world ... When a reader becomes that engrossed, that connected to the tale and its people, that is the sign of masterful writing!
Tome Tender

Strasser's descriptive writing style made me feel like I was actually watching this on the big screen ... I recommend this series to science-fiction and fantasy lovers. In particular those who like stories centered around epic journeys like *The Lord of the Rings*.
Readers and Writers Connect

This one will set the heart aflutter for the true fantasy reader ... and with a dose of spiritualism and action tossed in the mix, it's bound to attract the attention of several genres.
For the Love of Books

Conquist

A Novel

Conquist

A Novel

Dirk Strasser

ROUNDFIRE
BOOKS

London, UK
Washington, DC, USA

CollectiveInk

First published by Roundfire Books, 2024
Roundfire Books is an imprint of Collective Ink Ltd.,
Unit 11, Shepperton House, 89 Shepperton Road, London, N1 3DF
office@collectiveinkbooks.com
www.collectiveinkbooks.com
www.roundfire-books.com

For distributor details and how to order please visit the 'Ordering' section on our website.

Text copyright: Dirk Strasser 2023

ISBN: 978 1 80341 603 8
978 1 80341 610 6 (ebook)
Library of Congress Control Number: 2023941511

A CIP catalogue record for this book is available from the British Library.

Design: Lapiz Digital Services
Cover artist: Alejandro Colucci

UK: Printed and bound by CPI Group (UK) Ltd, Croydon, CR0 4YY
US: Printed and bound by Thomson-Shore, 7300 West Joy Road, Dexter, MI 48130

We operate a distinctive and ethical publishing philosophy in all areas of our business, from our global network of authors to production and worldwide distribution.

Contents

For Lucy

Acknowledgments

Many fellow travelers have joined me at different stages on this long and perilous journey through the *Conquist* portal. I would like to thank, in historical order: Michael Pryor, Stephen Higgins, Jack Dann, Van Ikin, Avan Stallard, Robert Goodman, David Catt, Karen Parks, Paul Kots, Samantha McHenry, Kami McArthur, Scott Vandervalk, Terry Wood, Genni Matty, Andrew Saltmarsh, Peter Allert, Simon Walpole, Lynette Watters, Matt Bissett-Johnson, Emma Weakley, Kim Lennard, Leah Clementson, Beth Mason, Linda Sengsourinho, Lorraine Cormack, Nathan Phillips, Paula Boer, Jon Oliver, Alejandro Colucci, John Romans and Gavin Davies.

Author's Note

This novel is based on the first English translation of a diary that came to light in an archive in the *Museo Nacional de Arqueología, Antropología e Historia del Perú* in Lima. The extracts are included with the kind permission of the translator. Cristóbal de Varga was a distant cousin of both Hernán Cortés and Francisco Pizarro who, unlike Pizarro and many of the other conquistadors of his time, was highly literate. This very facility with words has lent credence to those that claim his journal comprised merely the fevered imaginings of a man frustrated by his own lack of success in an age where others were making their fortunes. A recent spectral analysis of the cover of the diary, however, has shown that what was thought to be solidified droplets of gold may, in fact, be a previously unknown chemical element.

Dirk Strasser

Chapter 1

El diario de Cristóbal de Varga

We conquistadors suffer from a disease whose symptom is an insatiable thirst for gold. Unlike other fevers, ours cause those innocent of infection to die. I know this, yet I still write these words in the fervent hope that my name will echo with Francisco Pizarro and Hernán Cortés.

On the eve of All Souls in the year of Our Lord 1538, I, Cristóbal de Varga, humble servant of His Imperial Majesty Charles V, King of Spain and Holy Roman Emperor, led my six hundred conquistadors through an *entrada* into a new world.

But that is not when my tale truly began. Was it when I first felt the bright ache for the riches of New Spain as I stood on the banks of Seville's Guadalquivir River and saw the square-rigged galleon sails swell in the gusting wind? Or was it the day my family lost the last of its noble pretenses and was overcome by grinding poverty with the death of my father? Or perhaps it began when I gained my commission from His Majesty King Charles V. No, I know when my tale took flight. It began when I first tasted the acrid sweetness of conquest, the day I fully experienced the florid symptoms of the conquistador's disease. It was the day many innocents perished in the grip of our contagion. The day we sacked Machu Picchu.

Chapter 2

At Sun's Gate

As dawn broke across the blue-ice Andean skies, Capitán Cristóbal de Varga breathed in the tension of the six hundred conquistadors at his back. He had always believed that those on the verge of victory could smell it in advance. And right now the sharp tang of triumph seared his nostrils. He ran his fingers across his smooth-shaven face, feeling the creases from a lifetime of watching men grow rich while he merely grew older. Finally, after all the years since he and his cousin Diego had stowed away on that galleon to the New World, his moment of conquest had arrived. The Sun Gate to Machu Picchu lay before him.

His horse shifted restlessly. He nodded to the two men that flanked him. Lieutenant Héctor Valiente acknowledged him with his usual composed impenetrable look, his black African face stark against the snow-capped peaks. In contrast Lieutenant Rodrigo Benalcázar's lean frame and pinched features teemed with energy as his fierce eyes focused on the steps in front of them.

Cristóbal raised his sword skyward.

"For the glory of God!"

Battle cries of *"Santiago y cierra, España"* resounded behind him. He urged his mount forward and led the charge on Machu Picchu, his heart hammering his chest. He rode on the wave of surging conquistadors, breathless, sweat streaming from his pores despite the cold. This was what he had relentlessly pursued for most of his life. It was in his grasp.

Suddenly the morning rays poured through the Sun Gate and a bright flash filled Cristóbal's vision. The brief revelation that it was a sign of God's grace quickly dissipated. He was riding blind. He faltered.

A volley of slingstones struck his armor.

Shielding his eyes, he looked down. A distorted halo encircled the stone steps.

He struggled to regain his momentum.

More slingstones rang against his helmet, echoing into his ears.

A spear bounced off his horse's armor.

But nothing was going to block his path this time. Not now that the prize was so close. He gritted his teeth and pushed his horse back into a gallop.

As he reached the gate, Incan soldiers set upon him with axes and star-headed clubs. Determined to stay on his mount, he swung his sword furiously, slicing through their cotton armor and wooden shields. He led the thrust through the Incan defenses until the path was clear for his soldiers, who then poured through the Sun Gate hacking at any Incas standing their ground.

Cristóbal pulled back on his reins and let his men ride past him. The misshapen halo faded, and his vision cleared as he watched his conquistadors swarm into the defenseless citadel cradled between two peaks.

The Incas ran from their houses in a wild panic, some scrambling up the terraced hills while others sought to escape by the rope bridge that spanned the Urubamba River. The bridge was sagging under the weight of numbers when the conquistadors started cutting through the ropes with their swords. Then it collapsed and hundreds of Incas plummeted into the gorge. Screaming.

Cristóbal rode into Machu Picchu to the sound of despairing cries. He was joined by his two lieutenants, Héctor and Rodrigo, and they headed for the royal palace near the main square.

They entered the palace to the sound of flutes. In the center of the chamber were two Incan nobles sitting on a nest of embroidered cushions and surrounded by servants. The man's effete features were wreathed by a scarlet *llautu* crowned with two feathers, and his earrings stretched his lobes so that they hung half-way to his shoulders. The woman was draped in jewel-studded garments of vicuña wool. Her fringe framed the flawless copper-brown of her face and two snake ornaments hung from her ears.

In front of them was a pile of gold statues and jewelry.

The nobleman waved the flute players into silence and addressed Cristóbal in Spanish. "We wish you welcome to Machu Picchu. I am Huarcay and this is my sister Sarpay."

Cristóbal pointed to the pile of gold. "That can't be all of it."

"Machu Picchu is only an empire outpost," said Huarcay.

Rodrigo drew his sword and took a step toward the nobleman. "Where's the rest?"

Cristóbal gestured Rodrigo to wait. "It's not enough," he said to Huarcay. "It's nowhere near enough."

The nobleman gestured his flute players into silence. "I can give you much more."

Cristóbal noticed Sarpay looking at him and his eyes locked on hers.

Huarcay said, "I can give you the emperor."

Héctor nudged Cristóbal who returned his attention to Huarcay.

"You know where Manco Inca is hiding?"

"Yes, I can take you to the gold of Vilcabamba."

Chapter 3

The Entrada
Six months later...

Lieutenant Héctor Valiente led the pursuit as he and Jorge galloped through the snow-specked valley. Their horses kicked up wild snow clouds and sent wild llamas scurrying up the slopes. Héctor bore down on an Incan *chaski* runner clutching a quipu of colored knots to his chest. He knew he was pushing his mount to its limits, but he wasn't about to let a royal messenger get away.

The runner headed toward a large gap in the mountainside. He glanced over his shoulder, his eyes locking on Héctor's for a brief moment. As he plunged into the pass, lights shimmered across the entrance.

And the runner abruptly vanished.

Héctor pulled to a halt. He removed his crested helmet, his breath clouding in the frigid air. The sunlight was cold on his dark skin as he stared transfixed at the opening in the mountain.

Jorge pulled up next to him and pointed to the break in the rock.

"I know where he went," said Héctor, frowning. "I saw him enter the pass."

"Then why have we stopped? The capitán won't be happy if—"

"I'm not interested in what you think Capitán de Varga will say." Héctor swallowed hard. There it was again. Why did they always question his decisions despite his rank? As always, he forced the fury back so it settled deep in the pit of his stomach.

"Come on, we're wasting time."

Blood rushed to Héctor's face. "Is this how you speak to your lieutenant?" He steadied his voice. "Something strange happened."

"I'm going after the runner."

"I haven't given the—"

Jorge was already charging toward the pass.

Héctor dug his heels into his mount and gave chase.

The curtain of light flickered.

And Jorge and his horse disappeared.

Héctor panicked and snapped back hard on his reins. His mount reared, and the lieutenant was flung to the ground.

He got to his feet, too shocked to feel any pain.

"Jorge?"

The only answer was the sharp-edged silence of the Andean snowscape.

An unearthly chill pierced him. Something he had not felt since the dark days before he had escaped the copper mines of Hispaniola. A time when he saw a *bokor* make a goat vanish, leaving a sheet of blood suspended momentarily mid-air before it rained to the ground.

He drew his sword and tentatively moved forward. The curtain flashed in and out of his vision as he approached. Of course, it's just another pass, he told himself. There's no dark *maji* here. But the chill froze the words into a lie. It was as if the Spanish armor he wore to conceal his past was slowly dissolving, leaving him exposed to the cold scrape of an ice blade on his skin.

Was that the death rattle of an *asson* he could hear? Impossible. Not here in the snows of the Andes. Even in his youth he knew the staccato sound of the *bokor* calling the spirits was no more than snake vertebrae inside a gourd, but it had never lost its power to unnerve him.

He drew closer to the curtain, his hand shaking as he clenched the hilt of his sword. He couldn't let the runner escape. After so many months in the Andes, finally they had a sign they were looking in the right place. How could he explain his fear to the capitán?

"*Ago!*"

An African voice, an echo he had long suppressed, resounded in his head.

No, you aren't here. You can't be. Leave me. I'm not what I once was.

Héctor stopped in front of the shimmering curtain which extended the full width of the pass, hanging from an impossible height where it merged with the sky.

"Jorge?" His voice sounded thin to his own ears.

Héctor shivered as he looked through to the other side. The pass appeared to continue but there was no sign of anyone. Chillingly, there were no hoof prints visible on the ground.

The gossamer curtain glinted tantalizingly close. Héctor touched it with his sword and the tip disappeared. Drawing a sharp breath, he thrust the blade all the way in until his hand also vanished. He pulled back quickly at the sensation of heat on his skin, and his sword rematerialized.

Only now his blade was streaked with blood.

Ago! The *bokor*'s cry echoed inside his head again and his heart pounded.

He steadied his breathing. If he was able to control his anger, he could also control his fear. He was a conquistador now. Not a powerless slave.

Brandishing his bloodied sword, he stepped through the curtain.

The air suddenly warmed. His vision rippled as if he were looking under water. When it cleared, he became aware of something at his feet. Looking down, he saw the crumpled figure of Jorge, blood pooling from a deep wound in his thigh, his eyes fading but still alive.

Héctor stared at his sword and then back to Jorge. "You... you weren't there..."

He heard whinnying. There was no sign of Jorge's mount, although strangely, a trail of hoof prints was now visible in the pass. He realized the neighing was coming from his own horse beyond the veil. Yet, looking through the curtain he could only see the empty, untouched snowscape beyond the entrance. It was as if the curtain revealed a scene frozen in time beyond it.

Grabbing Jorge under both arms, Héctor dragged the conquistador back through the curtain until the Andean cold bit his face once more. His horse was there, stamping its hooves in agitation. After heaving Jorge onto its back, he remounted.

He headed back along the snow-covered mountain path to the distant bone rattle of an *asson*.

Chapter 4

The Honor of the Fathers

Surrounded by snowdrifts from the previous night's storm, Cristóbal and Diego fought to stand firm against the mountain wind. Cristóbal pushed his crossbow hard against his shoulder and took aim at a herd of alpacas on a far slope. He cherished these moments alone with his clever cousin, free from the burden of command which had grown every day since they had left Machu Picchu.

"You really think I'll be able to hit one of the alpacas from here?"

Although Diego had some of his cousin's height, in all other ways he was physically his opposite. Diego was soft where Cristóbal was firm. He stooped where the Capitán stood unflinchingly rigid. His beard grew in wild tangles while Cristóbal's face defiantly laid every blemish bare.

"The bolt will make the distance," said Diego. "I can't speak for your aim."

Cristóbal smiled and widened his stance. "We both know it's not my aim that's the problem."

"No, it's usually *what* you aim at that we need to worry about." Diego took a deep breath. "Cristóbal, please don't tell me you've asked for her."

"I like the feel of this new crossbow of yours."

"Have you forgotten Incan emperors marry their sister? How can you install Huarcay as emperor when you're obsessed with his sister?"

Cristóbal lowered his crossbow and glared at Diego. Although they had been inseparable since boyhood, tending the horses on his father's diminishing lands, he often wished his cousin didn't share his family's stubborn streak. "Maybe instead of disapproving, you should find yourself a companion among the Incan servants."

"Do you really need a princess?"

"Spain wouldn't have an empire without the marriage of Isabella and Ferdinand. Great power comes from great alliances."

"I can remember our fathers talking about honor above all else. *Honra sobre todo.* But when did our families ever speak about great alliances?"

"Isn't that why we stowed away to the New World all those years ago, Diego? To find greatness?" Cristóbal lifted the crossbow to his chin again. "Can we finally put your new invention to the test?"

"Yes, Capitán."

"Let's make certain there's no chance involved." He raised his nose in line with the bolt. "Do you see the white one...there in the middle of the herd? That's the one I'm aiming for."

"The Incas believe the white alpacas are sacred."

"Don't worry. After we skin it, the Incas won't be able to tell the color of its coat."

Cristóbal welcomed the familiar surge of confidence as he took aim. His breathing steadied to a calm rhythm, his crossbow now part of his arm, the bolt head tingling as if it was his fingertip. Of course, he wasn't going to miss.

The white alpaca raised its head as if sniffing a sudden wind change. A sharp twang pierced the crisp high-altitude air. The alpaca moved with lightning speed, but the bolt struck it in the throat mid-leap. It collapsed onto a snow drift as the other alpacas scattered in confusion.

Cristóbal turned the weapon around to examine it. "I have the feeling that this crossbow of yours will do something important."

A clap of thunder echoed in the distance.

"Maybe," said Diego, "but no crossbow can help us if we can't find Manco Inca." They led their horses toward the white alpaca. The snow-crested Andean peaks jutted from the low clouds in the distance, piercing the blue sky. "I hate telling you something else you don't want to hear, but—"

"Ha, you love nothing better." Cristóbal removed the bolt from the alpaca's throat. "I'll save you the trouble this time. I know the men are getting restless. We need to find Vilcabamba."

"It's more than restless. I hear things they would never say to your face."

A sudden snow flurry stung their skin as they slung the animal over Cristóbal's horse.

"Come, let's get this alpaca back to camp," said Cristóbal. "If we approach from the south, the Incas won't see it's white."

***

By the time they had reached the campsite, the mountain peaks had disappeared behind billowing clouds, and it was clear another storm was on the way. The stench always drew Cristóbal back to the reality of his campaign. As usual he gagged. He fought to control his breathing, knowing he only needed to bear it a while and the pungency would fade. A man can grow numb to anything. Smells. Frustration. Even failure.

They had all been stuck on the plateau far too long. A company this size had to keep moving or it would drown in its own excrement. The storms had kept them trapped here for two weeks, and worse, they had no obvious path forward. Many of the soldiers had stopped donning their armor. They played card games, gambled for shares of future fortunes, and traded insults. Melting snow for water wasn't a fit duty for a conquistador, and only so many hunters were needed each day. Worst of all, since leaving Machu Picchu six months ago, Cristóbal had seen no sign he was looking in the right place for Manco Inca's hidden city. All he had were Huarcay's assurances that they were close, while other conquistadors were searching elsewhere.

Lieutenant Rodrigo Benalcázar approached with the three soldiers he always seemed to have in tow, Carlos, Luis and Martín. The wiry lieutenant gave Diego a sideways glance, as if he was the cause of the stink that shrouded the camp. Although there had been no threat since Machu Picchu, Rodrigo was wearing his full armor, including breastplate, gorget, and arm and leg greaves.

Cristóbal asked, "Any news from the patrols, Lieutenant Benalcázar?"

"No, Capitán, but Lieutenant Valiente hasn't returned yet. Should I send out a search party?" He glanced back at the three soldiers with a half-smile through his thin beard and collapsed cheeks. As always, he was keen to present his fellow lieutenant in the worst possible light.

"That won't be necessary. He knows where we are." Cristóbal indicated the alpaca behind him. "Could you get this skinned? And make sure the Incas don't see it."

"Why?"

"Diego tells me the white ones are sacred to them."

"So? Are we now appeasing pagans?"

"No, of course not, but our campaign will falter without Huarcay's support."

"You mean it hasn't faltered already, Capitán?"

Lightning lit up the clouds crowding the nearest mountaintop. Cristóbal said, "When the storms finally ease, we'll leave."

"To where?" A clap of thunder rolled down the slopes.

"Wherever Huarcay directs us. He tells me we're close to Vilcabamba."

"Is it time for one of the other Incas to direct us, Capitán?"

Cristóbal stiffened. As usual Rodrigo was trying to test his authority. He was a hard and cunning man who had fought his way to where he was from the slums of Extremadura, the poorest region of Spain. He was the sort of man you wanted on your side in a fight, and who instinctively inspired obedience. "What are you saying, Lieutenant Benalcázar?"

"There are rumors, Capitán. The men talk."

Were the three soldiers behind the lieutenant smirking? "If the men are wasting their time with gossip, then maybe you should make sure they have extra duties."

"Yes, Capitán. I'll see to it."

Cristóbal dismounted and looked up at the darkening sky as Carlos, Luis and Martín carried the alpaca carcass away. Where was Héctor? This was not like him.

Chapter 5

The Silence of Sin

Sarpay sat with her brother, Huarcay, in his tent with musicians playing on bone flutes and *wancara* drums as the Andean storm howled outside.

"So, he's finally asked for me?" Sarpay sipped coca tea from the cup that a servant raised to her lips. "You were right."

Although she had known from the beginning that this time would come, it was always better to give Huarcay the credit. Her nostrils widened as the coca gave her clarity, its bitterness lingering on her tongue. Although she was playing a dangerous game, and much more was at stake than in the usual courtly intrigues, she had the same advantage as always. Men underestimated her.

"Yes," said Huarcay, "though the way he looks at you I thought he would have come to me much earlier." He addressed the musicians without looking at them. "Play louder, I can still hear the wind."

Sarpay twirled one of her snake earrings as she spoke. "Did you protest?"

"I said I was honored but he would need to convince you."

"I see. He thinks he needs to persuade me?" She laughed. This was going to make things much easier. Despite their hairiness and pale skin, these Spaniards weren't so different to the Incan courtiers she had encountered.

"Grandfather was pleased," said Huarcay. "He believes that if the capitán needs to earn your respect, it will give us a great advantage."

"You spoke to grandfather again last night?"

"Yes, the bearded ones don't suspect. Now that you'll be sharing the capitán's bed, you will need to rely on me to ask him for advice." Huarcay gestured for the cup to be brought to his lips. "All you need to do is win the capitán's confidence while he's keen to please you. Do you think you can do that? After all this time, he still doesn't really trust me."

"It will be much easier for me to gain his trust. A man's desire is his weakness."

"Of course...louder, I said play louder! I don't want to hear the storm."

"I don't find loud flute and drums any more pleasant than the wail of the wind," said Sarpay. "You can't shut out that we're a long way from Machu Picchu with music."

"I can shut out a lot of things, my sister. I can shut out that the Spaniard will be making love to you tonight."

"It should only be a concern to you if you become emperor."

Huarcay waved away the cup that a servant brought to his mouth a second time, annoyed that the servant had misread his gesture. "You'll need to be careful. He and several others can speak Quechua."

Sarpay smiled. "That only makes it easier to tell him what he wants to hear."

***

Cristóbal shivered as he stood inside the entrance to Padre Núñez's tent shrouded by the chill Andean night. He wasn't looking forward to this. The padre was never easy to deal with.

"Why can't this wait until morning?" The Franciscan glared at Cristóbal. He sat at a small wooden table where a single oil lamp shed light on an open Bible. As always, he wore the coarse sackcloth of his order loosely tied at the waist and exuded an intensity belying his youthful face.

"I'm sorry to disturb you at your time of contemplation, Padre," said Cristóbal, "but I need to speak to you. Tomorrow will be too late."

"Well, quickly, close the entrance. The winds are biting tonight."

"Of course, Padre. I'm sorry."

Cristóbal tied the cords of the tent flap and sat down in silence.

"You'll need to tell me what sin you've committed before I can give you absolution," said Padre Núñez, drumming his fingers on the table.

"The sin hasn't occurred yet."

"So, you wish me to stop you from sinning?"

Cristóbal shifted awkwardly in his chair "I've already made up my mind to sin."

"I see. Half your men have asked me for absolution for fornication with the Indians. You're the first to ask forgiveness for a sin you haven't committed yet."

"I'm not like my soldiers."

"No? Capitán, our Lord forgives. Just make sure you confess in the morning with the others and you'll escape the fires of hell." Padre Núñez turned his attention back to his Bible.

"I don't wish to lay with an Incan servant girl," said Cristóbal. "I wish to marry an Incan princess."

Padre Núñez laughed. "Like your hero Francisco Pizarro? Marry? You wish to marry Sarpay?"

"Why do you find that humorous, Padre?"

"I've yet to persuade a single Inca to be baptized into the Church, so you may have quite a wait. Please, I wish to return to my contemplations."

Cristóbal felt the familiar ringing in his ears as blood rushed to his head. The padre had been difficult from the start of the campaign. "Is that all you can say to me?"

Padre Núñez's eyes bored into Cristóbal's. "We both know why I'm on this campaign. I give legitimacy to the Spanish Crown's conquest of new lands. When the Indians refuse to accept Christ, it gives us the right to enslave them and take their wealth and lands."

There was commotion outside the tent. Then a voice. "He's with the padre. You can't see him now."

"This can't wait." Lieutenant Héctor Valiente burst into Padre Núñez's tent. Cristóbal rarely found the African's face easy to read, but this time it was etched with exhaustion and fear. "Capitán, I've found the way to the hidden city."

"I'm pleased we won't be stuck here much longer," said the padre, "but could both of you now leave me to my solitude?"

"I'm afraid you're needed outside, Padre," said Héctor.

"Am I to get no peace tonight? What's so important?"

"It's Jorge. He needs the last rites."

Chapter 6

Kissing the Gods

Cristóbal's temples throbbed as he waited for Sarpay. He sat at a candlelit table with his open diary in front of him, tensely running his fingers across his chin, unable to write. Jorge's death and Héctor's strange tale unnerved him, and now he had only one night with the princess before they broke camp and faced Manco Inca's army. He listened to the mountain winds howling outside, battering his tent, and he poured himself a cup of red wine. With his supplies running low, he was determined to savor it.

Why was he so nervous? He had left Spain to find his fortune too young to think about marriage, and Spanish women were few and far between in the New World. There had been some dalliances with Indians, but he had barely given them a thought. What he was now considering was a world apart. This was a princess. True, an Incan one, but a princess of an empire of millions, one that dwarfed his homeland. She wasn't someone he could command. And that both excited and terrified him.

Would she find him too old? Would his creased face repulse her? Would she shrink at his touch? After all, what was he but a poor horse-tender whose little family wealth had disappeared after his father's premature death? Was he anything more than a man who covered his insecurities with bravado and bluster?

A gust of wind riffled the pages of his diary. He looked up as the tent flaps opened and two female Incan servants wearing the decorated sash of Huarcay's house ushered Sarpay in.

Cristóbal stared at her and she met his gaze in silence. She wore a golden wraparound skirt that reached to her ankles and was clasped on her right shoulder, leaving her left shoulder bare. Her headdress was a fringe of red woolen tassels that hung from golden tubes. Her eyes were a deep brown and her skin wore the delicate softness of youth.

Cristóbal had watched her many times since the campaign had begun, and now here she was. Looking at him the way no other woman had ever looked at him—with the haunting eyes of a princess.

"Thank you for your kind invitation, Capitán de Varga," she said, breaking the silence with an expression on her face he couldn't read.

"Your Spanish is excellent."

"I have much still to learn. I hear you have also mastered our Quechua tongue?"

Cristóbal coughed. "Maybe mastery isn't accurate. Could we stay with Spanish for now? Please come and sit with me. Can I offer you a cup of wine?"

"Huarcay speaks very highly of your Spanish wine. Thank you." Sarpay sat down at Cristóbal's table as he poured wine into a goblet and handed it to her awkwardly. "I hear we have finally found the path to Vilcabamba."

"Yes, we're breaking camp at dawn..." Cristóbal fell silent.

"Perhaps this isn't the best time for us to speak?"

Cristóbal cleared his throat. "What has your brother said about my request?"

"My brother can sometimes misunderstand requests. I think it's better I hear your words."

Was the princess smiling, or was it his imagination? "Yes... well...I wish to put a *proposición* to you."

"A *proposición*? I don't know this Spanish word."

Cristóbal took a sip from his goblet. "You know our plans are to find and capture Manco Inca and put Huarcay on the Incan throne."

"My brother has always been ambitious, and you have flattered him, Capitán de Varga. He would do anything to become emperor. Even sell his sister."

Cristóbal choked on his wine. Sarpay stared into his eyes, as she had done since she had entered the tent, and he couldn't look away. "I don't wish to buy his sister. It's not possible to purchase a princess."

"But is it possible to make arrangements without her consent?"

"No, that's not possible either."

"I see. So, what is it you want me to consent to?"

Cristóbal glanced nervously at the two servants.

"It's all right, Capitán de Varga, they speak no Spanish."

"Please, call me Cristóbal."

"Well, Cristóbal, what is it you wish to call me then, because I've noticed you haven't called me anything since I entered your tent. Perhaps I am...what's the Spanish word...a *prostituta*?"

Cristóbal coughed, spilling his wine on the table.

"You know, Cristóbal, we Incas have nothing like what you call money. That means there's no such thing in our empire as a *prostituta*. We exchange, we don't buy."

"Please...you're an Incan princess and that's how I speak to you."

"Then let me speak to you as an Incan princess, Cristóbal. You Spanish want our gold. It is a thing of beauty to our people, but for you it has value far beyond its beauty. It gives you wealth."

"That's true."

"Do you know what makes Incas wealthy? Influence. The person with the greatest number of followers is the wealthiest."

"Which makes the emperor the most powerful Inca."

"Of course, and it makes our gods Inti, Mama-Kilya and Viracocha the most powerful of all."

"I don't know much about your gods."

"No, but you know the true wealth of followers. Your conquistadors follow you across mountains in search of Vilcabamba. But they're not enough for you. You want more followers. You want to rule what remains of the Incan Empire."

"Huarcay will be emperor."

"In name, yes, but we all know the truth. You'll be wealthier than Huarcay because through him you will also have all his Incan followers."

"And Huarcay knows this?"

"My brother is blinded by his own ambitions, as are most men. He believes he'll be able to usurp your rule, or at least pretend it doesn't exist."

"I see, so where does this honesty leave us?"

Sarpay drew closer. "Men aren't the only ones to desire wealth. The difference is I keep my eyes open when I sense ambition." Cristóbal felt her breath on him as she ran her finger along his cheek. "Why is it, Cristóbal, that unlike your conquistadors, your face is hairless like an Inca?"

Cristóbal flinched. He couldn't remember the last time a woman had touched him this way. "My face isn't hairless. I shave it every morning."

"Why?"

"I...I find it a good discipline."

"Ambition and discipline. They make good companions, don't you think?" Sarpay drew even closer. "You know, I think you shave your skin to look different to the men under your command, the way the Incan Emperor wears the red fringe and gold tassels."

"Maybe you're right." It was as if Sarpay was breathing him in.

"Tell me what it is you really want of me."

Cristóbal tried to look away but Sarpay held her hand against his cheek so that it was impossible. "I wish you to be my wife." His voice was hoarse.

"I see. The way my serving girls are wives with your conquistadors?"

"No, the way a man and a woman are joined within the Church."

"And what if we cannot be joined this way? What would you want of me then?"

Cristóbal tried to turn away again, but she still held him firmly. "I...would still want you with me."

Sarpay drew so close their cheeks were now touching. A knot tightened in his stomach.

"Do you know, Cristóbal, that we Incas only kiss our gods."

She pressed her lips against his. A gust blew into the tent as the two servants left.

***

Huarcay had no sense of being watched when he made his way through the darkness. Why would he? He had done this many times since the company left Machu Picchu. The wind had abated and had left a biting chill behind. After entering a small tent on the northern edge of the encampment, he carefully tied the entrance and lit a candle.

He placed a jug of corn beer and a plate of roasted guinea pig at the feet of a dark figure propped up on a low wooden bench. "I've brought you fresh *chicha*, Grandfather, and the *cuy* has been cooked in the earth oven until it's soft and sweet."

The dark figure seemed to nod in response as it contemplated Huarcay with bottomless eyes.

"We've finally had the news we have been waiting for, Grandfather," said Huarcay. "The *chaski* has been sighted and the bearded ones are preparing to follow."

He reached down and started taking off the dark figure's sandals. "But as usual, I'm too absorbed in my own concerns, Grandfather. How are you? Have the servants still been treating you well?"

He held one of the figure's feet in his hands and started rubbing it. "You're cold, Grandfather. I'll ask the servants to bring you an extra blanket."

The figure's grimace was almost a smile.

"I'm at the crossroad now, Grandfather. There's no path back from this decision. I need to know what I'm doing is right."

He reached out for the figure's desiccated hand and kissed it. "Whisper the words to me."

Huarcay stood up and leaned forward, his cheek touching the mummy of his long-dead grandfather. He lowered his voice so that not even the wind could capture it. "Grandfather, give me your wisdom."

The air around Huarcay froze and the words echoed inside his head.

You are worthy. Do what will make you great.

Huarcay smiled and kissed the mummy on the lips.

Chapter 7

The Second Death

Cristóbal's heart was still pounding as he lay with Sarpay on his bed of alpaca wool and ran his fingers through her rich dark hair. Finally, his fortunes had changed. After years of frustration, he was on the verge of something momentous. That very morning, he still had no confirmation that he was even looking in the right direction for Manco Inca. The Pizarro brothers were hunting for him in the distant eastern suyu of the empire. But now he was certain he would be the one to find Vilcabamba, the golden city from which the emperor was waging his resistance against the Spanish rule. The previous night he had slept alone, as he had done every night since the conquistadors had left Machu Picchu. Now he slept with a princess.

For the first time in a long time, all his doubts vanished. For a moment, he again felt the pure joy of expectation that surged through him when he and Diego were not much more than boys, eluding soldiers as they stowed away to the New World and leaving behind the familiar patchwork fields and olive groves of Andalusia. A time when they were convinced that fortune and renown awaited them and all they had to do was grasp it.

Cristóbal kissed Sarpay and slowly, as his heartbeat eased, fell asleep.

***

The condor swept across a fire-red sky, fighting wild erratic winds. Battling the savage currents, it flew higher and higher, shimmering in fierce swoops through the heavens. Then the air stilled. The great bird's immense wings burned with light as it flew ever closer to the golden sun, arcing upwards, always upwards. Finally, its feathers began to shrivel and turn to ash. And it started to fall.

It tried to cry out. But it had no voice.

***

Cristóbal woke up in darkness, bathed in sweat, sucking air into his lungs. When he opened his eyes, Sarpay was looking at him.

"What were you dreaming?" she asked.

His breathing slowed. "A condor."

"That's a sign of good luck for the Incas."

"But this condor, it was burning under a red sky."

"Condors are always a good omen for my people. Try to go back to sleep. I'm sure all will go well tomorrow."

She started stroking his face and he felt himself relaxing.

"I don't believe in good luck," said Cristóbal. "I believe our fates lie in the decisions we make."

"Then forget about the dream. It doesn't matter."

Sarpay continued to stroke his face and he closed his eyes.

***

Flames lit up the night sky and crackling sounds of burning wood broke the silence of the Andean slopes. Huarcay staggered out of his tent, sleep-confused, his tunic twisted around him. He let out an anguished scream. What in Inti's name had these Spaniards done? He raced toward where Padre Núñez stood with Rodrigo and several conquistadors in front of the burning tent which housed his grandfather's mummy.

"Chay-qa wasi-y!" cried Huarcay, only able to voice his disbelief in Quechua, his face flaming with rage as if he himself was burning.

"I won't have the devil's work in my domain," said the padre.

"You have killed my grandfather."

Padre Núñez's lips were thin and hard. "Your grandfather died long ago. What was in there was an abomination before God."

"Your God has no place in these mountains. These peaks belong to our ancestors." Huarcay could barely spit out the words.

"I can't have this sort of worship among us."

"You…you…" Huarcay lunged at Padre Núñez, but Rodrigo pushed him back.

"If we had known what was in there earlier," said Rodrigo, his cheeks hollow in the firelight, "we would have burnt it down months ago."

Huarcay, distraught, tried to rush toward the flames, but Rodrigo ordered him to be seized. How dare they? He fought against the two soldiers that held him but finally fell limp. As the bitter smell of smoke filled his nostrils, his heart hammering his chest, he saw Cristóbal and Sarpay, wrapped in alpaca furs, emerge from their tents.

"Who gave the order for this fire?" demanded Cristóbal, glaring first at Rodrigo and then the padre.

"This is a command of faith, not a command of battle," said Padre Núñez. "As soon as I saw what was in this tent, I had no choice but to have it destroyed immediately. I couldn't let this evil fester in our midst."

Sarpay's eyes were on fire. "How could you commit this crime against our people?"

"There's no such thing as a crime in the name of God," said Padre Núñez.

"What was in that tent, Padre," asked Cristóbal, "that was so evil you couldn't wait to discuss its burning with me?"

"A black idol. The petrified body of an Inca," said the padre, his face twisted in disgust. "They speak to it as if it's still alive. They place food and drink before it as if it still feels hunger and thirst. It's been with us since we left Machu Picchu. No wonder we've had nothing but ill fortune. How could God bestow His grace on us when the devil lies amongst us and poisons our quest?"

"There'll be no more burning without my consent. Do you understand?"

Padre Núñez didn't respond.

"Huarcay is our ally. *Do you understand?*"

Padre Núñez met his gaze for a long time, but finally nodded.

Cristóbal turned to Rodrigo. "And you, Lieutenant Benalcázar, what was your role in this?"

"The padre showed me what he had discovered inside the tent. What else could I do except set it on fire immediately since we were breaking camp in the morning. I didn't think there was any need to disturb your...sleep." He looked across at Sarpay.

"In future, Lieutenant Benalcázar, I don't want you to concern yourself about my rest. You don't take orders from anyone but me. Is that clear?"

"Of course, Capitán."

"It's too late," cried Huarcay, dropping to his knees. "Goodbye, Grandfather." He had lost the man who had counseled him since he was a small boy. How could the Spaniards be so blind to the ways in which he had still been alive?

The flames had reached their maximum height and were now subsiding.

"Let the fire run its course," said Cristóbal. "I want all of you to return to your tents."

Huarcay remained on his knees, pulling out his eyelashes, as darkness slowly engulfed the light of his ancestor's flames. He felt Sarpay put her arm around him. "The bearded ones will suffer for what they've done," he whispered. "We'll wrench them from their God, and they won't find peace even in their dreams."

"First, we need them to sleep soundly," said Sarpay. "We're so close. Don't do anything that will endanger our plans."

"Look what they've done. We need to kill that God of theirs."

"And we will, brother. And we will. But not tonight."

Huarcay trembled.

"One night. In just one night," said Sarpay, holding out her open hand, "I have the capitán. We've always said that to control the body, you only need to control the head. We now have the head."

Huarcay felt his heartbeat ease. "Of course. You're right, sister. Go back to him. We'll finish what we've started."

***

"Is Huarcay still out there?" asked Cristóbal as Sarpay, holding an alpaca fur tightly against her body, peered out of his tent flap.

"Yes, he's torn off his tunic and is naked."

"He'll freeze to death. Go to him and take him back to his bed."

"You don't understand, Cristóbal, I can't. He needs to do this. He'll stay there until morning. For us the second death is worse than the first. There's no afterlife possible once your body has been burnt. That's why we go to such lengths to preserve our bodies."

"It's foolish to let your lives be ruled by *superstición*."

"I don't know this word, Cristóbal."

"It's...it's a false belief."

Sarpay frowned. "How do you know what's a false belief and what's true?"

"God tells us."

"Our gods tell us to worship our ancestors."

"But your gods are false, Sarpay."

"Only according to *your* God."

Cristóbal gestured for her to return to the bed. "Ours is the one true God."

Sarpay came back and sat down. "Of course, a god will inflate his power. It's the same with men."

"You need to speak to the padre about these matters. Come, you must be cold." Cristóbal lifted one of the alpaca wool blankets for Sarpay to re-join him.

"I don't wish to speak to your padre; I wish to speak to my grandfather. Why can't you Spanish allow the people you conquer to continue to worship their gods, the way we Incas have always done? Your one God claims too much power."

How was he going to explain it so she could understand? "God doesn't claim power. He has it."

"So, you believe it's not possible for our gods to prove they are more powerful than yours?"

"Come, it's too cold to speak of gods in the middle of the night. We have a long journey in front of us tomorrow. It would be better if we managed to get more sleep before dawn." He held out his hand to her.

Sarpay appeared to be deep in thought for some time. "You have a problem."

"I saw you speaking to Huarcay. Did he say he would break our agreement?"

"No, your interests and his are one. From what I saw tonight your problem is with your own men. Neither Huarcay nor I want you to lose your command."

"I won't." He reached out further toward her.

"Even gods can lose their command." She stared at him, but eventually took his hand, letting the fur she was wrapped in fall open as she lowered herself toward him.

Chapter 8

Behind the Shimmering Curtain

The next morning the sky was clear for the first time in days, and the sun revealed a brittle blue against the snow-capped Andean peaks. With his two lieutenants on either side, Cristóbal led the army as it traced the path of Héctor's patrol the day before. He looked back to see his company stretch out along the trail. Immediately behind him rode the standard-bearer carrying the flag of the red Cross of Burgundy as a sign that they were ready for battle. Behind the flag were three hundred mounted swordsmen, fifty mounted harquebusiers, foot soldiers and a dozen cannoneers. Then came Huarcay and Sarpay, borne on litters by powerful-shouldered carriers while other servants kept pace as they led pack llamas. Following them marched three hundred Incan warriors, and bringing up the rear were armored Spanish war dogs pulling at their chains, clearly venting their frustration after weeks of inactivity.

Cristóbal scanned the skies for condors, searching for a sign of good fortune despite himself. Of course, it was actions that mattered, not luck. He knew, though, at his age this would be his last chance, and even the greatest men in history benefited from good fortune. The gold of Machu Picchu had amounted to very little after the Crown received its royal fifth and the rest was distributed among his large company. He needed so much more. And now he had found the way. If he was the one to conquer Vilcabamba, he would be lauded as the greatest conquistador of all. Others were scouring the remote corners of what was left of the Incan Empire. They were all wrong. This shimmering curtain that Héctor reported explained how Manco's warriors could always disappear so quickly after each raid on the Spanish. He was certain he was looking in the right place.

He shivered as the soaring shape of a condor in the distance caught his eye.

***

By mid-afternoon Cristóbal gave the command to halt as dense storm clouds billowed across the surrounding peaks. Despite his faith in Héctor, he was still surprised that the pass was just as his lieutenant had described it. The play of light danced in front of him, gossamer-thin hues bleeding into each other. Beautiful, yet strangely frightening.

He rode toward the curtain with his lieutenants until they stood directly in front of it. All three horses were on edge, but Héctor's mount was particularly nervous. While Rodrigo wore an expression of gaunt determination, Héctor's usual mask was shrouded in a barely suppressed dread.

"Do you hear anything?" asked Héctor.

The long tail of the company was still coming to a halt in the valley behind them, and the wind sang a mournful song across the slopes. "The howling sound?" asked Cristóbal. "Is that what you mean?"

Héctor didn't look at him. "You don't hear a rattling noise?"

"*Rattling*?" said Rodrigo, spitting the word.

Héctor shook his head. "Never mind. It's gone now. Do you want me to show you what happens, Capitán?"

Rodrigo said, "This looks like nothing to me."

He sliced the curtain with his sword and his blade vanished and reappeared.

Cristóbal urged his mount forward, and as its nose touched the curtain, its head started to disappear. He heard gasps behind him. When the horse's neck had completely vanished, he pulled on the reins and slowly backed out until its head was fully visible again.

Although his heart was pounding, he couldn't show fear in front of his men. He leaned forward to stroke the animal's neck. It felt warm, and the animal was breathing normally.

"I don't like the look of this, Capitán de Varga," said a voice behind him. Padre Núñez had ridden up to examine the curtain. "This strikes me as the work of the devil."

"You see the devil in too many places, padre," said Cristóbal. "My horse doesn't seem to have suffered."

Padre Núñez removed the wooden cross he wore around his neck, pushing it through the curtain and then quickly withdrawing it. "Satan isn't beyond tantalizing us with lights and tricks."

"Are you suggesting we don't pursue Manco Inca through this veil?"

"I'm saying we need to tread carefully until we know what we're dealing with."

"Understood, Padre. I'm certainly not looking for a fight with Satan."

A clap of thunder rolled down from the peaks.

With his heart pounding again, Cristóbal turned to Héctor. "You went through without injury?"

Héctor nodded.

Cristóbal rode his horse forward again, this time not stopping when its neck vanished. His vision blurred as he passed through. Why was he holding his breath? Then the heat struck. A dense, airless heat. His skin started tingling, something he hadn't felt since the summers of his youth in Andalusia.

He spat out sweat that trickled into his mouth. The rocky walls came into sharp focus. Looking around, he saw the pass continue deep into the mountain.

Héctor suddenly appeared next to him, materializing out of thin air. "See. The signs of Jorge's horse and the chaski's footprints are still there," he said, pointing at the ground.

Cristóbal arched his neck at the steep cliffs on either side to see the sliver of daylight at the very top.

"Look back," said Héctor.

Cristóbal peered through the curtain which still shimmered behind him.

"Where have my men gone?"

"I don't understand it, Capitán, but I know they're still there, even though we can't see them from this side."

Another crack of thunder crashed through the veil and the rock walls reverberated.

"Should we send a patrol through to see where this pass leads, Capitán?"

"This isn't a time for caution. We've all waited long enough. I'll lose the men if I ask them to weather out another storm. There'll be a battle at the other end, and I want to attack with full force."

Cristóbal straightened his back. Holding his sword above his head, he galloped back through the curtain to where his men stared open-mouthed as he appeared.

"Come, conquistadors," he cried, "draw your weapons. We have found the entrada to the hidden kingdom. Manco Inca is within our grasp. The gold of Vilcabamba awaits us."

A wild cheer erupted as lightning flashed above the company.

***

Cristóbal and Héctor rode through the twisting pass with the company snaking behind two abreast. An eerie emptiness enveloped them, a nothing, as if the air was holding its breath. The silence was broken only by the sound of hooves reverberating from cliffs that reached impossible heights on both sides. Pale light slanted at bizarre angles from an unseen source above them, casting half-shadows onto the rocks. The ground was soft and even, making it easy to traverse, but the path twisted so many times Cristóbal could no longer be sure which direction they were going. At times it seemed that they were heading back the way they had come.

The inexplicable heat started to make breathing difficult and sweat pooled under his armor. He had given the order for swords to be drawn. Speed would be crucial once they reached the other side of the pass. They didn't want to be picked off two-by-two by Manco Inca's slingers or bowmen when they exited.

As they rounded yet another bend, Héctor stopped. "Can you see it?"

Cristóbal nodded, halting his horse and gesturing to Rodrigo and the standard-bearer behind him to stop. Just ahead, bright daylight streamed through a gap in the rock. Unlike the gossamer veil at the start of the pass, this was a curtain of intense sunlight, contrasting so vibrantly with the dark shadows it was impossible to make out what lay beyond.

He turned to Rodrigo. "Lieutenant Benalcázar, make sure my command is passed down. All horses need to exit the pass at a gallop and those on foot should be running. Follow my lead. We want to strike fear in the hearts of Manco Inca's warriors if they're lying in wait for us."

Rodrigo nodded and started the process of forwarding the orders down the long line that wound back to the entrada.

Cristóbal caught a look on Héctor's face. "You don't agree with my plan, Lieutenant Valiente?"

"It sounds…unnecessarily reckless to me, Capitán."

"Why am I not surprised?" said Rodrigo. "Lieutenant Valiente is counseling caution. Let me guess. You want to send an advance party through to give the Incas plenty of warning that we're on the way?"

Héctor ignored him. "If they have an ambush waiting, then—"

"Then we'll fight our way through in full force," said Rodrigo, "rather than send through a small number to be slaughtered."

"I've given my order." Cristóbal raised his sword. "Come, there's a time for caution, Lieutenant Valiente, and a time for conquistadors." He dug his heels into his mount and rode toward the light.

They pushed their mounts into a gallop and burst out of the pass. A sharp flash blinded Cristóbal. When his focus returned, he was stunned. He squeezed the saddle tightly to stop himself from toppling. How was this possible?

He and Héctor raced through a vast golden-grassed plain encircled by dark serrated mountains whose peaks were crowned by bright sparks. And instead of the fragile blue of the Andean heavens, above them was a deep crimson sky dominated by a sun twice the size it should be.

Cristóbal pulled back on his reins. He turned full circle, barely able to take in what he was seeing. The conquistadors poured out of the black mountainside, shouting battle cries. Like he and Héctor, they all galloped furiously before stuttering to a halt, overawed by what they saw. The Incas who followed were immediately transfixed, kissing the air in the direction of the bloated sun, then scattering as the snarling war dogs entered the valley.

One of the mastiffs broke free and raced toward a herd of golden deer-like creatures. Rodrigo gave chase, but the dog had already mauled it by the time he grabbed the mastiff's chain.

He slung the dead animal over his horse and rode to Cristóbal, pulling the dog along with him. "Look at this, Capitán." He pushed his finger into one of the creature's wounds and then held it up. "The *ciervas* in this valley have golden blood."

"Where are we, Capitán?" asked Héctor.

Cristóbal scanned the landscape, instinctively trying to find something familiar to focus on, but there was nothing. "This truly is a new world beyond the New World."

Diego rode up to the officers nursing a large bruise on his forehead. "There's something wrong here."

"We don't have time for this *mierda!*" said Rodrigo. "How are you the only one in this company who can injure themselves without doing anything?"

Cristóbal turned to his cousin. "Can we speak later, Diego?"

"I think it's better if we spoke now. Has anyone tried to re-enter the pass?"

Rodrigo turned his back on Diego. "Capitán—"

Cristóbal said, "Show us what you're talking about, Diego."

Rodrigo scowled as they made their way back to the pass, which from the valley looked like a dark scar in an even darker mountainside.

Diego pointed to the opening. "Push your sword into it, Cristóbal."

"What do you mean?"

"Pretend there's a curtain there like at the *entrada* and pierce it with your blade."

Cristóbal thrust his sword into the opening. It clanged and the sword jarred in his hand like it had hit rock. What was happening here? He swung at it at full strength, with the same result. Frowning, he ran his fingers along the invisible barrier. It had the smoothness of polished stone. This made no sense.

Rodrigo and Héctor also tried with the same results. All four of them threw rocks at the opening with no effect. Other conquistadors had seen what was happening and joined in the attempt, with several getting bruises like the one Diego had on his forehead as they tried to force their way through.

When Cristóbal shot a crossbow bolt into the entrance, it bounced back at him. He shot another to the very top of the pass, but it also fell back to the ground.

Growing increasingly desperate, Cristóbal ordered his harquebusiers to fire bullets into the pass, but they ricocheted back. There had to be a way to break the barrier. What else could he do? Finally, he cleared the area and told his cannoneers to fire their largest cannon ball directly into the invisible wall. The impact echoed across the plain, but the ball fell limply to the ground at the base of the pass.

Cristóbal's stomach knotted. This wasn't how he had pictured his triumphant assault on Vilcabamba. Not only was there no way back, but he had also loudly alerted Manco Inca to their presence. He saw the unease in his soldiers, who were now milling around aimlessly, and knew his authority was draining away. Padre Núñez and Rodrigo were making no attempt to disguise their animated conversation, and that worried him. The glistening black mountains appeared more ominous than exotic now, the wide plain suddenly constricting. And above all the red sky weighed down on his thoughts like a blood-soaked blanket. Were they in a trap? Would Manco Inca's warriors kill them one by one with their mobile tactics in this unfamiliar terrain? He needed to do something, or the campaign was lost.

"Lieutenant Valiente," he said, "assemble the men."

***

Sitting on his horse holding the battle flag, Cristóbal gathered his thoughts as his soldiers crowded in front of him.

Drawing a deep breath, he addressed them. "All of you have seen that the way we entered this valley won't allow us to return. The entrada we've found has proven to be just that. An entrada. The way out, the *salida*, is somewhere else."

"How do we even know there's a way out?" shouted Martín. Murmurs of agreement rippled through the company.

"Manco Inca has a path back to New Spain. Otherwise, how has he fought his war against us?"

"So where is Manco?" shouted another soldier. "I don't see him."

"Are you surprised his city is well hidden? We will find Vilcabamba, and once we've emptied it of gold, we will use Manco's path to return to New Spain. Remember, Cortés sank his own ships so that he and his men had no easy retreat. Are we not their match as conquistadors?"

There were shouts of approval from the soldiers. He had won them back.

"Men destined for great things see what others don't. I ask each of you what you see. I see a new world before us. *Nueva Tierra.*" He waved his hand at the engorged sun and crimson sky. "And what is the greatest achievement a man can accomplish in his lifetime?" He paused. "To conquer a new world."

The conquistadors raised their swords and echoed Cristóbal's final words.

"To conquer a new world!"

***

When the sun started to set, turning the sky the purple of bruised skin, silence fell across the company. A strange silence in a strange land. The standard-bearer staked the Cross of Burgundy flag into the ground at the entrance to the pass, and soldiers erected a large wooden cross next it.

Cristóbal then stood in front of his men and spoke the words that he had long dreamed of saying. Words that only a true conquistador could say. "I, Cristóbal de Varga, claim this land of Nueva Tierra and all who inhabit it in the name of His Imperial Majesty Charles V, King of Spain and Holy Roman Emperor."

As a blood-red moon hung in the sky and the wind howled around the assembled soldiers, Cristóbal was no longer certain that God could hear his words.

Chapter 9

Nueva Tierra

Cristóbal battled with his doubts even as he made furious love to Sarpay, pushing into her as if somehow it would give him the answers he sought.

He quickly disentangled himself from her after he had finished and lay back in the pile of furs, awash with sweat and confusion, the red-tinged moonlight shining through the tent entrance.

"Something has changed for you, hasn't it?" asked Sarpay.

"Yes, is it so obvious to you?"

"It's easy to tell a man's moods by how he makes love."

"Doesn't the strangeness of this world affect you?"

"It doesn't feel so strange to my people." Sarpay traced a path across Cristóbal's face with her finger.

"Is that why you all kissed the sun when we first entered Nueva Tierra?"

"The moment we saw its size we knew this was the abode of Inti, the sun god."

"So, if Manco Inca believes this, he would seek Inti's protection?"

"Yes. I'm certain Vilcabamba lies in the direction of the rising sun." Sarpay pulled her hand away and looked at Cristóbal's face. "What's happened to your cheek?"

Cristóbal reached up and felt small ridges where he had always been smooth. "They feel like pockmarks. How could they appear in a day?"

"I've seen the pox disease the Spanish brought to my people, but the scarring only appears in survivors. You haven't been ill."

"No, my father was struck down by the black pox when I was a boy. I know the suffering he endured. I've felt nothing."

Cristóbal ran his hands along Sarpay's cheeks. Her skin felt as smooth as when he had first touched it. "You don't have any marks."

She reached up and pulled his hands away and then examined them.

"What are you looking for?"

"There's nothing wrong with your hands."

Cristóbal frowned. "Why would there be?"

Sarpay held up her left hand. "What do you see?"

"Nothing...what's happened to your little finger?" It was twisted like a twig. "I've never noticed that..."

"It wasn't like that before today."

"Is it painful?"

"No, it feels the same as always."

Cristóbal leaned back, his doubts gnawing at him with vengeance. Could the padre be right after all? Was the devil somehow at work here? He shook his head to throw out the thought. It made no sense. Some pockmarks and a crooked finger were not monstrous things. Why would the devil bother with such trifles?

Sarpay was staring at him. Was that uncertainty in her eyes? He had never seen that before.

Smiling, he took her hand and kissed her twisted little finger. "Can you feel that?"

She nodded.

"Then it doesn't matter."

He drew her toward him again and tried once more to expel the doubts.

***

Staring at the open page of his diary as Sarpay slept, Cristóbal strived to capture his thoughts and shape them into words. His fingers obsessively brushed the new pockmarks on his cheek. Although he often struggled to start writing, he knew his persistence would be rewarded with a blade-like clarity, the moment he could truly banish his uncertainty. He lowered his hand to touch the smoothness of the blank page. The words started to come to him. Finally, he felt himself a true conquistador. He allowed the elation to overwhelm him.

He had found the way to Vilcabamba. From now on men would speak of de Varga in the same breath as Cortés and Pizarro. He shared with them the unique sensation of what it felt to lead men into unknown territory. New Spain was already well-established by the time he and Diego arrived carrying little more than the clothes they wore, and he had to admit the Spanish settlement had grown increasingly familiar after so many years. Nueva Tierra was a new world in more than name. And like the man who didn't know he was hungry until he saw food, Cristóbal realized he craved the strangeness that lay before him.

As he picked up his quill, he sensed he was on the verge of triumphs even greater and more profound than those of the conquistadors before him. And unlike the others who had scribes to record their exploits, the words that would speak his conquests to the world would be his own. He could shape how history saw him. The power lay in his own hand.

Was it best to give his actions a sense of destiny? Had he truly always known he would be the one who would find the emperor's hidden city? Perhaps it was better to appear humble. Great men had no fear of expressing their doubts because they knew they would ultimately prevail.

He dipped his quill in the pot of ink and began to write.

Chapter 10

El diario de Cristóbal de Varga

It is an unmistakable truth that the prison of command requires a leader to conceal his fears. We are all, the most elevated and the most downtrodden alike, trapped by our lives. The most fortunate of us are ensnared by our obsessions rather than the physical circumstances of our existence.

Those who learn of my tale must understand that at this moment a deep fear entered the heart of this humble servant of the Empire. And yet I, Cristóbal de Varga, must also declare the true nature of a conquistador's heart. Although we feel fear, the heart of a conquistador will always hone this fear into action. It was the conquistador heart that led my countryman Hernán Cortés to scupper his own fleet and overcome the evil sacrifices of the Aztecs Motecuhozuma and Guatemoc, and it was the conquistador heart which gave Francisco Pizarro the courage to conquer the Empire of Atahualpa with a smaller company than I command.

And it is this same conquistador heart that now drives us to embrace the unknown rather than seek to escape it, and for the glory of God we will forge deeper into the heart of this strange new world we called Nueva Tierra.

Chapter 11

The Devil's Fire

Cristóbal always knew when he was being watched. He kept the main body of his soldiers in the middle of the plain, ensuring he couldn't be ambushed, while patrols scoured the terrain for water sources and signs of Manco Inca's warriors. The swollen sun bore down relentlessly on the conquistadors and ash-winds parched their throats. The valley they were crossing seemed endless, the surrounding jagged crags unforgiving.

For Cristóbal, though, the greatest threat wasn't heat or thirst, or even imminent attack. The elation of the first few days in Nueva Tierra had been overwhelmed by a deep sense of unease that had befallen the company. The further the conquistadors pushed east from the entrada, the more disturbing the surroundings felt. And with each day Cristóbal heard new reports of minor afflictions among the company. An eye that began weeping, a scar that seemed to have appeared overnight, a nose that had grown inexplicably swollen, a previously healthy tooth that suddenly fell out, a small facial blemish that appeared one morning. Though only a few seemed to be affected, Cristóbal began to wonder how widespread the problems really were. Perhaps there were many more who were suffering from ailments so minor that they either didn't notice them or felt they weren't worth mentioning to anyone.

As Cristóbal shaved the new ridges in his face each morning, it became increasingly difficult to dismiss the thought that Nueva Tierra was hostile to them. This new world had cast a pall over them that weighed on every waking thought. Where *were* they? Cristóbal heard the mutterings of his men. He knew what lay behind their anxiety. He felt it too. They didn't belong

43

here. The landscape shunned them. And not just the red sky and bizarre mountain formations. The air itself seemed different, the days oppressive, the night sky with its strange constellations unsettling.

On the twelfth day in Nueva Tierra, the company reached the entrance to the next valley. Cristóbal was riding beside his lieutenants with Padre Núñez and Diego immediately behind when he gave the signal to halt. He stared grimly ahead as waves of furnace-like heat hit him and the smell of sulfur stung his nostrils. Before him lay a terrain cracked with a web of fissures where fountains of flame rushed skyward at irregular intervals, a furious roar accompanying each eruption. He shuddered despite the heat. These were no ordinary fires. The moment each flame reached its peak, it turned into a fragile shimmering image of itself and quickly dissipated, falling in countless glittering grains before fading into nothingness. Past the scorching landscape, the ground appeared normal, but there was no obvious way to get safely to the other side. How was he going to lead his men forward?

The horses were clearly agitated, so the men dismounted and approached the valley entrance on foot to get a closer look, each brandishing their weapon while the padre held his wooden cross in front of him.

"That's why Manco Inca hasn't attacked us yet," said Cristóbal, his skin prickling under the heat. "He thinks we won't get past this."

"If Manco can do it," said Diego, staring at one of the flame fountains, "there must be a way."

"Maybe the fires die at night?" suggested Héctor.

"Why would they?" said Rodrigo. "They come from the ground, not the air."

Héctor glared at him. "Then what's your plan?"

"Don't you see what these are?" asked Padre Núñez, stepping forward.

"Are you telling us you see more evidence of the devil's work here?" said Cristóbal.

"You haven't answered my question."

"I've never seen eruptions like these, but that doesn't mean the devil is blocking our path."

Padre Núñez's voice grew hoarse. "This is much worse than I feared."

"What are you saying?" His intensity frightened Cristóbal now. What could be worse in his eyes than being beset by the devil?

The padre grabbed Cristóbal shoulders, staring at him, his eyebrows joining in a single severe line—why hadn't Cristóbal noticed that before? "Can't you see?" he demanded. "The way the flames change. The glimmering. We've seen it before. Do you know where we are? We're hopelessly trapped in a place under blood-red skies where the earth beneath us shoots fire. And each monstrous flame is tantalizing us with a fleeting glimpse of a way out." He could barely say the next words. "We've entered hell itself."

Cristóbal pulled the padre's arms away. "You think these are elusive entradas or salidas created to torment us through all eternity? I don't want to hear any more of this foolishness. That would mean we were all dead."

"Maybe we died when we rode through the bright light into the valley."

"I'm not sure about you, Padre, but *I'm* still breathing."

"Or is it the devil's illusion of breath?"

"Why would all of us be sent to hell at once? It makes no sense."

"Doesn't it? You lead a company of Spaniards whose greed for gold, fornication and conquest knows no bounds and a band of pagans who refuse to be baptized."

Cristóbal frowned. "Then why are you as a man of God here with us in the *infierno*?"

"I make your ignoble quest possible and have failed to baptize even one pagan. I'm a failed Franciscan. How could my fate be anything else?"

Cristóbal fixed his gaze on Padre Núñez. The idea was dangerous. Men who thought they were in hell couldn't be commanded. "I don't want you spreading this nonsense amongst the men." Cristóbal reached for his crossbow. "Let's see what we're dealing with first before we argue about what it means."

He loaded a bolt, took aim at one of the flames and waited for it to reach its maximum height before it changed. The moment he pulled the trigger, he knew his timing wasn't right. The flame was already collapsing into fragile specks of light when the bolt flew through it, landing unscathed near a fissure in the distance.

Grabbing another bolt, he tried again, but this time he released it too early and struck the peaking flame. The bolt traveled a short distance but then collapsed into ashes.

On his third attempt, he knew he had it right. He hit the flame at the precise moment it transformed into an insubstantial image.

And the bolt simply vanished.

"Do you still doubt me, Capitán?" said Padre Núñez.

"It doesn't mean—"

"I think I've found something that could help us," said Diego, interrupting. "There's a pattern." He pointed to the right. "See there, the flames are higher, but they come at longer intervals. I think we can predict them. Watch while I count."

A giant flame fountain shot skyward near the southern slope. When the last light speck faded as it hit the ground, he started counting. He had reached fifty-nine by the time the fire flared again.

"I've counted fifty-nine each time for that particular eruption. It looks like there may be a path that we can take on the southern side. There should be enough time between the explosions for us to move from one safe location to another. Let me map out the exact path and count out the intervals before we decide."

Héctor shook his head. "A count of fifty-nine is enough for the cavalry, but what about the hundreds on foot? And the cannons and provision carts? Maybe the Incan warriors can run fast enough, but I don't think a conquistador in full armor would make it."

"And there's not enough space between the eruptions for the whole company anyway," said Rodrigo.

"You're right," said Diego, "but I still think it will work. We should divide into ten smaller groups. The horses will need to make the crossing several times, each time carrying two riders. When I know the pattern, I'll be able to tell you the counts. Each group will know exactly how long they have to move to the next safe position."

"Well done," said Cristóbal. "Lieutenants, let's make ten groups, pick counters for each and ask them to wait for Diego's instructions."

Héctor nodded and walked back to his horse. Rodrigo hesitated for a moment as if he was going to respond, but then seemed to think better of it and joined Héctor.

Cristóbal turned to Padre Núñez. "I'm going to prove to you we're not in the infierno of the scriptures. We'll cross this forest of fires. All of us, down to the last dog."

"I pray I'm wrong," said the padre.

Diego stared at the flame fountains for a long time, silently mouthing the count of the intervals between eruptions.

***

"...forty-six, forty-seven, forty-eight." Cristóbal joined in as the ten chosen counters matched Diego's speed.

"Good," said Diego. "You're all with me. Remember the pattern is fifty-nine, eighty, and seventy-five, repeated twice, with a forty-eight on the last stretch which gives you very little time."

Cristóbal pointed to the jagged map he had drawn in the dirt in front of them which showed the stages of the path they needed to travel. "The horses shouldn't have too much trouble, even carrying two riders, but those on foot will need to run."

"How will the cannoneers move quickly enough?" asked one of the counters.

"And the dogs?" asked another.

"We'll add extra horses to the cannon and supply carts. And the dogs just need to be released and called across with the right timing. They'll be fast enough."

***

When the first group of riders was ready, Cristóbal raised his sword as if leading them into battle. "We need to show the way to the others. Remember the pattern. Fifty-nine, eighty, and seventy-five. Listen carefully to Diego." He held out his hand to help Huarcay onto the back of his mount.

The nobleman looked terrified. "I prefer that my servants carry me."

"I don't want to take the risk. Your bearers should be able to sprint across with an empty litter, but they'll struggle with you in it."

"Nonetheless, I don't—"

Cristóbal lifted him up into the saddle despite his protests. "Lieutenant Valiente, when we've safely navigated the fires, start your crossing. Lieutenant Benalcázar, stay on this side to prepare each group." He looked at Sarpay. "Once Huarcay is safe, I'll return for you."

A wild font of flame spurted on the southern slope a short distance away.

"That one wasn't part of your plan," said Rodrigo, glaring at Diego.

"There are sometimes random eruptions that don't fit the pattern."

"And when were you going to tell us that?"

"Cristóbal said not to. Why worry about something you can't control?"

Rodrigo's eyes narrowed as the first group moved into position with two soldiers on each horse, and Diego started counting at the top of his voice. "One, two..."

Turning his head toward Huarcay, Cristóbal said, "Hold on tightly to me," and then to the other riders in his group, "When I give the command, follow me to the first location and go no further until I give the next command."

Cristóbal tried to shut out the roar of the explosions across the expanse in front of them. His face burned. The fate of his company lay with him. Fight fear with action. That was the conquistador's way.

"...fifty-six, fifty-seven, fifty-eight, *fifty-nine.*"

The flames shot into the air as Diego had predicted. They exploded into the sky and finally shrank into pricks of light before disappearing completely.

"Now," cried the capitán, leading his mounted conquistadors across the fissure.

A deep red turbulence swirled under the surface as he galloped across. His horse balked a little as it stepped over the crack, but everything went to plan. With Huarcay's fingernails digging into him and Diego counting out the time for the second fountain, he located the next safe area.

Swathed in sweat, his heart pounding, Cristóbal forced himself to listen. This one was a count of eighty.

When the final number was called, he gave the command to move again. He made it across on the count of fifty-five, but this time one of the other horses reared as it crossed the fissure, throwing both its riders from its saddle and running on in a wild panic. The two conquistadors got up, but one of them couldn't put his weight on his left leg.

"...fifty-three, fifty-four..."

Cristóbal flung the protesting Huarcay to the ground and galloped back frantically shouting "Run! Run!" to the uninjured conquistador, who charged toward safety. He reached out to the injured soldier and hauled him onto his horse.

"...sixty-seven, sixty-eight..."

The numbers swarmed in his head. How much time did he have? The safe area still seemed so far away, and his horse showed signs of distress. Sensing it trembling and slowing under the weight of two riders, he jumped from his mount, hitting it on the flank to urge it on, and started sprinting.

"...seventy-six, seventy-seven..." Diego's voice strained.

A final charge and Cristóbal reached safety as fire burst out of the crevice at the count of eighty.

Before anyone could let out a cheer, an agonizing high-pitched whinny pierced the air. The panicked first horse had been crossing another cleft just as fire exploded from it and the poor beast, engulfed in flames, appeared to become its own shadow as it rose on its hind legs and disintegrated into ashes.

Cristóbal's chest heaved. He sucked in air, barely able to take in the horror of the scene as Diego started another count.

And that wasn't the last horror Cristóbal witnessed that day. The counts burned into his soul. Fifty-nine, eighty, and seventy-five. Fifty-nine, eighty, and seventy-five. Then the final, gut-wrenching, forty-eight. He returned again and again to the other side to pull a new rider onto his horse and make the crossing one more time. Exhaustion overwhelmed him, but he rode back and forth throughout the day. When his horse needed to rest, he took one of his soldiers' mounts, refusing even a moment's respite. With each loss, his determination grew. When one of the cannon carts was too slow and the gunpowder caught light, incinerating the cart, cannoneer and four horses instantly, he ordered extra horses to be added to the next cart. When the first group of llamas panicked while being led across and were consumed by the flames along with their Incan handlers, he changed the strategy and ensured the next llamas were tied up in horse-drawn carts. When a random eruption struck one of his men, he began to pray.

Finally, as he approached the last group before the war dogs were to make the crossing, Cristóbal's eyes met those of Padre Núñez. Coughing uncontrollably and with his eyes stinging, he reached down to help the padre onto his horse. He no longer needed Diego's count; the numbers now sounded unbidden inside his head.

He raced across the first set...seventy-five...then the next... seventy-five. After counting the last forty-eight aloud, he slumped forward in his saddle.

Padre Núñez dismounted and helped Cristóbal from his horse. Both sat down on the ground and wiped ash and sweat from their eyes.

When Cristóbal finally finished coughing, he said, "Tell me Padre, have we just defeated the devil in his own playground?"

"Perhaps we've had a minor victory over him."

"So, you still believe we're in hell? A dozen men have died. How can that be possible?"

"You have the wrong view of eternal damnation, Capitán. Hell has nothing to do with dying an agonizing death. It's failing again and again in the one thing you most strive for."

"I don't want to hear any more of this talk."

"What is it you desire most, Capitán? What would eternal damnation be for you? Let me guess. Perhaps slowly to lose your command until you have no one left? Or could it be for your sense of honor to leak away until nothing remains? Or is it for you to achieve greatness, without anyone ever knowing what you've accomplished?"

"I've had enough." Cristóbal tried to stand up but found he didn't have the strength.

"Rest, Capitán," said Padre Núñez, getting to his feet. "Whoever you've fought today, you've fought well. It's the devil's way to make us unsure. All of us need to accept we're fallible. Until we discover the truth about where we are, I'll continue to pray that I'm wrong."

Chapter 12

El diario de Cristóbal de Varga

Is it possible to know what it is that you most desire? I battle with this most deceptive of all questions, the beating heart of all our actions. For the mind can play itself for a fool. How can a man be certain that what he believes to be his most ardent yearning isn't merely the hungers of others? Do we crave only the golden prizes that are held aloft by others to entice us? Do we conceal our true passion behind a mask of the passions of others? Are we ashamed of what the truth will reveal to ourselves?

So it was that Nueva Tierra imposed this most dangerous question on me. I realized that a man who has no answer is squandering his life. And one who has a false answer is a shallow pool. Thus, the padre's words led me to contemplate the desire whose loss would weigh most heavily on my soul. Does the answer lie in the command of men, or in the honor my father would have chosen?

Or do I value above all else the renown that great deeds bring?

Chapter 13

The Chaski

Cristóbal's anxiety grew after the ordeal of flames. The harder he sought to hide it from his men, the more it gathered strength. He felt like a cocked crossbow bolt, stock-still but harboring unbearable tension. The mountains loomed larger, the air was increasingly oppressive, and the crimson sky bled ruthlessly across the horizon every new day. Was he blindly leading the company into Manco Inca's trap? How could he conquer an enemy he couldn't see? The only time Cristóbal purged his fears was when he was alone with Diego. On mornings like this when they hunted together, for brief moments, it no longer mattered where he was.

"You know," said Diego as the cousins rode through high grass, their crossbows by their sides, "we call them ciervas, but they're not deer. They're closer to very small horses."

"I don't like to think we're eating horses."

"It's like when we used to call llamas *sheep*. We're always trying to take the old world—"

"Shh." Cristóbal pointed into the distance where a herd of ciervas were grazing. "They're almost in range."

Slowly they drew nearer. Diego's horse gave a snort and the animals suddenly darted away.

"How can you make so much more noise riding than anyone else?" asked Cristóbal, laughing.

"I can't help it if you gave me the noisiest horse in the company. It keeps me awake most nights."

"I've told you to take one of the Incan servants to help you sleep."

"I don't have the stomach to battle for one."

"Nor the sword skills, I'd have to say."

"True." They rode in silence for a moment until Diego said, "Can you feel the eyes on us?"

Cristóbal nodded. "I've felt them for days. Manco Inca can see us coming. He has the advantage."

"He's waiting for something," said Diego. "If he was going to attack us out here in the open, he would have already done it. I'm more worried about what will happen when we leave this valley."

"Sometimes you make more sense than my lieutenants."

"That's why you should make me one."

"If you could actually use a weapon of some kind, you may have a chance."

"Watch this. I've been practicing."

The cierva was now within range and hadn't sensed their presence. Diego took aim with his crossbow and released the bolt. He missed badly, and the animal raced into the distance. "These cierva are like lightning."

"And your hand still shakes when you take aim as if you were shooting in a storm. Come, we can't afford to lose a bolt."

They combed through the high grass until Diego gave a shout. "Over here, Cristóbal, you need to see this."

Cristóbal joined him, his stomach spasming as he saw the brutally butchered Incan body holding a blood-stained quipu of colored knots.

They both dismounted, waved away the insects that swarmed from the body and started examining it. Cristóbal turned his head to avoid the full force of the stench. "So, the chaski didn't get his message to Manco."

"No animal could have made these wounds," said Diego. "They're in rows of three."

"And I've never seen a weapon that leaves these sorts of marks." Cristóbal pulled some decaying flesh aside. "Look. Bone's been punctured in several places. Incan stone can't do damage like that." He picked up the bloodied quipu. "It appears Manco Inca and his army aren't the only threat in Nueva Tierra."

***

That night Cristóbal stared at the chessboard, planning his next move, while Huarcay frowned as he inspected the blood-stained quipu. In the months since Cristóbal had introduced the game to him, the Incan noble had mastered it quickly, playing surprisingly well and often making unexpected moves.

Huarcay said, "You say the chaski was stabbed many times, his flesh torn from the bone?"

"Yes, and the wounds came in threes," said Cristóbal without looking up. "Do you know what weapon would cause this?"

"No."

Cristóbal moved his bishop. "Sarpay tells me your people believe we are in the land where your sun god Inti rules."

"It appears that the pass was what we call a *huaca*, a sacred entrance to an abode of the gods. My servants are convinced that if they journey long enough, they'll come face-to-face with Viracocha the Creator."

"You have a Creator god?"

"Yes, of course. You think yours is the only god that claims creation?"

"How is it that something in the home of one of your gods is butchering an Inca?"

Huarcay was still frowning. "I...don't know. Perhaps the chaski displeased Inti."

"Is it possible that we're not where you thought we were?"

"It's...possible."

"If that's true, then we have no idea that traveling toward the rising sun is the right direction, do we?"

Huarcay handed Cristóbal the quipu. "I find this news of the chaski disturbing."

Cristóbal ran his finger along the length of one of the knotted strings. "So, what can you tell me about the message on this?"

"The quipu is addressed directly to Manco Inca. There's no doubt. Some of the colors have been covered in blood, so I can't decipher everything, but it says that an army of bearded ones is nearing the path to the place of hiding."

Cristóbal smiled. Manco might not know they were on his doorstep after all.

Huarcay moved his queen. "Check."

This was a move Cristóbal didn't see coming. "Ah, you've finally shown me your true intentions."

"The intentions of you Spaniards are always clear and your desires simple. Stopping you is another matter."

Cristóbal moved his queen to protect his king. "Now our queens threaten each other."

Before Huarcay could respond, Héctor rushed into the tent, sword in hand. "Capitán, there are lights moving in the distance."

Chapter 14

The Ñakaqs

Cristóbal, his two lieutenants and Huarcay peered into the night as bright flames drew closer to the conquistador camp.

"I count only twenty," said Rodrigo.

"Yes, but there may be more out there in darkness," said Héctor.

"I agree," said Cristóbal. "We need to be prepared for an ambush. Give the orders for the harquebuses to be primed. Everyone should be ready for battle but remain out of sight inside the tents until I give a command."

"We know Incas don't fight at night," said Rodrigo.

"We used to know the sky was blue," said Cristóbal. "I'm not taking any chances."

Was Manco Inca himself approaching? Cristóbal doubted it. The emperor wouldn't have forgotten the treachery of past conquistadors. It didn't matter. His company was finally at Vilcabamba's gates. The search was over. The advancing lights reached the torches fringing the campsite's edge. Finally.

As the light-bearers came into view, he drew a sharp breath. Instead of Incan warriors, hideous, misshapen, wild-bearded men in armor confronted them, each wearing high gold-inlaid helmets with shooting flames and carrying *horcas* almost twice their height. Cristóbal stared at the three sharp points at the ends of their monstrous weapons. He shuddered, remembering the damage done to the chaski.

Cries of "*Ñakaq! Ñakaq!*" from the Incas filtered into the night air.

"Do you know who they are?" he asked Huarcay.

"We have tales of hair-covered mountain-dwellers like these beyond our empire. I've never seen one. We call them *ñakaqs*.

They're known for their frenzied attacks and are said to get their strength by eating the flesh of men."

"I see."

A ñakaq with a twisted, bulbous face crowded by tangled red hair stepped forward, his helmet towering above the others. He staked his horca in the ground and began speaking with a series of growls and sounds made in the back of his throat, while flames streamed high into the darkness above him.

Cristóbal shook his head. "I'm sorry, I can't speak your language."

The ñakaq stared at him in silence.

"My name is Cristóbal de Varga. I bring greetings from His Imperial Majesty Charles V and wish to pay our respects to your leaders and trade for gold."

The red-bearded leader scanned the camp and then spoke in a guttural version of the Incan tongue. "Why have you entered our lands?"

"You speak Quechua?" said Cristóbal.

"You must turn around and go back in the direction you have come."

"We have no quarrel with your people. We seek Manco Inca and will leave once we've found him."

"We don't permit you to enter. You will leave our lands now." The ñakaq's helmet flames burnt brighter every time he spoke, as if feeding from his voice.

"We can't. We have no way back to our lands without finding Manco Inca. Let me speak to your king."

Padre Núñez approached the leader. He held a Bible in one hand and a document in the other.

"Not now, Padre," said Cristóbal. "He speaks no Spanish."

"You know our duty to God and Crown, Capitán de Varga. It must be in Spanish and it must be now."

Padre Núñez addressed the ñakaq in Spanish. "The *Requerimiento* requires you to recognize the Church as your

Mistress and Governess of the World, and with her authority the High Priest, called the Pope, and His Imperial Majesty, King Charles V."

The ñakaq leader said something in his language, but Padre Núñez continued without hesitating, taking several steps closer, so that he now stood directly in front of him.

"If you do not do this, then with the help of God we shall come mightily against you, and we shall make war on you everywhere and in every way that we can."

One of the horses neighed from deep in the central area of the camp where they were tethered, and the ñakaqs shifted nervously.

The padre's words grew louder until they reached a crescendo. "And we shall subject you to the yoke and obedience of the Church and His Majesty, and we shall seize your women and children, and we shall make them slaves, to sell and dispose of as His Majesty commands, and we shall do all the evil and damage to you that we are able. And should this death and destruction befall you, be aware that the responsibility will be yours alone."

Padre Núñez, flushed and breathless, now stood in front of the leader and held out the Bible, offering it to him to take. "Do you recognize the Church as your Mistress and submit to the Will of God?"

The leader simply stared at Padre Núñez. His features were hidden behind the tangle of his beard, making it impossible to tell what he was thinking.

The padre continued to hold out the Bible, his voice hoarse. "Do you submit to our Lord?"

More horses whinnied. Then one of the war dogs started barking. The ñakaqs looked around, increasingly uneasy.

The leader pointed to the nearest tent where shadows were moving. "Those who are hidden should show themselves immediately."

Padre Núñez pushed the Bible into the leader's deeply lined hand and continued to speak in Spanish. "Do you submit to our Lord Jesus Christ?" The two stared at each other in silence for a moment. The ñakaq then released his grip of the Bible and let it fall to the ground.

"Attack!" cried Padre Núñez. "Attack these demons!"

Cristóbal shouted, "No!" but a boom from a harquebus gun masked his command, and one of the ñakaqs clutched his bloodied face as he fell to the ground while the others stood stunned.

Cries of "*Demons*" filled the air, and in the confusion, the war dogs were released. They charged at the ñakaqs who quickly crouched in battle formation, brandishing their three-pronged horcas.

A mastiff was skewered, writhing as it was lifted high into the air and the horca blades pushed deeper into its belly.

The dogs continued barking, standing their ground but no longer moving forward.

Then the ñakaqs suddenly switched to attack, stabbing their weapons at the conquistadors on the edge of the camp and bringing one of the Spaniards to the ground in a barrage of thrusts. Soldiers hiding in the tents dashed out with their swords drawn, shouting their battle cries.

"*Santiago y cierra, España!*"

Despite being grossly outnumbered, the ñakaqs fought fiercely, stubbornly defending their position and making no attempt to escape. Cristóbal could barely believe their determination to stand their ground despite the hopelessness of their situation. This was a disaster. Corpses were no use to him. A conquistador fell as a horca pierced his armor and Cristóbal pulled him back to safety through the tangle of legs.

"Hold them in position," he ordered, but the ñakaqs made it impossible. They pushed forward when they saw the slightest gap or hesitation, their eyes wild and their helmet fires burning.

The conquistadors stayed out of reach of the horcas and drove their lances into the ever more tightly bunched ñakaqs, who soon had little room to wield their weapons. Cristóbal repeatedly shouted "Surrender" to them in Quechua, while they were slaughtered one by one, furiously refusing capture.

Until only the red-haired leader was left.

"We need that one alive," said Cristóbal. "Do *not* kill him."

The leader charged at the wall of conquistadors, spit flying from his lips. Two of them grabbed his arms, trying to disarm him, but he hurled them off and almost severed the arm of one of them with a thrust of his weapon.

"Clear the way!" Héctor's voice rose above the others as he galloped toward the last ñakaq and grasped hold of his horca. The leader clung to his weapon with manic determination and was dragged along, battered by the horse's hooves. As Héctor slowed his mount, two conquistadors grabbed the leader's legs and tried to wrench him from his horca.

Still, he wouldn't release his grip. Instead Héctor was pulled to the ground from his horse. Four soldiers then joined the attempt to force the horca from the ñakaq's hands, but he refused to let go, his face burning a grotesque crimson and his eyes bulging.

Finally, as Rodrigo wrapped his fingers around his neck and choked him until he passed out, his fingers slipped from his weapon.

Before the leader revived, the conquistadors bound his feet and hands. Cristóbal removed his helmet, quenching its fire. Then he ordered that they carry him to the command tent.

***

Cristóbal couldn't suppress his rage as he charged into Padre Núñez's tent. His blood pulsed and sang in his ears. The padre had jeopardized his campaign. How dare he command his men to attack. He needed to be brought to heel.

Padre Núñez looked up from his prayer.

"I hope you're seeking forgiveness for what you did tonight," said Cristóbal.

"Don't speak to me of forgiveness, Capitán."

"Do you understand what you've done? The deaths you've caused? The further deaths your actions may cause." Cristóbal's chest heaved as he struggled to breathe.

"The deaths I've caused? I warned you at the entrada that I saw the devil at work. You ignored me."

"And now you declare the ñakaqs demons?"

The padre fixed his intense eyes on Cristóbal. "Where do you truly think we are, Capitán? You talk of new worlds, but beyond the world of men there is only heaven, hell, and purgatory. And we know we're not in heaven."

"These ñakaqs are men whose territory we've invaded. That's all. We're not in hell."

"The fires, the obscene sun, the bloodied sky, the godless demons. How can you still believe we're in the world of men?" He stood up from his kneeling position. "Do you know what day we entered this place?"

"All Souls Day. The day of the dead."

Padre Núñez shook his head. "Not the day of the dead. The day we pray for all the souls in purgatory who are not good enough to enter heaven, but not evil enough for hell."

"You now think we're in purgatory?"

"I think our souls are being tested, and we need to make certain we're not on the side of demons."

Chapter 15

In the Name of the Demon

The red-bearded ñakaq prisoner was the key to everything. Cristóbal was convinced of it. He spoke Quechua, so he had to know where Vilcabamba was. Yet the captured leader had proved to be surly and uncooperative, and fear of his strength and battle fury meant his hands and feet remained constantly bound.

The ñakaq refused to reveal anything of any value to Diego, whom Cristóbal had entrusted with the questioning. He barely responded to Cristóbal at all, offering little more than stares and silences from behind his beard—although he appeared to be rapidly increasing his understanding of Spanish. Even his name, Tagón, had to be drawn out of him with difficulty, as if it was a powerful secret. And, in the end, there was no certainty that it was his actual name, adding fuel to the padre's conviction that he was a demon.

When he did speak, the ñakaq continually warned the conquistadors of an imminent attack if they didn't turn back, while both Cristóbal and Diego kept explaining that returning was the one thing they couldn't do. They were at an exasperating stalemate which Cristóbal knew he needed to break.

He lay awake each night next to Sarpay, his hands behind his head, with his thoughts spiraling in the search for a way forward.

Tonight Sarpay wasn't sleeping either. "You're...what's the Spanish word...*preocupado* again, Cristóbal."

"You often say I'm worrying, when I'm actually just thinking, Sarpay."

"There's a time for thinking and a time for making love."

"Of course, you're right."

"Is Tagón still not revealing anything?" Sarpay ran her fingers gently along his chest.

"I don't even know whether he is an enemy or an ally of Manco Inca." He shifted restlessly. "I've agreed to let Lieutenant Benalcázar interrogate him."

"Is that wise?"

"I don't know what else to try."

"Can you ever trust forced information?"

"I've treated the ñakaq well and it hasn't worked."

Sarpay drew back. "You know his name and yet you don't use it."

Cristóbal looked at her for the first time. "What are you saying?"

"You haven't treated him well. He's still just *the ñakaq* to you. You've treated him as a prisoner."

"You think he'll stay if I don't have power over him?"

Sarpay shook her head. "Men have such simple ideas about power."

"Power *is* a simple thing, isn't it?"

"Maybe, but it isn't just about chains and force. Find what he desires and offer it to him. You offered Huarcay what he most desired and he gave you his sister."

"I'm not sure if that's true."

Sarpay pulled his hands away from his head. "Come, enough thinking for tonight." She smiled and swung her leg so that she now sat astride Cristóbal and began to move in slow rhythmic rotations.

***

Deep into the night, Sarpay carefully slid from the bed and headed toward Huarcay's tent. It was a risk because Cristóbal would often wake from the recurring nightmare where he was a condor plummeting from the sky. Yet it was a risk she needed to take. She had been waiting for the chance to speak to her brother since Tagón had been captured, and she couldn't wait any longer. The encounter with the ñakaqs had changed everything.

Although Sarpay had no doubt that Cristóbal trusted her fully now, she had to concede that it made her more than a little uncomfortable. That wasn't something she had anticipated. She suspected her deceit was the source of his nightmares. While she sought to ease his tensions and doubts in many ways, she couldn't stop what happened in his dreams. He was a complex man whose actions and thoughts were not as easy to predict as those of the other men she had known. That made him more dangerous to deal with. And she also had to admit to herself, it made him more intriguing.

Huarcay appeared pleased to see her at first. She knew it wouldn't last.

"What have you found out about the prisoner?" he asked. "Cristóbal won't let me speak to him."

"Nothing," she said. "Cristóbal says Tagón isn't cooperating."

Huarcay scowled. "And you believe him?"

"He doesn't lie to me."

"Are you certain, sister?"

"I know when a man is lying to me."

"What's the point of sharing a bed with him if you can't find an answer to our most important question?" Huarcay's face flushed. "We can't make our next move until we know more about these ñakaqs."

"They speak Quechua," said Sarpay. "Perhaps they are Inca allies."

"Speaking our tongue proves nothing. Some of the Spanish speak Quechua. It doesn't make them our allies. These ñakaqs killed the chaski, remember."

"I haven't forgotten that," said Sarpay. "One death doesn't make them our enemies. We need to know the reason."

"Grandfather used to say it doesn't matter how many enemies you have, what's important is knowing who they are." Huarcay clenched and unclenched his fist several times. "I wish he was still with us. He always gave me clarity."

"Right now we don't know anything. We don't even know where we are."

Huarcay stared at her. "There must be a way you can get to the ñakaq."

"No, he's well-guarded. Even the God-man isn't allowed to see him...but I do have a strategy. I'm certain whatever Cristóbal finds out, he'll tell me, and I've already sown the seeds with Cristóbal on how he can draw more information from Tagón."

"Seeds?"

"You know that's what I do well."

Huarcay nodded slowly. "Yes. Yes, I know what you can do. Sometimes I think you've planted everything about our plan into my head."

"You know that can't possibly be true," said Sarpay.

Chapter 16

The Demon's Pact

Rodrigo entered the prison tent carrying Tagón's helmet. He stared at the repulsive ñakaq who sat in front of him with his feet and hands tied. Finally, he would have his chance to find out what they needed to know. There was no point being soft with this *malparido*. He had to almost choke him to death to get him to let go of his weapon, so the ñakaq wasn't going to easily give them the information they wanted.

"I know you understand some Spanish," said Rodrigo. "Now, listen to me."

Tagón met the lieutenant's gaze, but there was no flicker that he'd heard Rodrigo's voice, let alone understood what he was saying.

"This here on your helmet, we call this *oro*, gold." He ran his fingers along one of the inlays. "This is why we're here. You need to take us to your source of gold. You understand. Only then will we leave your lands."

Tagón remained immobile.

Rodrigo pressed his lips together and switched to Quechua. "You have to show us your gold source."

Tagón shifted slightly but remained silent.

Rodrigo drew closer and pulled out his knife. "I see you don't quite understand me." He dug the knife into the edge of one of the small gold inlays and pried it loose.

Tagón winced as if he had been cut.

"Ah," said Rodrigo, "you don't like your helmet damaged." He began to force out one of the other inlays.

"We have no gold," said Tagón in Quechua, adding in rasping Spanish, *"No hay oro."*

"What do you mean you have no gold? All your helmets are decorated with it. Gold is soft. It has no use in armor. Why do you have it in your helmets? It has value to you, doesn't it?"

"The gold isn't ours."

"Do you take me for a fool?"

"It belongs to the mountain."

"You mean you mine it? You dig it out of the ground?"

"The gold chooses to come to us."

"What?"

"We can't take it for ourselves."

"Pah!" Rodrigo spat on the ground. "Don't you lie to me, you ugly brute. I want to know where your source of gold is. Believe me, I'll find out."

Rodrigo started prying out each gold inlay in the helmet.

"No!" the ñakaq shouted and then reverted to his own language, which came out as a torrent of deep-throated venom.

The lieutenant continued to flick the gold pieces onto the tent floor as Tagón grew increasingly enraged. Despite his hands and feet being tied, the ñakaq lunged at Rodrigo, stunning him with a blow. The Spaniard recovered, swinging Tagón off balance so that he fell to the ground, and then jumping on top of him and holding his knife to the ñakaq's throat.

"Your beard won't offer you much protection," he sneered. "Now tell me where we can find your gold."

Tagón pushed back hard against the Spaniard's hand so that the knife was no longer at his throat. The last thing Rodrigo saw was the ñakaq's bulging eyes coming toward his own.

Then there was blackness.

***

When light finally returned, his head ached, and Héctor and two other conquistadors were staring at him.

"What's happened here, Lieutenant Benalcázar?" asked Héctor.

"The demon. He must have escaped."

"Tagón is still here."

Rodrigo looked across to see the ñakaq's inscrutable face staring at him. He reached up to his throbbing forehead and saw his hand was now covered in blood. "The demon attacked me. We need to deal with him. He needs to know what the consequences of attacking a conquistador are."

"How could he attack you?" asked Héctor, obviously enjoying Rodrigo's discomfort. "He's our prisoner. His hands and feet are tied."

"Let me deal with him," said Rodrigo, as he struggled to stand.

Héctor pointed to the gold inlays strewn on the ground next to Tagón's helmet. "It looks like you've done enough dealing with the ñakaq for one day."

"The demon needs to tell us where his gold comes from."

"Does he? Come, let's explain to the capitán how a prisoner with his hands and legs tied can best you in a fight."

The other two conquistadors smirked as they tried to help him out of the tent door. "Get your hands off me," cried Rodrigo. He scowled back at Tagón as he walked out. "I haven't finished with you yet."

***

"I forbid you to speak with Tagón again. Is that understood?" Cristóbal paced up and down as he fired the words angrily at his lieutenant. "I don't want you antagonizing him further."

"You gave me permission to question him." Rodrigo wiped blood from his forehead. "What did you expect? It's not like you were doing so well. And, anyway, since when is it a crime to antagonize a prisoner?"

"I asked you if you understood, Lieutenant Benalcázar."

"Yes...Capitán."

"Why damage his helmet? Why demand the source of his gold? That's not what I told you to do. Isn't all the gold of Vilcabamba enough?"

"Incan gold, demon gold—does it really matter?"

"You think I haven't thought of that?" asked Cristóbal. "I've seen the gold in the ñakaqs' helmets. Have you thought that maybe it was stolen from Vilcabamba? Or perhaps given as a reward? You can't just demand gold from Tagón without knowing whether or not his people have an alliance with Manco. It's not that easy."

"You're making this too complicated, Capitán. We grab as much gold as we can and then find our way back to New Spain. It seems simple to me."

"Does it?" asked Cristóbal. "Tell me, how many ñakaqs like Tagón have you seen outside Nueva Tierra?"

"Don't play games with me, Capitán. None, of course."

"Correct. So it follows that these ñakaqs don't have a way into our world. Only Manco Inca does. The key to making our way home is still to find Vilcabamba. Forget this idea of stealing ñakaq gold."

Rodrigo continued to wipe his forehead. "Why not take what demon gold we can find as well?"

Cristóbal felt the fury ringing in his ears. While Rodrigo had a rat-like cunning, he didn't understand the finer points of strategy. Deliberately slowing his breathing, he said, "You're no student of the ways of the conquistadors, are you?"

"I'm no student of anything, Capitán. I'm a lieutenant."

"We should all remember we're following in the footsteps of Pizarro and Cortés. They achieved greatness in the face of almost impossible odds. I always ask myself, what would they have done."

"You can tie yourself into knots with too many questions."

Cristóbal stopped pacing. "Maybe that's why you'll never be a capitán." He grabbed Rodrigo by the arm. "Lieutenant Benalcázar, we don't want these ñakaqs as our enemies. We need allies in this strange land."

Rodrigo pulled his arm from his grasp. "It'd be better for all of us if you took less notice of those books you read and more of what's in front of you every day."

"No conquistador has ever had any success without enlisting allies. That's why I made certain Huarcay joined the campaign." Cristóbal's temples were throbbing now. "We need these ñakaqs. We need to treat Tagón well so he'll help us find Manco Inca."

"The padre says they're demons." Rodrigo scowled. "Are we now seeking demons as allies?"

"I'll decide who we seek allegiances with. I just hope I can undo the damage you've done. Now, go and wash that wound — and stay away from Tagón. If you do anything like this again, I'll relieve you of your command. Is that clear?"

Rodrigo turned to go.

"I didn't hear your response, Lieutenant Benalcázar."

"Yes, Capitán." Rodrigo's reply came through gritted teeth.

***

When Cristóbal entered the prisoner's tent, Tagón's eyes followed him. With the ñakaq's face hidden under that monstrous beard, it was impossible to tell what he was thinking. Cristóbal ordered the guards to leave and then said, "I think it's about time we spoke frankly with each other."

Tagón blinked once but otherwise gave no indication he had heard anything.

Cristóbal held out the wineskin and two cups he was carrying. "It's time the two of us spoke as leader to leader."

The ñakaq stared at him.

"The attack on your people was a mistake," said Cristóbal. "I'm sorry for what happened. I didn't give the order. Do you understand?" Cristóbal put the wineskin and cups down and took out his knife. Tagón's mouth twitched slightly. "I'm releasing you. My battle isn't with your people."

Cristóbal cut the cords binding the ñakaq's hands and feet. "I also apologize for my lieutenant's actions. He won't be speaking to you again."

Tagón rubbed his wrists as he stared at his helmet on the ground. Cristóbal handed it to him, and Tagón started picking up the scattered inlays. "My people will still attack you." His words rasped from the back of his throat.

"You don't want us in your lands," said Cristóbal. "We would love nothing more than to leave. I have an offer for you. Do you want to hear it?"

Tagón nodded in the direction of the wineskin. "First we drink."

Cristóbal put down his knife and poured wine into both cups. "This is the finest wine in New Spain and I have very little of it left."

Tagón took one of the cups from him and, raising it to his lips, swallowed the wine in one draft.

Cristóbal took a sip from his cup.

"It's our custom for the giver to match the receiver," said Tagón. "Swallow it all."

Cristóbal was taken aback. "I'm not trying to poison you."

"I didn't accuse you of poisoning me, I accused you of being impolite."

"Impolite?"

"If you want our conversation to continue, empty your cup."

Cristóbal hesitated for a moment and then gulped the wine down.

"That's better," said Tagón, "now fill my cup again."

"My people would consider that comment impolite."

"You're in my lands asking something of me, so you have the responsibility for politeness."

Cristóbal squeezed the skin so that a stream of wine poured into the ñakaq's cup.

"To the top this time," said Tagón. Cristóbal filled it until it was almost overflowing and the ñakaq immediately drained it again. Nodding at the Spaniard, he said, "Your turn."

Cristóbal filled his own cup to the brim at Tagón's insistence and drank the wine without taking a breath.

"Now I wish to put my offer to you."

"Wait, we haven't finished our wine yet."

"We can finish it after we speak."

"That's not how my people discuss offers. We need to finish what you've brought. Anything else would be impolite."

Cristóbal was already feeling the effects of the wine. He repeated the ritual, although this was not how he usually savored his wine. By the time the skin hung limp and deflated, Cristóbal's head was swirling and he was finding it increasingly difficult to think straight.

The only effect the wine appeared to be having on Tagón was that his glare had mellowed and his eyes were now partly closed. "Tell me this offer," he said finally.

Cristóbal gathered his thoughts. "You speak Quechua. That means your people have contact with Incas."

Tagón nodded.

Cristóbal continued. "The Incas here have a way back to our lands. If you lead us to where they're hidden, we'll leave your lands forever—and take them with us.

"I take you to the place of the beardless ones and we'll be rid of all of you?"

"Yes. Do we have an agreement?"

Tagón tried to push the inlays back into his helmet, but they kept falling out. He looked up. "Have you truly released me?"

"You're free to go."

"Even if I don't agree to your offer?"

"Yes."

"Good." Tagón gathered up the inlays and stood up. He took a step, swaying a little, and then eased himself back down again. "This wine of yours has strength."

He leaned back, his eyes closing.

"You haven't given me your answer," said Cristóbal.

The ñakaq's eyes were now shut.

"Tagón?"

"We're agreed." With that Tagón started snoring.

Chapter 17

El diario de Cristóbal de Varga

What man has the right to denounce another a demon? Who can truthfully make such judgment with the acuity of the unblemished? Should we not first be vigilant for demonic shadows that blight our own being? Should we not first watch the dark dance that plays our thoughts and dreams? Should we not first peer into our own souls?

It was thus that I struck a bargain with Tagón the ñakaq to, for good or ill, follow the direction he chooses for us. Would this pact prove to be the portent of our triumph or the harbinger of our downfall? I cannot, in truth, confer any certainty on the elusive answer to that question.

A leader must decide who to trust. Even the greatest leader does not absolve himself of this most intimate of necessities. Yet to forge a path that your own men spurn takes the ultimate courage. I can only hope that I have trusted wisely.

Chapter 18

Fight or Flee

Cristóbal ignored the mutterings when Tagón first joined him at the head of the company. In his men's eyes the ñakaq was either a demon or a fierce enemy. It wasn't an easy decision to give him his freedom. But great leaders didn't make easy decisions. For his part, Tagón held true to his word, his stamina prodigious as he led the way south on foot, refusing the offer of a horse.

Late that afternoon, a sharp wind sprang up as the conquistadors reached the dark jagged cliffs of the southern mountain range. Cristóbal gave the signal to halt and stared at the barrier in front of them, aware of the restlessness in his company.

Tagón walked along the cliff face, studying the formations. "Here," he said finally. "This is the way in."

Cristóbal frowned. "Where?"

"You can only see it from here," said Tagón, waving him over.

Cristóbal rode with Héctor and Rodrigo to where the ñakaq was standing, and to his surprise he could see an entrance to a pass hidden by a wall of rock, invisible except from their angle.

"Come," said Tagón, gesturing them to follow him. He took one step into the entrance and half his body disappeared.

Cristóbal gasped. Another entrada?

"I don't like this, Capitán," muttered Héctor.

Tagón again signaled them to follow. "It's safe."

"How do we know what's on the other side?" asked Cristóbal.

Tagón stepped back out and his body was whole again. "I told you I'm taking you to the beardless ones."

"What color is the sky on the other side?"

Tagón seemed confused by the question. "The color it always is."

"Red?

"Of course." Tagón looked nervously over his shoulder in the direction they had marched. "We don't have much time."

"Why?"

"I've given my word to lead you to the Incas, but I can't protect you from my people."

Héctor asked, "Will we be able to return once we leave the pass on the other side?"

"No, but—"

A single drumbeat like a roll of thunder echoed through the valley, overwhelming the rushing of the wind. Several horses reared and the war dogs started whimpering.

Tagón glanced around. "If we don't enter the pass now, you need to prepare for battle."

"*Mierda!* This is a trap," cried Rodrigo. "The demon has led us into a trap."

A chill snaked down Cristóbal's spine as he turned his distressed mount around. Before the last drumbeat faded, thousands of armored ñakaqs wielding horcas emerged from hidden places on the slopes to the west and began marching across the plain toward the conquistadors.

"I know my people," said Tagón. "They won't follow us into the pass because they'll expect an ambush."

"Don't believe him, Capitán," said Rodrigo, his horse rearing as another drumbeat sounded.

"Hurry!" said Tagón. "My people will take the only other way from here into the valley of the Incas, a twisting mountain path. You'll be well ahead of them and safe from attack for days."

The drumbeats started again. Louder this time.

Cristóbal was frozen with indecision. What was the best course? He looked around. The curve of the cliffs on both sides gave some protection to their flanks.

"Are we fighting or fleeing, Capitán?" cried Rodrigo. "Give the order."

Ñakaq helmet flames moved inexorably toward them. Each new drumbeat merged with the echo of the one before, the sound pulsating to a crescendo.

Cristóbal drew a sharp breath. "We are conquistadors. We fight." His voice drowned the echoes of the drumbeat. "Prime the cannons! Load the harquebuses and crossbows!"

The conquistadors unsheathed their swords and grasped their halberds. Small breech-loading cannons were uncovered on carriages. The crossbowmen assumed their positions and loaded the first rounds of their weapons.

The ñakaq horde started running, a malformed mass of contorted limbs, shouting guttural battle cries as a river of fire surged across the valley.

To his dismay, Cristóbal heard Padre Núñez's voice rise above the tumult.

"The *Requerimiento* requires you to recognize the Church as your Mistress and Governess of the World..."

The padre stood on a wagon next to the largest cannon with gusts of wind blowing his robes into a wild fury.

"...and if you do not do this, then with the help of God we shall come mightily against you, and we shall make war on you everywhere and in every way that we can..."

"Get him down from there!" shouted Cristóbal, the incessant pounding of the drums exploding inside his skull.

Two conquistadors dragged Padre Núñez away as he continued to recite the *Requerimiento*, his last words drowned out by the battle cries of the ñakaqs, who now swarmed toward the Spaniards.

Cristóbal raised his sword in a call to battle, praying that his voice would not betray his fear. *"Santiago y cierra, España!"*

He brought his blade down quickly, signaling for the cannons to be fired.

The cannon shots struck the oncoming hordes, drowning the battle drums and scattering dozens of bodies in a blood-filled series of blasts. The ñakaqs were stunned for a moment, but it wasn't long before they gathered pace again.

"Load," cried Cristóbal, shocked that the first round hadn't given him more time. Then he pointed to Tagón and Padre Núñez. "Take these two out of the line of fire and don't let them out of your sight."

The advancing ñakaqs had made considerable ground by the time the cannons were fired again. Rolling toward the conquistadors was wave after relentless wave of tangled hair and wild eyes. The second round of cannon fire killed just as many as the first and a fountain of fire helmets shot into the air, but this time the attack didn't slow.

This was going to be a hellish battle. The Incas had always dispersed in a blind panic when faced with cannon fire, but these ñakaqs just kept coming.

Cristóbal galloped toward his mounted gunmen shouting "Harquebusiers! With me!" knowing the ñakaqs were now in range.

He quickly organized them into two rows. "Prepare to fire… first line…fire!"

The crack of gunshots drowned out the drumbeats and battle cries. Dozens of ñakaqs collapsed and the attack stuttered.

"Second line…fire!"

The ñakaqs looked around in confusion as more fell. While the harquebusiers reloaded, the ñakaqs regrouped and charged again.

"Fire at will! We need to hold them as long as possible."

The acrid smell of burning gunpowder stung his nostrils as the Spaniards continued to fire their harquebuses. Still the ñakaq army charged toward them, pushing the bodies away and manically focused on the conquistadors.

A scream. One of the harquebuses had exploded in a soldier's face.

Horcas flew through the air and pierced several gunmen's armor.

Was nothing going to stop them? Firearms were taking too long to reload. He gave the signal to his crossbowmen to shoot. Then he ordered the Incan slingers to unleash their storm of stones onto the oncoming ñakaqs. The barrage finally had an effect on their advance as they raised their shields and stopped in their tracks. Now was the time to press home his advantage. Cristóbal gave the signal for the cavalry to attack with Rodrigo leading the charge.

The mounted conquistadors crashed into the ñakaq mass, piercing their armor with lances. Rodrigo lifted a skewered ñakaq high above the fray and flung him free from his spear so that he whipped through the air. When the ñakaqs began grasping at the lances to haul the riders from their horses, the cavalrymen used their height advantage to stab down into their necks with their swords. The ñakaqs still managed to push forward, thrusting their horcas at the horses and bringing several to the ground. Four of them dragged a conquistador from his mount and managed to pierce his face with their horcas after pulling off his helmet—just before Rodrigo hewed them to death with his sword.

With the release of the war dogs, the ñakaq advance faltered again. Then the Spanish foot soldiers, brandishing swords and halberds, entered the fray followed by the Incan warriors with axes in hand, and the battleline became a brutal stalemate of furious face-to-face fighting.

***

As the sun started to set and cast long shadows across the increasingly frantic combat, Padre Núñez was deep in prayer, holding his wooden cross and sitting with his back to the rock face that concealed the entrance to the pass. He had positioned himself so that he couldn't see the fighting, although the rage of battle still reached his ears.

Tagón sat next to him, leaning against the rocky wall. "Who are you talking to with your eyes closed?" he asked, his voice raw and ragged.

Padre Núñez looked up from his prayer position. "Don't speak to me with your demon Spanish." He clutched his cross and held it up at the ñakaq.

"Why do you insult me when I speak in your tongue?"

"Knowledge of languages you can't possibly know is the sign of a demon."

"My people forget nothing. I remember the words I hear." Tagón gestured at the cross. "What is this? You hold it as if I should fear it, but I see nothing to fear."

Padre Núñez held it up to the ñakaq's face. "In the Name of Jesus Christ, our God and Lord, I command you to flee before the cross."

Tagón reached out and touched the cross, but the padre pulled it away from him. "I want to know about this word *demon* you call my people. You used it to command an attack on us. What does it mean?"

"Are you playing some monstrous game with me?"

"My people don't play games. Tell me what a demon is."

"An enemy of God. A servant of the devil. A creature with no soul."

"These are too many words I do not understand." Tagón's unblinking stare locked onto the padre's, unnerving him. "Do you wish me to be a demon?"

Padre Núñez hesitated. It had grown dark around them. "I only want to know the truth."

"We all have wishes. What do you wish the truth to be?"

The padre fell silent. He hadn't expected a question like this from the ñakaq.

Tagón stared at him intently. "Come, give me that cross of yours."

Padre Núñez slowly handed it to him.

Tagón moved it from one hand to the other and turned it around. "This would not be a good weapon."

"It isn't a weapon. It's a way of getting closer to God."

"I know nothing of this God you and the other Spanish speak of."

"God is all-seeing, all-knowing, and all-good."

"Does God carry a weapon?"

"No."

"Does he wear armor?"

"No."

"Then the only way he could survive in these lands is if he was hidden. Is he hidden?"

"Well...he is not seen, but he is around us."

"He is here with us now? Unseen?"

"Yes, he's watching us. He watches all of us."

"Even demons?"

Padre Núñez pulled away. "Are you mocking me?"

"I'm just trying to understand this God. We do not have these sorts of beliefs."

"But you have your own pagan gods, don't you? Like the Incas. The sun, the moon, the god of rain or fire perhaps?"

"These are all *things*, not invisible beings."

Padre Núñez's brow furrowed. He had never heard of a race with no gods. "Don't your people believe in a power greater than themselves?"

"We rely only on our own strength."

The padre's furrows deepened. This ñakaq surprised him. "Tell me then, where do your people believe you go after you die?"

"We bury most of our bodies deep in the mountains."

"I don't mean your physical body. What do you believe happens to your soul, your spirit, the part of you that isn't your physical body?"

"For us, there's nothing after death. Before birth there's nothing and after death there's nothing."

The padre shrank back further as the battle sounds continued to rage through the darkness. Of course, claiming no beliefs could just be a clever demonic trick. Somehow, though, it felt like the ñakaq was telling the truth. If so, it provided him with the ultimate challenge. How could one bring someone to know God's glory if he had no concept of a power higher than himself?

Tagón handed back the cross. "Is it possible to prove someone is not a demon?"

Padre Núñez pressed the cross to his own chest. "There is a way. If you choose of your own free will to be baptized into the Church, it would prove you had a soul. A demon could never allow itself to be baptized."

Chapter 19

Valley of the Incas

Cristóbal's stomach cramped. The ñakaqs were pressing them against the cliff wall. The battle was reaching a brutal pitch. He had lost men. Too many men. He knew he had made the wrong decision. A good commander chooses his field of combat. A good commander gives himself time to prepare. He'd failed on both counts. Could he not trust his instincts under pressure? He straightened up. This wasn't a time for guilt. He had no choice but to trust Tagón's word.

Calling Héctor and Rodrigo to him, he said, "Get your best men. We need to hold the ñakaqs while the others escape into the pass."

"We're running?" Rodrigo glared at him.

"A conquistador picks his battles." Cristóbal waited until his lieutenants had passed on his command, then he forced his voice above the tumult. "Retreat! Retreat! This way."

The mounted soldiers doggedly maintained the conquistador line while the rest of the company disappeared into the mountain behind them.

"Go, Capitán," shouted Héctor, fending off two ñakaqs. "The others need you. You're no use to any of us dead."

"My decision sent us into battle. I'm not leaving until you're all safe."

The ñakaqs continued to fight with unabated fury, seemingly unaware that the territory between the battleline and the cliffs had emptied in the darkness.

"Wait for the command," cried Cristóbal as he pierced another ñakaq in the face.

"Now!"

The conquistadors abruptly turned their horses and galloped toward the mountainside. Cristóbal glanced over his shoulder, expecting to see the horde charging after them. To his surprise, they stood stunned for a moment by the sudden retreat. Then a volley of horcas arced through the air, striking two soldiers. By the time the ñakaqs started their pursuit, the conquistadors were safe. Cristóbal was the last to enter the pass where Héctor and his patrol members were waiting.

"We'll hold them," panted Héctor. "You keep going."

"There's no need for any of us to stay. Tagón said the ñakaqs won't enter the pass."

"And you trust him?"

"I have to trust him now. Come, let's go. I want to lead the way when we enter this valley of the Incas."

Outside, past the serrated mountain wall, the war drums stopped beating.

***

Cristóbal was too weary to welcome the scar of red sky that appeared above the pass when morning broke. Veins of light twisted their way down the rocks toward the riders. The conquistadors had moved slowly through the night as battle exhaustion weighed heavily on them and their mounts, and now the sun's heat threatened to punish them further. Cristóbal felt the extra burden of the fifty dead Spaniards, at least as many Incan warriors, and a dozen horses killed by his decisions.

Tagón, as always on foot, had dropped back, and Diego tried to pull his cousin out of his stupor as they rode side by side. "We're almost at the gates of Vilcabamba, Cristóbal. Now's not the time to disappear into your thoughts."

"If I had trusted Tagón earlier, lives could have been saved."

"You were right to be cautious."

"There's a time to be cautious and a time to be bold. A great leader chooses his times wisely."

"You are a great leader, Cristóbal. Surely Pizarro suffered casualties?"

"He suffered very few."

"But he didn't fight armored ñakaqs with horcas. Incan warriors wear only cotton and their weapons are made of copper and stone. You've fought a much more formidable foe than Pizarro."

"Maybe, but the deaths could have been avoided. It's my duty to know who to trust. And now because I failed in my duty, fifty Spaniards won't be given a Christian burial."

As they continued, Cristóbal gradually grew aware of a rushing sound. Was that one of the phantom sounds that your head sometimes tricks you with? Or was it the muffled moans of the dying conquistadors he'd left behind? He focused on his breathing to drown out the ghosts.

But it didn't work. The rushing sound grew louder and louder until it was a roar. His head throbbed under the onslaught. Was he going mad? Was his own mind now threatening him? He cupped his hand to his ears instinctively although he knew the roar would persist.

But it didn't.

The roar muffled to something softer and more indistinct when he covered his ears.

It wasn't in his head.

The noise wasn't in his head.

He took his hands away, and the roar was even louder, increasing with every step his horse took.

And then it dawned on him. It was a noise he hadn't heard for a long time. The sound of rushing water. Digging his heels into his horse's flanks, he urged it from a walk into a canter.

The pass widened into brightness in front of him, and his hand tightened instinctively around his sword. As he left the pass, he swung his sword behind him. His blade clanged as if the opening was solid rock. Tagón had been right. They couldn't return the same way.

He had just come through another entrada. Cristóbal found the predictability of it almost soothing. Then, just as he felt he was beginning to understand this new world, it surprised him once more. From the cliffs to his right a magnificent waterfall seethed from the rocks, plummeting into a wild river that rushed through the valley.

But something was wrong.

The water churned and foamed in a way he hadn't seen before. The spray and mist plumed skyward in an odd way.

Some of the other conquistadors galloped toward the water's edge.

"Wait!" he shouted. "Don't touch it. The water is boiling."

Chapter 20

The Cold Metal

The conquistadors marched downriver and made camp a distance from the waterfall where its roar no longer dominated. After accepting Huarcay's invitation to join him in one of the steaming rock pools, Cristóbal now sat naked as the air chilled into evening and thick mist spread across the valley. The aches of battle slowly dissolved as he watched Incan servants carry drinking water from the river, allowing it to cool before filling the company's sagging water skins. Across the campsite his soldiers nursed their wounds after yesterday's battle and all-night ride.

Huarcay stepped out of his litter, and two servants helped him into the pool while others screened him from view with several embroidered blankets.

Once settled, the nobleman said, "Two of my carriers were killed last night, and their replacements are not giving me a smooth ride. My back pains me." He signaled for coca tea.

"Maybe you could try horseback instead," suggested Cristóbal.

"I don't trust your beasts. They're too unpredictable."

"You sound like Tagón."

Huarcay sipped from the cup a servant brought to his lips. "How far does the ñakaq say we are from Vilcabamba?"

"Tagón says it's a day's march," said Cristóbal leaning back so that the water touched his chin.

"And you believe him?"

"Yes."

Huarcay indicated for a servant to pour more scented oil into the water. "Does he call it Vilcabamba?"

"He calls it the place of the beardless ones. What else would it be?"

Huarcay motioned for their hair to be washed. "And don't rub too hard." He turned to Cristóbal again. "Did he say why the ñakaqs allow these Incas on their lands?"

"He said the beardless ones started coming here a long time ago in small numbers and were allowed to live in this valley as long as they didn't settle ñakaq territory beyond it. That means for Manco Inca to move freely between this valley and New Spain, there has to be both another entrada and a way out here."

"I see. Then what's your plan?"

"Tagón tells me we have two days before the ñakaqs reach this valley via the mountain path and by then we'll be a day's march ahead of them on the other side of the valley. That doesn't leave us a lot of time to destroy Manco Inca's army, collect all his gold, and return to New Spain to crown you emperor."

Cristóbal heard someone clearing their throat.

"Excuse me." Diego's head appeared over the top of the blankets. "When you've finished having your hair washed, Cristóbal, I've got something to show you."

***

"I've been thinking," said Diego as Cristóbal joined him at the campfire with his hair still wet.

"It worries me sometimes that I let you do too much thinking for me." Cristóbal wiped away some water trailing down his cheek.

"We can't avoid another battle with the ñakaqs. You know that, don't you?

"I've come to that conclusion." Cristóbal stared at the flames. "Why are you roasting that helmet?"

"I put it there when you started your bath, so it's been there a long time."

"You know," said Cristóbal, "you only notice other people's unpleasantness after you've rid yourself of your own. Maybe you should bathe while you've got the chance." He laughed. "Now, tell me what that ñakaq helmet is doing in the fire."

"I'll show you." Diego used his sword to lift the helmet out of the fire and swing it around for Cristóbal to see. "This ñakaq armor is made of a remarkable metal."

"We know that. It's difficult to pierce."

"Yes, but it's even more remarkable than I first thought. Come closer. Here, touch it."

"What?"

"Just feel the metal, not the gold inlays."

Cristóbal tentatively brushed the helmet with his fingertip. He frowned. Reaching out again, this time he kept his finger on the metal. Then he lifted the helmet from Diego's sword and held it as he ran his palm across the metal surface both inside and out. "There's no heat anywhere. That's impossible."

"Impossible for any metal we know." He took the helmet from Cristóbal. "Something didn't make sense to me. Why do the ñakaqs have fire inside the upper cavity of these helmets?

"To strike fear in their enemies?"

"No doubt. And to provide light for night battles. But then I thought, why would they take the risk of heating their scalps?"

"Yes, it would seem a high price to pay."

"Clearly there's no price to pay," said Diego. "The metal used in their armor is not only difficult for our weapons to penetrate, it also protects against fire."

"So, how does knowing this help us?"

"It gave me an idea. Let me tell you what I have in mind."

***

Sarpay rarely enjoyed sharing a litter with her brother. Huarcay was always too ready to complain that the carriers were too clumsy and causing his back to ache. This time the ride was worse than usual because she guessed what Huarcay was going to say to her at the end of it—and she wasn't looking forward to the conversation.

She stared at the river, watching the steam clouds rise from its roiling waters and join the ever-thickening mists of the evening air. How was it possible she was now torn? She had to admit that, despite herself, she'd grown fond of Cristóbal. There was something about the doubts that lay behind his mask that she found appealing. She craved him not because he was great, but because he was flawed. And part of her hated herself for it.

Some distance upriver from the camp, the carriers lowered the litter. Huarcay dismissed them, and Sarpay walked with him toward the riverbank.

"We need to change our plan," said Huarcay, without looking at his sister.

Sarpay felt suddenly cold. "Why?" she asked, although she knew the answer.

"These ñakaqs are a complete surprise. They don't seem to distinguish between us and the Spaniards. I've lost so many warriors already. We could all be killed."

"You don't know that for certain."

Huarcay turned to face his sister as mists blotted the purple hue of the sky. "Have you been lying in the capitán's bed too long, sister?"

"He's not the same as the others." Sarpay's voice sounded thin to her own ears.

"Yes, you're right. He's worse than the others because his actions have led us here."

How had it come to this point? She'd always been so certain of her convictions. "I don't regret any of our decisions, even though the circumstances have not turned out as we expected."

Huarcay stepped toward Sarpay. "You know, sometimes I feel you've enjoyed the role of the capitán's *prostituta* a little too much."

The Spanish word jarred Sarpay in the stream of Quechua. "Don't call me that word."

"Of course, sister." He reached out and held her hand. "You've done well."

Sarpay pulled away.

She hated herself, but she knew what she had to do now.

Chapter 21

Betrayal

Sarpay sat astride Cristóbal as she massaged perfumed oils deep into the aching muscles of his back. He winced as her fingers pushed too firmly into the vulnerable area behind his shoulder blades.

"Careful, you know not to press too hard there."

"I'm sorry. One of my other fingers now doesn't seem quite straight anymore."

"You're the one who seems *preocupado* tonight, Sarpay. Is something wrong besides your finger?"

"I'm worried that the ñakaqs will attack again."

"There's no need to worry. We have a plan once we reach Vilcabamba tomorrow." He turned and looked up at her. "Come, let me massage you tonight."

"You need gentle hands for massage. Your hands are made for battle."

"Give me a chance. I may surprise you."

"Just lie there and stop talking."

"You think I'm just a coarse conquistador, don't you?"

"No, you're different to the others."

"Let me show you how different." Cristóbal got up on all fours so that Sarpay now sat on him like a horse. He tilted to the side so that she could no longer hold on and she fell from his oiled back onto the nest of furs, laughing. How rarely he had heard that laugh! He twisted to face her and grabbed her by the arm, leaning back into the furs and pulling her so that she lay on top of him. Then he started to gently knead the muscles in her shoulders.

She pressed her cheek into his face as he continued, her body moving in a gentle rhythm across his.

"Have I told you, Cristóbal," she said, "that Incan noblemen have servants pluck the hair from their faces?"

"Do they? For a Spaniard that would be torture. We have too much hair."

"On our first night, you agreed that you shave your beard because it helps you command."

Cristóbal moved his hands lower down Sarpay's back. "That's only partly true. The other reason is that my beard is so streaked with gray it makes me look older."

"Vanity, not just ambition and discipline."

"No, not vanity. I'm...not a young man anymore. I need to keep the respect of my men, especially my lieutenants."

"You have the vigor of a young man," said Sarpay. "That's what matters."

She reached back and enveloped him.

***

That night Cristóbal dreamed again of the condor as it flew over seething flame-clouds under a deep red sky. This time he knew *he* was the condor and saw through its eyes the strange fire that burned below him. He stretched his mighty wings and felt the currents lift him. The purest of joys coursed through his body. *Nothing can touch me because I can fly higher than anyone.* He wanted to shout the words to the heavens—but the only sound he heard was a screech.

And the screech wasn't his own.

He felt a sharp pain in his back as talons dug deep into his flesh.

Something had attacked him from above. One of his wings was shredded in the onslaught and his neck torn open so he was unable to turn his head to see his attacker.

The two were locked together.

They started to fall.

Together.

Forever.

***

Cristóbal awoke, vaguely aware of shouting outside his tent. He reached over for the now familiar form of Sarpay. To his surprise, he grasped only furs.

He sat up, holding his head as Rodrigo and Martín burst into his tent.

"They're gone!" cried the lieutenant.

"Who?"

"The Incas. All of them. Huarcay. The servants. The warriors. They must have drugged the guards."

It took a moment for Cristóbal to clear his thoughts. He looked across at the indent where Sarpay usually lay. "And Sarpay." He threw away the blankets that she'd obviously pushed up against his back to make it feel as if she was still lying with him.

"We've been betrayed," said Rodrigo. "The *malparidos* have joined Manco Inca and left us at the mercy of the ñakaqs."

Cristóbal was gripped by a wave of raw anger. He struggled for breath. "I've...been made to look a fool."

"They're on foot. There's a chance we can chase them down with the horses and dogs before they reach Vilcabamba. I have my men saddling the fastest horses."

"Wait. We don't know what sort of defenses Manco Inca has. A small party will be vulnerable."

"Are you going to let Huarcay do this to us, Capitán? My men are ready to ride."

"No, our goal is to take Vilcabamba. Prepare the whole company. We'll move in full force."

"But—"

"And remember, Lieutenant Benalcázar, *you* have no men. They are all under my command."

Cristóbal stared down Rodrigo until he finally nodded, and then he and Martín left.

***

Cristóbal jerked compulsively at his reins as he rode downriver through the morning mists, flanked by his two lieutenants. How could he have allowed the Incas to do this? Wave after wave of rage pulsed through him. With each upsurge he suppressed, another stronger one formed and rose from the pit of his stomach up into his head. His face was on fire. His ears rang. *Stay calm. Good decisions are never made in fury. Stay calm. Don't let the white heat consume you.* Huarcay had made him look a fool, yes, but it wasn't as if he'd ever fully trusted the nobleman. And the other Incas, of course they were just following orders. But Sarpay...he had opened his dreams and fears to her. Sarpay's betrayal was the one that wounded him.

The snarling mastiffs leading the chase put him on edge, making it even harder for him to control his anger. They had been baited by the robes that the Incas had left behind and were in a hunting frenzy. The trail always veered back to the river which twisted and cooled throughout the day's march. When the mists finally cleared, it became obvious the path to Vilcabamba lay south toward the foothills.

"There's something that doesn't make sense to me, Capitán," said Héctor. "What does Huarcay hope to achieve by joining Manco Inca now? Why lead us to the gates of Vilcabamba and then betray us?"

"He lost warriors in the last battle," said Cristóbal. "I could see the ñakaqs preyed on his mind. There's no doubt Manco Inca has come to some sort of agreement with them, so Huarcay probably believes Vilcabamba will hold until the ñakaqs reach us, and we'll be battling on two fronts."

"That would be a disaster," said Rodrigo.

"I think Huarcay is wrong," said Héctor. "Vilcabamba won't be as well-defended as we expect."

Rodrigo didn't hide his contempt. "So now we're hoping the emperor's citadel is unprotected? Maybe he'll hold the gates open for us."

"Look at the lengths that Manco Inca has gone to ensure his city is hidden," said Héctor, ignoring Rodrigo's sarcasm. "You either protect yourself through strength or you protect yourself through secrecy."

"Or both," said Rodrigo.

"I'm not sure it's ever both," said Cristóbal. "You might protect yourself with the secrecy of feigned strength, but that's not the same as actually having strength. Héctor may be right and Vilcabamba will fall more easily than we think."

It was late afternoon when they found the truth.

They arrived at a recently abandoned Incan village huddled on the banks of the river, surrounded by a cluster of hills that merged into a giant mountain range in the distance. The houses were built in threes with distinctive interlocking trapezium-shaped stones and thatched roofs. There were signs of hastily extinguished fires and partially eaten meals on the floor. Corn and potatoes grew on the terraces carved into the hills behind the settlement where alpacas grazed. Dozens of large balsa rafts dotted the riverbank while the river churned a path into the rocks, disappearing into the shadows of a steep-sided gorge. There was no sign of where the inhabitants had gone.

The conquistadors had come to a dead-end.

Cristóbal ordered Rodrigo to get Tagón, and when the ñakaq joined him, he said, "We can no longer follow the river. Which direction is Vilcabamba?"

Tagón appeared confused. "This is the home of the beardless ones I spoke of."

"I can see this is an Incan village, but the people have fled to the city for protection. Where's the city?"

"I don't know of any city of beardless ones."

"Then another settlement where the Incas live."

"There's no other settlement."

Rodrigo spat on the ground. "The demon has lied to us."

"My people don't lie. I've brought you to the place of the beardless ones." Tagón turned to Cristóbal. "You said you'll leave our lands if I brought you here. We have a bargain."

"I thought you were taking us to Manco Inca. I can't fulfill my side of the bargain if you haven't fulfilled yours."

"I've done what I said I would. There's nothing more I can do."

Was there no one he could trust? Cristóbal's suppressed anger exploded to the surface. "Tell us where we can go," he demanded.

Tagón said, "I've been honorable. I'm unable to do anything more for you."

"This time the *malparido* has led us into a trap with no way out," said Rodrigo, seething. "Look around. How can we escape the next ñakaq attack?"

"You say you can't leave our lands," said Tagón. "I can't help you anymore."

A hot wave of fury rolled through Cristóbal. "Put him in chains!" he barked.

"What? You have the honor of a duende!"

Several conquistadors closed in on Tagón with swords in hand. They overwhelmed him and then took him away.

"Look here," said Héctor, pointing to tracks, "the Incas have headed into the hills."

"Then that's where Vilcabamba lies." Cristóbal snarled the order to move forward.

***

At first the slopes proved to be easy to negotiate on horseback, and the trail left by the fleeing Incas was clear. The sun threatened to set and mists billowed around the company, reducing visibility. The conquistadors were forced to rely solely on the war dogs still on the scent of Huarcay's people.

"It's here," said Cristóbal, peering ahead. "Vilcabamba is here and Huarcay knew it was here. Why else would he flee?"

"I don't see how Manco could hide a large city in these hills," said Rodrigo.

Cristóbal squinted. "Nueva Tierra is a place of hidden things."

"Maybe the way to Vilcabamba is through another entrada," said Héctor.

"At least Huarcay is leading us straight to it," said Cristóbal. "And the dogs are getting frantic, so we must be getting close."

As the mists thickened, the chase led the conquistadors onto a plateau. The air suddenly whistled with a deluge of Incan slingstones, striking the Spaniards and denting their armor. Two horses were hit in the legs and collapsed to the ground, taking their riders with them.

Cristóbal pointed into the mist. "That's where they came from."

A second volley of slingstones hit the conquistadors from another direction. Cristóbal was suddenly disoriented. He spun around. Where were the attackers? It was like fighting an invisible enemy. The war dogs had now whipped themselves into a frenzy and were tugging on their chains with manic ferocity.

"Release them," ordered Rodrigo, and the armored mastiffs charged through the mist.

"This way," he shouted.

The conquistadors broke into a gallop after the dogs.

Another hail of stones rained down on the Spanish and several horses reared. Cristóbal was thrown from his mount after a number of rocks struck it simultaneously. He hit the ground hard and pain shot from his hip down his left leg. As he struggled to his feet, a sudden gust of wind momentarily cleared the mist and the final rays of the setting sun revealed the Incas, slings and *bolas* in hand, in a far corner of the plateau.

"There," cried Rodrigo, leading the charge straight at the Incan warriors.

As Cristóbal called his horse back to him, he saw the conquistadors push their horses into a wild dash. Despite an avalanche of stones coming at them, only one of the soldiers fell. As they drew closer, the Incas swung *bolas* around their heads and released them at the horses' legs, bringing down several of the mounts. The barrage of projectiles only stopped once the war dogs reached the warriors and they were forced to brandish their copper axes to defend themselves.

Cristóbal lunged to grab his horse's reins and then tried to calm his mount as he watched the charging conquistadors reach the Incas, hacking and butchering them without mercy, easily shattering their wooden shields and penetrating their cotton armor. Shrill cries pierced the dusk, and the plateau was awash with a blood-red sunset. Soon there was no resistance and Rodrigo pushed through to the servants and villagers cowering behind the warriors, leading a massacre of the old, the young and the defenseless.

"Enough!" Cristóbal's voice rose above the screams. "I said enough!"

He had remounted and now galloped into the fray. Most of the conquistadors stopped at his command, but Rodrigo continued hewing into the Incas until Cristóbal was right in front of him. "I said stop, Lieutenant Benalcázar."

Rodrigo had his sword high above his head, ready to strike another Inca when he seemed to become aware of Cristóbal for the first time. "I didn't hear your command, Capitán." He lowered his sword.

Cristóbal pushed his way past him toward a group of servants huddled around Huarcay and Sarpay. He glared at the Incan nobleman but couldn't bring himself to look at Sarpay. "Where is Vilcabamba?" he demanded.

Huarcay struggled for breath. "I don't know."

"You don't know?" Cristóbal's voice strained. "You still claim not to know where Vilcabamba is? You stand there after you've betrayed me, and you expect me to believe your lies. This is the last time I will ask you this question as a reasonable man. Where is Vilcabamba?"

"I...I don't—"

Cristóbal sheathed his sword, his hand shaking with rage as the darkness grew. "Tie up the ones that are still alive and march them back down to the village. Lock them all up and place them under guard. All except Huarcay. I want him tied to a stake in the town square for me to deal with."

Chapter 22

The Rage of the Conquistador

When the conquistadors started piling firewood at Huarcay's feet as Cristóbal and Diego watched, the blood drained from the nobleman's face. "No!" he cried, straining at the cords that held him to the stake. "Please hang me, shoot me, anything else."

Cristóbal's words were measured with venom, his ears ringing and temples pounding. "No, you're going to burn like the pagan that you are, knowing that your body will be ash and you'll never reach your afterlife."

"Please..." Huarcay started whimpering.

"Hold your tongue. How dare you plead for mercy after what you've done. You've more than deceived me, you've made a mockery of me. You've destroyed my authority and even now you seek to frustrate my life's ambitions."

Huarcay fell silent.

"Where is Manco Inca?"

Huarcay shook his head. "I...I can't take you to him."

"Do you still take me for a fool? You drug my men and abandon us in the middle of the night. You were on your way to Vilcabamba. You know where it is."

As Cristóbal stood watching Huarcay tremble, he suddenly felt cold. Something had changed. No longer was he fighting the waves of fury. He had surrendered. The heat of anger had grown into a chill that now burrowed into his soul. "Prepare the fire!"

"Can I speak with you?" asked Diego as Cristóbal turned his back on Huarcay.

Cristóbal didn't answer as the two of them walked to the far corner of the square.

Diego said, "You know killing him won't help us find Manco Inca."

"I'll find him. The villagers will know where he is. Don't you understand, my command is at stake here."

"You think you'll regain respect if you kill him?"

"How can I let a man who has humiliated me live?"

"Cristóbal, there are things more important than your humiliation. We can still do what we set out to do. You have no idea what these villagers will be able to tell you. There are things that only Huarcay knows. You need to find out what they are, not kill him in anger."

Cristóbal put his arm on Diego's shoulder. "You're right, Diego. But this time I want to make sure he's telling me the truth."

He walked back to the stake where wood was now piled high around Huarcay. "Bring me some embers," he commanded.

When the soldiers returned from the campfire, he pointed to the ground in front of them. "Place them here."

Cristóbal looked into Huarcay's terrified eyes. "If I burn you, you won't live on after death. You need your body to die intact, don't you?"

Huarcay struggled against his bonds.

"What a shame you didn't let yourself be baptized as a Christian."

"Baptize me now." Huarcay's voice cracked. "I want to be a Christian."

"You're a weak man," said Cristóbal. "A liar and a coward."

"Let me...let me become a Christian. Get the padre."

"And now you're lying to me again." Cristóbal lifted some of the glowing embers, balancing them on the broad blade of his sword. "You fear this fire more than anything, don't you?" He approached Huarcay, holding the ember over the firewood piled at the nobleman's feet.

"No...no..." His words trailed off into a whisper, his eyes closing.

"Now listen to me," said Cristóbal. "You will die at my command, but answer my questions truthfully and I won't burn you."

Huarcay opened his eyes wide and stared at Cristóbal. "I will tell you the truth."

"Good. How far are we away from Vilcabamba?"

"A long way."

Cristóbal turned his sword and the embers fell onto the wood.

"How far?"

"I don't know because I don't know where we are."

"You deserted us to join Manco Inca. You must know the distance."

"Please, I don't know...*I don't know.*"

Cristóbal bent down and blew on the embers and the flames sprang to life. "The fire will take hold soon and I won't be able to stop it."

Huarcay started laughing hysterically. "Vilcabamba is not even in the mountains. It's in the Amazon forests deep in the eastern suyu on the Chontabamba River."

Cristóbal frowned. "The jungle? What are you saying? You've led us away from Vilcabamba from the outset?"

"You wanted to hear the truth. Stop the fire..."

The wood started crackling and the flames began to take hold.

"You don't have much time. Where have you led us? What is this land?"

"We only know that anyone who disappears through the veil and exits the pass never returns. The villagers are descendants of the Incas who strayed through the sacred huacas over the centuries."

"You're saying there are more huacas, more ways into Nueva Tierra?"

Smoke spiraled up Huarcay's body. "Yes, yes, there are other huacas where people vanish."

"How many?"

Huarcay started coughing as the smoke reached his mouth. "Please, put out the fire while I can still breathe."

"We haven't finished. How many huacas are there?"

"Seven. There are seven huacas. All have a veil of light and a point of no return beyond it."

"So you led us deliberately into this one? Who was the chaski?

"He was one of my chaskis, not Manco Inca's."

"He wanted to be seen? He was part of your plan to lead us into a trap?"

"Into a trap. Yes...yes, into a trap." Smoke now billowed from the wood. "I've told you everything now."

Cristóbal struggled to make sense of what Huarcay was telling him. "You've imprisoned the largest battalion of conquistadors in New Spain to stop us finding Vilcabamba?"

"Yes, we wanted Manco Inca to prevail and regain our empire."

"While I'm imprisoned in Nueva Tierra forever."

"Now you have the truth. Please, please quench the fire." The wood now crackled and groaned loudly as the flames took hold. "It's almost too late."

Cristóbal's thoughts whirled and he felt off balance. "So all of you freely chose to lock yourselves in the same prison?"

"We thought we were joining our gods...it was a risk we were all prepared to take for our people. Please...ahh...I can feel the flames." He screamed.

Cristóbal looked at Huarcay as if he had just seen him for the first time. "Douse the flames and clear away the ashes."

***

Cristóbal fingered the blood-stained quipu knots as a soldier led Sarpay into his tent with her hands bound. For a long time, he simply looked at her, trying to steady his breathing and regain his balance. "Tell me," he said finally, "why I shouldn't strangle you with this quipu."

"I can't give you a reason, Cristóbal."

"*Cristóbal*? You still call me by my first name?" He held up the quipu. "This obviously doesn't say anything about Vilcabamba, does it?"

"No."

"What does it say? The Spaniard is a fool? He believes anything we tell him? What about condors bringing good luck? Is that what it says?"

"Condors do bring good luck, but only to Incas."

"A clever lie then. Good fortune to you means bad fortune for me. What does the quipu actually say?"

"It counts the number of llamas in the southern suyu."

"Bah!" He whipped the quipu at the tent wall. "Are you going to lie to me again and say you knew nothing of the plan to send me and my conquistadors to this prison?"

"No, Cristóbal."

He grabbed her by the jaw, his face so close to hers he could feel her breath. "Again, you call me by my first name. How dare you!"

"I'm sorry." She tried to look away but Cristóbal held her so that she had to face him.

"Sorry? What are you sorry for, Sarpay? That you didn't escape as you planned?"

"There's no escape for me either. We're imprisoned together."

Cristóbal squeezed her jaw and she winced. "You wanted so much to destroy me that you were prepared to sacrifice your own freedom. But you had a choice. I didn't. I was blind, and you led me into a trap."

"I did it for my people and my gods."

Cristóbal released his grip. "Your gods? Your plot won't bear fruit, you know. Another conquistador will find Manco Inca. Your empire will disappear anyway, and your gods will be forgotten."

"Our gods have abandoned us. I can see that now. We haven't entered the abode of Inti and joined our great Incan ancestors. Inti showed his contempt when he shined his light through the mist and exposed us to be butchered like animals."

Cristóbal turned his back on her. "You lied to me. Every day."

"Just as the Spaniards have always lied to the Incas. Your great hero Pizarro is a monster."

He faced her. "I never lied to you, Sarpay."

"Those with power don't need to lie, Cristóbal. They just do what they wish." Sarpay reached out to Cristóbal with her bound hands. "We're in a place neither of us understands. Don't you think we need each other? Come, our battles are over now."

"And you've won." Cristóbal pulled away and addressed the soldier. "From now on treat her as one of the servants. Get her out of my sight."

***

A veneer of calm settled over Cristóbal's turmoil the next day as he walked past the bodies of the Incan warriors hanging from makeshift gallows. Huarcay hung higher than the others, the blood-stained quipu still around his neck. As the wind sprang up, the gallows creaked and the corpses began to sway. He looked at Huarcay's face. The Incan's expression was frozen and hard to read—but it wasn't fear.

I gave you respect and you made a mockery of my leadership.

Why did Huarcay's eyes appear defiant in death?

I honored your sister, and both of you conspired against me.

Perhaps it was simply the look of someone who had done what they set out to do, a look that had evaded Cristóbal his whole life.

Are you savoring the joy of your victory over me from your afterlife?

The thin crust of stillness cracked. Cristóbal felt bile rising from his stomach like an elemental force. Once he started retching, he couldn't stop until he crumpled to the ground and passed out.

Chapter 23

El diario de Cristóbal de Varga

Are noble words the dawn that inevitably follows the night of death? If that is true, I am now blind to the light of day. I have found no solace, let alone any nobility, in the deaths I've commanded in my anger.

As the silence of past screams echoes in my ears, I hear the words my father held fast. *Honra sobre todo.* Honor above everything. Hold firmly to your honor, he would say, and all else will follow. He remained true to his belief even in times of his deepest suffering when his family fell into the grinding abyss of poverty and the black pox sores punctured his body. I have always thought I too believed those words. Now I am no longer certain I can claim their nobility.

Perhaps nobility isn't a dawn but is, in truth, a flame which burns brightly, shedding heat and light on those in its orbit. Like any flame, it can be quickly extinguished by a gust of ill wind, vanishing as if it never existed and bestowing only darkness on all those that once flourished in its radiance.

And as with any flame in a storm, once it is extinguished, it is impossible to rekindle.

Chapter 24

Before the Storm

Cristóbal put his quill down and looked up from his diary at the candle. The last words he had written resounded in his head. He reached out and put his finger into the flame, holding it there and watching the light flicker around his skin.

"What are you doing?"

Cristóbal pulled back quickly. He'd forgotten Diego was there. He glanced across at his cousin. "I hope you're enjoying that because that's the last of our wine."

"Looks like we'll need to make do with corn beer from now on." Diego took another sip from his goblet. "Do you ever wonder what those two boys who stowed away on that galleon in Seville are doing here?"

Cristóbal blew on his fingertip to cool it. "If you didn't want any gold, you should have told me."

"Do you remember the time we stole that prize black pig?"

Cristóbal chuckled. "We didn't think that through, did we?"

"Children often don't. What do you do with a pig? How could you hide it?"

"And we thought we could just carry it out of the pen in the middle of the night and it wouldn't make any noise."

"Lucky Señor Arantes didn't see it was us."

Cristóbal put his hand on his cousin's shoulder. "You know, I always value what you say, Diego. I need you by my side even if we don't always agree."

"We both know it's never been about the gold for us. I've followed you into two new worlds. I'm not going to stop now. Besides, I don't have a choice. There's nowhere to go." They sat in silence for a moment in the flickering candlelight. "Do you think we'll ever see Spain again, Cristóbal?"

"I don't know. Most conquistadors never return. I want to go back to Señor Arantes and buy every black pig he has."

"He'll be an old man by now. Who knows if he owns pigs anymore."

"It doesn't matter. I'll put a blanket over his legs as he sits in the sun and read him from my diary the tale of how two failed pig thieves became famed conquistadors."

Diego leaned forward to look at the open pages of Cristóbal's diary. "Why are you writing your journal when the two of us and Padre Núñez are the only people in Nueva Tierra who can read?"

"Great deeds only matter if they're remembered."

Diego drank the last of the wine. "So far we have a great number of bodies, but not so many great deeds."

"Did Pizarro count the bodies he left in his trail?"

"I don't know, but he couldn't read or write, could he? Why not have a chronicler like the other conquistadors?"

"Maybe I'm not like the other conquistadors." Cristóbal closed his diary. "And unless I find the gold we're seeking, no one will remember the name Cristóbal de Varga—no matter how much I write."

Diego stared into his empty goblet. "Please, Cristóbal, strike my name from your journal. I would rather disappear than be remembered for this."

Shouts broke the tense silence that had settled on the village. A conquistador, eyes wide with fear, pushed his head through the tent flaps. "Capitán, it looks like the ñakaqs are massing."

***

Cristóbal, Rodrigo and Diego surveyed the scene in the distance as Héctor rode toward them. In the darkness beyond the village a swathe of fire helmets spread out across the valley.

"Is the army as large as it appears?" asked Cristóbal as Héctor pulled up next to him.

"Larger, Capitán. There are many ñakaqs not wearing fire helmets, so I'd estimate the army is at least ten thousand strong and growing."

Rodrigo said, "I'll give the orders for the cannons."

"There are no signs they are about to attack," said Héctor. "They seem to be waiting as more arrive."

"That gives us a chance to attack them first," said Rodrigo.

"Attacking them first started this war," said Héctor.

Diego ran his fingers through his tangled beard. "There may be a way to avoid more deaths."

Rodrigo shook his head. "Look at the mountains, you fool. And the river. There's an enemy about to strike from behind. How can we avoid fighting?"

Diego ignored him and addressed Cristóbal. "I've tested the Incan rafts, and they're strong and buoyant. We can use them to escape downriver."

"Will they be able to keep our horses afloat?" asked Héctor.

Rodrigo spat on the ground and glared at him. "How can we call ourselves conquistadors when we run like slaves and women?"

Héctor grabbed the hilt of his sword. "That's the last time you insult me."

"Enough!" said Cristóbal, holding up his hand. "The first one of you to draw your sword against the other will be thrown in chains."

The two lieutenants faced off, frozen in fury, while Cristóbal's intense gaze switched from one to the other. Slowly, Héctor and Rodrigo unclenched their fists and lowered their hands.

"Remember, I'm the one who decides what we do," said Cristóbal.

"Then what's your decision, Capitán?" said Rodrigo, his teeth clenched.

"There's something worrying me about Diego's plan," said Cristóbal. "When the Incas abandoned this village, why didn't they take the rafts downriver through the gorge? We would have been unable to follow them. My guess is the river's too dangerous right now."

"So we fight?" said Rodrigo.

"We fight, and after our victory we'll find a way back to New Spain. Lieutenants, prepare the defenses." Cristóbal turned to Diego. "That plan of yours to defend ourselves against the ñakaqs—make sure it's in place. There's someone I need to speak to."

As he turned to go, he thought he heard the sound of fluttering wings from the darkness.

***

Tagón sat on the floor, looking at the ground, as Cristóbal entered the Incan building he was using as a prison.

"I'm here to free you," said Cristóbal. "You can return to your people as we agreed."

Tagón made no eye contact as he spoke. "You're no better than a duende. I no longer trust what you say."

"I'm truly sorry, Tagón. I was angry." Cristóbal used his key to unlock Tagón's chains. "I thought you had deceived me. I know now there are no Incan cities here."

Tagón rubbed his wrists without looking up. "We were right to forbid your entry to our lands. I will tell my people we now have *two* great enemies."

"Are these duendes your great enemy?"

"Yes, you are both the same. Your word means nothing."

"Did a duende ever release you from imprisonment and say they were sorry for what they'd done in anger?"

Tagón continued rubbing his wrists.

Cristóbal drew a deep breath. "I made a poor decision and am trying to make amends. Do your people not make poor decisions?"

"My people have made many poor decisions. They may be about to make another, but there's nothing either of us can do about it."

"Nothing?"

"We're a relentless people. Our king will attack, no matter what I say. If you stop us the first day, we'll attack you again the second. If we don't destroy you on the second, then we come for you on the third. If not the third, then the fourth."

"Then my only course is to defeat your people in battle. I just hope the two of us don't face each other."

Outside a drumbeat resounded into silence.

Cristóbal instinctively grabbed his sword and glanced out the open door into the darkness.

"So, I'm free to go?" said Tagón.

"Yes, I'll walk you safely through the camp."

Tagón stepped toward the door and then hesitated. "I was also filled with anger." He looked at Cristóbal for the first time since he had entered the building. "My people won't attack before dawn. They may not attack for another day."

"Why?"

Another drumbeat echoed in the dark.

"They're waiting for more to join them."

"*More*?" Cristóbal joined Tagón and they stepped outside. He stared at the countless fire helmets burning in the distance. "Exactly how many more?"

"Many, many more."

Tagón headed in the direction of the lights. "I'm sorry my release will make no difference."

The sound of war drums filled the air as Cristóbal walked with him through the village, ignoring the mutterings of his men.

Rodrigo approached the pair, his sword drawn, with Martín and Carlos in tow.

"Step back, Lieutenant Benalcázar," ordered Cristóbal. "I'm releasing him."

"You're giving up our only hostage?"

"Put away your weapon, Lieutenant Benalcázar. Tagón and I struck a bargain and he kept his word. He's not at fault here."

Héctor joined them. "Is there a problem, Capitán?"

Rodrigo reluctantly sheathed his sword.

Tagón took a step and then stopped. "There's one possible way my king may listen."

"Say whatever you can to him."

"No, the words need to come from you, not me."

"You want me to come with you?"

"Yes."

"Unarmed?"

"Not just unarmed. You would need to come as my prisoner."

After the stunned silence, Rodrigo said, "You're not considering this, are you, Capitán? Are you mad?"

Cristóbal ignored him. "What will happen to me after I've spoken to your king?"

"You'll be set free, no matter what the outcome. According to our customs, those that come as willing prisoners have the right to freedom."

"How can you believe what a demon says?" Rodrigo's voice was strained.

"Don't call me a demon."

"Tagón, will you give me your word of honor that I'll be set free?"

"Can't you hear the drums?" said Rodrigo. "We're about to be attacked."

"Yes," said Tagón. "Our king will listen to you and you'll be unharmed. There will be no attack until you return."

Cristóbal looked at the mass of ever-growing flame-lights. "I accept your word, Tagón." He held out his hands with his wrists touching. "Tie me, then."

Rodrigo spat on the ground.

Cristóbal turned to Héctor. "Lieutenant Valiente, you have the command until I come back."

Chapter 25

By the Throne of the King

The stars shed light like weeping wounds above Cristóbal and Tagón as they walked together across the valley. Although Cristóbal took Tagón at his word, he could feel sweat on his palms. It struck him that for the first time since he had left Machu Picchu, he had made a major decision without considering what Pizarro would have done. He knew he hadn't asked the question because the answer was that this would never have been a course that the great man would have taken. For once, he didn't care.

As they drew closer to the milling hordes, helmet flames illuminated a sea of wild-bearded faces that didn't seem quite as grotesque to Cristóbal as before. The ñakaqs surrounded him as he calmly entered the throng of fierce eyes and grasping hands. Tagón said something in his guttural tongue to them, and they backed away, leaving a path through the vast army.

"I need to blindfold you now," said Tagón. "Then I'll take you to our king."

Cristóbal was engulfed in darkness and felt an extra cord being tied around his wrists.

"I'll lead you." With the blindfold covering Cristóbal's ears, Tagón's voice sounded muffled. "Just go in the direction I pull you, and you won't stumble."

Cristóbal continued, tentatively at first, but gradually gaining in confidence. Soon the ground sloped upwards, so he guessed he was heading into the foothills. Occasionally he heard voices around him, but with his limited knowledge of the ñakaq tongue he only rarely picked out a word he understood.

After what seemed like an eternity, Tagón spoke to him again. "I'm going to take off your blindfold."

Spears of light shot into Cristóbal's eyes, and he blinked to focus his vision. He was in a large canyon where torch flames burnt from every corner. Above was a massive stone throne carved directly out of the dark mountainside, flanked on either side by huge sculptured horcas with their three prongs pointing skyward. On the throne sat a ñakaq, his beard falling to the floor in a tangle, and on his head was a helmet-crown of prodigious height encompassing a monstrous fire.

Tagón untied Cristóbal's hands and covered his own eyes for a moment before he spoke to the king in the ñakaq tongue. The king replied and then shifted his gaze to Cristóbal.

"Cover your eyes with your hand each time before you speak," said Tagón in Spanish. "It's a sign that you respect his secrets."

Craning his neck, Cristóbal held his hand briefly over his eyes as Tagón had done and ventured a greeting in ñakaq.

"I am told you speak the beardless ones' tongue," said the king in Quechua.

"Yes, though it's not my mother tongue."

"That means neither of us is at a disadvantage."

"My name is Capitán Cristóbal de Varga. I bring greetings from His Imperial Majesty Charles V, King of Spain."

The king didn't respond, and Tagón gestured that Cristóbal had forgotten to cover his eyes before he spoke.

Cristóbal repeated his introduction, this time starting with the gesture.

"I am King Malín."

"I am honored to meet with you as a prisoner of Tagón," said Cristóbal.

"And I am honored that an invader in our lands chooses to speak to me in this way."

"We're not invaders. We were seeking the king of Incas, who you call the beardless ones."

"The beardless ones have no king."

"Not here in your lands, but in our lands they do. We thought he was hidden here, but we were wrong."

King Malín ran the fingers of both hands through his massive, tangled beard. "When did you discover you were wrong?"

"When we arrived at the Incan village two days ago."

"So you wish to return the way you came?"

"We entered your lands through a pass and it's no longer possible to return through that pass. We need to find another way."

"That is unfortunate. We allow no one in our lands. If you had returned when Tagón first warned you, much bloodshed would have been avoided."

"We had no choice."

"You travel as an army. Have you claimed ownership of our lands in the name of your king?"

Cristóbal hesitated, running his palm across his cheek. "Yes," he said finally.

"Can a claim like this be relinquished?"

"Only our king is able to do that."

"Tagón tells me your people do not always speak truths. I am glad you have chosen to answer in our way."

Cristóbal's neck strained as he continued to look up at King Malín. "Does that mean there's a way we can avoid further bloodshed between our peoples?"

"No. Your army entered our lands ready for battle, claiming our land for your king. We told you to return and you killed our party and imprisoned its leader."

"The deaths were an error. I didn't give that order."

"You continued deeper into our lands, broke an oath to release your prisoner, have killed beardless ones who have lived under our protection for centuries, and have slain my people in battle. On what basis could our enmity end?"

Cristóbal fell silent, unsure how he could possibly defend his actions. To the ñakaqs, he and his conquistadors were the demons.

"My only defense," said Cristóbal finally, "is that I've been misled by the beardless ones from our lands, and we now find ourselves searching for a way to return. Since we can't go back the way we came, please allow us to pass through your realm."

"This isn't how we deal with our enemies." King Malín seemed affronted by the suggestion. "We allow no one to cross into the duende mountains from ours. The border is closed."

"There has to be some way. Even if you eventually defeat us, you'll lose countless lives. We'll defend ourselves to the last. Don't you wish to save the lives of your people?"

"Our people have always died to protect our lands and will continue to die. If we lose our lands, we lose our secrets."

There had to be something he could offer them. Cristóbal swallowed. "We have gold from a city called Machu Picchu. You could melt it for your helmets."

King Malín seemed stunned. Tagón quickly said something to him in the guttural ñakaq tongue. They appeared to be arguing.

"I've told our king that you meant no insult," said Tagón in Spanish.

Cristóbal wasn't sure what offense he had caused. He covered his eyes before he spoke. "I am truly sorry, King Malín."

There was another flurry of words between the two ñakaqs.

"You've been honored to be told our king's name," said Tagón. "Please don't use it when addressing him."

Cristóbal swallowed again. There had to be something he could offer. "Tagón has said you have a great enemy, these duende you talk of. We can help you gain victory over them."

Tagón and King Malín looked at each other. Had he finally found something that swayed the ñakaqs?

"You said yourself we travel as an army," said Cristóbal. "Why not make an ally of that army?"

The two ñakaqs spoke heatedly to each other while Cristóbal waited.

King Malín finally addressed him. "We can't accept your offer because you don't have the power to fulfill it."

"Are you saying I don't have command of my men?"

"I'm saying you don't know these duende," said King Malín.

"Then tell me about them."

"We also call them wind-whisperers. They live on the far high peaks. Their voices shift with the wind and they use their words like weapons."

"I don't understand," said Cristóbal. "We can fight words."

"No," said King Malín, shaking his head so that his massive beard swayed all the way to the ground. "I know you believe what you say, but you don't understand. Your offer is refused."

Cristóbal had a leaden feeling in his stomach. "So, is there nothing that I can do that will end this battle?"

"No."

"Nothing?"

"Nothing."

Cristóbal fell silent for a moment. "Then allow me to return to my men with the news."

"Of course. There will be no attack until our army is complete."

"You mean there are more of you?"

"Many more are still to arrive."

"Tagón, take me back. I need to prepare."

"Wait," said Tagón. "It's almost dawn."

The ñakaqs covered their eyes and a stillness fell across the mountainside as if the air itself waited in anticipation. Slowly a deep-throated chant filled the void, growing from a low earthen rumble to a force summoning the mountain peaks. Soon the sun's crimson rays began to creep across the dark rock, mingling with the shadows to form bright patterns that pulsated to life. The forms gyrated and danced in rhythm with each surge until they were indistinguishable from the sound. And, finally, as the chant reached its crescendo, the ñakaqs removed their hands from their eyes, and the mountain was ablaze with the piercing fire of the sun.

Tagón blindfolded Cristóbal again and led him back down the mountain and into the valley. Cristóbal heard the rasping voices of the ñakaq soldiers all around him and then they faded into the distance. When Tagón removed the blindfold and cords, Cristóbal saw they now stood on the middle ground between the two armies.

"It seems we won't be sharing any more of your Spanish wine," said Tagón.

"I'm afraid I have none left anyway."

"I told you my people don't sway from their path."

"The Spanish word is *obstinado*."

"Perhaps our peoples are not so different."

"Are these wind-whisperers also *obstinado*?"

Tagón frowned. "Don't compare the duendes to my people. I've fought them and felt the sting of their arrows. They've caused our people untold grief."

"So, you are grave enemies?"

"We're more than enemies. The duendes have been determined to eliminate us for thousands of years. They fight without honor, from places where we can't harm them."

"It sounds like King Malín should have accepted my offer."

"I think it's time for our farewells." Tagón said something in his tongue. "It doesn't translate well into Spanish or Quechua, but it means something like, may you have the death that you wish for."

"I'm not ready to die yet." Cristóbal put his hand on the ñakaq's shoulder. "Thank you, Tagón, for being someone who doesn't lie to me."

"Farewell, Cristóbal de Varga."

With that, each walked slowly to their own camps as the sun bore down on them. Out of the corner of his eye Cristóbal thought he saw a shadow cross the red sky beyond the valley, but when he looked up it was gone.

Chapter 26

The Cry of Battle

The drums grew louder throughout the day, reverberating until the valley shook. The ñakaq army continued to swell until just before sunset. Cristóbal rode from one station to the next as the conquistadors made their final preparations. He stopped by the cannon carts where Diego was checking the new mechanisms.

"You still believe this will work?" asked Cristóbal.

Diego shook his head. "I've had no time to test it. The most important thing is to get the timing right."

Guttural battle chants merged with the drumbeats. Cristóbal scanned the plain where the flaming helmets of countless ñakaqs burnt furiously.

The rhythm of the chants began to dominate and soon the drums were drowned out by a sound even more terrifying. Ñakaq voices merged to form a wall of deep-throated calls that avalanched from the surrounding slopes like an elemental force.

Cristóbal's heart pounded deep in his chest. Rodrigo obsessively wiped spit from the side of his mouth. Héctor was on the other side of the camp, but Cristóbal could see him on his horse, moving from conquistador to conquistador.

Then the lights of the helmet fires flooded toward them.

Cristóbal held up his hand to the cannoneers. "Wait for my signal," he shouted, his voice barely audible above the ñakaq battle song.

Onward they came, brandishing their monstrous horcas. Cristóbal glanced at Diego, nodded almost imperceptibly, and then let his hand drop.

The first round of cannon fire crashed over the other battle sounds. This time, though, there was no pounding of the valley floor. Instead a canopy of water formed above the heads of the oncoming army and fell like a waterfall onto the ñakaqs, extinguishing their helmet fires and clouding the air with dense smoke.

In the confusion, Héctor led his men straight into the enemy ranks. Rather than hacking at them brutally as they had done the last time, they aimed with precision at the few vulnerable places in their armor. They thrust their blades into their faces. They pushed their lance tips into the exposed regions between the chest and shoulder and on the upper leg. High on their horses, the conquistadors had the advantage that the smoke wasn't as thick, while the ñakaqs were still coughing and gasping for air, fighting almost blind. The first ñakaq battalion soon lay decimated.

A second battalion from the eastern slope met the same fate, as another round of water doused their helmet fires. Rodrigo led his soldiers out to slaughter the choking and confused ñakaqs.

A horn toned above the tumult and the survivors retreated, disappearing into the surrounding slopes, and leaving a valley littered with the dead and the dying. Those under Rodrigo's command chased the fleeing ñakaqs until Rodrigo finally responded to Cristóbal's frantic signal to call the men back to their defensive position. The lieutenant raised his sword in victory.

Cristóbal removed his helmet as Rodrigo returned. "Don't you have control over your battalion, Lieutenant Benalcázar?" he demanded angrily. "The plan was not to pursue the retreating army."

"My men were a little over-enthusiastic, Capitán."

"Show me an over-enthusiastic conquistador, Lieutenant Benalcázar, and I'll show you a dead one. We need to keep our discipline."

"They're doing as ordered now, Capitán."

"If you can't control those under your command, maybe I should give the command to another lieutenant."

"My men won't break ranks again."

"Do I have to remind you, yet again," said Cristóbal, glaring at his lieutenant, "they are not *your* men?"

Rodrigo gave an expressionless nod and turned to go.

"Wait, Lieutenant Benalcázar, I haven't given you your orders yet. Make sure no one kills any ñakaq who are still alive. I want the survivors imprisoned."

After Rodrigo had left, Diego said, "I'm no friend of his, but don't you feel you were a little harsh? He performed well, didn't he?"

"Until the end."

"But it was only a moment's hesitation before he called the soldiers back."

"It's one thing for him to argue with my strategy in private. I can't have him hesitating to follow my commands in public, even for an instant."

"Isn't there a danger you'll make him more defiant?"

"You have skills in preparing for battle, Diego, but please leave the battle's pitch to me. A hesitation like the one he showed could have meant multiple deaths. There was no point chasing the ñakaqs up the mountain. There were still so many of them that when the smoke cleared, our soldiers would have been surrounded and overwhelmed."

"As always, I'll leave the leadership to you, cousin."

Cristóbal's expression softened. "You did well today, but you know that we won't be able to use that trick a second time, don't you?"

"Yes, I know."

***

The conquistadors cheered Cristóbal when he returned to the village. For the briefest of moments, he allowed himself to embrace the triumph, knowing that he had fashioned a victory almost equal to Pizarro's in Cusco. Then his thoughts turned to the eight conquistadors and three horses they had lost in the attack. His soldiers erected a cross and buried their dead, staunching the wounds of the injured soldiers and horses with the fat of fallen ñakaqs because their dressing supplies were limited. The ñakaqs had died in such numbers that the soldiers ended up leaving them where they lay after collecting the helmets so that the gold inlays could be removed. Cristóbal gave the order that they should be buried in mass graves the next morning.

Later that night he sat alone in his tent when the celebrations began.

***

"Tie him to the cross!" After Rodrigo gave the order, the camp fell silent.

A moment ago, the conquistadors had been wildly reveling in their victory. They drank Incan corn beer, bellowed, and acted out moments of the battle to each other. Eight ciervas rotated on a spit with golden juices hissing as they dripped onto the fire. Several soldiers had donned ñakaq helmets with embers in their upper cavities, and ran around, coughing and spluttering to gales of laughter until they collapsed to the ground in mock bewilderment.

Rodrigo's head swirled with chicha. He was past the point where he could recognize having a ñakaq prisoner brought to the celebrations was a bad idea.

The conquistadors were now all staring at the large cross that had been erected in the village square. Something didn't quite make sense to Rodrigo at that moment. He looked around, swaying slightly, waiting.

Then there was an avalanche of drunken cheers and laughter.

Carlos, Luis and Martín dragged the bound ñakaq toward the cross and lashed him to it.

Rodrigo grabbed one of the horcas and faced the ñakaq, who thrashed to try and pull himself free. Rodrigo reached back and flung the horca forward, stumbling, with the weapon barely making half the distance to the cross. His drunken miss was met with raucous laughter.

"Here, give it back to me. I can do better than that," he said.

Luis handed the horca back to him and he took aim again.

This time he almost made the distance but was off target.

"If he'd been a little less ugly, I would have hit him," he said, taking another draft of chicha. "Even his own weapon doesn't want to go near him."

More laughter.

He took several unsteady steps closer. "I'll get him from here. Give it to me again."

Luis had just handed Rodrigo the horca when Héctor gripped him by the arm, saying "Enough."

Rodrigo scowled. "Enough? You say enough to me?"

"The capitán doesn't want any of the prisoners harmed."

"I don't see the capitán here."

"Which is why I'm the one stopping you." Héctor turned to Carlos and Martín. "Cut the ñakaq down."

Rodrigo, staggering, brandished the horca at Héctor. "Who are you to give orders to my men?"

Héctor grabbed the horca, and the two lieutenants glowered at each other as they both held onto it.

"You're defiling a great victory," said Héctor.

Héctor pushed at Rodrigo with the horca and Rodrigo stumbled and fell backward. He tried to get up but Héctor placed his foot on his chest to stop him while the soldiers finished taking the ñakaq from the cross.

"The ñakaqs were not captured for your sport, Lieutenant Benalcázar." And then to the soldiers, "Put this one back with the other prisoners."

Rodrigo seethed as Héctor lifted his foot. Luis reached out to help him stand, but he pushed him away.

Chapter 27

Battle's Dawn

Cristóbal could barely take in what he was seeing the next morning. He scanned the swathe of fire helmets that clustered just outside the range of his cannons, his blood churning through his veins.

"There are even more than before," said Diego. "How is that possible after we killed so many?"

Héctor returned after riding as close as he dared. "My guess is it's tripled in size overnight, Capitán."

"Thirty thousand?"

"At least. And there appear to be more arriving."

Cristóbal's stomach tightened.

"And there's something else, Capitán."

"What is it?"

"The bodies of all the ñakaqs we killed have disappeared."

"That's not possible," said Cristóbal, struggling to grasp what he was being told. "There were thousands of them."

"I couldn't find a single corpse."

"Are we dealing with demons after all?" said Héctor.

"I don't want to hear any more talk of demons," said Cristóbal. "Ñakaqs we can defeat. Demons we can't."

"So, what happened to the bodies?"

"They must just be very quick in retrieving corpses. We've been so busy celebrating tonight, no one would have noticed them removing their dead." Cristóbal struggled to stop his thoughts from spinning. Why had he been so eager to let his men enjoy the victory? "When do you think they will attack?"

"They're still building, so hopefully not soon. I don't know."

"I thought our victory would give us several days at least. If they attack today, we're lost. How many of the men are too drunk to fight?"

"About half."

"Let's hope the ñakaqs wait until at least tonight."

***

The dusk air had a bitter tang to it as Cristóbal checked the battle provisions. He offered encouragement as he walked past each group of soldiers, hoping that his words didn't sound quite as hollow as they seemed to his own ears.

Héctor was sharpening his sword with a whetstone when Cristóbal reached him. "If the ñakaqs attack tonight," said Héctor, "we'll make sure they die with the taste of Toledo steel."

"Any sign of movement?"

"The mists have fallen, so it's difficult to see. It looks like the helmet fires are still multiplying, but none are moving toward us."

"Do you think they will try a surprise attack?"

"That doesn't appear to be how they engage in battle. I don't think they'll attack tonight. They know we won't sleep, so they may wait until sunrise."

"Then it makes sense that some of us try to get some sleep once the preparations are in place."

"I agree. We'll hear their battle drums long before they start advancing."

Cristóbal put his hand on his lieutenant's shoulder. "Héctor," he said, "I need to ask you this." He paused. "It will be difficult to keep Diego from the heart of the battle this time. Please—"

"There's no need to ask me, Capitán. I understand. As long as I have a sword in my hand, I'll keep Diego safe."

***

Cristóbal closed his diary and watched Diego pushing his food aimlessly around his plate as the light of the blood moon shone through the canvas of the tent.

Cristóbal said, "For once you don't seem to be enjoying your meal."

Diego's laugh was empty. "Some would say that it will do me good to enjoy my food a little less."

"You need to eat. We're depending on you again. Your idea saved us last time. We need your new plan to work."

"The beauty is that we'll be using the inaccuracy of our cannons to our advantage. The metal shards from a single shot could kill or blind dozens of ñakaqs. It will work, but I'm not convinced it will be enough. Unlike water, we don't have a limitless supply of *metralla*."

"We'll have the ñakaqs on their knees by the time we run out."

"Hopefully."

"You're not yourself tonight. What's wrong?"

Diego stared sullenly at his food. "I don't think I'll survive the coming battle."

"Conquistadors conquer their fears."

"I don't feel fear, Cristóbal. Only despair." Diego spoke without looking up.

"Pizarro was hopelessly outnumbered. So was Cortés. We'll also prevail."

Diego started pushing his food around again. "That's the problem. I don't know if we deserve to prevail. Hanging all those Incas. It wasn't right."

"I was angry."

"You were angry with yourself."

Cristóbal nodded slowly. "As usual, you're right."

"And still you write each day in that diary of yours so that you can be remembered. What will be remembered will be the shame you left behind."

"As long as I remain alive, my story is worth telling."

"Who will read it, Cristóbal?"

"Who knows? I used to be so certain my words would be heard. Now, I don't know. I write my diary out of habit."

"We do so much out of habit. Sometimes I think our quest is a habit."

Cristóbal placed his hand over Diego's arm and stopped him obsessively moving his food. "I've told Héctor to watch over you when the ñakaqs attack."

"Then I'm an even heavier weight in battle than I am in life." Diego pulled his arm free from Cristóbal and held out his hand. "Will you show me what you've written this one time?"

"No, I don't want anyone to see it until it's finished."

"It may finish tomorrow."

"True. Then it won't matter what I've written."

Cristóbal looked away as if he was watching something in the distance. "Tell me, Diego, if a salida suddenly appeared before us, right here, and there was a way back to New Spain just for you and no one else, would you leave?"

"Why waste your time with these sorts of thoughts?"

"Would you?"

"I don't want to think about it."

"These are the sorts of things I think about at night.

"Have you answered your own question?"

"I would like to be the capitán who stayed with honor."

"To save his soldiers from what appears certain annihilation?"

"No, to die fighting with them."

"So, have you decided what you would do?"

"I have, but I don't like my answer."

"And what's that?"

"I would leave only if I could take my diary with me."

***

As dawn broke, Cristóbal realized he had fallen asleep over his open diary. He stepped outside his tent. The morning sun burnt brightly into his eyes and it took him a moment to see what lay before him. The ñakaq numbers had swelled further since midnight. Fires no longer burned in their helmets, but the army had moved closer. It now formed a monstrous arc of shining armor stretching from the edge of the river in the west to the mountain range in the east, so that the conquistadors were backed into the corner of the valley where the Incan village lay.

Rodrigo had obviously been waiting for him to wake. "Capitán, the demons have moved within cannon range. We should start our attack."

"If that's your strategy, Lieutenant Benalcázar, it sounds to me like you still haven't recovered from your drunken celebrations."

"It was only corn beer. We had won a great victory."

"I'm happy for my men to celebrate great victories—but look around." Cristóbal waved his hand in the direction of the seething mass of ñakaqs. "Does this look like a great victory for us? We can count ourselves fortunate that they didn't attack while you and the others were staggering drunk."

"We shouldn't simply be waiting for them to come for us," said Rodrigo.

"No? That's exactly what we should do. We have one more surprise for them, thanks to Diego, and you want to waste it on some frontline soldiers who are in range? It looks to me like they're tempting us to show them what we have."

"It appears you're giving your cousin the credit for our victory in the last battle. I don't remember him killing a single demon."

"We'll stick to our plan, Lieutenant Benalcázar, so please return to your station and wait for my orders."

Rodrigo turned to go, then stopped. "There's a demon walking toward us."

Cristóbal could see he was right. A lone ñakaq without armor or a helmet was striding across the valley in their direction. "It's Tagón!"

The red-bearded ñakaq approached and walked through the line of cannons toward Cristóbal. He moved in a straight line and the conquistadors backed away from his path.

When he finally stood in front of Cristóbal he reached into his leather tunic and pulled out a three-pronged knife.

Rodrigo drew his sword and took a step forward.

"No, wait," said Cristóbal.

Tagón slowly placed the knife on the ground at Cristóbal's feet. His voice rasped in the back of his throat. "I wish to be baptized."

***

"He's come of his own free will," said Cristóbal.

Padre Núñez eyed Tagón curiously after Cristóbal and Rodrigo brought him to his tent. "Are you mocking me? You want me to baptize you?"

"Yes."

"Then you are truly evil. Even now you tempt me to believe your words."

"You still call me evil?" said Tagón. "You said yourself, a demon would never willingly allow itself to be baptized."

"He's unarmed, Padre," said Cristóbal. "Why else would he put himself in danger?"

Padre Núñez closed his eyes for a moment. When he opened them, he asked Tagón, "Why is it important to you?"

"My people aren't demons. I want to prove it."

"That's the only reason?

"Yes. I accept the actions of my people could be seen as the actions of demons. Soon you'll all be dead. I want to be certain we're not creations of evil."

Cristóbal said, "Then this won't affect the coming attack?"

"The attack will still occur."

"The baptism is for you?" asked Cristóbal.

"Yes, and I want all of you to know in your hearts before you die that we aren't evil."

"Why does this matter if you believe your people will kill us all anyway?"

"It's a matter of honor."

Rodrigo glowered. "He's wasting our time. It's pulling us away from our battle preparations."

"My people have a saying," said Tagón. "Those without honor can't recognize it in others."

"Pah! There's no point in talking of honor when flies are infesting your corpse," said Rodrigo.

"It makes a difference if you've accepted the Lord before your death," said Padre Núñez.

Rodrigo's eyes widened in fury and disbelief. "*Mierda!* You're doing a baptism when we're under siege?"

"It's always a good time to bring another soul to the Lord. God's work is often a mystery. Perhaps this action will save us."

"It may save your place in heaven, Padre, but it won't help the rest of us."

***

Although the river flowed powerfully at its heart, the waters just beyond the river's edge where the rafts were moored formed a natural harbor. Tagón stood waist high with Padre Núñez in the calm waters that reflected the flame-red of the sky, while Cristóbal, Rodrigo and several mounted conquistadors watched from the bank.

Padre Núñez's words floated across the water.

"What do you ask of the Church of God?"

"Faith," said Tagón in his harsh-edged Spanish.

"What does Faith offer you?"

"Life everlasting."

Padre Núñez exhaled three times on Tagón, making the sign of the cross with his thumb on the ñakaq's forehead and breast.

"I exorcise thee, unclean spirit, in the name of the Father and of the Son, and of the Holy Spirit."

Padre Núñez placed his hand on the matted hair of Tagón's head.

"Do you believe in God the Father Almighty, Creator of Heaven and Earth?"

"I do believe."

"Do you surrender to God's will and accept the mercy of Christ our Lord?"

"I do surrender."

"Do you choose to be baptized of your own free will?"

"I do so choose."

Padre Núñez poured water from the river over the head of Tagón twice. "I baptize you in the name of the Father, and of the Son and—"

Just before he invoked the Holy Spirit, guttural battle cries exploded into the air from behind the conquistadors. The massive ñakaq army, this time without fires flaming from their helmets and drumbeats heralding their attack, swarmed across the valley toward them.

Rodrigo rode into the water and pointed his sword at Tagón's throat. "You'll pay for deceiving us."

Cristóbal shouted, "Withdraw your blade, Lieutenant Benalcázar."

"You've been fooled again by an enemy, Capitán," said Rodrigo. "You think it's chance the ñakaqs attack just now when we have our backs to their army?"

"Tagón chose to come to us unarmed. He can walk free."

Rodrigo glared defiantly at Cristóbal, his ferocious eyes tearing into the capitán.

They could hear cannons blasting behind them. Rodrigo withdrew his sword and turned to enter the fray.

Cristóbal waved a farewell to Tagón. "We both know this is the final battle. I just hope the two of us don't come face-to-face."

"As do I," said Tagón. "That's why I've chosen not to fight."

Chapter 28

The Final Battle

The ñakaqs shouted guttural war cries, wielding black shields and horcas as they surged toward the Spaniards with terrifying intensity. Cristóbal charged through the conquistador camp toward the cannon stations, knowing they were at risk of being overrun. The cannoneers continued firing, but each time a shot struck into the heart of the swarming army, the ñakaqs changed their formation so that the next one missed its mark.

"*Metralla!*" cried Cristóbal as he reached the cannons in full gallop. "Use the metralla now."

The cannoneers began loading the artillery with canvas bags filled with tiny pieces of jagged metal. The first wave of the new scattergun explosions caused mayhem among the swarming horde, injuring large clusters of ñakaqs and impeding the onslaught. The second wave created further destruction and the advance faltered.

Cristóbal's command had come too late, however, and an advance enemy line, now separated from the rest, reached the cannon stations and assailed the cannoneers. Diego drew his sword, but Cristóbal shouted at him to get back. One of the cannoneers was hacked down by a succession of horcas before Héctor and his men raced in, savaging the ñakaqs and ending their penetration of the Spaniards' defenses.

While the cannons had been silent, the ñakaqs had regrouped and were now bearing down on the village in full force. Renewed metralla explosions again spawned havoc, with each shrapnel strike from the cannons bringing down dozens of ñakaqs. The harquebuses and crossbows also felled large numbers, but nothing slowed the charge, and a large bulk of the army now advanced on the conquistadors' defensive line.

Héctor signaled the mounted soldiers to attack. "*Santiago y cierra, España!*"

As the conquistadors rode out to meet the enemy, a sharp whistling sound pierced the tumult, and many of them were suddenly pinned down by a flurry of large, weighted nets thrown over them. The horses panicked and entangled themselves further, falling to the ground. Trapped soldiers and their mounts were then met with a hail of stones before the ñakaqs converged on them. The conquistadors slashed at the netting, but the terrified horses made it difficult to stand their ground, and soon horcas were being thrust at them from all sides.

"Now!" Cristóbal gave the order to release the war dogs, and the mastiffs bounded toward the ñakaqs, tearing their helmets from their faces and mauling them with brutal ferocity. Rodrigo then led a charge which pushed the advancing army back, so that the conquistadors and their horses could be released from the nets.

The metralla was still bringing down countless ñakaqs and making it impossible for them to bring their full weight of numbers to bear on the Spaniards. Despite their heavy losses, though, they continued to surge, forcing the conquistadors to retreat toward the cannons. The fighting became increasingly desperate and brutal. Foot soldiers entered the fray, and the battle became close-quarter combat, with the clash of Toledo blade on ñakaq horca ringing through the air. The conquistador swords pierced the weaknesses in their armor, but the overwhelming numbers inexorably swung the balance toward the ñakaqs.

The cavalry tried repeatedly to break through the front line but was forced to retreat each time the nets flew toward them. Although the ever-growing wall of bodies hampered the attack, the ñakaqs climbed relentlessly over their fallen comrades, pushing forward with unyielding resolve. Conquistadors continued to fall, and the Spanish defenses weakened one soldier at a time. With the cannons finally overrun and most of the war dogs slaughtered, the horde now pressed on unhindered toward the village.

Cristóbal backed away from the front line to try to find a weakness in the attack. He looked around urgently to see where his cousin was. To his dismay, he saw Diego's horse was being dragged down. He raced in his cousin's direction, but ñakaqs swarmed across his path and he struggled to fight his way through. Slashing furiously to clear the way, he looked up to see Héctor already at his cousin's side. The lieutenant was swinging his sword in wild arcs at the ñakaqs who had smothered his cousin.

To Cristóbal's astonishment, Diego emerged from the onslaught, helmetless, but still brandishing his sword. He looked across and his eyes met Cristóbal's.

And Diego smiled.

Just as a horca pierced through his eyes from the back of his head.

Cristóbal screamed to the heavens in anguish, but all he saw was a massing of giant condors in the distance.

**

Padre Núñez knew from the high-pitched cries now filling the air that the ñakaqs had reached the village. He was on his knees at the banks of the river, desperately praying, saying every plea for mercy and salvation he knew, repeating the words over and over again.

"Father, hear our prayers. Precious Blood and Word of God, lead us to salvation. Protect your humble servants from the evil that has beset us. Bring us out of darkness into Your light."

When the turmoil grew to an intensity where he could no longer hear his own words, he looked up and saw Tagón walking toward him. "You murderous demon," he cried. "You were never going to allow yourself to be baptized."

"I said it would make no difference to our attack."

"I believed you, you creation of the devil."

"The timing of the attack had nothing to do with me."

"Spoken with the smooth tongue of evil." He crossed himself. "Are you here to kill me?"

"No, but my people will reach you soon."

"What do you want with me?"

"I want you to finish the baptism."

"Is this another trick?"

"Neither of us can control this battle, but we can do this one thing that's important to both of us."

Padre Núñez hesitated. *Lord give me the strength to know your divine path.* The battle cries outside grew louder. *Can you hear me, Lord?*

"Baptize me. Now, before it's too late."

The padre reached out for Tagón's hand. "Come with me."

Padre Núñez led Tagón into the water as the battle drew deeper into the village. "Quickly."

He placed his hand once more on the ñakaq's head and asked, "Do you believe in God the Father Almighty, Creator of Heaven and Earth?"

"I do believe," replied Tagón, his voice barely rising above the tumult.

"Do you surrender to God's will and accept the mercy of Christ our Lord?"

"I do surrender."

Weaponless Incan servants and villagers ran screaming toward the river.

An inexplicable surge of joy coursed through the padre. He knew it was going to happen. Finally, his life's work was coming to fruition. He was about to bring a soul from having no conception of a higher being to understand the glory of God.

"Do you choose to be baptized of your own free will?"

"I do so choose."

Padre Núñez spoke his next words while he poured water over Tagón's head three times, invoking the Holy Trinity. "I baptize you in the name of the Father, and of the Son, and of the Holy Spirit."

As he said the last word, a brilliance suddenly streaked the air around him, and it seemed as if the sky itself had taken a breath and sprung to life. He looked up, barely comprehending what he saw. High overhead was a gleaming host of powerful winged women, armed with silvered bows and glistening arrows, descending from the clouds. A trail of light traced their paths, and their hair streamed with the wind against the crimson heavens.

The firmament above the battlefield brightened as if a second dawn had broken. A wordless song of cold beauty froze the air. Both men and ñakaqs were paralyzed, their weapons hanging limply in their hands as they stared upwards for a moment in awe.

Until the arrows started raining down on them.

The ñakaqs put their shields up, but for many it was too late as their numbers fell under the attack, the shining arrows easily piercing their armor. Although the conquistadors also put up their shields, they lowered them when they realized the arrows were directed at the ñakaqs.

Padre Núñez crossed himself. "Thank you, Lord."

***

Cristóbal raced to the riverbank where Tagón was now emerging from the water. "Are these the duendes you spoke of?"

Tagón looked nervously at the sky and turned to go. "Yes," said Tagón, "these wind-whisperers are our great enemy. Trust them like you trust the wind."

Cristóbal ordered a renewed charge, despite the conquistadors' depleted numbers. The ñakaqs were now caught between two armies, unable to defend against both the hail of arrows from the sky and the conquistador blades from the ground. Being simultaneously attacked from above and below was devastating. The ñakaqs were slaughtered in colossal numbers. The wide, open valley left them dangerously exposed. When they lifted their shields to protect themselves against the arrows, they were vulnerable to the conquistadors' swords. When they hurled their horcas into the air, their weapons rarely got close to their targets, and without their horcas, the ñakaqs were left defenseless against the Spanish.

Yet, they continued to fight, seemingly unable to change their course. And they died in their thousands. Tens of thousands. Relentlessly fighting a battle they couldn't win, a battle that became a massacre. An inexorable, stabbing massacre. And still they fought. Grimly, stubbornly. And still they fell. When one flank finally attempted to retreat, those fleeing were pursued by the duendes and butchered in even larger numbers, leaving the rest of the army with no alternative but to keep fighting to the death. And fight to the death they did, until the massive ñakaq army was eventually reduced to a shadow of its might, and little more than fifty fought the remaining conquistadors. And in the heart of the combat, towering above the other ñakaqs with his massive beard tied around his waist, stood King Malín, wild-eyed and brandishing his horca.

"Take them alive!" cried Cristóbal. He glared at Rodrigo who obviously wasn't happy with the command.

The two hundred surviving conquistadors surrounded the remaining ñakaqs, tightening the noose so that they had little room to wield their horcas effectively. Several perished, but most of them including King Malín were finally disarmed and subdued.

After the ñakaqs were bound and taken to join the other prisoners, and the cold wordless song of the angels circling high above the battlefield reached a triumphant pitch, a wind-blown silence settled on Nueva Tierra.

Chapter 29

El diario de Cristóbal de Varga

After fifty days and nights in Nueva Tierra, we were exposed without a path of retreat, and no conquistador ever fought with such courage and skill against an overwhelming adversary. It was then it appeared that despite the trials and tribulations that had beset us in this new world, our Lord had finally found his lost flock. When it appeared we would all die in that strange and far-flung land, at the very moment as our deaths were at their greatest imminence, the sky seemed to lighten like a bright dawn springing to life at midday and a frosted wailing filled the air.

Despite the danger that lay upon us, we all looked up, as if entranced, to see a luminous army of angels descending from the heavens. The ñakaqs, too, ceased their battle fury and stared skyward, and both our peoples were thrown from our entrancement only as the first hail of arrows hurtled toward us. As we lifted our shields to protect ourselves from this new onslaught, I sensed that the arrows of these duendes were intended for the ñakaqs, and not my soldiers. And as our padre shouted praise to the glory of God for our salvation, the ñakaqs were slaughtered like no army in history, leaving a carpet of dead and dying bodies across the battlefield.

In the silence of our victory, we erected a cross as the golden-winged leader of the duendes alighted before us with her lieutenants, her face shimmering like sunlight on water, and spoke to us in a tongue so strange it sounded to our ears as the wind passing across mountain peaks.

Chapter 30

The Duendes

The duendes continued to circle like condors above the carnage long after the meager remnants of the ñakaq army had been imprisoned and the surviving soldiers had collected conquistador bodies. As the Spaniards buried their four hundred dead, Padre Núñez performed the final rites for those men who would not survive their injuries. In the eerie after-battle stillness, Cristóbal stood over his cousin's grave and wept. A hand fell on his shoulder. Héctor's.

"I'm sorry, Capitán." Héctor was clearly distraught. "I couldn't keep my promise."

Cristóbal struggled for control. "It wasn't fair for me to ask it of you, Héctor. It was my duty to keep Diego safe. I should have forbidden him from entering the battle. He wasn't a skilled swordsman."

"Was he supposed to cower in one of the Incan houses? You know he wouldn't have done that."

"He would have been alive now if he had hidden after the ñakaqs had breached our defenses."

"We were making a final stand. How could we have known that God would send these angels to save us?"

Cristóbal wiped his stained face and looked up at the winged beings who so far had made no attempt to contact them.

There was a shout from the riverbank where Tagón had been struck by an arrow. Cristóbal and Héctor rushed to the ñakaq who was gritting his teeth and pulling the arrow from his thigh.

"What happened?" cried Cristóbal as Padre Núñez and others ran to join them.

Tagón shook his fist at the sky. "The wind-whisperers don't like that I'm walking here among you unharmed."

"Is that why they don't come down?"

"Yes, they won't land while I'm free."

"Is the hatred you have for each other so bitter?"

"You've seen how my people were prepared to attack yours with our full might. Our hatred for the wind-whisperers is well beyond this."

"Why?"

"I can't answer your question."

Cristóbal hesitated. "I need to speak to them, Tagón."

"I would not advise you to do this. They're not like my people. Their words will ensnare you."

"They've saved my life and those of almost two hundred conquistadors. It's my duty to thank them. Do they speak Quechua?"

"Some do."

Cristóbal looked up at the circling duendes. "What happens if you remain here with us?"

"They'll wait for another chance to kill me. If not before dusk, they'll fly back to their mountain, and return in the morning and start circling again."

"I think the best thing for your safety is to shelter in one of the buildings."

"It's not just me who needs protection if you're going to call them down, it's those you hold as prisoners, especially King Malín. If you must talk to them, make sure you meet some distance from the village."

Cristóbal spoke to Héctor. "Place extra guards around the ñakaq prisoners for their protection and tell Lieutenant Benalcázar that I want both of you with me."

***

Padre Núñez insisted on accompanying Cristóbal, Héctor and Rodrigo as they made their way past the legion of ñakaq corpses strewn across the valley floor beyond the village. Flies already swarmed the bodies and the stench of rotting flesh was starting to filter through the air. The conquistadors pushed through to a large stretch of riverbank that remained free of corpses.

Cristóbal looked up at the circling duendes and gestured to them to land, calling to them in Quechua. "It's safe. Please, I wish to speak to you."

"Are these angels, Padre?" asked Rodrigo.

"I believed so at first, but now I'm less certain. I have no doubt that God's work brought these winged ones to us in our hour of need, but we've just seen them try to kill a baptized Christian. It's possible that, like all of God's children, these duende are capable of both good and evil."

"I know we owe these people our lives," said Cristóbal, "but we need to be wary. From what Tagón has said they can't be trusted. They may have only saved us because we gave them an opportunity to destroy a vulnerable enemy."

"Then it looks to me like we've finally found some allies in this world," said Rodrigo.

"Look," cried Héctor, "they're coming."

Several of the duendes descended in ever decreasing spirals until they landed in front of the four Spaniards, gracefully folding their giant wings behind them, their diaphanous raiment settling on the contours of their bodies. They were taller than the conquistadors, had lean, well-defined muscles, powerful shoulders and golden hair, and their smooth skin shimmered with a delicate light.

Despite Tagón's warnings Cristóbal felt the mesmerizing power of their beauty drawing him in. How could the ñakaqs be at war with such magnificence? These exquisite creatures, by their very presence, demanded to be held in awe, to be worshipped, not engaged in an eternal battle.

One of them, a duende with pale eyes and a face of porcelain, stepped forward.

Cristóbal spoke in Quechua, fighting the effect she was having on him. "I am indebted to your people for saving us from certain defeat."

The duende looked at Cristóbal curiously. She walked up to him and then lowered her forehead so that it touched his. A jolt surged through him.

When she stepped back, she spoke with a voice like the wind. "You have allowed us to have a great victory over our eternal enemy. I am Ithilia."

The name swirled through his head. He struggled to coalesce his thoughts into words. "My name is Capitán Cristóbal de Varga." For the first time in his life he felt shame at the ugliness of his own name. "It appears we have benefited each other today."

"Where are your lands, Capitán Cristóbal de Varga?" asked Ithilia, somehow lifting his name and spinning it into something greater.

"We come from New Spain, a land of blue skies."

"*Blue* skies? Where does this strange world lie?"

"Far from here. We entered your red sky world through an entrada, and we seek our way home."

"And to trade for gold," added Rodrigo.

"Can you help us?" asked Cristóbal.

Ithilia seemed to be studying Cristóbal's face. "We always help our friends."

The duende's nostrils flared slightly. "I can smell ñakaqs."

"The stench of the corpses will get worse, I'm afraid. It will take some days to burn them all."

"No, I smell live ñakaqs. You captured what remained of the army. I also saw one in your company."

"Yes, we also took ñakaq prisoners from a previous battle."

"How many ñakaqs do you have?"

"Over sixty."

"Please give us the honor of killing them."

Her voice softened the harshness of her words, and Cristóbal struggled to grasp their true intent. "I...can't let you do this," he said finally. "They are my responsibility."

"Then please kill them yourself."

"Are you saying that the countless ñakaqs who have died today are not enough for you?"

"An enemy that lives will always rise again with greater vengeance. You must have seen the secretiveness and stubbornness of the ñakaqs. These prisoners you have are the last males of their kind. In time they will breed and build another army and wage war once more. We need to finally eliminate them completely. You do understand, don't you?"

Cristóbal watched Ithilia's shimmering form as she swayed from side to side. He understood, of course he did. He desperately wanted to understand. And yet, how could someone so exquisite say such vile words? "What's caused this great hatred between your peoples?"

"You've seen what they do. Did they not attack you unprovoked?"

"So, you also entered their lands?"

"No, they entered ours."

"That doesn't explain the hatred. I sense more than just enmity."

"The answer to your question should be obvious."

"How?"

"You've seen them. They are repulsive in every way. They violate our world with their presence."

Cristóbal frowned. "You hate them because they're ugly?"

"Do your people not value beauty?"

"Yes, we admire it very much. We seek it out. We want to possess it."

"My people...how can I say this to you? We *worship* beauty. Our essence is beauty. These ñakaqs, they assault what should be worshipped."

Cristóbal found himself taking in the breath-filled music of her words more than the words themselves. "I see."

"You say *you see*, but you don't. My people fall ill in the face of ugliness."

"Then why not stay away from them and remain on your mountain?"

"Their existence sullies our world. All sickness and death come from them. Look what they've done to your people. We won't recapture the perfection we once had until we have wiped them from our world."

Cristóbal ran his fingers along his cheek. "You want to kill each and every ñakaq?"

"Yes, and we have almost achieved it during our history, but always some of them escaped to breed again, like vermin. And soon we are facing another army."

"Why have you been unable to defeat them?"

"They hide in crevices and underground where our wings are a disadvantage. We can never enter their domain. Together your people and mine have had a great triumph today, and with your help, we will have a final victory over them."

"And if I refuse your request to kill the ñakaqs in our camp, Ithilia?"

The duende reached out for Cristóbal's hand. Her skin felt like silk. "Let us speak as friends. If you kill the remaining ñakaqs, there will be no barrier to us finding a way to return you to your blue-sky world laden with gold."

Cristóbal had spent a lifetime striving for the precise meaning of words. His diary was a testament to his obsession. He sensed Ithilia was making it difficult for him to grasp the full significance of what she was saying. He forced the elusive words to settle in his mind so he could see them for what they were. Pulling his hand away, he said, "I understand what you're asking."

Ithilia pointed to the sun sinking toward the peaks in the distance. "We need to leave now. We do not stay in the lowlands overnight. Please, Capitán Cristóbal de Varga, either kill the ñakaqs tonight or allow us to when we return after sunrise."

"We'll speak again in the morning."

Ithilia smiled, bending down again so that their foreheads touched. "I look forward to celebrating our great victory with you in our High Palaces once the last of the ñakaqs are dead."

She spoke to the other duendes in words of breaths and sighs, and as the sun's rays fractured across the peaks, they spread their huge glimmering wings and flew skyward.

Chapter 31

The Curse of Honor

Cristóbal left the sounds of the conquistador camp behind as he headed toward the river. With Diego gone, he was now truly alone. This would have been a time when his cousin lent him an ear and offered some advice he probably didn't want to hear, but which often was right. Too many of his past decisions had been wrong, and he needed to clear his head.

He weaved his way past the balsa rafts, toward the riverbank. The nightly mists had fallen again, and he could hear the rush of the central surge of water beyond the calmer waters at the edge. As he removed his armor, it felt like the weight of command had been lifted from his shoulders. Although he knew it was an illusion, he embraced the feeling that, for a brief moment, lives didn't depend on him.

His cotton undergarments stuck to his skin with grime and sweat, and he made no attempt to rip them off. He entered the warm waters and waded until he was chest deep. When his garments began to billow, he peeled them off and threw them back onto the riverbank.

He lay on his back, floating, and let the current wash through his body. For a moment, it was as if Diego was with him again.

So, Cristóbal, you've finally grown tired of your command?
There have been too many deaths. Spanish. Inca. Ñakaq. I've lost so many of my conquistadors. I've lost you, Diego.
And it's not over.
No, I need to kill more.
Some of the deaths you couldn't help. Others you could.
Maybe, but the responsibility remains with my command regardless.

Why not worry about the ones that you can help?
I don't know who to trust, Diego.
Yes, you do. Honra sobre todo.

Cristóbal felt a surge around his shoulders and couldn't regain his footing. He'd entered the strong currents in the middle of the river and was being carried away. He fought against the flow, but despite being a strong swimmer, he was dragged further into the river's maw.

Ahead was the gorge that split the mountain in two and through which the wild waters concentrated all their force. He tried to stand, but the spiraling currents dragged him off his feet. He kicked furiously and his arm strokes became frantic, but he couldn't escape the river's pull.

Was this how his conquest ended? Ingloriously. With a single foolish decision he didn't need to make?

His arms started to tire and he swallowed water.

It would be a relief to stop thrashing, to let everything wash over him.

"Grab hold of the rope!"

What rope was Diego talking about? And why was he speaking to him in Quechua?

Something brushed past his arm.

Of course, Diego wasn't helping him. And there was no rope in the middle of the river. Just give up and let the current shoot you into the raging waters of the gorge.

"Grab the rope!"

There was that voice again.

Something brushed past him again.

He reached out. It *was* a rope. He grasped hold and immediately it started to pull him against the flow.

His arms strained and his shoulders burned as he clung to the lifeline. His fingers were slipping.

And slipping.

Foaming water poured into his nose and mouth.

He couldn't breathe.

He couldn't breathe for an eternity.

And then he could.

He gasped, coughing the river from his lungs. His vision swam. He had been pulled into the calm waters. His heart pounding, he started wading while still holding onto the rope.

Diego, you've saved me.

When he clambered to the bank, he looked up and saw the broad features of an Incan youth from the village who stood there holding the other end of the rope which now lay coiled at his feet.

"The river is dangerous at this time of the year," said the Inca. "You need to take care."

Cristóbal coughed, unsure what to say. He had barely spoken to any of these villagers on whom he'd wreaked so much destruction. Mumbling a thank you, he looked for his clothes and armor.

When he had finished putting on his wet cotton garments, the Inca was placing the rope on one of the rafts.

Cristóbal said, "I'm sorry we brought this war to you. It was all a mistake."

The youth nodded.

"I'm the capitán, you know. It was my fault."

"I know." The youth shrugged.

How different this youth was to Cristóbal at his age. Where was the fire, the outrage? What had happened to these Incas here in Nueva Tierra?

"When will you leave?" asked the youth.

"I don't know. Soon, I hope. You'll have the village to yourselves again."

"Will the wind-whisperers come back?"

"They say they're returning in the morning."

"I don't like them," said the youth. "The ñakaqs have always treated us well."

"How have the wind-whisperers treated you?"

The youth shrugged again. "I need to go."

"What's your name?" asked Cristóbal, but the Inca had disappeared into the mist that hung between the river and the village.

Cristóbal picked up his armor and walked back to his tent.

Chapter 32

El diario de Cristóbal de Varga

There was a time when I knew where my path lay, but this world, where a man must choose his own angels and demons, has stripped me of all certainty. How does a man, untethered, judge his past deeds, let alone the choices before him? I saw in the enmity of these two ancient races the dark mirror of my own conquest.

Was I on the brink of being cured of the conquistadors' disease? Were we Spaniards any better than thieves and barbarians? What rights did we truly have to the gold and land we claimed in the name of God and King? How could we raid and plunder with the unshakable conviction that we had a host of angels at our backs?

So I came to this mortal decision. Is a man ever in greater danger than when he finally questions what he has always believed to be his most fundamental truth? Is his sanity ever nearer to breaking? Is he ever closer to staring into the void of madness and dissolution?

Chapter 33

Honor and Folly

Cristóbal knelt at his table with his diary open in front of him, praying. The words in his head seemed hollow. With a shock, he realized he was no longer talking to God. The raging thoughts were his own mind battling with itself. What were sixty more deaths after the tens of thousands he had been responsible for? Sixty weighed against two hundred of his men returning safely to their homes. Two hundred conquistadors that had followed him to a new world measured against sixty ñakaqs hell-bent on killing his entire company. And yet...the choice was impossible.

He swiped at his diary in frustration, sending it tumbling to the ground. Why weren't his decisions simple anymore? He cradled his face in his hands. *Diego, not only don't I know who to trust, I can no longer trust myself.*

When he looked up, he saw Tagón standing in front of him. The ñakaq was holding out his helmet which had several gaps where gold inlays had once been.

For a moment he thought he was seeing an apparition.

"I'll be forging a new one," said Tagón. "I want you to have this."

"Why?"

"It's almost impossible to resist the wind-whisperers. Yet my people are still alive in your prison."

Cristóbal shook his head. "All I've done is delay my decision."

Tagón stepped closer to Cristóbal, offering the helmet. "Please take it. It's our custom. When an enemy acts with honor, they earn the right."

"I...can't."

"These are my people's most precious works. Each of us forges our own. When we die, no fire ever burns in it again. The helmet is part of us...what you would call our soul."

"You can't create your own soul."

Tagón glanced at the open diary on the ground. "No?"

As Cristóbal picked up his diary, he heard loud voices outside. When he looked up, Tagón was gone and the helmet now sat on the table. Cristóbal placed his diary next to it as Héctor, Rodrigo and Padre Núñez entered the tent arguing.

"Why isn't this simple, Capitán?" said Rodrigo. "We just give the angels exactly what they want."

Padre Núñez quickly added, "Except we must keep Tagón from them. We can't allow a baptized Christian to be killed."

"Why are you suddenly offering us your views on our strategies?" asked Rodrigo.

"This isn't a battle plan," said Padre Núñez, "or a debate on how we can get our hands on gold. This is a moral decision. Tagón is a baptized Christian."

Héctor said, "Capitán, I can't see why we're allowing these duende to tell us what we should do. The ñakaqs are *our* prisoners. Our war with them is over. We should refuse to hand over any ñakaq, whether they're baptized or not."

"It's no small thing when a soul is brought to God," said Padre Núñez.

"We should treat all the ñakaqs the same way. Does Tagón even know what he's supposed to believe?" demanded Héctor.

Padre Núñez shot back, "If I had ever heard a confession from you, perhaps I would value your views on Christians more."

Rodrigo's face was flushed now, and he made no attempt to hide his impatience. "Have you all forgotten the angels saved our lives? *Is there any choice?* We hand over all the ñakaqs, and for the first time since we entered this God-forsaken land, we have no one trying to kill us."

The three started shouting at once.

"Enough!" cried Cristóbal above the uproar. "I've made my decision. I don't trust Ithilia's words. These duendes are no angels, just as the ñakaqs are no demons. We've killed ñakaqs when they've attacked us, but there's no honor in murder."

Rodrigo spat on the ground. "Honor? Are you mad? First you trap us into a world with no escape, and now you lead us to our deaths." He unsheathed his sword.

"You draw your blade on your capitán?" said Cristóbal. "Guards!"

Héctor drew his sword and brandished it at Rodrigo. Several conquistadors rushed into the tent.

"Disarm Lieutenant Benalcázar!" ordered Cristóbal.

Rodrigo nodded to the guards, and they moved quickly to disarm and hold Cristóbal and Héctor who both looked around bewildered. To Padre Núñez, he said, "Please return to your tent. I have the command now."

"What's this?" demanded Cristóbal. "How dare you!"

"You still have no idea who to trust, do you?" sneered Rodrigo. "I'm making sure your decisions won't be causing any more conquistador deaths."

"You'll pay for this treachery!" cried Héctor.

"Not before your corpse has been rotting a long time." He nodded in the direction of Carlos and Luis. "Put the slave back in his chains." And with that they led Héctor out.

"You're executing us?" cried Cristóbal, still barely comprehending what was happening. "You barbarian!"

Rodrigo drew closer and Cristóbal could smell his breath as he spoke. "You know something? At least I'm a true conquistador. You think you're following Pizarro and Cortés? *I'm* the one like them. We're from the poorest of the Spanish poor, not from families who talk fine words about honor."

He spat the last word onto the ground like it was poison. Turning away, he ordered, "Take the *malparido* out of my sight."

Chapter 34

The Lost Command

Padre Núñez searched frantically for Tagón, questioning several of the villagers. He finally found him sitting on the floor, sharing an evening meal with an Incan family in their dimly lit house. Other than the elderly woman who sat in darkness in the far corner, they all looked up from their meal of corn and flat cakes when he burst through the door.

"Tagón, you need to leave," cried Padre Núñez.

"What have the wind-whisperers said? Do they want Cristóbal to give me to them in the morning?"

"Yes, he refused—but you don't have until morning."

"Why?"

"Lieutenant Benalcázar has just imprisoned the capitán and has taken command. As soon as he can find you, you'll join the other ñakaqs in chains."

Tagón pushed his plate way. "I see."

"You need to hurry. Lieutenant Benalcázar has his men searching for you."

Tagón stood up. "Are you doing this because you baptized me?"

"Of course. You're a Christian now. You have to be saved."

"Do I? There's much I don't understand about being a Christian."

"I know. It doesn't matter. You've been blessed by God. Your baptism was the source of our salvation. I need to protect you."

"From demons? Do you now believe the wind-whisperers are demons?"

"I now suspect there are no more demons in Nueva Tierra than there are in other lands. There are Christians and those who I'm duty-bound to bring to our Lord. That is all."

The sounds of conquistadors searching Incan houses came through the open window.

Padre Núñez ushered him out. "Quickly."

Tagón thanked the family for the meal and turned to Padre Núñez. "I am forever grateful." And with that he slipped outside and disappeared into the mist and darkness.

When Rodrigo and three conquistadors including Luis entered the house soon afterwards, they eyed Padre Núñez suspiciously, as he sat on the floor with the Incas, a plate of half-eaten food in front of him.

"Why are you here, Padre?" demanded Rodrigo.

"Is there a problem with me sharing a meal with an Incan family?" asked Padre Núñez. "How can I bring anyone to God without speaking to them?"

"We have more important things to concern ourselves with now."

"Nothing is more important than God's work."

"We're looking for Tagón."

"Well, I'd suggest you move on to the next house before he realizes you're after him."

"Why would he have any idea we're searching for him?"

"The mist doesn't seem to muffle sounds. I could hear you as you moved through the camp and it was clear who you were after, so I suspect he could have heard you as well."

Rodrigo narrowed his fierce eyes. "You wouldn't be thinking of protecting the ñakaq now that you've baptized him, would you, Padre Núñez?"

"No, but I still think you shouldn't give him to the duendes, Lieutenant Benalcázar."

"It's *Capitán* Benalcázar."

"Of course, Capitán Benalcázar. I've told you my view on Tagón, but I wouldn't presume to contradict your command."

"I'd always thought we saw eye to eye on how to deal with pagans, Padre." Rodrigo looked around the single room dwelling, convinced there were no hiding places. His eyes settled on the old woman in the corner who hadn't moved since he'd come in. "Don't you know you're sharing a meal with an abomination?"

Padre Núñez looked closely at the figure for the first time, realizing it was a mummy. "My eyesight must be starting to fail me, Capitán Benalcázar."

"Luis, take the abomination and burn it," ordered Rodrigo. After he shot one last look of suspicion at the padre, he turned and left.

***

Cristóbal sat on the dirt floor, his hands bound, legs chained, and his back cold against the stone wall of the Incan building. Héctor sat slumped on the opposite side staring into space while outside two soldiers guarded them.

"Don't look so forlorn," said Cristóbal. "I don't believe Rodrigo has the loyalty of all my men. Mark my words, Héctor, there will be a revolt later tonight."

"I don't think so, Capitán. Rodrigo has been sowing the seeds of this for a long time."

"Of course they'll—"

"No, Capitán. You rarely spoke to the soldiers man to man. I'm surprised this hasn't happened earlier."

"Are you saying I've brought this on myself? That I should have been drinking chicha at the campfire rather than wine in my tent?"

"I'm saying you acted like you were above them. Believe me, I know what that feels like."

"Doesn't a leader need to stay apart from those he commands to hold their respect?" Cristóbal shifted uncomfortably and his chains clanked. "What about those men I placed directly under your command, Héctor? Are none of them still loyal to you?"

Héctor stared directly at Cristóbal. "Look at my face, Capitán. I know you don't see it, which is why I'll follow you to the ends of the world, but I still have the face of a slave to the men. None of them respected me. They followed my commands only because they were your commands."

Cristóbal suddenly felt the full weight of the position he found himself in. "So the two of us are alone?"

"It appears that way, Capitán."

"And Rodrigo will execute us tomorrow?"

"Yes."

"And the ñakaqs I was protecting will die tomorrow anyway."

"You made the right decision."

Cristóbal shifted his feet, feeling the tug of the chains that bound him. "Did I? How can it be the right decision if it leads to the very thing it was supposed to stop?"

"Sometimes decisions work out that way."

"No, the good ones don't." Cristóbal fell silent for a long while and then said, "Do you believe my decisions have been foolish, Héctor?"

"Remember Rodrigo agreed to install Huarcay as emperor, and he didn't hesitate to enter the entrada. It was only later he claimed he knew better."

"You haven't answered my question."

Raucous laughter from the village square filtered through the night air.

"They're celebrating," said Héctor. "Almost four hundred conquistadors died today and they're celebrating!"

Cristóbal listened to the voices of the soldiers whom he used to command, catching snatches here and there above the increasingly wild cries of festivities, realizing he barely knew who they were. What had he done? How had everything he had strived for come to this moment? He could have avoided this. It wasn't inevitable. He could have told the conquistadors what they wanted to hear tonight. That he would hand over the ñakaq prisoners to be killed by the duendes, and that the conquistadors would be shown the way home, laden with gold. It would have been the easiest course of all. He knew what to say to keep their loyalty for another night, but instead he agonized over a moral decision, nearly drowned, and then decided to save prisoners hell-bent on killing him.

Yes, he knew the words he could have said.

Conquistadors of Nueva Tierra, let us not forget that today we overcame the greatest army any Spanish battalion in history has ever faced. No Christian army has fought with such courage and skill against a horde of unbelievers. And in the end God in his wisdom chose to reward our valor and send to us the instruments of our salvation. Never forget that we fought gloriously against overwhelming odds, and in doing so ensnared our enemy in a fatal trap. Tomorrow we'll wipe the remaining ñakaqs from our midst and strike our new path to gold and glory. But tonight, let us celebrate our mighty victory.

He knew the words. But he'd chosen not to use them.

Chapter 35

Sarpay's Curse

The strumming of a six-stringed *vihuela* floated across the village square where a raging campfire threw flames into the night sky. The conquistadors had discarded their armor and were openly cavorting with Huarcay's surviving servant women. Soon, though, emboldened by copious cups of chicha, they started ransacking the village houses and dragging young Incan women from their beds and out to join the celebration.

Sarpay tried to move quickly as she poured large amounts of corn beer into the conquistadors' cups. Sometimes she wasn't quick enough and a soldier would grab hold and paw at her. Laughing, she would always manage to pull away. She knew what she had to do. Keep them drinking and keep them laughing.

"Drink," she implored. "Quickly before the chicha runs dry."

"Yes," shouted Rodrigo, "let's all drink, because tomorrow we will share our cups with angels."

He pulled Sarpay to him and held her firmly on his lap. She gritted her teeth, pouring corn beer into his mouth as he fondled her. What was the Spanish insult he always used? *Malparido!* "Am I still welcome in the Capitán's tent?" she asked, smiling.

"You're still welcome in the Capitán's bed," replied Rodrigo.

Sarpay filled her mouth with chicha and bent down to kiss him, releasing the beer so that it entered Rodrigo's mouth and trickled down his chin.

He continued to grope Sarpay, reaching out and pulling any passing Inca to join them, until he realized the flames were starting to subside.

He released his grip on Sarpay and got unsteadily to his feet. "Listen to me," he shouted as the music stopped, his slurred voice betraying the large amounts of corn beer he had already drunk. "This is your capitán. Do you all hear me? Capitán Benalcázar. The fire is dying. Find more wood. We can't let it die. There's still more chicha for us."

Several of the conquistadors had started to leave the square when he cried, "No, wait. You don't need to leave the village. These Indians all have abominations hidden in their houses. I know it. Go find them. Look in every dark corner and uncover every rug. Then spike them on ñakaq horcas and bring them to the fire so we can burn away the evil from Nueva Tierra."

As the conquistadors left to ransack the village buildings, Sarpay realized Rodrigo was smiling at her look of horror. "Are you going to tell me that Capitán de Varga would have never given a command like that?"

She forced all expression from her face. "It no longer matters what command Cristóbal would have given."

"A good answer." He leaned down and kissed her breasts. "A very good answer."

The soldiers soon started returning with the mummies skewered on horcas, throwing them on the fire with each one feeding the flames to greater heights. The villagers cried out as if they themselves were being burnt each time sparks shot skyward when another mummy hit the pile.

"Make them look," shouted Rodrigo. "The pagans need to see how easily we destroy what they believe."

Sarpay stared impassively at the fire, shutting out the screams of the villagers.

"You see now how powerless your gods are, don't you?" asked Rodrigo.

"I do," said Sarpay.

"I'm more powerful than your gods. Can you see that?"

"I can."

"You should remember that."

"I will." Sarpay gestured to her servants. "More chicha for the Capitán. More chicha for everyone."

When the last mummy was heaved into the flames, the music started again.

***

Cristóbal was half-asleep when he became aware of a figure in front of him.

"Padre Núñez?"

The padre nodded. "The guards have let me in to hear your confession."

"I don't think I asked for a confession."

"We both know Rodrigo will execute you and Héctor in the morning. Don't you think this is a good time?"

Cristóbal became aware of Héctor's ragged snoring. "I don't feel the need to confess, Padre. I made the right decision tonight. If you can't break my chains, then maybe it would be better to just prepare to give me the last rites."

Padre Núñez looked over his shoulder at the shadowed outlines of the guards through the window. "You know I can't release you." He drew closer, speaking softly. "I made sure Tagón escaped."

This was unexpected. Despite everything, he smiled to himself. "I suppose you were never one to take your orders from the capitán. Be careful, or you'll end up in here with me."

Padre Núñez shrugged. "You know, I think we're all trapped by our ambitions. We build our own prisons with the bricks of our passions. Whether it's the desire for gold or the desire to save souls."

"So, what do we do, Padre? Do we shed ourselves of our ambitions?"

The padre shook his head. "We can't shed our ambitions any more than we can shed our skin. What am I without my desire to bring pagans to God? What's a man's life worth once he abandons his life's work?"

Héctor continued to snore and Cristóbal suddenly became aware that the music had faded.

"Here," said Padre Núñez, revealing a gourd from under his sackcloth, "it's the last of my sacramental wine. Please take it and make both your fates a little more palatable."

Cristóbal lifted his bound hands in protest. "No, Padre, I can't give up on my ambitions yet. You drink your wine tonight. You're still a free man."

"Of course, Cristóbal, of course. Just because we know our obsessions will destroy us in the end, doesn't mean we should forsake them. Farewell, Cristóbal, I feel we won't see each other again."

With that Padre Núñez turned to go.

***

Deep into the night, Sarpay moved through the village square. She stopped at each soldier, checking his breathing. The conquistadors had collapsed comatose around the campfire and many were snoring. Even Padre Núñez appeared to have drunk too much and not quite made it back to his tent.

When she reached Rodrigo, Sarpay held a knife against his throat for a long time while he slept on the ground. She was trembling as she mouthed curses at him.

He reminded her so much of Francisco Pizarro. The same hollow features. The same twisted smile. The two men were hewn from the same brutal stone. The day Pizarro captured Cusco was carved in her memory, the day the Incan capital burned, the day he installed her seventeen-year-old cousin Manco Inca to the throne as his puppet.

She raised the blade and ran it down the length of Rodrigo's cheek, drawing blood.

Most of all she would never forget the tortured look of Manco's wife the day she was seized by Pizarro to become his loathsome brother's consort, the day the rebellion began.

Sarpay rasped a curse from the back of her throat. "Die in this prison we've led you into."

She lowered the knife and left.

Chapter 36

The Long Night

Despite the silence that now reigned across the village, Cristóbal couldn't sleep, his thoughts storming inside his head—until he noticed a shadow pass across the open window.

Then a figure wielding a knife stood in the doorway.

"Sarpay," he whispered.

"You sound surprised."

"I...I am."

"You may deserve to be imprisoned under these red skies, Cristóbal, but you don't deserve to die."

She started cutting his cords.

"Where are the guards?"

"They've had a little too much to drink, like the others."

"You've drugged them all?"

Sarpay smiled. "How easy it is to fool men when they hold so little regard for you."

The cords fell off and Cristóbal rubbed his hands. Héctor woke as Sarpay started cutting his bonds.

"Unfortunately, you'll need more than a knife to get these chains off our legs," said Cristóbal.

"It looks like you're in luck tonight." She pulled a set of keys from under her tunic and started unshackling him.

"So Rodrigo was not to your taste?"

"I must be hard to please." Her face was lined with grim determination. "We're leaving now. All my servants and the surviving villagers."

"Where will you go? Rodrigo will hunt you down before you can get out of the valley."

Sarpay moved across to unshackle Héctor. "We're taking the rafts downriver. He won't be able to come after us."

"Through the gorge? It's too dangerous, isn't it?"

"The villagers are masters of the river. They give us some chance of survival, even when the waters are as treacherous as they are now. They're loading the rafts. Are you coming with us or not?"

"Leave my command?"

"I know you'll find it hard to accept, but you don't have a command anymore."

"There is another choice, Capitán," said Héctor.

"I'm not a cold-blooded murderer. No one will be butchering drugged Spaniards while I have a breath in my body." Cristóbal stroked his chin, annoyed at the stubble. "Where are the ñakaq prisoners?"

Sarpay said, "We've already released them, and they're coming with us."

"Then let's all get on these rafts."

As Cristóbal and Héctor stepped over the drugged guards outside their door, they saw the ñakaqs standing silently in the darkness, waiting for them. At the front were Tagón and King Malín.

"I thank you, Capitán Cristóbal de Varga," said King Malín. "Tagón has told us what has happened to you since you chose to protect us against the wind-whisperers."

Cristóbal remembered to cover his eyes for a moment before he spoke to him. "Killing someone in battle is one thing, murdering the defenseless is something else entirely."

"Then we understand each other," said King Malín. "That is why we'll allow your people to sleep in peace."

"Sarpay tells me you'll join the raft journey through the gorge. Is there no other way?"

"Our people are not fond of the water, but we need to get back to our wives as quickly as possible."

"Why not simply go home the way you came?"

"If we marched back to the other side of the valley," said King Malín, "we would be exposed to the wind-whispers for the entire journey."

Cristóbal shielded his eyes again. "Then our fates are bound together."

***

The moon still shed its blood-red light on the village as Cristóbal and Sarpay made their way to the riverbank. Cristóbal had donned his armor and was carrying a sack of his belongings, including his diary and Tagón's helmet, which he had collected from his tent. None of the sleeping conquistadors who littered the village square showed any signs of waking as they walked past.

"This drug you use must be very powerful," said Cristóbal. "Huarcay could have slain us all in our sleep the first time you fled."

"We only drugged the guards last time, and Huarcay wasn't a conquistador. He never had the stomach for killing." Sarpay stared at Cristóbal. "You could kill your enemy right now. Why not run your sword through Rodrigo while he snores?"

"As I said to King Malín, I'm not a murderer."

"Perhaps not now."

The Incas continued to load the rafts with the last of the supplies, including several live alpacas and ciervas, while Cristóbal struggled to find a response to Sarpay's accusation.

Héctor led two horses toward them. "Should we risk taking these on the river, Capitán?" he asked.

Sarpay called over a villager who had been adjusting the sail on the nearest raft. To Cristóbal's surprise it was the Inca that had rescued him from the water earlier in the evening.

They acknowledged each other with a nod of mutual recognition.

"This is Tiso," said Sarpay, "but it appears you know him."

"He's already saved my life once tonight." Cristóbal smiled. "Tell me, will the rafts bear the weight of horses?"

Tiso looked at the stallions that Héctor held. "Yes, but what do they eat?"

"Corn if there's no grass."

"And they're not afraid of water?"

"Horses can swim. We've crossed rivers with them early in our campaign, but they were small streams compared to what we're facing here. They'll need us to calm them."

"Then you can put those two on this raft and you'll need to travel with them."

Cristóbal studied the fleet of balsa rafts in the final stages of preparation. "Can we have two more horses on another raft with Héctor?"

"Four horses?" asked Héctor. "Are you sure, Capitán? Only two of us can ride."

"It would be good to have replacements ready, and in the meantime, they can carry supplies overland." Cristóbal smiled. "And make sure we take the two fastest horses, including Rodrigo's."

"Of course, Capitán."

***

Cristóbal watched dubiously as the Incas swung the two crescent-shaped sails around to catch the night wind. The bamboo upper deck felt insubstantial underfoot. His horse shifted nervously, pulling at its tether, and Cristóbal stroked its mane to calm it. This fleet of rafts was nothing like the Spanish galleons he had sailed on.

"Where's the rudder?" he asked Sarpay as the riverbank receded. "Are we simply going to be at the mercy of the winds and currents?"

"No," said Sarpay, pointing to several Incas including Tiso who stood at the front and back of the raft, raising and lowering several centerboards by their handles. "See how the *guaras* are used with the sails to control the direction of the boat."

To Cristóbal's surprise the rafts appeared to be navigated efficiently and with precision into the middle of the river. He felt a sudden surge as the raft left the calm waters of the port and entered the racing current. The Incas adjusted the guaras into another pattern, and Cristóbal's raft sped toward the gorge with the rest of the fleet close behind.

Wild waters soon began pouring over the logs lashed with hemp-like ropes, but rather than weighing the raft down, they immediately disappeared through the cracks, passing through the structure like a sieve. The deck bucked under Cristóbal's feet and he grabbed hold of the thatched hut in the middle of the raft to steady himself.

Glancing back at the village, he felt a pang of remorse at what could have been, mouthing a wordless goodbye to his cousin. Then the roar of the looming gorge commanded his attention.

The water foamed around the vessel and spray hit his face like rain. Sarpay was shouting something at him, but he couldn't hear above the tumult. While he had thought the raft was moving quickly before, it now sped up to breakneck pace in another surge of current. The waters swirled in all directions, and giant waves towered up ahead. Unlike ocean waves, these didn't roll toward the vessels, instead they remained static, drawing the rafts to them like lodestones and battering them mercilessly until they escaped.

With the raft now completely enveloped by spray, Cristóbal lost all sense of direction. A wall of water suddenly reared up like a foaming beast and crashed across the deck. The raft began spinning, caught in a monstrous whirlpool. The Incas pulled at the two curved masts and frantically adjusted the centerboards to break away.

After an abrupt jolt, the vessel started moving forward again. Cristóbal looked back at the fleet and saw one of the other rafts crash into the rock face and splinter in two. The Incas on board were flung into the raging torrent. They desperately tried to stay afloat by clinging to the balsa logs, but one after the other, they were smashed into the jagged rocks and disappeared under the surface.

Cristóbal's own raft now rapidly headed toward the cliffs. The razor-like rocks sped toward him so swiftly he covered his face with his arms, anticipating impact. But the navigators changed the raft's direction just in time, and when he uncovered his eyes, he saw they were sailing in the middle of the gorge again.

Another raft to his right was swamped by a standing wave and everyone on board was hurled into the river. Cristóbal felt his stomach heave when he realized Tagón was one of those struggling in the water. Tiso and the other Incas on his raft threw out rescue ropes, and several, including two ñakaqs, escaped drowning by using the lifelines to fight their way through the current. Cristóbal grabbed one of the ropes to help reel in those at the other end. His heart was pumping furiously when Tagón finally crawled onto the deck, choking and gasping and still clutching his horca, his beard a tangled mat across his chest. The ñakaq nodded his thanks before both of them were upended by another wave and had to grab hold of a cabin wall to avoid being swept away.

The gorge narrowed, concentrating the current to even greater speeds and making it more difficult to avoid the encroaching cliffs. Cristóbal, Tagón and Sarpay crashed to the deck as the raft bucked like a wild horse. They struggled back onto their feet just as a swathe of water tore across the raft and upended them again.

The vessel picked up impossible speed, then suddenly turned full circle before it shot out of the gorge like a cannonball. Only then did it finally slow, the roar of the river easing and the spray thinning. One by one the gorge spat the rafts out into a large flat expanse of calm water surrounded by clusters of trees with tangled roots exposed above the water line.

The navigators readjusted the sails and centerboards and headed for the trees. Cristóbal spoke to Tiso as he comforted his distressed horse. "This doesn't look like a good harbor."

"It's not, but it's almost dawn and the wind-whisperers will soon be flying overhead on their way to the village. If they see we have ñakaqs with us, they'll attack us. We need to hide quickly."

Silence swallowed the distant roar of the gorge as the Incas found a way through the maze of roots and entered the stillness of the canopy. Soon the morning sun began to filter through the leaves, washing a pale green light onto the rafts.

Not long after, a flock of shadows passed across the tangled branches above them.

No one spoke.

Tagón became a statue. One of the horses neighed, and the shadows were gone. The Incas waited a while and then headed back out to the middle of the river.

Chapter 37

Whispering the Flames

As dawn broke across the village, Rodrigo awoke dazed where he had collapsed the night before. Struggling to his feet, he blinked at the morning sun and ran his fingers along a thin cut that had appeared on his cheek. He kicked Luis who was lying near him until he stirred.

"Get up," he cried. "The duendes will be here soon."

Carlos and Martín ran toward him.

Martín shouted, "The Incas are gone. All of them."

"What?" Rodrigo squeezed his eyes shut to escape the growing light of the morning.

"It looks like they took the rafts onto the river," said Carlos.

"*Mierda*! They've drugged us again." Panic hit him.

Carlos said, "They must have freed the ñakaq prisoners. They're gone as well."

Rodrigo felt his gut twisting.

"So have Capitán de Varga and Lieutenant Valiente. And they've taken some horses, including yours," said Martín.

Rodrigo leaned over and vomited onto the ground. As he wiped his mouth, he looked at the glowing embers of the fire. He suddenly knew what to do. "We had sixty-two ñakaq prisoners, didn't we? And with Tagón, that's sixty-three."

***

By the time the army of duendes appeared in the distance, the campfire flames had sprung back to the heights of the previous night, smoke poured into the sky, and the stench of corpses hung heavily above the village square.

"Quickly," cried Rodrigo. "Stoke the fire."

Ithilia flanked by a dozen duendes alighted, all of them folding their glistening wings behind them, while others continued circling above the valley.

Ithilia stared at the fire.

"We decided to save you the trouble and killed the ñakaqs ourselves," said Rodrigo.

She looked around. "Where is Capitán de Varga?"

"We had a disagreement," said Rodrigo, trying to ignore the taste of corn beer vomit in his mouth. "He wanted to let the ñakaqs live. I said we should kill them, so now I'm the capitán. Capitán Rodrigo Benalcázar."

"How have you killed them?"

Rodrigo pointed to the charred bodies engulfed by flames. "As you can see, we burned them alive."

Ithilia's nostrils flared. "Strange, I don't smell any freshly killed ñakaqs."

Rodrigo forced a smile. "The stink from the corpses surrounding the village must be overpowering everything."

Her nostrils widened again. "My people have a very acute sense of smell. Particularly when it comes to our enemies." She glared into Rodrigo's eyes. "Is someone lying?"

An icy shiver coursed down Rodrigo's spine. "The Incas... drugged me last night. I've only just woken up, so I'm taking the word of my men that the ñakaqs in the fire are our prisoners."

"I know that they can't be."

"Then I've been lied to."

"Perhaps it would be better if I spoke to Capitán de Varga."

"That's impossible. He's escaped with the Incas through the gorge."

"I see. And could it be possible that he took the ñakaqs with him?"

Rodrigo prodded the nearest conquistador. "Luis, why didn't you tell me the ñakaqs had escaped as well?"

"I—"

"Why would you hide that they'd escaped?" demanded Rodrigo, "and then pretend that burning corpses were our prisoners?"

"Lieutenant Benalcázar, I—"

"It's Capitán, remember. *Capitán*."

"It appears someone under your command has lied to you," said Ithilia.

"I apologize for what Luis has done."

"The offense is not to me, it is to you, Capitán Benalcázar." Ithilia's voice wafted through him, seeking deep recesses.

"Yes, of course."

"To lie to those in command is a most serious offense."

"Yes. Yes, it is."

"He has humiliated you before an ally. He has made you look weak and foolish. Isn't that true?"

"Yes, that's what he's done." Rodrigo couldn't look at Luis.

"What will you do to show your leadership, Capitán Benalcázar? What will you do so that none of your men lie to you again? What will you do so that no one will ever again make you look foolish?"

"I'll punish him."

"And what sort of punishment does someone who lies to their superiors deserve? A light one? Something that others will quickly forget?"

"No, it needs to be something that others remember."

"Something that shows you are in authority, isn't that right?"

"Yes."

"Something as deathly serious as lying to you needs a deathly serious punishment, doesn't it, Capitán Benalcázar? Or is it still *Lieutenant* Benalcázar?"

"It's Capitán Benalcázar."

"So, Capitán Benalcázar, you know what you must do. There's only one possible punishment. Only one punishment that no one will forget. You need to put him to death, don't you?"

Rodrigo was trembling.

"You can't do this!" cried Luis, his voice strained with fear. "You know it's not right."

"You've lied to me."

"No, Capitán. I haven't lied to you. I followed your orders. You know I have."

"You've lied to me and made me look foolish."

"Look at me," said Luis, increasingly frantic. "Look me in the eyes and tell me I've lied to you."

"You know which punishments are remembered most clearly, don't you, Capitán Benalcázar?" asked Ithilia, her voice grabbing hold of him again.

"Stop listening to her," cried Luis. "Can't you see what she's doing to you?"

Ithilia continued. "We all know those punishments that fit the lie are the ones that aren't forgotten. The lie was to burn corpses and pretend they were still alive, wasn't it? There's only one possible punishment here."

"Yes, there's only one."

"No!" shouted Luis.

"Throw him on the fire," said Rodrigo.

The conquistadors hesitated.

"I said throw Luis on the fire!"

Luis started screaming as several soldiers grabbed him, his eyes wide with an incomprehensible fear. He struggled to break free as they dragged him toward the flames, but with so many holding him it was impossible. He jerked and fought as the soldiers lifted him from the ground. And with an almighty heave they threw him into the middle of the blaze. He immediately tried to clamber down the pile of flaming ñakaq corpses, tumbling so that he was encased by a mass of charred bones and leering skulls. He fought his way to the surface, but his skin and hair had caught alight and he wailed in agony.

"Use the horcas to keep him in the fire," commanded Rodrigo.

"What's happening here?" Padre Núñez staggered into the village square, eyes bloodshot.

"This isn't your concern, Padre," said Rodrigo.

"Why are you setting fire to one of your own men? How is it we're burning Christians?" Two soldiers held him back.

"Leave this to me, Padre. You're not thinking clearly. You were drugged by the Incas, and they've escaped and taken the ñakaqs."

"And this is Luis's fault?"

The conquistador's wails grew louder. "Save me, Padre."

"Luis lied to protect the ñakaqs. Now let me deal with this."

"It's her!" Luis's voice was a hoarse scream as he reached out with a flaming arm and pointed to Ithilia. "She's evil."

Somehow, he managed to make it to the edge of the fire. The conquistadors thrust the horcas at him until he fell into the flames. Each time he struggled to his feet and attempted to escape, he was pushed back again. Until finally he didn't get up.

Ithilia approached Rodrigo and leaned forward, touching his forehead with hers. "I'm glad you have chosen to punish those that stand in our way. The great victory is still in our grasp. Will you now help us to hunt down the escaped ñakaqs before they reach the hidden abodes of their maidens?"

"Of course, but we can't follow them through the gorge."

"There is another way."

Chapter 38

The Chase

The rafts raced downriver with both the current and wind behind them, the forest of exposed tree roots on both banks rapidly giving way to flat expanses of sand. Cristóbal loaded his crossbow as Tagón obsessively scanned the skies above the gorge.

"Any sign of the duendes?" asked Cristóbal.

"Not yet," said Tagón. "I would have thought they would be after us by now. If this wind holds, we may make it into the mountains without another battle."

"You can't afford to lose anyone else. Are you sixty-three truly the only males of your kind alive now?"

"Yes, apart from some young boys who have had no training yet. We sent all our forces against you."

"Maybe that wasn't wise."

Tagón glanced over his shoulder again. "You were trapped and the valley was wide enough for a large army."

"But with the duendes being such a great enemy, you should have expected them to attack while so many of you were exposed."

"It had been a long time since the duendes attacked us in full force in open battle, and we were focused on stopping you. Our stubbornness is our weakness as well as our strength. King Malín couldn't think past making certain you could never enter our heartlands."

"So, are you taking the Incas to your homes?"

Tagón looked shocked at the suggestion. "Of course not. We've offered them another smaller valley, hidden deep in our realm, for them to rebuild their village. You're welcome to stay there—if we make it." Something caught his attention and he pointed to the mountains behind them. "It looks like your conquistadors have allied themselves with the wind-whisperers."

Cristóbal followed the line of Tagón's gaze, and there, coming over the cliffs that formed the gorge, was a sight he could barely comprehend.

Etched against the cloudless red sky was an army of duendes, golden wings spread to twice their height, with each duende carrying an armored conquistador in front of them. And at the rear were horses, each tethered by ropes to four duendes, their legs flailing for purchase mid-air so that they appeared to be galloping across the heavens.

"We won't have a chance if they catch us," said Cristóbal. "The duendes can shoot us at will."

"I think the wind is dropping," said Tiso, adjusting the sails.

The raft was noticeably slowing.

Behind them, the duendes swarmed down and landed on the treeless stretches of the valley, releasing their grips of the conquistadors and untethering their horses. The soldiers quickly mounted their steeds and raced downriver, while the duendes surged skyward again, resuming their pursuit of the rafts unencumbered.

"Can't we go any faster?" cried Cristóbal.

"The current will pick up soon," said Tiso, "but we need to watch out for rapids. The rocks will damage the rafts if we hit them."

A small group of duendes were now flying well ahead of Rodrigo and his men, although the conquistadors were also drawing closer to the Incas. A sudden surge drew the rafts into the faster current, and the navigators raised and lowered the centerboards to adjust to the new conditions. Up ahead, the river disappeared into what looked like a cave within the rocky face of the mountain.

"Is that another gorge?" asked Cristóbal.

"No," said Tiso, "it's a tunnel. If we can reach it, we'll be safe."

The duendes, however, were now almost within striking distance. Cristóbal took aim with his crossbow, flexing his knees to absorb the raft's movement. He released the bolt, and one of the lead duendes plummeted from the sky, splashing into the river. As he loaded his crossbow again, he gave a silent thanks to his cousin's weaponry skill. The second bolt also met its mark and another duende fell from the sky.

Clearly the duendes hadn't expected an attack from this distance and their pursuit stuttered.

Tagón clapped him on the back. "Well done."

Cristóbal smiled grimly. "It should slow them a little. It won't be enough, though."

The duendes soon picked up speed again, swerving in erratic formations to avoid being struck. When they came into range, Cristóbal took aim, although it was more difficult because the raft was now veering left and right to avoid the ragged rocks that loomed out of the water.

He released the bolt, but it failed to hit a mark this time.

This seemed to embolden the duendes and they drew closer.

The next time Cristóbal allowed for the swerving of the raft, and he struck another duende. She faltered but continued flying. He shot further bolts in rapid succession, with a mixed strike rate, but it was enough for the duendes to be more cautious.

They flew higher, out of reach of the bolts, and then drew their bows again. The ñakaqs lifted their shields to protect themselves and the Incas from the volley of arrows. Fortunately, with the increased height, the duendes lost accuracy and missed their targets. They then changed tack again and swooped toward the rafts.

The Incas flung their slingstones at them, but theirs was the accuracy of farmers and sailors rather than warriors. When Héctor started shooting bolts from his crossbow, he and

Cristóbal were the only ones having any impact. The duendes were now almost directly overhead, and although they were wheeling in wild circles to avoid being targets, they managed to shoot with devastating precision.

To Cristóbal's dismay, Rodrigo and his conquistadors had now almost caught them and were riding along the river's edge, crossbows and harquebuses in hand. Fortunately, the harquebuses lacked accuracy from a galloping horse, but the crossbow bolts were dangerous.

Cristóbal fixed Rodrigo in his sights. Their eyes met and he hesitated. Why was he unable to pull the trigger? Despite what the lieutenant had done, did he still feel he owed him something? Why couldn't he shake off the feeling that it was dishonorable to kill those who had been under his command, even after they had usurped him? He lowered his crossbow. Then a wind gust caused a surge in the raft and it raced toward the dark opening in the mountain that was suddenly close.

All the other rafts had caught the same gust and the entire fleet was hurtling toward the tunnel. The duendes and conquistadors were caught off-guard and it took them a moment to increase their speed.

Cristóbal realized the sudden spurt wasn't quite going to give them enough breathing space as Rodrigo bore down on the rafts again. This time, though, he could see that their horses were tiring after their long gallop across the valley. Slowly, they were dropping further back, until he was certain they weren't going to catch them.

The powerfully muscled duendes, however, obviously hadn't tired and were once again within shooting range. Arrows hailed down on the rafts, and although many of them fell harmlessly into the water or failed to penetrate the ñakaq shields, some hit their mark.

Cristóbal raised his crossbow again, and suddenly everything went dark.

He thought for a moment that he had died, when he realized they had just entered the tunnel.

The entrance was the only source of light and it was rapidly receding into the distance. A few duende arrows splashed into the water near the rafts at the rear of the fleet, but the pursuit was over.

A cheer erupted inside the cave, echoing sonorously until it eventually faded.

Tagón again gave Cristóbal what must have been his highest praise, clapping him roughly on the back and saying, "You've done well. You've done well."

The Incas lit torches to help guide them through the tunnel, and the flames created curious patterns on the rocky walls. The current wasn't strong, and there was no wind, so the rafts moved slowly. The only noise was the sound of dripping from the walls.

"What happens at the other end of the tunnel?" asked Cristóbal. "Will the duendes be waiting for us?"

Tagón said, "No, the river cuts deep through our heartlands, and we have the advantage over the wind-whisperers in our terrain. There are few places where they can attack us from the air."

"Then you believe we're safe, Tagón?"

"As safe as we can ever feel. All we can do is hold tightly onto our secrets and hope it's enough."

A clap of thunder reverberated from the tunnel entrance.

Chapter 39

In the Palace of Angels

Rodrigo signaled a halt to the chase, silently cursing Cristóbal for taking his horse. At the end of the chase it would have made a difference. Thunder crashed overhead and erratic winds gusted in his face. Padre Núñez was still lagging well behind when Ithilia and several of the other duendes landed next to the conquistadors as they stood on the rocky banks at the entrance of the tunnel.

"Can you carry us into the next valley?" asked Rodrigo. He strained his neck, looking up at the steep cliffs towering toward the increasingly cloud-filled sky.

Ithilia didn't seem pleased. "That will be difficult."

"Why?"

"There is no valley beyond the tunnel. The ñakaq heartlands lie at the other end. They are a maze of mountain paths and ravines. The ñakaqs know their own territory and are impossible to find."

"They might be impossible to find from the air, but my men will be searching for them from the ground."

"You will continue the pursuit?"

"Of course. The Incas have made us look foolish for the last time, and they have to pay with their lives, and when we find the Incas we'll find the ñakaqs."

"You will hunt and kill the ñakaqs?"

"Yes."

"That would please me greatly. The two of us together can finally lay the ñakaq secrets bare." She looked up to the sky where the gathering clouds were taking on a purple hue. "But there is a tempest on the way. We will need to return to our High Palaces. The storms in these mountains are wild and

188

often last for days. It will be impossible to continue the pursuit now."

"Do we wait out the storm here?" Rodrigo looked around at a cluster of thick-canopied trees to their left.

Ithilia held out her hand to Rodrigo, the sun breaking through the clouds for a moment and enveloping her in a halo. "Let us make our plans for the final demise of our enemies together, Capitán," she said. "We would be pleased to carry you and your men with your horses to our High Palaces as our guests."

Rodrigo smiled. "We would be the ones who are pleased, Ithilia." He turned to his soldiers. "Prepare yourselves, conquistadors! Tonight we will be the guests of angels."

***

The winds buffeted the conquistadors as the duendes carried them ever higher into the skies of Nueva Tierra. Storm clouds crowded above them, looking increasingly ominous. Rodrigo felt Ithilia's warm contours along the length of his back as she held him tightly, and her great wings powered effortlessly through the air. He could barely keep his eyes open as gust after gust struck his face.

When Ithilia entered the cloud mass, Rodrigo's vision fogged and he lost the sensation of flying. Ice pricked his face and moisture sheathed him like cold sweat. He struggled to breathe, the air so damp it felt like he was drowning.

Finally, the duendes broke through the clouds and the heavens burnt red again. There in the distance soared an impossibly high peak, stark against the sky. And at the summit stood a cluster of golden towers striving to greater heights than the mountain itself.

Ithilia said something to Rodrigo, but although her mouth was close to his ear, it was as if the vast open sky dispersed the sound so that it was impossible to hear.

The higher they flew, the colder it became and the harder it was to breathe. A crack of thunder sounded below, but the storm now seemed to belong to a different world. Up ahead, many figures were standing on a series of platforms, flanked by flaming torches, jutting out from the mountainside. As he drew closer, to his surprise the figures appeared to be Incan men. As Ithilia landed on one of the platforms, Rodrigo was light-headed, the way he had felt when he first entered the Andes. His legs buckled and one of the Incas rushed to support him.

Ithilia said, "Please, each of you will be taken to bathe before the feast."

Rodrigo started to shiver in the bitter cold now that his back was exposed, and the Inca led him through a jewel-encrusted doorway into the gleaming tower. Once inside, he immediately felt heat that seemed to be generated inside the walls.

"My name is Puyu," said the Inca. "I am at your service."

He took Rodrigo through a high-arched hall, festooned with a series of mountain-scape paintings stained in a red light. They came to a narrow doorway and the Inca beckoned him in, saying, "This is your cleansing room."

Rodrigo entered the humid chamber which was clouded with a heady aroma from a sunken bath. In the corner was a full-length mirror.

"Please," said Puyu, "remove your clothes and enter. Take care not to allow your head to go under the water."

"Why?"

"The cleansing waters are not suitable for your face."

Rodrigo eyed the Inca curiously. "How is it your people are here in duende palaces?"

"I've served the winged ones since I was born."

"Do they pay you?"

"I don't understand the word *pay*."

"Are you free to leave?"

The Inca laughed. "Of course not. What a thought! Where would I go?"

"Down to the valleys."

"Why would I do that?" Puyu frowned. "I would die. Now please take off your clothes. The water will feel hot against your skin at first, but you'll soon become accustomed to it."

"The other Incas seem to survive down below."

"What others?"

Rodrigo still felt unsteady. He took off his armor and cotton undergarments slowly and stepped into the steaming water, sliding so that he was sitting on a ledge and the water level came up to his neck. "How long have your people been serving the duendes?"

"I don't know. A long time. I once heard a tale that our ancestors lived in a place where we were the masters, not the servants, but it was just a story."

The warmth seeped into Rodrigo's bones and his skin tingled faintly.

"I'll need to shave your face," said Puyu.

"Is that necessary?" asked Rodrigo.

"Ithilia won't have beards in the feasting hall."

"Well then, you'll need to shave me."

"Remember not to swallow any water."

Rodrigo leaned back as Puyu softened his beard with hot water and a sweet-smelling soap. "Take care that you don't draw blood," he said when he first felt the keenness of the blade on his throat.

"You're not a ñakaq, are you?" asked Puyu.

"No."

"And yet you have a beard."

"Spaniards always have beards. Some shave every day to hide them."

"Then you'll need to be shaved every day you're here."

"Because Ithilia doesn't want to be reminded of the ñakaqs?"

"The winged ones find hair other than on top of your head and around your eyes offensive. You'll also need to bathe before every meal."

"I see."

Puyu finished the shave and then disappeared for a moment, returning with several small bottles and a set of shimmering garments. "I'll leave now. Please allow yourself some time before you get out of the water. There are fires under the base which keep the bath warm. When you're ready, come into this recess." A rope dangled from the ceiling and he pulled it, releasing a rain-shower. "See, this allows you to wash away the residue. Pull on this rope again and the water stops falling."

"How do I get to the feasting hall?"

Puyu pulled the rope a second time to stop the flow. "Once you've dried yourself, you can use the mirror to help you put on these clothes correctly. After that, choose the perfume that's to your liking, and then ring this." He reached out to pick up a small bell sitting in an indentation in the stone wall and rang it. "I'll return for you when I hear it."

Rodrigo nodded.

After Puyu left, the tingling sensation on his skin grew to a point where it was unpleasant, and he got out and walked to the recess from which the rope was dangling. He pulled the cord and a warm rush of water surged over him, relieving the tingling. He closed his eyes for a moment, and when he opened them a dark mass was clumping at his feet.

To his horror, he realized it was his own hair.

He raced to the mirror and saw that all his body hair had fallen out. He leaned on the wall to steady himself. What sort of water had he been bathing in?

He quickly toweled himself dry and wrapped the robes he'd been given perfunctorily around himself and then rang the bell.

When Puyu returned, he shouted, "What have you done to me?"

"This won't do," said Puyu. "Not at all. Let me show you how these garments should be wrapped so that Ithilia will approve."

Rodrigo pulled away. "Why didn't you tell me the bath was going to remove all my hair?"

"It's part of the cleansing. I told you not to put your head under the water."

"You should have warned me."

"The winged ones require cleansing. There's no choice."

"Maybe for you, but we're guests here."

"I would suggest you don't argue with Ithilia."

"I'll argue with anyone I want to argue with."

"Please, your hair will grow back. Let me help you with the garments or you won't be allowed in the feasting hall." Rodrigo clenched his teeth and let Puyu adjust his robes. "And which fragrance have you chosen?"

"I don't care. Just pick one for me."

Puyu applied one of the perfumes to Rodrigo and then led him through a series of corridors. As they walked, they were joined by other conquistadors, all of them shaved. To their embarrassment, Carlos and some of the others had clearly ignored the instruction to keep their head above water and were now bald.

The conquistadors were awe-struck when they entered the giant feasting hall. The ceiling was painted in the most stunning colors, showing full size duendes in mid-flight. The walls were decorated with sky-scapes and myriad cloud formations of delicate beauty, while the floor depicted winding rivers, treetops and rocky crags, the terrain of Nueva Tierra as seen from great heights. In the middle of the hall was an enormous crimson spiral-shaped table at which the duendes sat with each second seat vacant.

And in the center of the spiral was Ithilia.

"Welcome," she said. Standing up, she spread her wings and flew across the spiral of the great table, so that she now stood in front of Rodrigo. As she touched foreheads with him, her nostrils flared. "You are pleasant to me. Come sit by my side."

She reached out and embraced him, wrapping her powerful arms around his chest, and then became airborne again, carrying him back to her chair. This time, unlike the previous occasions, she flew with their bodies facing each other.

Other duendes followed her lead and each carried a Spaniard to a seat at the table.

Incan servants then began serving a staggering selection of foods. There were steaming potatoes of every color imaginable, blue corn, roasted grains, beans in the shape of stars, stuffed peppers, marbled meats swollen with seasoned juices, and all manner of fruits and spices the conquistadors had never tasted before. It grew increasingly dark outside and flaming torches lit the feasting hall. Cloud wisps floated in from the giant open windows as the conquistadors gorged themselves and servants continuously filled their gold-inlaid goblets with honeyed wine.

"Tell me, Capitán Rodrigo Benalcázar, do you have feasts like this in your lands?" Ithilia seemed to exhale rather than voice her words.

"A feast like this would be for a king or maybe a high noble."

"And are you a high noble in your land?"

"A capitán who returns to his land with much gold will become a high noble."

"Is this why you speak with such desire of the gold you wish to take with you?"

Rodrigo picked up his goblet, examining it as it shone in the flame-light of the torches. "Yes, I see you have much gold here."

"We have more gold than you could ever imagine, Capitán Rodrigo Benalcázar. And we will grant you more than you can possibly carry if you are successful in your hunt for the remaining ñakaqs." Ithilia leaned toward him. "Tell me, have your people ever experienced the bliss of wiping an enemy totally from your lands?"

"We've found enslaving a conquered people is better than killing them."

"Do your people make good slaves?" asked Ithilia.

"All people can be enslaved. What counts are chains, power and punishment."

"Then the ñakaqs are the one exception. They refuse to be enslaved and they refuse to stop fighting. We have no choice but to kill every last one of them."

"But they can be captured," said Rodrigo.

"With extreme difficulty. However, did your imprisonment of them aid you in any way? Could you use your prisoners to bargain with them? Did they give you any of their secrets?"

Rodrigo put his goblet down. "No."

"That is our dilemma with this repulsive enemy." Ithilia looked at him with her eyes glowing in the flame-light. "Have you not noticed that you never see any ñakaq maidens?"

"It's not that surprising," said Rodrigo. "We also have no women in our armies."

"Then perhaps you have more in common with the ñakaqs than you believe."

"But if their maidens don't fight, then surely they'll have no defense against an attack?"

"That may be true. If we knew where they were." Ithilia took a bright red berry from a bowl and offered it to Rodrigo. "But we have *never* seen a single ñakaq maiden. They are hidden. The ñakaqs have many secrets. Even after millennia, we have never found their Great Halls."

Rodrigo frowned. "I think I'm beginning to understand the full nature of our enemy."

"We have inflicted grave defeats on the ñakaqs in the past, but they simply hide from us until many years later when a new generation of ñakaqs has grown into an army. Then they resume their eternal war with us."

"So we need to find the ñakaq women?"

"And the children, before they can grow to avenge their fathers' deaths."

"Of course, the children."

"You do understand me, don't you?" Ithilia moved closer.

Rodrigo looked into her eyes. "The ñakaqs have attacked us since we entered their lands. I would love to bring you the head of the last ñakaq in Nueva Tierra."

"Perhaps you could present it to me surrounded by a scattering of golden jewels. You have no idea how much pleasure that would give me." Ithilia ran her fingers along Rodrigo's smooth forearm, and her wings started trembling.

He said, "You know, I haven't seen any male duendes. Where are they?"

"We have no need of males."

A distant rumbling reverberated through the open windows of the grand feasting hall.

Chapter 40

In Storm's Dark

The sky lit up as the rafts emerged from the tunnel, revealing a barren terrain of serrated rocks and narrow defiles. Though Cristóbal braced himself for the crack of thunder to follow, it still hit him like a hammer blow to the head.

Now that the sailors were out in the open, rain slammed into them like slingstones. The ñakaqs raised their shields for protection, but it wasn't enough. With the winds blowing from erratic directions, the Incan navigators struggled to keep the rafts away from the rocky banks. Soon the current began to surge again as the rains from upstream swelled the river.

"I thought you said you felt safe in your homelands," Cristóbal cried over the top of the howling wind as he and Tagón held on to keep their balance.

"Not out in the open during a storm," shouted Tagón.

"Is there no place where we can shelter?"

"There are some caves not far from here, but we'll need to get to them without destroying the rafts."

As the darkness of the dusk started to overwhelm the darkness of the storm, the rain froze to hail and ice-pricks stung Cristóbal's face. He shivered, wondering for a moment where his conquistadors were sheltering. Until he remembered he no longer had any men under his command.

Tagón pointed to a gap which had opened in the sheer rock face that lined the riverbank. The Incan navigators swung the raft to the right as sheets of ice pounded them and waves crashed over the deck. Slowly they made progress toward the cave entrance, fighting the current by precise angling of the crescent sails and lowering of the centerboards.

A rush of water lifted them, sending them directly into the cliff. Tagón grabbed his horca and thrust it at the rock, stopping the imminent impact. Another raft behind them appeared to be heading to the same fate but was saved when the ñakaqs on it followed Tagón's example and used their horcas to stop their vessel crashing into the cliff.

With the ñakaqs' help, the rafts made their way parallel to the rocks until they entered the cave. The wind still swirled near the entrance and hailstones continued to lash them, but as they continued further into the cave, the air fell still and the fury of the storm became a distant echo.

The Incas retrieved torches that had been kept dry in the cabins and lit them to reveal a cavern of sharp-toothed stalactites jutting from the ceiling, grotesque stone formations threatening to spring to life, and water teeming with fast-moving creatures. They then grabbed their long-oars and paddled deeper into the cave until the water level became too low for them to continue.

The rafts clustered against a smooth rocky shelf jutting out above the water line, and the Incas lashed them together so that they formed a large floating platform.

"We can wait out the storm here," said Tagón.

The Incas prepared to settle down for the night on their vessels while Tagón joined the other ñakaqs as they walked across the rafts and onto the rocky shelf. "My people always prefer the feel of stone," said Tagón.

Cristóbal and Héctor fed the horses, and then took a blanket each and followed the lead of the ñakaqs.

The torch flames were kept low to reduce smoke, so the cavern was plunged into a deep darkness dotted with small pockets of light.

Cristóbal and Héctor sat down with their backs against the cave wall and their blankets wrapped around them, desperately trying to stop shivering.

Despite the faint rumble of the storm still reverberating from the entrance, a deep silence reigned over the cavern.

Then a Quechua voice filled the silence.

Oh, Creator Viracocha!
Ever-present Viracocha!
Where are you? Without? Within?
In the clouds? In the shadows?
You who are in the highest heavens,
And among the clouds of the tempest,
Accept this our sacrifice.

In the faint light on one of the rafts, an Inca stood, knife poised, above a squirming cierva being held down by two other villagers. As he intoned the last word, the Inca plunged the knife deep into the chest of the beast, and a spurt of golden blood glinted in the torch flames.

"I'm sorry, Héctor," said Cristóbal, now shivering uncontrollably.

"Why, Capitán?"

"For this. For bringing you to this, instead of the fame and fortune I promised you."

"You only promised the *chance* of fame and fortune. You were careful with your words, I remember."

"I'm always careful with my words. It hasn't helped me."

"Your words have helped me, Capitán. No other conquistador would have appointed a freed slave as lieutenant."

"You were by far the best soldier."

"And yet, Capitán, without your authority I couldn't command a dog."

"Héctor, I no longer have any authority. There's no need to call me Capitán anymore."

"You still have your authority while I'm alive. If you lose yours, I lose mine. Call me what you wish, but I'll continue to call you Capitán."

Cristóbal's shivering started to ease. "I'm very grateful to you, Héctor, for standing by me, but for once I have no idea where we go to from here. I can no longer lead anyone."

"We're both still alive, aren't we? Despite everything. That gives us a chance. Rodrigo isn't good enough to keep his command."

"If he gives the men what they want, he will."

"We both know that isn't as easy as it sounds, Capitán."

"Maybe Rodrigo *is* more like Pizarro and Cortés, and I've been foolish to try to measure myself against them. They would never have allowed themselves to lose their command, or to be hunted down by their own soldiers, or to find themselves shivering in a cold cave with a storm raging outside."

"I went from copper mines to *portero* guard to conquistador to lieutenant. Good fortune plays a part in every success, Capitán."

"I've always thought that's the excuse of someone who will never achieve anything."

"Or the lament of someone who really hasn't had much luck. Believe me, as long as you're not in chains, you've reason to think your fortunes can change."

"Maybe you're seeing things more clearly than I am, Héctor." Cristóbal shifted position to try to release some of the pressure from the rocks. "Did you know this creator god Viracocha that the Incas just made a sacrifice to is bearded, pale-skinned and destined to come from the West?"

"Like a conquistador?" Héctor considered this for a moment. "So, the reason Pizarro wasn't attacked in overwhelming numbers the way we were attacked by the ñakaqs was that the Incas at first believed him to be Viracocha?"

"Yes, and Cortés was also believed to be a god. It's a shame the ñakaqs didn't have a white-skinned god."

"Or even a black-skinned one." Héctor gave a wry smile.

"It looks like they don't have *any* gods. Maybe this world we're in is beyond such things. Sarpay believes their sun god Inti has abandoned them in Nueva Tierra. That's how she explains that the Incas here are simple villagers under the protection of ñakaqs instead of rulers of a great empire. My fear is maybe our Lord also has no power here."

"You don't truly believe that God has forsaken us, do you Capitán?"

Cristóbal shrugged. "That's what it feels like right now, but I'm far too tired to be contemplating God's intentions tonight." He pulled his blanket higher. "Let's both try to get some sleep. Who knows what the morning will bring?"

Cristóbal rested his head on the cold stone and searched the torchlights for Sarpay. She could have easily left him to his fate. There was no need for her to take him with the fleeing Incas. Maybe he'd already had his stroke of luck. He found her settling down in the middle of their raft, pulling a blanket across her shoulders. She met his gaze as if she knew he was looking at her, but he turned away.

Chapter 41

Dance of the Duendes

Music wafted through the walls from an unknown source, filling the feasting hall with an aching decay-tinged sound, as the Incas cleared the spiral table.

"What instrument is that?" asked Rodrigo.

"Death," said Ithilia.

Rodrigo barely heard the word as the dark notes swum through his befuddled head.

"You know," she said, "my people make no distinction between our lives and our art."

What had she said? He felt her fingers trail along his arm.

"Everything we touch and everything we are is our own creation. I'm glad you have chosen to create with us." Ithilia smiled and for a moment the light behind her seemed to illuminate the skull under her face, glowing bright red under the surface of the skin.

Rodrigo shook his head to banish the image and the angelic face returned.

"Come, Capitán Benalcázar, let me show you."

She stood up, holding Rodrigo's hand as he joined her, and all around the feasting hall the other duendes and Spaniards followed their cue. The Incan servants quickly removed the chairs, and the couples formed a procession out of the spiral until the last pair, Ithilia and Rodrigo, joined the others in the open space near the arched doorway.

The Incas folded the spiral table inwards until it formed a giant sun-like disk in the center of the hall. Then the duendes each embraced their partners in unison and together began circling the disk in time to the exquisitely mournful music emanating from the walls. And after they had completed a full revolution, the duendes began singing in their own voiceless tongue a song of yearning and pain, until the hall filled with the susurrus of countless breaths.

Cloud tendrils drifted in from the open windows as if answering the duendes' call, and the voices became more breathless and the music more turbulent, pulling the dancers into its spiraling urgency. The duendes spread their wings, lifting themselves and their partners so that they continued their dance with their feet stepping across an invisible floor. The higher they flew, the more the movements seemed to be infused by the music's dark notes. Swirling through the warm air, the dancers moved in waves, predictable yet unique, like wind-blown sand.

And as the gyrations became more frenetic, the tempest of dance created by the beating of the great wings captured the cloud wisps, and they too joined the eddying in the high arches. And, finally, when the music dwindled into an echo and the dancers descended languidly to earth, a dark shadow passed fleetingly across the hall.

***

Ithilia led Rodrigo by the hand along a hallway decorated with cloud-scapes of wild storms.

"For us to truly know each other, you must see this," said Ithilia.

He followed her through an archway onto an exposed platform that jutted out into the night sky.

Rodrigo shivered as the two of them stood on the edge of the open balcony. Below was a vast crater filled with countless ñakaq helmets, their gold inlays gleaming like stars in the moonlight. For a moment he lost sense of where the heavens lay. His head swirled. His feet no longer belonged to the ground.

"Do you see both the beauty and the death here?" said Ithilia. "Just imagine if all this was yours."

Surrounded by a stark silence, Rodrigo fought the urge to dive into the star-filled crater. He felt Ithilia's arm holding him back.

"I see we understand each other now," she said.

***

Ithilia and Rodrigo stood naked in front of each other in the duende's chamber. She ran her hands across his smooth chest, her nostrils widening each time she took in a breath. The stars burned ferociously through the open window and the distant sounds of the storm cocooned the moment.

Rodrigo reached out to touch her breasts.

She shook her head, gripping both his arms and drawing them firmly down by his sides. Then she ran her hands slowly down to his wrists until she held his hands in hers.

"This way," she whispered.

Ithilia took the Spaniard's fingers, drawing them around her back, and showed him how to stroke her wings so that they trembled. She led him to her bed which appeared to be swathed by white summer clouds. As she eased him onto his back and straddled him, despite the power of her limbs, he felt a softness on his skin gentler than the rarest of vicuña wool. Ithilia enveloped him first with her arms, then with her wings and finally with her whole body.

Conquistador and duende pulsed like rhythmic flurries of wind. And as the gusts intensified, Ithilia spread her wings, lifting them both into the air as they climaxed.

First like the stab of a knife.

Then like the urgent arcs of a sword.

And finally, like the silent flight of an arrow.

Until, still entwined, they wafted gently back onto the bed.

Chapter 42

The Padre and the Angel

"I am told you refused to bathe." The porcelain-skinned duende who stood under the door arch of Padre Núñez's chamber spoke in a wind-inflected Quechua.

The padre looked up from the Bible on the ornately carved table and saw the night-lamp frame the perfect features of her face and golden hair that cascaded across her strong shoulders. He recognized her as the duende who had been carrying him.

"Baths are indulgences of the devil."

The duende frowned. "We cannot allow you to move freely around our palaces if you don't bathe."

"I'll wash myself, providing no one is in attendance, but I won't allow myself the immoderation of these hot baths you have here."

"This is most disturbing for us. You will be unable to enjoy any feasting or the company of our people while you are with us."

"If that's the price I have to pay, then so be it." He looked at her more closely. "Tell me, though, you carried me across the mountains, and then here into your palaces, didn't you? Why is my unbathed body only now offensive to you?"

"It was always offensive. We tolerate what we must, but we cannot have our palaces sullied."

"What's your name, my child?" he asked.

"Ariathe." It sounded like a soft breeze.

He closed the Bible. "Do you understand, Ariathe, that purity of the spirit is what's most important, not purity of the skin?"

"For us there is no difference."

"I see."

"So, you will allow me to take you to a bathing chamber?"

"No, but can you tolerate my state of uncleanliness a little longer and speak with me?"

"Is there a possibility if we speak that I will be able to persuade you to bathe?"

"Yes, if there's a possibility that you'll accept my reasons for not doing so."

Ariathe appeared to contemplate what Padre Núñez was asking. "Then, let us listen to each other."

She sat down next to him, her wings folded tightly against her back.

"Who tells you how to live your life, Ariathe?"

"I don't understand. We have always lived how we now live."

"Then how do you know bathing is so important?"

"It just is."

"But someone must tell you this."

"Ithilia perhaps."

"Is there no one above Ithilia who tells you how to live your life?"

"No, Ithilia is our leader and we follow her."

"Is she the one who has made the rule about bathing, and all your other rules?"

"I don't know. I don't think so. The rules have always been there."

Padre Núñez ran his fingers along the edge of the Bible. "How can you be certain the rules are right?"

Ariathe looked confused. "Rules are always right, aren't they? That's why they're rules."

The padre smiled. "You're very young, aren't you? How old are you?"

"I'm not sure what you mean."

"Do your people not measure the seasons?"

"Measure? No, why would we?"

"You appear as if you have much to learn."

"I simply need you to bathe. Ithilia will not be pleased with me if you continue to refuse."

"If you're going to follow a rule, Ariathe, don't you think you should be certain it's right?"

"I suppose so."

"I know the rules I follow are right because they are made by God."

"You're using another word I don't know. Who is this God?"

"He created the world we live in and watches over us and judges us."

"I've never thought of anyone creating the world."

"He gives us the rules that we should live by." He touched the cover of the Bible. "And they're all here, in this book."

"I see," she said, although it was clear from her face, she didn't. "But you keep saying *he*. That's not possible, is it? The ñakaqs are *hes*."

"The ñakaqs aren't the only *hes*, but can we leave that for another time? What's important is that you learn more about our Lord God and come to know him."

"I suppose."

"You're very fortunate, Ariathe, because I am a padre, which means I'm the best person to teach you about our Lord. Do you want me to do that so that you know which rules you should follow?"

Ariathe fell silent. Finally, she nodded, her golden hair cascading across her shoulders. "Yes, it appears that I am very fortunate." Then her face crumpled. "But I don't think I'll be allowed to see you again if you haven't bathed. Even if the rule is wrong, I can't break it."

Padre Núñez looked at her angelic face. "All right, show me the bathing chamber."

Ariathe smiled.

Chapter 43

The Hidden Valley

Although the rain had eased by the time the Incas re-entered the river the next morning, the winds still whipped at the sails in wild bursts, causing the rafts to pitch and jerk without warning.

Cristóbal struggled to keep his two horses from panicking. "Wouldn't it be better to wait?"

"We're vulnerable from the air here," said Tagón. "The wind-whisperers won't fly in these conditions, so I'm hoping we can make it to the valley without another attack."

"Let me help," said Sarpay in Spanish, stepping across the deck to the second horse.

"Stroke its mane like this," said Cristóbal, "and breathe slowly."

Sarpay matched Cristóbal's rhythm and soon both horses had calmed, despite the raft's erratic movements.

"I saw you looking at me last night," said Sarpay.

"Did you?"

"Yes. Why?"

"The sacrifice to Viracocha...I wanted to see whether you were part of it."

"Why does it matter to you, Cristóbal?"

"I don't know."

Sarpay ran her hand along the full length of the horse's back. "Do you wish to share your bed with me again?"

Cristóbal stopped stroking. "I have no right to anything anymore."

"It was never your right, Cristóbal."

"Yes, I know, but now everything I thought was mine has become an illusion. You never chose me. You were with me for the sake of your people and your gods."

"Your horse is getting agitated again," said Sarpay. "You don't want to lose it as well, do you?"

Cristóbal grunted and ran his hand across its mane again.

Sarpay said, "You know I'll never become a Christian."

"There was a time you said your gods had forsaken you."

"I remember the pain of that time well, Cristóbal. I said our sun god Inti had abandoned us. That doesn't mean Viracocha won't keep his promise to the Incas and return from the West to protect his creation."

"So you'll always choose your bearded, white-skinned god over the Almighty?"

"Your Almighty doesn't allow anyone to believe in both."

"It's impossible for more than one Creator to exist."

"Not if there's more than one world."

Cristóbal folded the thought through his mind before he spoke. "You think Nueva Tierra is truly a different world, not just a new land?"

"Yes," said Sarpay, "and I think your God has no place here. Perhaps neither has Viracocha, but the Incas here haven't given up hope that he'll return to us."

Tagón gave a shout and pointed at the fork in the river up ahead where it split into three. "We need to take the left one."

"Are you sure?" asked Tiso. "Doesn't this one end in a waterfall?"

"We allow your people through our lands to trade your crops," said Tagón, continuing to point, "but we keep our secrets."

The other rafts followed Tiso's lead, steering into the left distributary.

They soon entered a terrain which, from a distance, appeared to be guarded by hundreds of ñakaqs with their horcas thrust high into the sky. As the rafts drew closer, Cristóbal could see they were life-size stone statues standing like a silent battalion before a cleft in the mountain, surrounded by overhanging rock.

As they sailed through the stone army that lined both banks, the ñakaqs on the rafts silently raised their horcas, mirroring the pose of the statues. They then passed through the cleft and entered a ravine where the cliffs on either side sloped steeply toward them.

Not long after, the river started winding. At several points the river doubled back and the wind pushed them in the opposite direction to the current. For a while the rafts seemed stationary, until the navigators turned the rafts at an angle to the wind and continued downriver by tacking from one bank to the other.

A faint rushing sound in the distance started to grow.

"That's the waterfall," said Tiso. "If we get too close, we'll be caught and won't be able to escape its pull."

"Strike for the right bank after the next corner," said Tagón, "but be quick."

As the rafts followed the next coil in the river, the full roar of the waterfall hit the sailors. Up ahead, plumes of spray shot into the air and the Incas frantically adjusted the centerboards to turn toward an embankment on the right with a high overhang.

The waters swirled and several of the rafts rotated so that the sails were now driving them toward the waterfall.

Tiso steered to the ledge and everyone disembarked before pulling the raft out of the river. By this time one of the other rafts was teetering toward the falls, almost disappearing in the churn at the lip of the cliff. Tiso threw a rope toward them and one of the Incas on the raft scooped it from the water and tied it to the base of the mast.

Tagón and the others clutched the other end and tried to draw them in, but despite their efforts, the raft didn't move any closer. Its navigator lowered the sail so that it was no longer working against the direction they were being pulled. Although it had some effect, those straining at the rope started to struggle.

Cristóbal grabbed the end of the rope and lashed it to the saddles of the two horses. Slapping them on their rumps, he urged them forwards. With the help of the horses, the raft escaped the turbulence of the waterfall and drew closer to the ledge until everyone could disembark, and the vessel was hauled out of the water.

Cristóbal studied the overhang, aware that they couldn't possibly be seen from the air. As the other rafts landed, the Incas and ñakaqs carried them high onto the embankment, safely away from the water.

Tagón then headed toward the cliff face and disappeared.

Moments later he re-emerged. "Leave the rafts here. They'll be safe. Bring everything else this way."

Cristóbal grabbed his belongings, loaded other supplies onto the horses and, holding their reins, followed Tagón. He wasn't surprised this time to see there was a hidden entrance through the mountainside. He looked at the rock closely as he walked into the gap and realized the regular markings meant it wasn't a natural formation and must have been made with tools.

After a short walk, the gap opened into a valley like no other he had seen in Nueva Tierra. There before him lay a lush green forest with trees stretching as far as the eye could see. Multi-hued birds squawked and chattered in the thick canopy and large ciervas grazed among the undergrowth.

"This is the valley for your new village," said Tagón.

The clouds started to disperse overhead, and for once Cristóbal was almost grateful to catch a glimpse of the crimson sky.

Chapter 44

El diario de Cristóbal de Varga

So my ambitions for great riches and power have come to this. I have made some unwise decisions, but what can a man do about unwise decisions except to undertake to make no more. But even in this time of regret, in the depths of my defeat, I find precious moments of consolation in the situation I have found myself. In my most loyal lieutenant, Héctor, I have discovered a friendship that was never possible when the burden of command weighed on my every action. In Tagón I now see a kindness and nobility that reflects its healing light onto my own tortured disposition. And in this valley, I now make my home, the dark strivings that once disturbed my waking thoughts have finally eased.

I write these words in the full knowledge that I can no longer truthfully call myself a conquistador. While this realization provides me with strange solace, there is a question that now troubles my soul. If I am no longer a servant of His Imperial Majesty Charles V, King of Spain, then what am I?

While the answer to this question continues to elude me, I have found that obsession is a beast that can never be truly tamed. After so many months in the safety of this wooded valley, the seed of my ambitions, which I thought had shriveled and died, has sprung back to life.

Chapter 45

The Crossbow

A cierva shot out in front of Cristóbal and Héctor, dashing into the forest undergrowth before either of them could react.

"We've grown too slow in our time here," said Cristóbal, lowering his crossbow. "It shouldn't have escaped both of us."

"The crossbow was never my weapon of choice, Capitán," said Héctor.

Cristóbal ran his hand across the gray-streaked beard he had let grow. "Are you saying I'm the only one who has slowed down?"

"We shouldn't be too hard on ourselves. The vegetation is so dense here, the cierva can disappear in two steps."

Cristóbal breathed in the warm air that filtered through the canopy. Despite the pleasant temperature and easy routine in the hidden valley, he never forgot that the bloated sun still burned beyond the protection of the trees. He couldn't shake the nagging doubt that they would be discovered and obsessively scanned the forest that surrounded the glade. By avoiding looking at the heavens, he could almost pretend he was no longer in Nueva Tierra. Almost. Inevitably, he ended up focusing on where the cliffs beyond the forest edged onto the blood sky.

A rustling sound from the trees grabbed his attention and he raised his crossbow. After a moment one of the horses appeared, grazing on the long grasses that grew on the glade's edge. With the undergrowth making riding difficult, the mounts had all lost their muscle tone over the months since Tagón had brought them here. This one was starting to look fat.

Cristóbal patted his own small paunch, until he realized he was being watched. Looking up, he saw Tagón had emerged from the forest, carrying a basket.

"You're early today, my friend," said Cristóbal. "What have you got for us?"

"Some field mushrooms," said Tagón, "and some of the purple potatoes you like."

"You feed me better than I fed you when you were my prisoner."

"We both know you're not a prisoner here."

"This valley is the most agreeable place I've seen in Nueva Tierra, but I can't really leave it, can I?"

"It's agreeable to be safe, isn't it?"

"Is any place truly safe when someone is determined to kill you?"

"Our lands are vast, and if you and the Incas are careful, even if the wind-whisperers fly directly over us, they won't see signs that anyone is here."

"But is it safe from a ground attack by Rodrigo?"

"They have no boats, so they can't enter the way we did."

"True, but there are small breaks in the canopy, like this glade here. The duendes could fly Rodrigo and the others here. Wouldn't it be safer if we joined you in your city?"

Tagón frowned. "I've told you that our Great Halls are our greatest secret."

"I know, Tagón, but I can't help but feel we'll eventually be discovered. The Incas have been building houses and planting crops. That can't go unnoticed forever."

"The wind-whisperers avoid flying at night, so if the Incas make sure there are no fires during the day, there should be no evidence that the valley is inhabited."

"The capitán is right," said Héctor. "Rodrigo will hunt us day and night. We've humiliated him and he won't forget. Hiding is something we can only do for a while."

"We need a plan to defend ourselves," said Cristóbal.

Tagón ran his fingers through the tangles of his beard. "There are too few ñakaqs left to risk a battle with anyone. And the Incas aren't warriors."

Cristóbal put his finger to his mouth and then pointed into the undergrowth to their right. There were two ciervas grazing downwind of them. He raised his crossbow, took aim, and shot the bolt, striking the first cierva clean through the neck and out the other side, with the bolt then piercing the second one in the chest. Both beasts collapsed.

"You haven't lost your eye, Capitán," said Héctor.

"I'm grateful that's at least one thing I haven't lost," said Cristóbal. The three of them walked over to where the two ciervas lay with golden blood pooling on the mossy ground. "It looks like the Incas will be feasting tonight."

"I've never seen a weapon do that," said Tagón. "Can I have a closer look?"

Cristóbal gave the ñakaq the crossbow, and he and Héctor proceeded to cut the throats of the ciervas.

"It's not like any other crossbow we have," said Cristóbal. "Diego designed it for power and long-range accuracy."

Tagón examined it closely, turning it through different angles. "You say Rodrigo and the other conquistadors don't have these?"

"No, Diego worked on it after we left Machu Picchu. There's only one."

"You know," said Tagón, "I believe we could make copies of this in our forges."

Cristóbal wiped the golden blood from his hands. "You're serious?"

"Yes."

"Without damaging it?"

"We're skilled at such work."

"How long will it take?"

"Maybe only a few days to make one. I'll bring the copy to you to see if it works the way it should before we make more. If you're happy with it, we wouldn't need your crossbow after that. We could use the copy to make the others."

"Let me think about it."

Tagón handed the weapon back.

"What's wrong, Capitán?" asked Héctor. "It seems like the best plan we have for our defense."

"I don't want to be responsible for a deadly Spanish weapon being used against Spaniards."

"You haven't really given up hope of winning back your men, have you Capitán?"

Cristóbal surprised himself. "Perhaps not."

"I think you're making a mistake."

Tagón said, "I will swear an oath we would only use the crossbows against the wind-whisperers."

Cristóbal looked at him. "You ñakaqs are a frustrating people. If a Spaniard said that, I couldn't have believed him. I know your oaths are ironclad, but I can't hold you to it if you're under attack."

Cristóbal felt the weight of his crossbow in his hand.

For an instant he stood again on that wind-blown Andean slope aiming for the white llama with Diego by his side. Was he reluctant to hand his weapon over to be copied because it was his last connection with his cousin? Would it be a betrayal? Or would Diego have insisted on it?

Cristóbal said, "I think Diego would be pleased with your offer. Here."

Tagón took the crossbow with reverence.

"When you've made them," said Cristóbal. "I'll train your people how to shoot."

He then called the wandering horse over, and he and Héctor heaved the two cierva carcasses over its back. Stroking its mane, he said. "It looks like it's not time to go out to pasture just yet. There's still work to do."

***

That night Cristóbal sat with Héctor by the campfire outside the hut that the Incas had built for him. Clusters of bright stars shone through breaks in the canopy as he wrote in his journal, his eyes straining in the low light.

"I haven't seen you write in your diary for a long time," said Héctor.

Cristóbal put down his quill. The trees crouching in the darkness beyond the fire's reach seemed comforting. "I haven't had much to write about."

"Do you want to read me what you've written?"

"They're not great words, Héctor. Not the sort I expected to write."

"Let me hear them anyway."

Cristóbal sighed and ran his palm along his beard. "If you really want to hear them, then..." He squinted at the open page. There was a time when, despite the poor light, he would have had no trouble reading.

"I write these words in the full knowledge that I can no longer truthfully call myself a conquistador. While this realization provides me with strange solace, there is a question that now agitates my soul. If I am no longer a servant of His Imperial Majesty Charles V, King of Spain, then what am I?"

"Do you truly believe, Capitán, that you're no longer a conquistador?"

"Look at me, Héctor. Conquistadors conquer. I haven't conquered anything."

"There are many different types of conquest. No matter how hard you've tried to make those words in your diary sound real, they're not. They're just fine-sounding words."

"You would think differently if you could read. Words are real, maybe more real than anything else."

"I understand the power of written words," said Héctor. "Written words set me free from the copper mines of Hispaniola. I saw the truth when you gave your crossbow to Tagón today. You know your conquest isn't over."

"You could be right. I can't see myself dying of old age in this valley."

The bushes just beyond the campsite rustled, and both Cristóbal and Héctor instinctively reached for their swords. Cristóbal relaxed when he realized an Incan woman was walking toward them, but he was surprised to recognize it was Sarpay carrying a large plate of roasted cierva meat.

"We thought it was only fair that since you killed them, you should have your share," she said.

"Your people have done so much for me," said Cristóbal, closing his journal and putting it on the ground. "The ciervas were my thank you for the kindness the Incas have shown me despite the horror I've brought down on them."

"The duendes have never been friends of the Incas here in Nueva Tierra. I'm told they keep many as slaves in their palaces."

"They're slave owners?" said Héctor. "Another reason we should kill them if we get the chance."

Cristóbal grabbed a knuckle of cierva roast and took a bite. "I would have thought you'd ask one of your servants to bring this to us," said Cristóbal.

"The Incas here in Nueva Tierra are different. They don't believe in nobles or emperors, and my servants appear to be adopting their ways."

"Does that mean you're no longer a princess?" asked Cristóbal.

"I suppose I made that choice." She put the plate down. "I'll leave the two of you in peace."

"Please join us," said Cristóbal. "It's good to hear someone other than Héctor speak Spanish."

Sarpay sat down by the campfire and picked up a piece of cierva. "One thing I can say about Nueva Tierra is that cierva tastes better than llama."

Cristóbal and Héctor reached out for more of the fat-laden meat. The fire crackled and feasting Incas in the distance cheered and sang.

"You could have had your huts with the others," said Sarpay.

Cristóbal wiped the yellow juices from the side of his mouth. "We don't really belong with the villagers."

"I don't think I belong with them either. All they have are stories of a distant land where their people ruled rather than lived in the shadow of two warring races." She stared into the fire. "I don't want to be the one to tell them that even in that distant land, the Incas no longer rule."

Sarpay looked at the journal that lay at Cristóbal's feet. "I see you're still writing in your diary."

"Yes, tonight is the first time for a long time."

"He read part of it to me just before you came," said Héctor. "Did he mention me?"

"No, but he didn't mention me either."

They laughed.

"You write, even though now no one can read your words," said Sarpay.

Cristóbal gave a wry smile. "Padre Núñez would never choose to read it anyway. I've never seen him read anything other than the Bible or the *Requerimiento*."

"Why not teach me to read?" asked Sarpay.

Cristóbal looked at her and then at Héctor. "I'll teach both of you."

Héctor shook his head. "I'm a simple man, Capitán."

"It's a matter of time, not a matter of how simple you think you are. And it appears time is what we have much of here."

"You would do this for me?"

"I would do it for the only man under my command who remained loyal to me."

He motioned for them to sit down either side of him and he opened his journal.

***

Later Cristóbal lay on his bed of furs with his eyes open, listening to the forest sounds, when a silhouette moved across the hut's open window.

It took him a moment to realize it was Sarpay.

As she appeared next to his bed, he said softly, "I've given enough lessons for one night."

"I've come for other reasons, Cristóbal," she whispered.

She let her robes fall and took Cristóbal's hand, placing it on her breast.

Cristóbal took a sharp breath. "There's no reason for you to come to my bed anymore."

"Except that I want to."

Sarpay bent down to kiss him.

Chapter 46

The Promise

"You were close that time," said Cristóbal as Tagón watched the bolt hit the far slope. "Are you sure you don't want to rest? The crossbows are heavy."

"They're lighter than horcas." Tagón lowered the crossbow to the ground, putting his foot in the stirrup and cocking the bowstring to the latched position with both hands.

"Remember," said Cristóbal, "you need to allow for the trajectory of the bolt and the tiny delay after you pull the trigger."

Tagón took another bolt from the quiver and placed it in the grooved track between the lath and latch. Then he raised the crossbow and planted his feet firmly on the stony ground.

Cristóbal said, "Lean your face over the stock a little more."

Tagón adjusted his position and indicated that he was ready. He didn't seem to be aware of the tense looks that King Malín and the other ñakaqs nearby were giving him.

Cristóbal signaled to the ñakaqs high on the distant slope. A horca arced through the sky from the mountain ledge, glistening silver against crimson. The only sound was the whistling of the wind, until a clang of metal on metal rang through the air as Tagón's bolt hit the horca mid-flight.

Cheers erupted from the ñakaqs who stood on the ledge with horcas in hand and those who stood in the valley below.

Tagón lowered his crossbow and smiled behind his red beard. He had hit the target on only his tenth try. "It works," he said. "You have just saved our people, Cristóbal."

"Diego made the original, and your people made the copy," said Cristóbal, "so I don't think I deserve much of the praise."

"You've shown me how to shoot this crossbow," said Tagón. "My people have tried to kill you from the day you entered our

221

lands, and now you not only give us a great weapon we can copy, you also show us the secret of how to use it against our eternal enemy. I think you're the one to be praised."

"I just hope Diego's crossbows give you an advantage in your battle with the duendes."

King Malín's beard flowed in the wind and his eyes gleamed with joy as he embraced Cristóbal. "We're forever indebted to you," he said. "Please allow us to show our gratitude."

Cristóbal covered his eyes before he spoke. "There's no need."

"Yes, yes there is. Name what you want," said King Malín. "Just say so, and if it is within my power, I will give it to you."

In the past his answer to such a question would have been so obvious it required no thought. This time Cristóbal was surprised which desire erupted to the surface. "Be careful. What I wish is within your power, but you may choose not to give it to me."

"Name it." King Malín waved his arms expansively.

"I want to see your Great Halls."

The wind whistled past, lengthening the silence.

"I am sorry, Cristóbal," said King Malín eventually. "I cannot take you to our halls. I know I made the promise to grant you what you wished, but this is the one thing I cannot do for you, even though it is within my power. You're asking me to reveal our greatest secret."

Cristóbal shielded his eyes. "If this is something you can't fulfill, I won't hold you to it."

"No, I have been shamed," said King Malín, lowering his head. "I made a promise I must break. There is no worse crime for a leader. You cannot absolve me of the consequences."

"What consequences?"

"There's no need for you to concern yourself with them," said King Malín, "but please let us divulge to you another of our deepest secrets."

Chapter 47

The Broken Campaign

The High Palaces of the duendes loomed just ahead, threaded by thin cloud wisps, stark against the red sky. Rodrigo struggled with what he was going to say to Ithilia after another failed search. She wouldn't be pleased. It had been months since she had personally carried him down to the ñakaq lands, but there could be other reasons for that. The duende who now carried him back from his most recent campaign hadn't told him her name, and barely said a word. She landed on one of the platforms, released him perfunctorily, folded her wings and walked inside, leaving the Incan servants to deal with Rodrigo and the other arriving conquistadors.

Shivering in the bitter high-altitude air, he asked the servant, "Where does Ithilia wish to meet with me?"

"She doesn't wish to see you now," said the Inca.

"What do you mean? She needs to hear my report. Where is she?"

"She is bathing."

"Then I can speak to her while she bathes."

"I'm afraid that's not possible."

"Not possible?" Rodrigo choked on the words. "I'll just go and see her in her bathing chamber."

"I don't think that's—"

Rodrigo marched through the arch into the palaces. The red-stained frescoes of battle scenes that lined the walls disturbed him more than usual as he strode along the corridor that led to Ithilia's chamber. He pushed past the two Incas standing at the entrance, despite their protests. Walking through a curtained doorway, he stepped into the ornate bathing room where Ithilia lay in the steaming water up to her chin.

"Why are you here?" she asked, without opening her eyes.

"It's been a long campaign this time. Don't you wish to hear my report?"

"Is it any different to the last report, or the one before that? Or any of them?"

"The region we covered was different to the last one, so we know another part of the ñakaq heartlands where the survivors can't be hiding."

"Thank you for your report. You can begin your next campaign."

"That's all you have to say to me?"

"The only thing you've done is add to the places where we *don't* need to look."

"That's some sort of progress."

"Is it?"

"Your scouts are making the decisions where to land us."

"Now you blame us for your failure to stay true to your word?"

"No, but this search is much more difficult than I thought it would be." He took a step toward her. "Can you at least open your eyes and look at me when we speak?"

Without moving anything else, Ithilia raised her eyelids and stared at him. "I'm not sure if I find what I see before me particularly pleasant. Look at you, you've let your beard grow again, and you smell as bad as the first time on the battlefield."

"I'll shave my beard and bathe, and we can talk later."

"I don't think there is much more for us to say to each other. The ñakaqs will still be busy impregnating their wives with future soldiers that will threaten us again. As I've told you, the only option we have now is to find their city and burn it to the ground with all its inhabitants in it. I know you've been unsuccessful again. Is there anything else?"

"There are other things for us to speak of."

"Perhaps there are. Let's deal with them now. We can begin with your padre preaching to us. I've warned you before to stop him."

"Padre Núñez doesn't listen to me when it comes to matters of the spirit. He says he takes his orders from God."

"I want him to stop talking of baptisms."

"I'll speak to him again."

"And so our discussions end with the same weak promises. Take the padre with you on your next campaign. Before you leave, pass me my towel."

She stood up slowly, revealing the size of her expanded belly as droplets of water dripped from her skin.

"You've grown since I last saw you," said Rodrigo handing her the towel.

"Yes, the births are now not far away."

She extended her wings and fluttered them so that a shower of droplets flew through the air, then started to towel dry her upper body. She looked up at him after a while as if she was surprised to see him. "Are you still here? Perhaps it would be best if you go and prepare for the next descent as soon as possible."

"But I would like to be in the palaces for the births."

Ithilia looked puzzled. "Why?"

"It's my child and I want to see it baptized. So do the others."

"I've told you that births from the Quechua-speakers were always still-born, so don't expect these to live."

"I think I can say we Spaniards are a little more vigorous than the Incas."

"We will soon see."

Rodrigo watched Ithilia step out of the bath, her skin translucent, and dry her lower body.

"It looks to me like we're your people's only hope of surviving."

Ithilia looked down at him, her nostrils flaring. "My people have an advantage over all others. Unless we are killed in battle or through an accident, we do not die."

Rodrigo stared at her. "You...don't age?"

"Once we reach adulthood, no."

He eyed her curiously. "How old are you?"

Without looking at him she said, "We don't measure such things." She wrapped her towel around herself. "Now go and prepare for the next hunt. You should leave again tomorrow. Don't fail me again."

***

Rodrigo slumped wearily in his saddle as the swollen sun burnt overhead. He and Padre Núñez rode at the head of the conquistadors through the ñakaq heartlands, crowded by a stark landscape of jagged rock formations. In the distance, the endless mountain chain and countless valleys stretched to the horizon. How had his promise come to this? One futile search after the other. With a jolt he straightened himself, aware that one misstep along the narrow mountain path meant the end of both horse and rider.

"I wouldn't have assured Ithilia success if I'd known the terrain was going to be this difficult," said Rodrigo.

"It isn't easy saying no to these duendes," said Padre Núñez. "She insisted I join you this time."

"She told me she doesn't want you threatening to baptize the newborns."

"Threatening? Since when is bringing someone to God a threat? Sometimes I feel I'm making progress with the duendes, and other times it's almost like they're corrupting me. Whatever happens, these children must be baptized."

"What if they have wings?"

"Angels are God's servants and they have wings," said the padre. "I believe in the end I'll bring all the duendes to God."

"I don't think they'll listen to us until we find the ñakaqs." He shifted in his saddle. "You know, Padre, the duendes are almost immortal."

"There's no such thing as being *almost* immortal."

"Ithilia told me that they don't age."

"That's impossible."

They turned a corner and rode onto a stretch of flat terrain under a rocky overhang bordering on a river. Rodrigo instinctively drew his sword before he was even conscious of exactly what he saw.

When the scene took form, to his horror, he saw an army of ñakaqs in front of him brandishing monstrous horcas high above their heads.

He yelled, *"Santiago y cierra, España!"* and the other conquistadors poured out from the pass behind him, swords drawn and battle ready.

It took Rodrigo a moment to realize that the ñakaqs in front of them were statues. "Hold!" he cried, but several of the Spaniards had already hacked into them.

The conquistadors pulled back on the reins of their horses and stared at the stone army in confusion.

Rodrigo looked closely at one of the statues that had been attacked by the conquistadors. The stone exterior seemed more like a shell. He swung his sword at it and the cracked shell now shattered, revealing what was underneath. To his shock, it appeared to be an actual ñakaq. For the briefest of moments, he had the mad thought that this must be where they had been hiding, but when it didn't move, he and Padre Núñez dismounted and walked up to the exposed ñakaq to examine it. They saw the deep wound in its chest and the look of anguish on its face. There was something deeply troubling about this place.

"I think these are entombed ñakaqs who died in battle," said the padre. "Somehow they've been kept from decaying inside the stone shell."

The conquistadors all drew back from the statues once it was clear Padre Núñez was right.

"I think we should leave," said the padre.

"No, wait," said Rodrigo. "This is an important place for the ñakaqs. Look at the rock formations above us, the sloping cliffs, the river. This can't be seen from the air and barely accessed from anywhere else. I think the ñakaqs are hiding somewhere nearby."

Chapter 48

The Mouth of Gold

Tagón led Cristóbal and Héctor up the rock-strewn slope toward a summit cloaked in thick clouds. At Tagón's insistence they rode in full armor and carried shields, although the ñakaq had assured them he wasn't expecting an attack.

Cristóbal still felt frustration at the ñakaq' furtiveness. King Malín had promised to share one of his people's great secrets but had refused to say in advance what it was. Tagón wasn't much more forthcoming, even now as the three of them trekked toward it.

"I think we need to walk from here," said Héctor, dismounting. "Maybe if the horses were fitter, we could keep riding a little further, but I don't want to take the risk."

Cristóbal reluctantly agreed. They were still a long way from the summit and the mountain reared up in front of them. His feet touched the loose stones that were proving so treacherous for the horses. He stroked his horse's neck. It had been good to be riding again.

He watched Tagón dismount, marveling at how quickly the ñakaq had acquired riding skills after he had finally been convinced to try. "Tell me," he said, "King Malín spoke of the consequences of breaking his promise to me. What are they?"

"He must lose his kingship."

"What? That seems a heavy price for breaking one promise."

"A freely given promise has more power than anything else for my people. For a king to break such an oath is unforgivable."

They tethered their horses to a tree. Cristóbal said, "I'm ashamed of breaking the promise I made to you."

"It was a truly shameful thing."

"But you've forgiven me. Why not forgive Malín?"

"It's not a matter of forgiveness. There are consequences."

"You say this as if it's a law, yet there were no consequences for me."

"No? You're no longer a Capitán."

As they continued their climb on foot with the cloud-shrouded peak looming above them, Cristóbal asked, "So has the new king been chosen?"

"Yes," said Tagón. "It's me."

A sound-dampening stillness enveloped them as they ascended into the clouds. Cristóbal felt his armor weighing heavily on his shoulders with every step. "Should I cover my mouth before I speak to you from now on?" he asked.

"No, a new king must earn respect. I'm king in name only."

"You have my respect."

"Please, Cristóbal, it's impolite to talk of kingship this way. Speak to me as you always have."

The cloud bank hugging the slope thickened, and Cristóbal could barely see more than two steps ahead. Only the incline of the ground under his feet convinced him they were still ascending. "So you're still not telling us where we're going?"

"You will see soon enough," said Tagón.

Strangely the air seemed to be warming and the cloud took on an increasingly pungent smell. Muffled explosions echoed high above them, and Cristóbal and Héctor instinctively fingered the hilts of their swords.

"Lift your shields above your heads." Tagón's words cut through the haze.

Just as they did, they emerged into clear air, blinded for a moment by the intense sunlight.

When Cristóbal's vision came back into focus, he stood transfixed. There above him, cradled by the mountaintop, thundering like a storm, was a flaming lake of molten gold, sputtering furiously and shooting plumes of smoke and golden spears into the air.

"This is the *Boca D'oro*," said Tagón. "The Mouth of Gold that's the source of our wealth."

A lance of liquid gold shot skyward and arced toward Cristóbal. He sidestepped it to avoid being hit as another one struck Héctor's shield and spattered across it.

"Watch me, but keep one eye on the Mouth," said Tagón, taking a metal urn from his pack. "There is danger here."

He held the urn in front of him and, showing great skill in anticipating the flight, he raced toward a spear of gold coming in his direction and caught it.

Cristóbal looked into the urn and saw the liquid cooling to a flawless shine before his eyes. He placed the palm of his hand on the urn and it was cold to the touch. Of course, it's made of the same metal as the fire helmets.

"Here, take these." Tagón handed urns to Cristóbal and Héctor, and they followed his lead, running in the direction of the arcing liquid, side-stepping if it got too close, and laughing each time they managed to fill their urn.

They stopped to catch their breath.

Then it happened.

A gust of wind momentarily cleared the smoke above the lake of molten gold, and Cristóbal gasped. There, framed against the crimson heavens of Nueva Tierra, hovering above the middle of the Boca D'oro, it was as if a window had opened in the air. And through it he saw a scene so achingly beautiful that he held his breath: a snow-capped mountain slope and the blue sky of New Spain.

Although the smoke soon obscured the vision, his heart continued to pound. He had glimpsed what had up until now merely been a hope. A wordless euphoria coursed through him. He looked at Héctor. They had found their salida, their way out of Nueva Tierra.

Chapter 49

The Art of Ice

Ithilia was sawing into a block of ice with a jagged-toothed tool when Rodrigo stepped onto her balcony. Clouds swirled past, just out of reach, and a series of frozen peaks stood out starkly against the surrounding sky. He noticed immediately that her belly had grown even larger in the week he had been away.

Rodrigo started shivering. "Can we talk inside where it's warmer?"

Ithilia interrupted her sawing long enough to say, "I've told you not to waste my time telling me you haven't found anything."

"I believe I've found where the ñakaqs are hiding, Ithilia."

Ithilia kept him waiting while she finished, then said, "You know, I prefer carving ice to wood. Wood yields too easily. It's weak compared to ice. Ice needs both force and subtlety. You need to strike it hard, but if you strike it without finesse, it will crack and shatter, leaving you with nothing to work with."

"I don't know anything about carving," said Rodrigo impatiently. "I want to tell you how close we are to finding them."

"Close? When it comes to defeating the ñakaqs, getting close is the same as if you had done nothing."

Ithilia picked up a chisel and hammer.

"We've found some—"

"I know. I've already been told. You found some statues containing dead ñakaqs."

"I would have come to you with the news immediately, but you said to bathe before seeing you."

"The problem is I have also been told these statues are next to a tributary surrounded by cliffs which ends in a waterfall. Where would the ñakaqs hide?"

Rodrigo said, "When we flew over a forested valley not far from the statues, I saw a thin line of smoke come up from the treetops."

"No one reported that to me."

"I'm sure that's where the ñakaqs are hiding. Just fly my men into this valley and you'll have the head of the last ñakaq by sunset."

Ithilia examined the block of ice. "You see, I now worry when you make promises because you have disappointed me so often in the past."

Placing the chisel on the ice, she searched for exactly the right spot. She lifted the hammer and struck the chisel, moving it slightly and then striking it again, and then again and again until a storm of ice shards flew into the air.

Rodrigo shivered, waiting for Ithilia to finish.

Still holding the chisel in one hand, Ithilia rubbed the section she had been working on with a cloth and smiled at her handiwork.

"Are you going to disappoint me again?" she asked. Without waiting for a reply, she said, "Come here. Give me your hand."

Rodrigo looked suspiciously at the chisel.

"There is no need for us to be this way," she said. "I am impatient after all these months, but you can still salvage our agreement." She put the chisel down. "Come give me your hand."

He held it out for her, and she took it, drew it to her mouth and then started licking his palm. Despite the cold, Rodrigo felt a warm surge through him as she moved her moist tongue across his fingers.

She then took his hand and pressed it on the half-finished ice sculpture, holding her hand firmly over his so that he was unable to move it.

"What are you doing?" he demanded.

"You've seen how we create, haven't you? Our music. Our art. Ourselves. For us beauty on its own has no emotion. We intensify the power of our art by spiking it with a tincture of death."

Rodrigo felt the cold seeping deep under his skin. He struggled to pull his hand away, but Ithilia continued to hold it in place.

"A touch of pain, a whiff of decay, a stain of blood. That's what's needed. You are helping me create my art."

"Take your hand off me."

A sharp pain burgeoned in his fingers and started spreading.

"Of course," said Ithilia, finally releasing, her grip, "but take care not to attempt to remove your hand from the ice."

Rodrigo tried to lift his hand but found he couldn't. "Mierda! What have you done?"

"Your hand is now frozen onto the ice. If you try to force it, you will tear your skin away."

Rodrigo felt a wave of panic.

"If you keep your hand there for too long, your blood will start to freeze, your fingers will first turn blue and then black. By that stage they will have started to rot and no longer be any use to you."

"No! Are you mad?" His voice was shrill. He looked around, desperately hoping there was someone who could help, but they were alone on her balcony and there had been no one in her chamber when he had arrived.

"What has happened to us, Capitán Benalcázar? We had such great plans. Can you see what you've done? You've broken my faith in you. And that makes everything difficult. I don't think I can trust you anymore."

Rodrigo saw his skin coming away as he tried to pull his hand free.

"You need to stop struggling. It is always much easier if you simply do what I ask. Can you do that? Just stop struggling."

He let his arm go limp.

"See how much better it feels. Doesn't it feel better?" She bent down over the block of ice and began blowing warm air onto Rodrigo's fingers. Gradually he felt the grip the ice had on his hand loosening as heat spread through his skin.

"Now lift it," said Ithilia.

To Rodrigo's relief, his hand came away easily. He wiped the moisture from his palm on his clothing.

"Do you see how easy I can make everything? Let's make things the way they used to be. All you need to do is kill the ñakaqs. That's all. No more reports of what you've been unable to do. Just kill them so that I can keep my promise to you."

She took his hand and raised it to her mouth. Extending his ring finger, she placed the tip in her mouth. When she took it out, it glistened with her saliva.

"Show me I can trust you, Capitán Benalcázar. Give my work of art power. Give it the touch of pain."

Rodrigo pressed the tip of his ring finger on the sculpture until he knew it had frozen onto the ice. He looked into Ithilia's eyes as he tore it away, leaving his finger raw and a circle of his skin on the carving.

Chapter 50

The Last Temptation of Padre Núñez

Padre Núñez lay in a large steaming bath with his eyes closed. He no longer fought quite so hard against the sensual feeling that overcame him. If this was what he had to endure to bring the duendes to the Lord, then it was a small price to pay. And it made sense, didn't it? A pure body belongs to a pure soul.

As usual, his thoughts jumbled in the heat. This time he felt a caress on his shoulders, which he thought at first was a ripple in the water. He drifted out of his contemplation to realize a duende was sponging him.

It was Ariathe.

He sat up quickly. "What are you doing?"

"I'm washing you."

He pushed her hand away. "No, please, you can't wash me. I agreed to bathe, but I must always do it alone."

She stared at his face.

"Do you understand me?" asked Padre Núñez.

"You do not wish me to touch you?"

"No. You need to leave."

"Why? Can I not help you?"

"I'm a Franciscan. A man of God. I have to eternally fight the weakness of the flesh."

"Your flesh does not feel weak to me."

"You don't understand. It's the same reason I didn't want to bathe."

"And yet now you bathe."

The padre shifted uncomfortably. "That's because you agreed to continue to speak to me if I did."

"Perhaps you can also allow me to touch you now for the same reason."

"No, I've fallen into sin already. I don't want to fall further."

"You are certain that your God would not want me to touch you?"

"No, that's not the sin, Ariathe. It's the evil thoughts that would enter my mind if you did."

"Evil? I don't understand what you mean."

"Bad."

"Bad for whom?"

"Just bad."

"Mmm. This God is even stranger to me than you are."

"He's your God too."

"If it is not evil for me to touch you, then shouldn't you be responsible for your thoughts?" She shook her head and her thick hair danced across her shoulders. "After all these months, I still don't understand you, Padre Núñez." She put the sponge down. "You know the births will be soon."

"Yes, I'm preparing for the baptisms."

"My people are rarely with child. It is a great event that so many will give birth at the same time. I hope they will live."

"They'll be born out of wedlock, but we're all God's children."

Ariathe looked at him with her exquisite face. "I can't help but feel sad."

"Why?"

"I should have been carrying your child."

Padre Núñez drew a sharp breath. "That's impossible."

"Are you not a man like the others?"

"Yes, but I am a man of God."

"Didn't you say God had a son? Why can he have child, but you can't?"

"It's not so easy for me to explain to you in a way you would understand."

Ariathe moved closer and let her wings fan out behind her. "Our wings are beautiful, aren't they? Do you wish to feel them? Or is there a law of God against touching wings?"

He shrank back.

"They are not made of flesh. It won't matter to God if you touch them, will it?"

"Perhaps not."

"But, of course, if there is a law in the Bible, then you must follow it."

"The only winged creatures in the Bible are angels and they are messengers of God."

"There can be nothing wrong in feeling the wings of God's messengers, can there?"

"No, there isn't."

She drew close so that he could reach out behind her to touch them.

The padre's hands left the water, and as they hung suspended, drops fell from his fingers back into the bath.

"It's all right," said Ariathe. "Your hands can be wet."

She knelt next to the bath and folded her wings slightly to make it easier for Padre Núñez.

He reached out and felt the softness of her feathers.

"Yes, be gentle," whispered Ariathe.

Her wings started trembling.

Chapter 51

A Weakness of the Flesh

The only light in the room was a small lantern on the table illuminating an open Bible. Rodrigo called Padre Núñez's name several times as he searched his chamber, but there was no answer. A noise came from the balcony and he walked through the arched door into the frigid night air.

Outside was the blackness of a sliver moon, and Rodrigo could barely make out the figure that stood in the deep darkness.

"Padre Núñez?"

There was no answer. The wind whistled into the silence.

"Padre Núñez?"

The voice that replied was muffled. "Please leave me, Capitán Benalcázar."

"Why are you out here in the bitter cold?"

"I need to pray."

"Since when do you need to pray outside?"

"My flesh has weakened during our time with the duendes."

"I have to speak with you, Padre. Can you come inside into warmth?"

"No, I will remain here."

"We have problems with the duendes."

The padre grunted. "I have my own problems."

"Ithilia is losing patience with us."

"That's no concern of mine." He grunted again.

Rodrigo pulled his robes tightly around him as the cold bit into his skin. "We can't afford to upset Ithilia. Once I've killed the ñakaqs, she'll be satisfied, but in the meantime you need to stop preaching to the duendes."

The wind moaned from the distant peaks, making it hard to hear the reply.

"What did you say, Padre? Please just come back into your chamber."

"You can't ask me to stop spreading God's word." He let out a cry. "These duendes are in need of it."

"Then at least stop insisting on baptisms for the newborns."

"If I can't bring any adults to our Lord, at least I can bring the children." His voice sounded strangely staccato.

"We need to avoid offending them."

"Is it now an offense to baptize a child? How has Ithilia convinced you of that?"

"She hasn't, but—"

"Beware these duendes, Capitán Benalcázar, they can knot your thoughts with their words." Padre Núñez now seemed to be grunting every second word.

"We need to keep in mind what we're doing here—why are you making those noises, Padre?"

"My only purpose is God's will."

"My purpose is to return to New Spain laden with gold, and to do that we need to please the duendes."

"The gold is your concern." His voice was strained. "The salvation of souls is mine."

"The duendes are flying us back down to the ñakaq lands tomorrow. I expect a battle this time, so I don't want you there. The children may be born while I'm away. You need to promise me not to attempt any baptisms while I'm gone."

A cry was the only answer.

"Did you hear me, Padre?"

There was no answer.

"Padre?"

Rodrigo peered into the darkness, not sure what he saw. He ran inside and grabbed the lantern from the table and then held it in front of him as he rushed back out onto the balcony.

"What are you—" He stopped mid-sentence, shocked by what he saw.

The lantern shed light on Padre Núñez who stood naked from the waist up. His face was covered with a white cotton mask with holes for eyes. In his hand was a six-tailed leather scourge that he was swinging to flagellate himself. The padre's body was torn and bloody, and large chunks of flesh hung in strips from his frame.

"What in the Lord's name are you doing?" cried Rodrigo.

"My flesh is weak." Padre Núñez grunted as he whipped the leather straps knotted with pieces of metal onto his back, tearing deeper into his open wounds, his eyes gleaming through the holes in his mask.

"What's possessed you, Padre?"

"I've sinned against God and I need to suffer as Christ suffered." He began lashing his body with increasing fervor.

Rodrigo stepped forward and seized his arm so he couldn't swing the scourge again. "You're bleeding too much, Padre. Stop."

"My body needs to be sanctified. It has dragged me into the devil's arms."

"Come, give me the scourge. It's enough."

"No, leave me. I have to be punished."

Rodrigo gripped him harder, shaking his arm until he dropped the scourge. Then he reached out and tore off his mask.

Padre Núñez's face was sweat-stained and drawn, his eyes the eyes of a madman. "I've fallen into temptation," he said, his voice hoarse and dying.

As his mania ebbed, his legs gave way. Rodrigo stopped him from falling and led him through the doorway into his chamber, laying him on his bed.

"Beware the duendes," said Padre Núñez as his eyes darted from side to side. "Beware of what they can make you do."

"I'm strong," said Rodrigo. "I don't fear them."

"You should. You should fear them. I thought I was strong too. I thought I could bend them to me."

"You'll need to bathe these wounds."

Padre Núñez's face suddenly went pale and he shrank into the bed, his eyes rolling back. "No, no more bathing. No bathing."

Rodrigo drew away. "I'll fetch one of the Incas to tend to your wounds."

As he left the chamber, the padre's voice was barely perceptible, a hoarse whisper endlessly repeating, "No bathing. No bathing."

Chapter 52

The Art of Birth

Ithilia was naked with her legs apart and was slowly and rhythmically beating her golden wings as she hung above her bed. Her wings were contorted to enable her to hover in mid-air while facing the ceiling. Ariathe and several other duendes attended to her as she grimaced with each convulsion.

She bit her tongue with the contractions to stop herself from crying out, but soon the stabs of pain became so great her chamber echoed with her tortured screams.

Her wing beats became more erratic as she struggled to find rhythm and her body vacillated between climbing higher and threatening to fall back down to the bed.

"It's close," said Ariathe. "I can see it."

She convulsed and an involuntary beat of her wings suddenly pushed her high into the arch of the ceiling. Ariathe and one of the other duendes flew up and grabbed Ithilia in case her wings failed her. She shrugged them off and managed to regain her rhythm, just as the baby emerged, letting out a strong cry that pierced the chamber.

Ariathe held it as Ithilia slowly descended onto the bed.

Other birth cries echoed through the High Palaces.

Ariathe stood next to Ithilia's bed, holding the child as the duende leader lay exhausted with her wings folded around her.

"Does it have wing-buds?" asked Ithilia, her voice like a gust of wind.

"No, see for yourself."

"I don't wish to look at it. Break the cord."

Ithilia closed her eyes and drifted for a time until another duende announced her presence. "I have news of the other births," she said.

Ithilia opened her eyes. "None of them have the buds, do they?"

"No, none."

"It appears these Spaniards are the same as the Quechua-speakers. No matter."

"Do you wish us to tell the Spaniards?"

"No, they won't understand the artistry, and they still have a battle to fight for us."

"So we let the sky decide?"

***

Ithilia stood on the platform, holding her swaddled baby as she sang to it softly in the wind-blown tones of her people. Spreading her wings, she soared into the night sky toward the stars.

Onward she flew, ever higher, until the sun's rays started to filter over the edge of the world. And then still higher until the air thinned and she struggled to draw breath.

Finally, she stopped her ascent and beat her wings so that she hovered high above the highest peaks. She unwrapped her baby from its swaddle. Its face contorted, but the keening wind took its cry.

She held the child above her head so that the sunlight hit it, her words merging with the air.

"To those who deserve flight, give them wings. To those who are worthy, grant them the power of the wind. To those who are gods, give them immortality."

As she spoke the last word, she released the child and it fell like a stone.

She continued to hover, looking in the other direction at the rising sun. Then suddenly she dived down after the baby and caught it in her arms.

Holding it tightly to her breast, Ithilia started to sing again.

Chapter 53

Discovery

Sarpay's soft curves were against Cristóbal as he lay next to her. If he closed his eyes, he could almost convince himself that everything had returned to how it had been. Almost. His Incan princess was by his side and his soldiers loyally awaited his next command of conquest. Of course, it was all a hollow dream, then as now. More gold than he could have imagined was within his grasp and he had seen the tantalizing vision of home, but there appeared no way of getting there. He opened his eyes to the reality of his crudely built hut and its barely rainproof thatch roof. As the first glimmer of a green-tinged dawn seeped through the trees, he heard the multi-colored birds that the Incas called *mayus* begin their morning chorus.

Outside Héctor emerged from his own hut and was reheating potatoes in the embers of last night's fire. Cristóbal slid his arm slowly away from Sarpay so as not to wake her and got out of bed. Pulling on his cotton shirt and breeches, he went and joined Héctor.

"I dreamed last night that we returned to Cusco with a thousand urns filled with gold," said Héctor, giving some of the steaming potatoes to Cristóbal.

"In the dream I had," said Cristóbal, "Francisco Pizarro welcomed us and said we had outdone his feats and could lay claims to be the greatest conquistadors of all." He gave a wry smile.

"There must be a way to get through the salida, Capitán. There must."

Cristóbal blew on a potato to cool it down. "I've tied myself into knots trying to find a way. Any raft would burn before it even touched the molten gold."

"Couldn't we cover the raft with the fireproof ñakaq metal?"

"Possibly, and there may even be a way to make it float somehow, but how would we climb up into the salida? With a long ladder?"

"Why not?"

"The main problem is the heat from the gold," said Cristóbal. "You felt it. We couldn't even get close to the lake let alone travel across it on a raft."

"Diego would have found a way."

Cristóbal nodded. "Yes, he would have found a way to build a cannon that could safely shoot us through to New Spain."

The mayus suddenly began squawking and erupted from the branches in unison. Cristóbal looked up to see Tagón and several ñakaqs in battle armor approaching. "What's wrong?" he said, putting his plate down.

Tagón was grim. "We had a report that the wind-whisperers and conquistadors flew over the valley before dusk yesterday."

"What could they have seen?" asked Cristóbal.

"Some of the Incas started their fires early last night. And there's always the risk that someone was standing in a clearing just as they flew over."

"We can't be certain that they saw anything, can we?" asked Héctor.

"No, but I'm told the flight was slow and deliberate. They suspected something was here and they were looking for it."

"So, we need to expect an attack?"

"Yes, and if I know the wind-whisperers, they won't wait long."

***

Cristóbal picked up a stick and drew several circles in the sandy ground in front of Héctor and Tagón. "These are the large clearings in the valley." He added a line. "And this is the river entry we came through. Do we agree that these are the only places the duendes can launch an attack?"

Tagón said, "Without rafts I can't see how they can get to the river entrance, but we can put some guards at the entrance to the valley just in case."

Cristóbal waved the stick above the circles. "And we also agree that the duendes won't try to attack us from the air because the canopy makes it impossible for them to see us?"

"Yes, and they'll never choose to fight on the ground where they're at a disadvantage," said Tagón.

Héctor nodded. "They'll want to release the conquistadors quickly and fly up to safety, leaving all the fighting to Rodrigo and the others. And the only places where they can land are in these clearings."

"Exactly," said Cristóbal.

"That means we need to prepare for a battle against conquistadors," said Héctor.

Cristóbal tapped the stick on the ground. "I know Rodrigo enough to say that if all two hundred of the conquistadors land successfully, it will be a massacre. We'll all be trapped in the valley and hunted down. We need to make sure they don't touch ground."

"Can we arm the Incas?" asked Héctor.

"No, these Incas aren't warriors. They'll be no help against armored soldiers." Cristóbal turned to Tagón. "How many ñakaq soldiers will you risk in this battle?"

"All sixty-two that survived the last battle against the wind-whisperers."

"Are you sure? Don't you want some to remain in your halls? It's you who the duendes want to kill."

"It's a matter of honor. We can't let the wind-whisperers attack our heartland. If they could find this valley with the help of the conquistadors, then our halls aren't safe."

"Even with every ñakaq," said Héctor, "we're outnumbered three to one."

Cristóbal ran his hand across his stubbled chin. "The key is not to let them land."

"How do we do that?" asked Héctor.

"All the ñakaqs have crossbows now, don't they, Tagón?" Cristóbal made several marks between the circles. "This is where you should position yourselves. That way it will be possible to move quickly to defend more than one clearing."

"Yes, but you required us never to kill Spaniards with them. We've made oaths."

"I don't need you to kill Spaniards. What you need to do is kill duendes."

***

The mid-morning sun flamed the sky as the duendes and conquistadors stood on the high cliffs surveying the densely-treed valley below.

"I know they're down there," said Rodrigo.

"I can't see anything below the canopy," said Martín.

"It doesn't matter what you can or can't see. I'm telling you they're hiding in that valley. All of them. Cristóbal. Héctor. The ñakaqs. The Incas. We'll destroy them all at once. This is the day we cover ourselves in glory."

He pointed to three large clearings. Speaking to the duende who had been carrying him, he said, "See, you can land us there, and then come back here to wait for my signal to return."

Rodrigo raised his sword. "Are we ready, conquistadors? Our moment has finally come."

The duendes lifted the soldiers and launched themselves from the cliff toward the valley below. Rodrigo signaled for the battalion to split and head for separate clearings so that they could all land at once.

When they were still some distance above the tree tops a volley of bolts arced up at them from different angles, with one of them striking a duende in the chest. Both duende and conquistador then plummeted from the sky, crashing into a tree and falling through the branches.

"I knew they were there," shouted Rodrigo, pointing his sword at the clearing. "*Santiago y cierra, España!*"

More bolts flew toward them and four more duendes plunged to the ground, releasing their hold of the conquistadors so that eight bodies tumbled from above the forest canopy into the undergrowth.

The Spaniards shouted their battle cry, but instead of continuing their descent, the duendes swerved back up and started circling out of reach of the bolts.

"I gave the order to land," said Rodrigo angrily.

The duende ignored him and instead spoke to the others in their wind-blown tongue. They then swerved and headed back to the cliff top.

"Didn't you hear me?" demanded Rodrigo after his duende released him. "We should have continued."

"We have no armor," said the duende. "There was too much risk."

"So that's it? They stay safely in the valley and there's nothing we can do about it?"

"The plan was to surprise them, but they were well-prepared for our attack. We would have been slaughtered if we had tried to land. I need to return to speak with Ithilia."

***

Cristóbal and Héctor joined the ñakaqs as they combed the undergrowth looking for the fallen. Cristóbal's stomach knotted when he came across the first dead conquistador.

"We'll give the Spaniards a Christian burial," he said.

"They would have killed us, Capitán," said Héctor.

Cristóbal nodded. They moved on, but none of the conquistadors had survived.

"This one's the only one still alive," shouted Tagón.

Cristóbal and Héctor joined him and saw a duende wedged in a tree. Somehow, she had managed to survive both the bolt and the spiraling tumble through the canopy. She was unconscious but breathing.

The ñakaqs lifted her out of the tree branches that had broken her fall and carried her to the clearing.

"What will you do with her?" asked Cristóbal.

"We rarely capture one, but we've always killed them quickly in the past. They are too dangerous."

Cristóbal looked at the duende's face. Her skin was gray and no longer shimmered. "Can we keep this one alive?"

"Why?"

"She may be useful."

"If we leave the bolt inside her, she'll be dead within a few days. Are you saying we should save her life?"

"Yes, but bind her wings, arms and feet."

"I think it's unwise, but if that's what you wish." Tagón gave an order in his tongue to the other ñakaqs.

"What will Ithilia do now, do you think?" asked Cristóbal.

"She'll come for us again. Soon. It's best to assume it will be tomorrow. She now knows we're here, but she'll think twice about attacking us directly the next time. Diego's crossbows are the perfect weapon against a direct attack."

"Then the valley isn't safe anymore?"

"No, it's no longer safe. The wind-whisperers are not like us. They'll try something different, to trick us. I think we need to prepare to move straight away."

"But they'll start searching for us wherever we go, won't they?"

"That's the nature of our enemy."

Cristóbal considered Tagón's words carefully. "If we could somehow convince them we're all dead, they would stop hunting us, wouldn't they?"

"Of course, but how is it possible to convince someone of your death."

"You need to trick them."

"My people are not good with tricks."

"Maybe you need to become better with them in your dealings with the duendes."

An unearthly scream ripped the air. The ñakaqs had pushed the barbed bolt through the duende's body and were now busy staunching the bleeding from both wounds.

***

"I can tell when you have a plan, Capitán," said Héctor, as he and Cristóbal walked back to their hut.

"You know me too well, Héctor."

"So, what is it? I know it has something to do with why you want that duende alive."

"It's only half a plan."

"Then tell me the half that you know."

"There is one way we can make it through the salida and back to New Spain."

"And what's that?"

"The duendes could carry us there."

Héctor frowned. "Why would they do that?"

"I don't know yet."

Sarpay greeted them at the hut, and then stared intently at Cristóbal.

"What's wrong?" asked Cristóbal.

"I don't know," she said, "but you look guilty."

Chapter 54

Ithilia's Demons

Padre Núñez winced in pain, struggling to keep pace with Ithilia as she strode down the long corridor. The fresco scenes seemed to scream at him in agony with every step. Here was a beast being skewered through the heart, there a warrior dying a horrific death mid-battle.

"I've told you I will speak to you later," said Ithilia, without slowing.

"I must insist." Padre Núñez's erratic motion contrasted with Ithilia's. "The timing is very important."

Ithilia waved him away. "You are getting more tiresome with every day. Don't abuse the freedom of movement we have granted you here in the High Palaces."

"I told you I have to baptize these children."

"And I've told you that they were still-born, so there is nothing you can do for them."

Padre Núñez grabbed her by the arm so that she would stop walking. "I don't believe you. I heard the cries last night. At least some of them survived the birth."

"You are mistaken, Padre. It was the same as with the Incas, the children were all still-born. What you heard were cries from the pain of childbirth."

"Then let me see the bodies."

"That's impossible. They have already been taken by the sky."

"What in God's name does that mean?"

Ithilia pulled his fingers back from her arm to free herself of the padre's grasp, bending them until they were at the point of breaking. "They were our creations, not yours. And not your God's."

Padre Núñez drew back, making the sign of the cross. "What have you done with the children? What evil have you committed?"

"We have no need of offspring because we do not age."

"But I've seen your people die."

"In battle, yes. If it wasn't for the ñakaqs, we would live forever. That's why all of them must be destroyed."

Padre Núñez felt his legs buckle as he realized the implication. "Did you kill all your males as well?"

"We have no need of males or children."

"Then why seek children from us?"

"Why do anything? Because it has beauty. You speak of creation, but you have no understanding of it. There is art in the creation of a child, of holding it within our bodies, in the pain of giving birth. And in the pain of giving death."

Monstrous. Abominations. What were these creatures? The padre staggered back. "How could I have been so wrong? You're pure evil. I've now truly seen a demon and it has gilded wings and a tongue of silver."

Ithilia started to walk away, but then turned back. "How dare you proclaim something beyond your understanding of evil? Can't you see our perfection? We have no conflict between what we *are* and what we *desire*. You Spanish, you have been created by your God, while we have always been. We are our own creation."

Impossible. Madness. Padre Núñez's head swirled.

Ithilia looked at him with contempt. "You are flawed and filled with contradictions that darken your every thought. You call us evil? *You* are the demons."

Ithilia turned her back on the padre and walked through the doorway.

Several duendes were in the chamber.

"We don't have good news, Ithilia," said one of them.

Ithilia pressed her lips together until they went white, glaring at each of the duendes in turn. Finally, she said, "Don't tell me the Spanish were defeated."

"No," said the duende who had already spoken, "they didn't get a chance to fight. We couldn't land them."

"Why? Are the ñakaq horcas suddenly an effective weapon against us?"

"No, they shot countless arrows at us from the weapon the Spanish call a crossbow."

"The ñakaqs shot these arrows? Is that what you're telling me?"

"Yes, as far as we could see. These crossbows have a long reach and can be shot with greater accuracy than our own bows. We will have the same problem no matter how we attack them."

Ithilia's wings opened and closed several times in quick succession.

"But we now know for certain that the ñakaqs are in the valley with the Quechua-speakers."

"Yes."

"So, the ñakaqs have decided to protect the Incas at all costs? They feel indebted to them for escaping the Spaniards' prison."

"Yes, Ithilia."

"And we know once they've made such a decision, they will never abandon them. They will defend them to the death." Ithilia smiled at the thought. "I believe I know what we have to do."

"Will you wish to speak to Rodrigo?"

"No, he is no longer needed. I have other plans."

Chapter 55

The Fallen Angel

The duende opened her eyes and Cristóbal watched her reactions closely. He saw the initial fog of confusion, then the wild panic followed by a deeper fear. Her powerful muscles tensed. She struggled against the cords, the full degree of her confinement striking her when her wings twitched.

"It's good to see that you've regained consciousness," said Cristóbal. "You've lost a lot of blood."

The duende looked around, the ropes giving her just enough slack so she could twist her neck to see she was tied to a tree.

"My name is Cristóbal de Varga. You were shot down when your people attacked us, but you managed to survive the bolt and the fall."

The duende's eyes darted in all directions, finally settling on Cristóbal's face.

She said one word. "Why?"

"Why what?"

"Why am I still alive?"

"The ñakaqs wanted you dead, but I told them I wished to speak with you."

"And they listen to your wishes?"

"Sometimes."

The duende shuffled her feet, obviously uncomfortable touching the ground. "Why would you wish to speak with me?"

"First tell me your name. As I said, I'm Cristóbal de Varga."

She stared at him for a long time, strain etched across the soft features of her face. "I'm Eleria." She said the name as a series of three breaths followed by a sigh.

"I can't say your name the way you do," said Cristóbal, "so you'll need to excuse me."

"Did you wish to speak to me about my name?"

"No, Eleria, I want to know if there's anything I can do to stop your people attacking us again."

"Why would we stop? Some ñakaqs remain alive, and you are protecting them here in this valley."

"Well, you see, that's not actually true. The ñakaqs are the ones helping to protect us here. Their homes are elsewhere. Even if you kill all the people here, it won't help you find them."

Eleria's nostrils flared. "I can't smell any of them nearby, but I can tell they've been here recently." She shuddered. "And I know they touched me."

"They tied you to the tree and bandaged your wounds."

Eleria's face paled and she retched.

Cristóbal gathered some leaves and wiped the bile from her chest.

She asked, "Are you going to force yourself on me?"

"Why would I do that?"

"To make your dominance over me complete."

"No, I'm not going to force myself on you. What I want is to stop another attack. What would Ithilia do if she was told she can't kill the ñakaqs by attacking this valley?"

"She wouldn't believe it. It doesn't matter that the ñakaq halls are elsewhere. It's obvious they've sworn to protect the Quechua-speakers here. They won't flee and leave the Quechua-speakers unprotected, so we will be able to kill them all here without finding their halls."

"The only problem for you is you can't launch a successful attack on the valley. You've seen what happened. We struck you before you even got close to landing. None of the others we hit survived."

Eleria almost smiled. "You think my people will stop now that we are certain you are here? We will return, but unlike the ñakaqs, we are quick to change our strategy. You won't be able to guess how we'll attack."

"I see." Cristóbal held up a plate of potatoes. "Would you like something to eat?"

Eleria eyed him curiously. "I don't understand why you want to keep me alive after what I've just said. There's nothing I can do for you. I don't want to die a slow, ugly death, which is what will happen to me if I stay like this. I would rather you killed me quickly."

"What if I don't want to kill you at all?"

"You don't want to force yourself on me and you don't want to kill me. I don't see any other possibility."

"I could release you."

Eleria looked genuinely surprised. "Why would you do that?"

"I'll tell you in good time."

Cristóbal heard footsteps on the forest floor behind him and turned to see Héctor approaching.

"I see our duende is conscious, Capitán."

"Yes, but she's refusing to eat."

"Leave her to me. Tagón is waiting for you."

Chapter 56

The Dead Ñakaqs

With the prevailing winds in their favor, Tiso and the other Incan navigators made good progress despite having to fight the current. Cristóbal stood with Tagón on the lead raft, the wind whipping the back of his neck. The familiar cliff faces crowded the vessels from both banks.

"It was your idea," said Tagón. "You said that we should convince the duendes that we're all dead."

Cristóbal ran his fingers across his beard stubble. "I don't understand what these statues have to do with it."

"Wait, Cristóbal. When we get there, I'll show you."

The rafts reached the plateau before the river divided. There, on the rocky shore under a large overhang, the hundreds of life-size ñakaq statues came into view, their horcas pointing to the heavens.

Cristóbal noticed that this time several of them appeared to have been damaged. He wondered again what purpose the statues could possibly serve as the Incas steered the rafts toward the plateau. The ñakaqs on the rafts held their horcas high in the air, mimicking the pose of the statues. Could it be that this was some sort of worship, even though they claimed to have no gods?

The Incas pulled the rafts onto the bank and Cristóbal followed the ñakaqs as they entered the forest of statues.

Tagón and the others each picked out one of the stone ñakaqs and thrust their horcas at them so that they punctured the surface. With repeated jabs, the holes became larger and the outer casing shattered.

Cristóbal was shocked to see what appeared to be a flesh-and-blood ñakaq inside the casing.

"They're not alive, are they?" he asked.

"No," said Tagón, "they died long ago in our greatest battle. We preserved them and encased them in a shell made in our forges that stops their bodies from rotting."

The ñakaqs continued breaking the corpses free.

"Of course," said Tagón, "now that they're exposed to the air, even though their flesh has been embalmed, they'll start to decay. That still gives us a number of days where they're indistinguishable from the corpses of those who have just perished in battle, and my guess is the wind-whisperers will attack soon, possibly tomorrow."

Once the bodies were without the support of the shell, they collapsed to the ground. The ñakaqs started picking them up and loading them onto the rafts.

Tiso approached Cristóbal as he watched. "Can I speak with you?"

"Of course. Anyone who saves my life can speak to me at any time."

Tiso coughed.

"What is it?" asked Cristóbal.

"There's talk among the villagers that you're the god Viracocha."

Cristóbal shook his head. "You saw me nearly die. You know that's not true."

"I know, but—"

"Tiso, please make it clear to your people that although I have white skin, I'm not Viracocha."

He shifted awkwardly. "They say you're leading us somewhere."

"I don't think I've ever led anyone to a place they've truly wanted to be. Wouldn't you rather be back in your village, living the life you had before I invaded with my conquistadors?"

"No, I'd rather be here."

Cristóbal swallowed. "Tiso, I don't believe there are any gods in this world. Not my God, and not any of yours. We all need to stop looking for them. We're on our own here."

The Inca nodded slowly. "Then, can you teach me how to shoot your crossbows?"

Chapter 57

Valley of Flames

Fire rained down on the valley before dawn the next day. Cristóbal had barely slept after spending much of the night helping prepare the rafts. He had intended not to sleep at all because Tagón had predicted the duendes were likely to attack in the morning. However, he now found himself sitting by his campfire, crossbow leaning against his side, as smoke woke him. At first he thought the smell was coming from the dying embers, but then he saw the treetops across the valley were aflame.

How could he have let himself fall asleep? Maybe he was getting old.

He looked up through the clearing to see the duendes, well out of reach of crossbow bolts, flying in an elegant formation, shooting arrow after flaming arrow into the valley's canopy.

Tagón raced toward him, his eyes red with anger and lack of sleep. "They must have flown in the dark to surprise us," he said. "Quickly, we have little time."

Cristóbal rushed into his hut, waking Sarpay before hastily collecting his few belongings.

"Come, Tagón is waiting for us."

They followed Tagón through the undergrowth. Above, the fire had taken hold and heat bore down on them. Tree trunks cracked and groaned under the assault and flaming branches crashed to the ground.

"I never thought they would attack before dawn." Tagón's voice was hoarse. "We managed to get the ñakaq statue corpses in place, but the rafts still need to be launched."

Low-lying bushes started smoldering, and Tagón was forced to take a twisting path to avoid them. Finally, they came to a clearing where most of the Incas were waiting.

Cristóbal was awash with sweat, and coughing smoke out of his lungs. All he could see was a tumultuous churning of smoke, ember and flames. Somewhere above the swirling roof, the duendes may still have been shooting flame-arrows into the valley, but it was impossible to tell any more.

Many of the Incan children were choking and crying while the adults watched in fear as the fire encircled them.

Tagón got down on his hands and knees near the edge of the clearing, the flames stretching dangerously close as he groped for something. To Cristóbal's surprise, when the ñakaq found what he was looking for, he pulled back and opened a hinged trapdoor that had lain invisible against the forest floor. A faint play of light shimmered across the opening.

"This leads to a tunnel system under the valley," said Tagón. "Be careful. The steps are steep."

The first few Incas had already vanished underground when several ñakaqs pushed their way through the undergrowth into the clearing, frantically putting out fires in their beards. Behind them were several of the Incan navigators, including Tiso.

"The rafts have been launched," said one of the ñakaqs.

"Good," said Tagón, ushering more Incas into the entrada.

Cristóbal began looking around anxiously. "Where's Héctor? He must still be with the captured duende." He stared in the direction of the tree Eleria had been tied to. A ferocious wall of flame stood in his way.

"Don't be a fool," said Sarpay.

"Follow the others into the tunnel. I'll catch up."

With that he pushed his way through a section of undergrowth where the flames had only begun to take hold and entered the smoke-choked forest.

The heat had an intensity he had never experienced. His skin prickled and the hairs on his arms singed and shriveled to almost nothing. Struggling for air in the furnace, he sucked smoke into his lungs and coughed violently. His eyes watered, and as his vision wavered in heat ripples with the forest collapsing around him, he could no longer be certain of what he was seeing.

A great beast appeared, shuffling toward him as if wounded. He waved the smoke from his face and for a moment could see what was really there. Héctor was dragging an unconscious Eleria across the forest floor, her wings torn and singed. Cristóbal rushed toward Héctor, whose eyes widened in surprise.

The two of them together lifted the duende and carried her back through the flaming forest.

Sarpay was still waiting there, one of the last to enter the tunnel.

"I told you to leave without me," said Cristóbal.

"And I told you not to go into the forest."

"Come," said Tagón. "We need to leave now. I don't know why you would bring the duende."

Sarpay walked down the steps, and Cristóbal and Héctor followed carrying Eleria.

***

High above the valley, Ithilia and the other duendes circled in formation, watching the smoke plume violently below.

Ithilia constantly scanned the valley, looking for any signs of death or life, imagining the chaos under the smoke clouds. The contrast of anarchy with the beautiful curves her people traced in the sky pleased her. Although she knew that until they saw the bodies nothing could be taken for granted, she savored the tang of ultimate victory like a fine wine.

One of the duendes pointed to the river. Though the distance and tendrils of smoke obscured the view, a series of rafts laden with passengers appeared to be leaving the cliffs on the valley's edge.

"They are heading toward the waterfall," said the duende.

"Come," said Ithilia, giving the signal to fly toward the river.

The sails billowed in the wind as the current drove the rafts relentlessly toward the precipice. Smoke from the fire continued to make it impossible to see clearly how many people were on the rafts, and the speed at which they were traveling meant the duendes couldn't reach them before they tipped over the edge of the falls.

Ithilia watched the rafts hurtle into mid-air dislodging all those on them. Passengers and rafts hung frozen for a moment in silhouette against the raging wall of white water and then plunged into the maelstrom at the foot of the falls.

The duendes flew across the precipice's edge and hovered above the broken rafts at the bottom, looking for survivors.

No one emerged.

They followed the river further downstream just to be certain, but there were no signs anyone had survived the drop.

Ithilia gave the signal to return to their High Palaces. The fire needed time to burn itself out, so it would be some days before they could establish how many ñakaqs had been killed.

Chapter 58

The Cavern

The underground passages were lit by strange glowing stones that had been placed in the rocky wall at regular intervals. The ñakaqs led the way through the maze of intersecting tunnels which had obviously taken generations to build. Incan children who started crying were quickly quietened by their parents. Everyone proceeded in silence, concentrating on their footing on the slippery surface. After the heat of the fire, the underground air felt biting cold to Cristóbal. He and Héctor continued to carry Eleria who still hadn't regained consciousness.

Eventually the tunnel widened into a vast cavern with a large crystalline lake in the middle. Above them, in the highest reaches, was an opening in the rock through which a patch of red sky shone. From the ceiling hung a tangle of vines and tree roots.

Some of the Incas immediately set about catching the dark fish that darted across the lake and began boiling water for tea.

Cristóbal and Héctor placed Eleria on the cavern floor and together with Sarpay made themselves as comfortable as they could on the rocky surface.

"These duende truly have the beauty of angels, don't they?" said Héctor.

"Is that why you risked your life to rescue her?" asked Sarpay.

"No," said Héctor, still looking at Eleria. "The Capitán believes she'll be useful."

Sarpay's eyes narrowed as she regarded Cristóbal. "What are you proposing that makes her so important?"

"You can't influence an enemy without speaking to them," said Cristóbal.

"This sounds like another lesson from Pizarro and Cortés," said Sarpay. "You think you can deal with her like you did Tagón?"

"You said yourself the key is to find what someone desires and offer it to them."

"Yes, but that's easy to do for men. Women are more complex. Do you have any idea what she desires?"

Tagón joined them, nodding in the direction of Eleria. "She looks dead to me."

"No," said Héctor, "she's still breathing."

"Make sure you don't untie her. If she escapes, our plan to fool the duendes will be exposed."

"Do you know what happened with the rafts?" asked Cristóbal.

"We had a watcher near the waterfall. He's just told me that the wind-whisperers followed the rafts and saw them go over the falls, then spent some time looking for survivors."

"So, we tricked them?" asked Sarpay.

"Yes. They couldn't get too close, and there was a lot of smoke in the air. I don't think they could tell the figures on the rafts were all made of straw. I'd say they believe all the Incas are dead."

Cristóbal said, "They'll probably think Héctor and I went with the Incas over the waterfall."

"I'm less certain about that, but it's more important that they find the burnt remains of the ñakaq corpses that we scattered around the valley. There were sixty-three, so they should be convinced they'd killed all of us and stop searching."

"Are we in danger of being discovered?" asked Cristóbal, looking up at the piece of sky visible high above them where clouds were now gathering.

"Even if a wind-whisperer flew directly overhead, they would only see darkness."

"How long do we stay?"

"Until the wind-whisperers can satisfy themselves there are sixty-three ñakaq bodies in the valley. They'll wait for the fires to die before the return, so it could be a few days."

"And then?"

"There are many other valleys, but none are as protected as the last one. Rodrigo and his men will be able to attack from the ground. Our best hope is our trick will work."

Eleria let out a groan. "Remember," said Tagón, "we can never allow that one to get away. If she does, all is lost."

"She won't escape," said Cristóbal.

"I could remove her wings, just to be safe."

"No, I'm trying to get her to trust us."

"Just be careful." Tagón looked across at Héctor. "Both of you. We call them wind-whisperers for a reason. They can twist anything with their words."

A flash of lightning lit up the cavern and a column of rain began to fall into the lake.

Chapter 59

A Dance of Ashes

The valley lay black and broken below them. Where once great trees reigned, now stood twisted skeletons. Where waves of green had washed from cliff face to cliff face, now ashen gray drifted aimlessly across a carpet of charred remains, and rainwater pooled in puddles the color of death.

The duendes separated in a graceful formation and spread across the valley in their search for corpses. Scattered amid the carcasses of alpacas, ciervas and smaller animals, they found ñakaq remains. They picked them up and carried them to the middle of the valley where Ithilia stood waiting.

She smiled, counting them as each one was piled in front of her, her nostrils flaring. When the last one was added, she intoned the number reverently. "Sixty-three."

After scouring the valley for most of the day, the duendes now stood in a spiral around their leader.

Ithilia spoke with the wind eddying ash around her feet.

"Victory. Finally, we have our victory over the great enemy. Finally, we are free once more to spread our wings in every corner of the world, to walk in the lands of our choosing, to claim earth as well as sky. Come, let us sing."

The duendes began a low wail, like a wind yearning to be a storm, growing in power, whipping the air into a furious climax, until finally dying and falling into silence. Then they unfolded their wings, and, opening like an elegant flower, flew into the sky in spiral formation. As they rose higher and higher, the spiral began to swirl in an aching dance. And as they span, they soared to even greater heights, so that the valley below receded into a black stain surrounded by a sea of mountains.

With Ithilia at the apex, they gyrated, piercing their way through the heavens, ever upwards.

And when the sun threatened to creep behind the peaks, they would climb further, so that it again came into full view. They stopped the sun from setting on them. Escaping the fate of the world. Higher. They fought the sun, refusing to let it abandon them, drawing on its power.

And as the air thinned to nothingness and they could no longer draw breaths, one by one oblivion captured them, and they started to fall.

And fall.

And fall.

Until their breaths returned and their great wings started beating again. And with dusk overtaking them, they flew home to their High Palaces.

Chapter 60

The Angel Wakes

Héctor watched Eleria as the others in the cavern slept. Her exquisite face now seemed to be glowing, although her eyes still hadn't opened since the fire. He wondered, not for the first time, how different everything would have been if he had abandoned Cristóbal like the others. What was happening at the duendes' palaces while he sat here underground in the dark with water relentlessly dripping from the opening above into the lake?

"Why are you looking at me?"

Héctor realized Eleria had just spoken. "You're alive."

"For some reason, you and the other Spanish are determined to keep me that way. I remember when the fire started you cut me from the tree. Why did you save me?"

"The capitán wants you alive."

"Do you always do what the capitán tells you?"

"He's the capitán."

"The capitán wasn't there when the fires started. You put your life at risk to save me. Why? He wouldn't have known."

"You were my responsibility. I was told to watch over you, so I did. It's simple."

"It doesn't explain why you were looking at me just now."

Héctor turned away. "Your face looked like it was glowing. That's unusual."

"I see." Eleria tried to sit up, but with her hands and feet tied it was too difficult. "Can you help me up? These rocks aren't comfortable to lie on."

He grabbed her around her well-muscled shoulders and pulled her up into a sitting position. Her skin was warm and smooth to the touch.

"That's better." Eleria looked around. "Where are we?"

"Underground, in a cavern."

"I can see that. What happened?"

"The ñakaqs helped us escape the fire and led us here."

Her nostrils flared. "How long have I been with them?"

"Half a day and half a night."

"No wonder I feel like I'm dying."

"Why can't your people bear being near them?"

Eleria's face contorted. "Look at them. They're repulsive. Unclean. Earth-bound. They are covered in hair. Their voices are harsh. Their minds have no flexibility. They have no sense of beauty. They are everything we're not."

"How do you find us then?"

"You're different to the ñakaqs."

"But we have beards. On this campaign I've rarely felt clean."

"You came to us as the enemy of our enemy, so we can tolerate your shortcomings."

"I see."

Eleria squinted to look more closely at Héctor through the gloom. "But you're not the same as the other Spanish, are you? Your features are different. Your skin color is darker."

"I *am* different. In our world I'm from different lands to the others."

"Then how do you come to be with the Spanish?"

"I joined them to make my fortune, and Cristóbal recognized that I was a good soldier."

"I think there's something you're not telling me."

Héctor turned away again.

Eleria said, "I much prefer it when you look into my face like you did before."

Héctor didn't answer.

Eleria said, "Now you're like you first were when you came to watch over me at the tree. You're not talking much."

"I was a slave," said Héctor finally. "I was owned by a Spaniard but was eventually able to buy my freedom."

"There's no shame in being a slave. The Quechua-speakers serve us because they are inferior. If the ñakaqs were a little more malleable and had accepted the same fate, perhaps we could have avoided a lot of bloodshed."

"My people aren't an inferior race to the Spanish, and the ñakaqs aren't an inferior race to yours."

Eleria looked surprised. "And the Quechua-speakers?"

"They may look weak here in your world, but their ancestors entered your lands confused and with nothing. In our world they ruled over a great empire of millions."

"Millions? Is that possible?" Eleria shifted awkwardly. "My wings are aching. They're not used to being bound like this."

"You also suffered some burns during the fire."

"You're not going to untie my wings if I asked you to?"

"No."

"I'm in a lot of pain. Do your people understand pain?"

"Yes, my people know pain all too well."

"It would help if someone stroked my wings."

"Are you asking me to stroke your wings?"

Eleria's face glowed. "Yes, would you?"

Chapter 61

Feast and Reward

Rodrigo was glad to be invited back to the feasting hall again. He sat next to Ithilia in the center of the spiral table and, if anything, the food was even more lavish than it had been the first time.

Ithilia appeared pleased with him once more. Laughing. Offering him wine from her cup. His men also appeared to enjoy the same attentions from the duendes as they once had. Also like the first feast, Padre Núñez was missing.

Something was different, though. Something below the surface. Ithilia was a little distant and her words had a slightly cold undercurrent.

"I'm glad our search finally found the ñakaqs," said Rodrigo, "but did you come across the bodies of Cristóbal and Héctor?"

"No, there were no Spanish corpses found in the valley. I believe they would have been killed with the Quechua-speakers when the rafts went over the waterfall."

"But you said you didn't find any bodies in the water."

"No, the turbulence made it impossible."

"I see."

"The deaths of ñakaqs were what was important to us. We have proof of those. Are you fearful that these two Spanish will return to threaten you?"

"No, no, of course not."

Ithilia smiled. "I've always found that more than one *no* usually means a yes." She held out a yellow apple-like fruit for him. "Have you tried these? They are the sweetest fruit we have."

She drew closer so that it was almost touching his lips. Rodrigo bent forward and took a bite.

"So, Ithilia, can we speak of the rewards you promised for our many months of hard work."

"Rewards?"

"The gold you promised. The help in finding our way home."

Ithilia took a bite of the apple herself. "Now, we're both aware you didn't really best the remaining ñakaqs in battle."

"That's true, but that was never our agreement. We found the hidden place where they lived."

"Well, no, you found the valley where the Quechua-speakers were hiding. The ñakaqs were only there to protect them. It wasn't their home."

Rodrigo drew back. "Our actions gave you your victory."

"Of course. Of course." Ithilia touched his arm. "There is no question you have been invaluable. Of course, our agreement stands. I'm only saying it wasn't quite how both of us envisaged it when you said you would bring me the head of the last ñakaq."

"Perhaps not."

"In fact, it was actually *our* flight over the valley that led us to think the ñakaqs were hiding there."

"But we found the statues that pointed the way. You would have never seen them from the air."

"There's no doubt you and your men were important in a number of ways, although we ended up losing some of our people in your attack on the ñakaqs."

"As did we."

"Yes, we both did. The only point I want to make is that nothing unfolded as we had planned."

"No, it didn't."

"So, we could perhaps say that you didn't quite fulfill your part of the agreement in the way we had envisaged. That would be fair to say, wouldn't it?"

"Well…"

"Which doesn't mean I won't keep my side of the agreement."

Rodrigo relaxed a little.

"It's just," said Ithilia, "it's just that we, in turn, may also not be able to fulfill our side of our bargain in quite the same way as we both envisaged."

"Why would that be?"

"You see, we promised you as much gold as you could carry."

"Yes, the gold you have here in your palaces is of high quality."

"That's where the problem lies. We can't possibly give you the works of art we have in the High Palaces. You can see that, can't you?"

"But you could give us the gold in the crater of ñakaq helmets you showed me."

"We planned to give you as much of the ñakaq gold as you could carry."

"Then give us this gold, Ithilia."

"There's the problem, you see. When we struck our bargain, I thought that by killing the ñakaqs in their halls, you would find their source of gold. Since you haven't fulfilled your part of the agreement in the way we foresaw, you have made it impossible for us to fulfill our part in the way we foresaw. We still don't know where the ñakaqs' gold source is, so I can't give you any of their gold."

Ithilia offered the fruit to Rodrigo again, but he pushed it away. "Then give us the gold from your source."

"Don't you think this is worth another bite?" She put the half-eaten fruit back on the plate. "You see, the ñakaqs are our *only* source of gold. We have no other. The last of the unused gold we have is in the crater of helmets, and we will need it for our own art. So that leaves us with a dilemma, doesn't it?"

Rodrigo sat back in his chair. "You have no gold to give us."

"You could return to the Quechua-speaker village where we destroyed the ñakaq army. The gold in the helmets there would be considerable. You would only need to give us half."

"What? You want us to scour the corpses of tens of thousands of ñakaqs and pry out each sliver of gold piece by piece? And then give you half?" Rodrigo couldn't believe what he was hearing. "And after all that, we won't have enough anyway. Nowhere near enough."

"There is an alternative. Search for the source of gold in the ñakaq heartlands. You may also find the way back to your lands. We can carry you to the inaccessible places the way we have been. You found the hidden valley. You can find the source of gold."

Blood rose to his face. "This is your best offer? Months or years of searching for a gold source you've never been able to find?"

"When you find it, as much as you want is yours."

Rodrigo leaped to his feet and hurled plates from the table so that they clattered across the stone floor of the feasting hall, splattering Spaniards and duendes with food. "No, we demand you give us gold from here in the High Palaces as reward for what we've done."

"Sit down," said Ithilia. "I've already told you that's impossible."

"I won't—"

He felt Ithilia's hand on his shoulder and her breath in his ear as she whispered to him. "This is not how a guest behaves."

Rodrigo felt her fingers digging deeply into his shoulder as she pushed him back down into his seat.

"You have our support in your quest for gold, Capitán Rodrigo Benalcázar."

He fought against the pressure, but her strength was enormous.

Slowly he sat back down.

The Incan servants quickly removed the scattered plates and food, replacing them on the table in front of Rodrigo and Ithilia.

Ithilia smiled and held another yellow apple in front of him, and he took a bite.

Chapter 62

The Last Valley

Tagón promised that the new valley was now not far as he led the way along the steep mountain path. Cristóbal was unused to trekking long distances on foot, and for the first time since the fire thought about his horse. The poor beast had been through so much with him, he couldn't bear the notion that its last moments alive must have been agony. What else could Nueva Tierra take away from him?

Eleria was now his only hope of reversing what had been a steady deterioration in his fortunes since entering this strange land. Although the duende was alive, she was struggling with the trek from the cavern, despite Héctor's support. She still had her hands and wings tied, making it difficult for her to maintain her balance on the descent, and she was obviously not used to walking. He would need to nurse her back to health if she was going to be any use to him.

When they finally entered the new valley, Cristóbal's heart sank. It was hardly more than a rocky gorge surrounded by high cliffs, with a small forested area and a stream trickling through the center.

"There won't be room for all of us to live here," he said to Tagón. "The huts will be cramped together."

"There won't be any huts." Tagón pointed to the southern cliff face. "That's where you'll all be living."

Cristóbal shielded his eyes against the sun and saw the myriad of small openings in the rock. "So we're living in caves now?"

"Yes, you'll be safe here."

Safe. Cristóbal felt the word scratching the back of his throat and wanted to spit it out. He wanted to write it in large letters in his diary and then tear out the page and rip it to pieces. "Tagón, I need to find some hope, not just safety. I need to know that Nueva Tierra is more than just an endless series of mountains and valleys. I need to know what I've been defending. I need a purpose." He drew a deep breath. "You're the king now. There has to be some way for me to see your Great Halls."

Tagón fell silent.

Cristóbal said, "Don't promise me anything. Just think about it."

Tagón didn't look at him.

***

Cristóbal and Sarpay climbed up to the entrance to one of the caves and stepped into the half-light. They placed their sack of belongings on the ground and sat down.

"Do you dream of condors anymore?" asked Sarpay.

Cristóbal ran his fingers through his hair. "Yes, I think I did once before the last attack. Why? Do you want me to have even more bad luck?"

"When you dreamed of condors you were anxious, but you were striving for something."

"I'm not anxious. Tagón says we'll be safe here."

"I know that's not enough for you, Cristóbal."

"Is it enough for you?"

"Yes."

"I suppose it would be. You've achieved your life's work by keeping the hope of an Incan Empire alive and stopping me from ever finding Vilcabamba. Me, I've achieved nothing."

"The condor dream was just after you came back with the gold-filled urns, wasn't it?"

"It may have been."

"What happened that day? You didn't tell me too much about it."

Cristóbal shifted position. "I told you Tagón took us to the source of the ñakaq gold. I...I just assumed he wanted me to keep the details a secret."

"Are you going to tell me what your plan is?"

"What do you mean?"

"I know you too well now. You've been acting differently since you returned that day. Do two urns full of gold matter that much to you?"

"They don't. I started thinking that with the knowledge of the gold source I could win my command back."

"You think you can gain the conquistadors' respect again? Does their respect still have value to you after what they've done?"

"I need my command back."

"Why?"

"Because without it I don't know who I am."

"I see. And this captured duende is part of your plan?"

"Yes, although I don't know exactly how yet."

Sarpay laid the alpaca fur she had carried with her on the ground. "Then you don't lust after the duende like Héctor does?"

"Does he?"

"Have you been too obsessed with your own thoughts to see it?"

"Possibly."

Sarpay walked toward the entrance of the cave, which was bathed in sunlight, and then turned to face him. "There was a time when you were obsessed with me. Do you remember? You barely spoke to me for a long time, but we both knew, didn't we?"

"I remember."

She took off her garments and the light contoured her slender body as she stood in front of him. "I don't have the strength of a duende, but you know I'm strong, don't you?"

Cristóbal nodded.

"And I have no wings; but you're a condor, so you don't need the wings of others, do you?" She walked toward him and he stood up. "I chose you. You haven't forgotten that, have you? Am I not enough for you anymore?"

"I'm still obsessed with you," he said softly.

He took off his clothes and lifted her up so that he took all her weight and her legs twined with his.

For a moment, they were one.

Chapter 63

The Final Requerimiento

"They killed the children." Padre Núñez paced up and down Rodrigo's chamber. His eyes were wild and spittle formed in the corners of his mouth as he spoke. Outside the open window clouds gathered across the peaks.

"Ithilia told me they were all still-born," said Rodrigo.

"Every single one of them? And you believe her? You believe her?"

"Why should she lie?"

"To cover up that they killed them, Lieutenant Benalcázar?"

"*Capitán* Benalcázar."

"Yes, yes, of course. Capitán. *Capitán.*"

"So why would they have killed them?"

"Because having children is no different to a dance for them. Because carrying a child is the same as a living sculpture. Because something needs to suffer or die every time they create a work of art. I don't understand what goes on in their minds, but they're beyond redemption." He wiped the spit from his lips.

"What do you want me to do, Padre?"

"These duendes are not going to come to God willingly. They won't. Their words are as difficult to hold onto as a gust of wind, but I know what to do now. I know what to do."

"What are you saying, Padre?" said Rodrigo. "And stop walking backward and forwards. It makes it hard to concentrate on what you're saying."

"You have to allow me to read them the *Requerimiento.*"

"What? Declare war on them?"

"We both know the *Requerimiento* isn't a declaration of war. It's our solemn duty to crown and God. It's why we're here. Have you forgotten our purpose?"

"You want to tell them that unless they submit to the will of the Pope and His Imperial Majesty, King Charles V, we'll attack them? Are you mad? How can we threaten them with war and enslavement if we're their guests here?"

"We need to leave these palaces. The longer we're here, the worse it will become."

"They saved us from slaughter by the ñakaqs. They're our allies."

"We can't be allied with them anymore. They've sent our children to purgatory without any hope of salvation."

"You don't know that, Padre."

"I was here the night the babies were born. I heard them cry that night. The duendes almost convinced me I didn't hear them, but I know I did. The children were alive. They've been killed and now their souls are lost forever."

"What do you think will happen after you recite the *Requerimiento* to the duendes?"

"We'll be on the right path again. It will return our moral authority to us. We should trust God's will. Has the path you've chosen without him given you anything?" The padre's eyes grew wilder and his voice more strained.

"Ithilia has promised to help us find the source of ñakaq gold."

"Just words. You must know by now that you can't trust the meaning of any of the duende words. They have the power to make you believe things you wouldn't otherwise believe. We need God's word to protect us against them."

"Stop pacing!" Rodrigo shouted. "Let me think."

Padre Núñez stopped in front of him, but he continued to shift weight from side to side.

"You'll read the *Requerimiento* in Spanish, yes?" said Rodrigo.

"That's the way His Imperial Majesty wrote it."

"It doesn't matter that the duendes know very little Spanish?"

"No, its force isn't diminished."

"Then read it to Ithilia, if it's the only thing that will give you peace."

Padre Núñez calmed instantly.

***

"Why would you come to my chamber?" Ithilia stood with Ariathe and several other duendes as Padre Núñez approached, holding a cross in one hand and the *Requerimiento* document in the other.

He walked toward her until he stood directly in front of her. "I am required by our Lord to read the *Requerimiento* to you."

"Your God's requirements are no concern of mine. Please leave us."

Ithilia waved him away as if he were an annoying insect, but Padre Núñez ignored her and began reading.

"The *Requerimiento* requires you to recognize the Church as your Mistress and Governess of the World, and with her authority the High Priest, called the Pope, and His Imperial Majesty, King Charles V. If you do not do this, then with the help of God we shall come mightily against you, and we shall make war on you everywhere and in every way that we can."

"Don't speak words to me in a language I barely understand."

Padre Núñez continued despite her protest.

"And we shall subject you to the yoke and obedience of the Church and His Majesty, and we shall seize your women and children, and we shall make them slaves, to sell and dispose of as His Majesty commands, and we shall do all the evil and damage to you that we are able. And should this death and destruction befall you, be aware that the responsibility will be yours alone. Do you recognize the Church as your Mistress and submit to the Will of God?"

He fell into silence and offered the cross to Ithilia.

She looked at the cross and then directly into the padre's eyes. "Are you demanding that I accept the authority of your God? This God that you wish to infect my people with? The God that requires baptism?"

Padre Núñez repeated his question in Quechua. "Do you recognize the Church as your Mistress and submit to God's will?"

"How do you know what the Will of your God is?"

"I'm a man of God."

"I see. A *man* of God."

She grabbed the hand with which the padre was holding the cross. He tried to pull away, but she drew his hand toward Ariathe and pressed both cross and hand firmly against her stomach.

"What are you doing?" he protested.

"I want to see how much of you is man and how much God."

"Let go of me."

"I'm touching your cross. Isn't that what you wanted? To touch the cross is a good thing, isn't it?"

"Release my hand." Padre Núñez's fingers began to go numb under the pressure. "Take the cross. Take it from me."

"Isn't it good for us to hold the cross together? There's no mistake that you are bringing your God to me." Ithilia's fingers dug into his tendons. "Tell me first how a man of God is different to a man?"

Padre Núñez grimaced.

"Tell me," she said, tightening her grip.

"We..." he grunted in pain. "Franciscans...take vows of poverty, obedience and chastity."

"Poverty? I see, and yet you perform your duties with men whose lust for gold has no bounds?"

"Please..." He could now feel pain shooting up his arm.

"Obedience? Which command from your God have you obediently followed? How many pagans have you baptized?"

Padre Núñez heard a bone in his hand crack. He gasped as pain shot up his arm.

"Tell me how many pagans you have baptized," demanded Ithilia.

"One." The padre's voice was barely audible.

"One? You have obediently baptized one?"

The padre grew faint as the pain spread to his shoulder and chest.

"And chastity?" said Ithilia. "Tell us how you have held your vow of chastity."

He trembled.

"Tell us. As you hold the cross of your God against the belly that carries your child, tell us how you kept your vow of chastity. Tell us in what manner you can call yourself a man of God?"

Padre Núñez whimpered as he fell to his knees.

"Come, stand up," said Ithilia. "We all fall short of what we feel we should be. Let me show you what my people do in times like these."

She and Ariathe helped him out onto her balcony. The wind whistled as they took him toward the edge and the open sky below.

"Do you see?" asked Ithilia. "The immensity of the heavens. What are your vows in the face of such vastness?" She still held his hand which clutched the cross. "Step closer to see it all for yourself. Don't be afraid. You have your cross and I will hold you."

He took another step and the empty sky yawned at his feet.

"Of course, you know your God will protect you. You have fallen short in his service but he will not forsake you. You know that, don't you?"

Padre Núñez began the Lord's prayer, his voice trembling. *"Our Father who art in heaven, hallowed be thy name."*

"What you're certain of is that you haven't failed him. You know it in your heart." Ithilia's voice blew through the padre's words as he spoke them.

"Thy kingdom come. Thy will be done on earth, as it is in heaven."

"And you don't need proof from him, do you? Why would you?"

"Give us this day our daily bread."

"Of course, if there is any doubt, any doubt at all that you may have failed him, you could put it to the test. You could give yourself to the heavens. If you have been true to your God, he will protect you."

"And forgive us our trespasses. As we forgive those who trespass against us."

"Why not banish any doubt? Give yourself to the heavens. It would be so simple, wouldn't it? So simple."

"And lead us not into temptation."

"And such a relief to finally be certain."

Ithilia released her hold of the padre's hand.

"And deliver us from evil."

"Such a relief."

"And...deliver us from evil."

"To finally, finally be certain."

"Amen."

And with the final word, Padre Núñez still clutching the cross in his crippled hand, let himself fall forwards into the open sky.

Chapter 64

El diario de Cristóbal de Varga

I dreamed of the condor again last night. On awakening I was beset by a question that now torments my soul.

If no one saw it soar across the vast heavens.

If no one saw it stretch its colossal wings to catch the updrafts.

If no one saw it dance with the mountain winds.

And if no one saw it disappear.

Did it exist?

Chapter 65

Valley of the Faces

The condor angled its great wings to swoop toward the dark bird below, tracing its path through the air with such precision that it felt as if it was tethered to the bird's flight. Screeching, the condor drew closer, thrusting out its claws for the imminent impact. It was almost upon its prey when the bird suddenly dropped like a stone, and the condor was left scrabbling at nothingness.

Cristóbal lay awake for a long time in the dark, his thoughts in turmoil, until he became aware of a figure standing at the cave entrance, silhouetted against the pre-dawn sky.

"Tagón, what are you doing here so early?"

"I want to show you something today, but we need to leave now."

Sarpay was still sleeping next to him, breathing softly. Cristóbal kissed her lightly so she wouldn't awaken, got dressed and stepped outside.

None of the others had yet emerged from the caves. The sky was a deep purple, and the only sound was the soft babble of the stream below.

"This way," said Tagón as they made their way to the other side of the valley, where he led Cristóbal through a hidden gap in the mountainside.

"How many more secrets do you have?"

"I told you from the start we were a secretive people."

"I remember. Now, are you going to tell me where we're going?"

"No."

"I thought so. It's fortunate I trust you."

Tagón held up his hand. "Wait. We're being followed."

Cristóbal reached for his sword. "Who's there? Step forward."

His tension eased when a familiar figure rounded the corner behind them. "It's only me," said Tiso sheepishly.

"Why are you following us?" asked Cristóbal.

"Because you looked like you were going somewhere important." He couldn't meet Cristóbal's gaze.

"If we are, then the last thing we want is someone following us," said Tagón.

"Please go back and leave us," said Cristóbal.

Tiso shuffled awkwardly. "My people...we know nothing. Great things happen around us, but we're herded like alpacas."

"We're keeping you safe," said Tagón.

"The wind-whisperers are also keeping my people in the High Palaces *safe*. I don't want us to be safe like an alpaca waiting to be shorn. I want us to be able to fight for ourselves. There are so few ñakaqs left. You need us."

"I've shown you how to shoot a crossbow," said Cristóbal.

"I know, and I'm grateful."

"But?"

"But I would like Tagón to make me my own crossbow. Maybe even two, so I can teach some of the others."

"Two?" said Tagón, raising his eyebrows. "Would two be enough?"

Tiso looked up and nodded. "For now."

"I see." Tagón glanced at Cristóbal then across to Tiso. "Don't follow me again. Now return to the valley."

"Will you make me the crossbows?"

"I haven't said no, have I?"

Tiso hesitated, half-smiled and then turned to go.

***

Tagón took Cristóbal through a series of narrow crevices and rock splinters until they finally came to a crater ringed by mountain slopes etched with bizarre formations. He led him to the middle of the crater and then sat down, inviting Cristóbal to do the same.

"What are we doing here, Tagón?"

"This has always been one of my favorite places in the heartlands."

The ground was hard and there was no vegetation, making it difficult for Cristóbal to share Tagón's enthusiasm.

"Why is this place special to you?"

"Look around, Cristóbal."

Cristóbal turned, staring at the surrounding rocks against the pale-red mid-morning sky. "I'm sorry, Tagón. I don't know what you mean."

"Give it time. You might need to wait until the sun is higher and there's more light."

"What am I looking for?"

"The faces. I call this place the Valley of the Faces."

"Where are they?"

"In the rocks all around us."

Cristóbal squinted at the western slope. "Can you see them there, Tagón?"

"Yes, and there, and there, and there," he said pointing. "We're surrounded by faces."

Cristóbal blinked, trying to force them into the forms that Tagón said were there.

"You need to calm yourself," said Tagón. "They don't appear if you're tense or your mind is agitated."

"If that's true maybe I'll never be able to see them."

Cristóbal let his mind wander, to a time with Diego when two boys were lying on their backs on the banks of the Guadalquivir River staring at the clouds and watching giant galleons with billowing sails being chased across the sky by fantastic many-fanged beasts.

Then the transformation came, unheralded. One moment he saw only rocky slopes and the next they sprang to life. He was unaware of how much time passed, but suddenly hundreds of giant faces peered out at him from the mountain. Some leered, some laughed. Some looked frightened, some triumphant. Some joyous. Some despondent. Some had the wide eyes of shock or surprise and others had the closed eyes of sleep—or death. Some appeared deep in contemplation, while others were frozen in mid-shout. Some of them appeared to be arguing, while others looked as if they had just found a loved one.

"I can see them," he said.

"I know."

"How did you know, Tagón?"

"I can see it in your face."

"What an amazing place. Are these ñakaq carvings?"

"If they were carved by our ancestors, we have no record of it. I always thought they were natural formations and it was our minds that were creating the faces."

Cristóbal smiled. "You're so very different from when I first saw you."

"As are you Cristóbal." Tagón put his hand on Cristóbal's elbow. "I'm going to take you somewhere else today."

A chill went through Cristóbal despite the increasing heat of the day. He knew what Tagón was about to say. From now on there would be no going back. "You're going to take me to the Great Halls, aren't you?"

Tagón looked at him and nodded in silence.

Chapter 66

The Words of the Wind-Whisperer

"Why don't you make love to me?" asked Eleria as Héctor brought her breakfast, placing the plate next to her. The morning sun slanted through the cave entrance.

"I've told you why. If I made love to you, you would no longer be a prisoner. I would have to release you."

"But you could still keep my hands and wings tied."

"Then I wouldn't be making love to you. It would be something else."

"I'm offering it to you freely. Cristóbal must be thinking you are anyway. We've been sharing the same cave for weeks."

"Eat your breakfast."

She held out her bound hands.

"I'm sorry I can't free your hands more often," he said as he untied her.

"I know you think I'll unbind my wings the first chance I get and fly away."

"Of course."

"The truth is with the fire damage to my wings and being bound for so long, I'm not sure if they work anymore."

"I hate it when you say *the truth is*. It means everything else you've said isn't the truth."

"You're being unfair."

"Maybe. Just don't ask me to stroke your wings again. I know what that does to you."

Eleria began spooning the corn into her mouth. "You still haven't told me what your plans are for me. How long do I have to stay in this cave?"

"Cristóbal is the one who has plans for you. It's up to him."

"But you know what they are, don't you? Am I ever going to be released?"

"I'll bring you some tea."

When he returned with a steaming cup from the fire on the ledge outside their cave, she said, "You're always so guarded when you speak to me."

"I have to be."

"No, you don't."

"I think I do, Eleria. Too often with you I find myself saying things, sometimes *thinking* things, that I shouldn't."

"And that disturbs you?"

"Of course, it does. The one thing I've always held onto in my life is that I remain in control of myself."

"But you do want to make love to me, don't you, Héctor?"

"I'm going for a walk. Hurry up and finish your tea so that I can tie your hands again."

Eleria took a sip. "You know what I think? I think you need to stop serving Cristóbal. You don't need to serve anybody."

Héctor glared at her. "Stop it. I know what you're doing."

"What am I doing? Trying to make you value yourself more highly. You're at least as good as Cristóbal at anything. I just don't understand why you serve him like you're not as good as he is."

He grabbed the cup from her and emptied it onto the ground. "Enough," he said. "I don't want to hear your words anymore. No wonder the ñakaqs call your people wind-whisperers."

As he re-tied her hands, she leaned over and kissed him. For a moment when he felt her soft lips on his, he returned the kiss, but then he pulled away and walked outside.

Chapter 67

In the Halls of Demons

Cristóbal gasped as he looked around the giant cavern. Huge ñakaq likenesses in full battle garb glared at him from the stone walls, their faces frozen in a frenzy with intricately carved beards cascading to the ground to form the floor under his feet. High above their heads burnt enormous helmet fires that filled the cave with light and warmth, while smaller lights studded the ceiling and walls, flickering like underground stars. In the distance was a stone bridge connecting to a staircase that descended into the depths.

"So this is one of your Great Halls," said Cristóbal, his eyes wide open as he tried to grasp what he was seeing.

"No," said Tagón, "This is just an antechamber. Come, this way."

Cristóbal followed Tagón over the bridge. Below, a series of staircases, arched bridges and vaults led further and further into the bowels of the mountain. "It looks like we have a long journey ahead of us."

"We do," said Tagón, "but you're looking the wrong way. Down there are our workshops and forges. We're going the other way."

Cristóbal followed the line of Tagón's sight, and he saw a series of staircases leading up well past the giant helmet fires into the upper reaches of the mountain.

"Our Great Halls are hidden well above the ground," said Tagón. "The duendes may live on a mountain, but we live *in* a mountain. Who knows how many times they've unknowingly flown past our home?"

"I'm honored you've brought me here, Tagón."

"Malín made his promise to you that you could have whatever you wanted. And this is what you chose."

"It wasn't *your* promise, Tagón."

"No, but I'm now king, and Malín made his pledge on behalf of all ñakaqs, so I decided I couldn't escape the burden of the oath."

When they commenced their ascent into the mountain, the dark walls changed to ones that glistened with gold. Cristóbal ran his fingers across the surface as he climbed. This was no natural phenomenon. The ñakaqs must have poured molten gold over the natural rock. Shafts of sunlight streamed in through small holes in the mountainside, merging with the glow of countless oil lamps to create a delicate dance reflecting from gilded wall to gilded wall.

"This isn't what I expected," said Cristóbal as they climbed another staircase.

"Like the wind-whisperers, you think that we're not capable of such things?"

"No, no, of course not, but how can anyone know what you're capable of if you keep so much hidden? What you've built here is something I could never have imagined."

They stepped into a vast cavern whose walls were dotted with gemstones of intense indigo, scarlet and crimson. In front of them were a series of steps leading up to a large ornate chair carved into the rock. At the base of the steps stood two ñakaq guards.

"This is the throne chamber," said Tagón.

Cristóbal was shocked when he recognized one of the guards was Malín.

"I'm sorry that I was the cause of you losing your kingship," Cristóbal said after an awkward silence.

"I lost the kingship through my own foolishness," said Malín. "You aren't to blame."

Cristóbal strained his neck to see the stone crown that hung from the ceiling above the chair. "So now you guard the throne you once sat on?"

"The kingship of the ñakaqs is a burden, not a privilege. It would never be given to one who seeks it. I don't think it's ever good to desire command."

"Maybe that's the mistake I made," said Cristóbal.

"I, too, am sorry that I was the reason you lost your command, Cristóbal."

"No, Malín, I also take responsibility for my foolish decisions. Most of them were made long before I saw my first ñakaq."

"Come," said Tagón, "I want you to see our Greatest Hall."

Cristóbal and Malín nodded silent farewells, and Cristóbal followed Tagón across a gem-encrusted bridge. They entered an even bigger cavern with an impossibly high vaulted ceiling, colored crimson so that it looked like the Nueva Tierran sky. Cristóbal turned a full circle, mesmerized. The rock wall was dotted with dozens of openings, each one veiled by a shimmering curtain.

"You seem to always be looking in the wrong direction," said Tagón.

"What do you—" Cristóbal lowered his gaze and saw someone standing next to Tagón.

"This is my wife, Sala," he said.

"I am sorry, but I speak the language of the beardless ones poorly." She smiled shyly. Masses of thick hair framed her large open face. "I'm pleased to finally meet you."

"As am I." Cristóbal embraced her. "It's an honor."

"Perhaps too much of an honor," said Sala, throwing a glance in Tagón's direction. "It is difficult to throw our men from their paths of secrecy. With so few men now, I think we have agreed it is time for a change."

Cristóbal raised his eyebrows. What else was going to be revealed?

"Come sit with us." Tagón pointed to four stone benches forming a square.

After the three sat down, Tagón said, "You've freely chosen to aid us in our war against the wind-whisperers, so it's important that you know the full nature of our enmity."

"The duendes are cold killers without honor," said Cristóbal. "I understand why you have to defend yourselves."

"It's not as simple as it appears," said Tagón, dragging the words from the back of his throat. "Our people came from far beyond the mountains after being driven from our ancestral home by hordes of what we call light-eaters. Our ancient tales speak of a path of escape, which we also knew to be a path of no return."

"You entered Nueva Tierra through an entrada the same way we did?"

"Yes."

This was a surprise. How much more did the ñakaqs have in common with the Spaniards? "And the duendes?"

"The wind-whisperers have always been in these lands."

"Did they see you as invaders?"

"No, Cristóbal. The duendes had not known other beings before we came. They'd always been alone. They had no experiences that allowed them to feel threatened."

"So, you were the ones who attacked?"

"That wasn't our way in those distant times. We were looking for a new home and Nueva Tierra was vast. Since the wind-whisperers lived on the mountain peaks, we asked if we could settle the valleys. We would trade precious metals with them and help build great palaces. There would be peace."

"But there was no peace?"

"At first there was, but it depended on us serving their needs. It was soon clear to our people that the wind-whisperers considered themselves so superior to us that our natural place was to grovel at their feet. There was no exchange as we had agreed, no trade. They treated us with disdain. They didn't age or die while our people fell into illness and frailty. I see now that they saw themselves as gods. They made us feel weak and unworthy, forgetting we had once been a proud people."

"The way they've done with the Incas?"

"Yes, we became their slaves. But then we discovered that it was possible to kill them and we revolted."

"Why are you telling me this tale with a sense of shame, Tagón? There's no dishonor in a revolt against injustice."

"That may be true, but as you've seen, we do nothing by half-measures." Tagón shifted uncomfortably and took a deep breath. "It wasn't just a revolt. It was a massacre. We butchered them in their sleep. We relentlessly pursued those that escaped through the High Palaces and slaughtered every single male wind-whisperer. Our ancestors believed it was the only way they could free themselves. Maybe they were right. The surviving females then branded us what you would call demons and have hunted us ever since. We were forced to find ways of hiding, of moving unseen. Over time we discovered more and more secret paths within our lands."

"Entradas? Huacas?"

Tagón shook his head slowly. "We give them a different name in our tongue. What the beardless ones call huacas lead *into* our lands. The hidden paths we found were ways to move quickly from one place to another *within* our lands. I've taken you through three of them—the last one today to our Great Halls. And in this, the Greatest Hall, we've uncovered more paths than anywhere else. From here we can travel to all the corners of our lands."

"So that's why the duendes haven't been able to defeat you?"

"Yes, we can appear as if from nowhere. Our armies are able to move in ways that seem impossible, and we can swiftly carry the bodies of our fallen to a place where we can honor them." Tagón lowered his eyes. "But there's a price to pay. You see, in fighting the duendes, it was almost as if we were becoming the demons they claimed we were."

"The price?" Cristóbal shivered. Did he really want to know the answer?

Tagón lifted his head. "Look at me. You can see it."

"I..."

"Every time we traveled through one of these hidden paths, we became more twisted, uglier, more misshapen." Tagón swallowed. "At first it was in small, insignificant ways, but over time the deformities multiplied. With each secret path we took, our bodies revealed what we suspected truly lay in our hearts. We were once a race as fair as yours. Now we had become monsters."

Cristóbal reached up to feel the pockmarks on his face. "That's why you were determined to allow yourself to be baptized and prove you weren't demons?"

"Yes, and it's the reason our helmets are so important to us. If we can create a perfection to crown our deformities, then we can't possibly be the monstrosities we appear to be. We always believed that, as long as our people remained alive, we could redeem ourselves."

Tagón hesitated, compulsively running his fingers through his beard. "And for us to hold to that belief, we needed to stop you at all costs. From the moment we saw your army, your war-beasts, and your weapons, we knew that our survival was at stake. You were heading ever closer to the wind-whisperer lands."

"But you gave us no chance."

"We knew what would happen. We'd seen it before. It was inevitable that you would become slaves of the wind-whisperers. Your ground weapons combined with sky attacks meant our very existence was threatened. We had to stop you by any means. It's why we killed the Incan runner. We thought he was showing the way forward for your army."

"And you were right about everything."

Tagón nodded again and glanced at Sala. "Anyway, enough of the past," he said. A female ñakaq approached them, carrying a bundle in her arms. "Let me introduce you to my newborn son."

Chapter 68

El diario de Cristóbal de Varga

Betrayal can numb your soul like the coldest of frosts. I do not accept its bitterness lightly and hope always to have the will to battle the illusive rapture that it promises. Yet I also recognize that loyalty to one must sometimes necessarily mean betrayal of another. And in a world untethered from the certainties of good and evil, where entradas offer stark choices which cannot be undone, I can only hope I have chosen wisely.

So it was that I willfully would contaminate my love for Sarpay and seek an agreement with the duendes so that my men would return to New Spain laden with gold, fulfilling my solemn promise to them and accomplishing all that we had set out to do.

Nonetheless, even as I write these words suffused with duty and honor, I must question whether I am driven by a noble oath with those who entered a new world under my command, or if my most ardent desire is that our tale will now be spoken of whenever the feats of Francisco Pizarro and Hernán Cortés are lauded.

Chapter 69

Unfurling the Demon

As Cristóbal wrote by the faint oil lamp light, his heart beat so furiously he thought Sarpay would hear the pounding and waken. He could barely grasp the grandeur of what Tagón had shown him and the possibilities that now opened for him. Finally, he had found a way forward. His mind whirred. He knew he wouldn't be able to sleep until he wrote the thoughts into his diary. The words tumbled from his quill like a river pouring into a gorge, only stilling when he wrote the last word. He drew several slow breaths and his heartbeat steadied. After closing his diary, he lay down beside Sarpay, feeling her warmth slowly seep into his body. He stroked her hair gently, vaguely aware through the haze of half-sleep, just before he fell into a deep slumber, that she had opened her eyes.

***

Early the next morning, Cristóbal ran his fingers along his jawline as he and Héctor sat by the stream at the far end of the valley. It felt good to be smooth-shaven again after so many months. Finally his plan was clear.

"He took you to the Great Halls?" said Héctor, his eyes wide open.

"Not so loud," said Cristóbal. "No one should know, especially not Sarpay."

"Why?"

Cristóbal's head was bowed. "I plan to tell the duendes that I know where the ñakaq halls are."

Héctor fell silent, eventually saying, "I don't understand."

Cristóbal swallowed, staring at the flowing water. "I'm going to strike a bargain with Ithilia. In exchange, the duendes will carry all the conquistadors home through the salida with more gold than any of us had ever dreamed of."

"You would do this for two hundred men who overthrew your command and attempted to kill you?" Héctor sat back.

"I deserved to be usurped. I betrayed my men's trust in my command, and I have to make amends." Cristóbal looked up at his lieutenant. "Most of all I'm doing this for you, Héctor. You should go home a free and wealthy man, not live here in poverty and captivity."

"But how can you betray the ñakaqs? Tagón and the others will be wiped from the face of Nueva Tierra."

"They won't be. I have a plan. My condition with Ithilia will be that you all need to be safely through the salida before I tell them anything."

Héctor frowned. "Do you think you can just refuse to tell Ithilia? She'll force the secret out of you and the ñakaqs will die anyway."

"Ithilia will try, if she gets the chance, but she won't find out where the Great Halls are...because I don't know. Tagón blindfolded me when he took me there."

Cristóbal saw something in Héctor's face he had never seen before. It was as if his lieutenant was looking at him for the first time.

"Then you'll die here in Nueva Tierra," said Héctor. "You're sacrificing yourself for your conquistadors."

The sound of the stream filled the silence for a long time.

"I...I haven't been a great man." Cristóbal struggled with the words. "It's a matter of honor. I've led these men to this point through my actions. They are my responsibility. I need to do this to make it right."

***

Eleria eyed Cristóbal and Héctor curiously as they entered the cave.

"I need to speak with you," said Cristóbal.

Eleria said, "You could have spoken to me many times since the day you captured me. Why do you have the need now? I see neither of you have brought any food. That is not a good start."

Cristóbal asked, "If we untied your wings, how long would it take you to be able to fly long distances again?"

Her gaze became more intense. "It…could take me a while to regain my full ability. After so long, my muscles have weakened. Why are you asking me?"

"Could you fly tomorrow morning if, say, we unbound them now?"

Eleria looked surprised. "You're going to untie my wings now?"

"And your feet and hands," said Cristóbal.

She cocked her head. "Why? Aren't you afraid I'll escape?"

"I want you to escape."

"So you can kill me while I try and not have it on your conscience?"

"No, so that you can send a message from me to Ithilia."

"A message? Do you want me to tell her where all of you are hiding?"

"She'll be interested to hear that because she, no doubt, believes we're all dead. That's how we made it appear to her when we left the burning valley."

"Why are you telling me this?"

"Ithilia will find out we're alive anyway when you speak to her. We can't stop you telling her, but the message I want you to give her from Capitán Cristóbal de Varga is that I know where the Great Halls of the ñakaqs are located, and I'm prepared to take her there."

"The Great Halls? You've been to them?"

"Yes, and I thought she would be very interested to hear that."

"I suspect she would, Capitán Cristóbal de Varga, and you're going to release me to tell her this?"

"Yes, I want you to fly to the High Palaces as soon as you're able."

"I could carry you there, and you could speak to her yourself."

"No, I want you to give her the message that Héctor and I wish to meet with her in the burnt valley where your people attacked us."

"Ithilia will be suspicious. She will think it's a trap."

"She can bring as many duendes as she wants. We'll meet in the very center of the valley. All the vegetation is burnt. There's nowhere for anyone to hide."

"If I know her, she will first want to see this valley where you are hiding."

"Can you make it clear that there are no ñakaqs living here and that the Incas should be left alone?"

"I can't promise that Ithilia will do anything, Capitán Cristóbal de Varga. What do I say to her that you require in return for this revelation?"

"I want her to carry all the conquistadors to a salida that will allow us to return to our lands."

Eleria turned to Héctor. "You've been silent. Are you the one who is going to free me?"

He nodded.

"Once I leave here, I can say and do whatever I choose," said Eleria. "You're aware of that, aren't you?"

"Of course," said Héctor, "but Ithilia will be intrigued by the offer."

"Now that you know what we want, are you able to fly from here before first light tomorrow?" asked Cristóbal. "I don't want anyone to see you leave."

"You're serious, aren't you?"

"Of course."

"Then if you untie me now, I can test my wings tonight. If they are working well enough, I'll leave before dawn."

"In that case, tell Ithilia we'll meet her in the burnt valley in two days' time." Cristóbal turned to his lieutenant and nodded.

Eleria stared intently into Héctor's eyes. "So, are you going to free me now?"

He knelt beside her and untied her feet first and then her hands. Finally, he reached around her and unwrapped the binding on her wings.

Eleria inhaled deeply and closed her eyes as the binding fell to the ground. She arched her back and flexed her shoulder muscles.

Slowly her wings unfurled.

***

Deep into the night, Eleria silently alighted at the entrance to Héctor's cave and stepped inside, folding her wings behind her back.

"Did anyone see you?" asked Héctor.

"I don't think so. Even if someone happened to look out of their cave, all they would have seen was a glimpse of a shadow."

"And your wings are strong enough to fly to the High Palaces?"

"They've healed well from the fire and are stronger than I thought they would be, but there's one last test I would like to do."

"What's that?"

"I want to see if I can carry you."

"Why?"

"At full strength I could easily have flown you to the High Palaces. I want to see if I can carry your weight."

Héctor held his hand up. "I don't want to be carried."

"Well then you need to wake your capitán."

"I can't do that. It would also wake Sarpay."

"Then it appears the only way I can be certain I can fly in the morning is to see if I can carry you. You're not frightened, are you?"

"No, why would I be frightened?"

"Then, come, if we wait too much longer it will be dawn and I'll have to wait another day." She held out her hand for him.

Héctor nodded reluctantly. "What do you want me to do?"

"Come here and stand just outside the entrance."

He did as Eleria said, and he watched her take off into the night sky, turn, and then fly back so that she was now hovering just above his head.

She said, "Reach out to me with both hands."

Héctor lifted his arms and they grabbed hold of each other by the wrists. The wind of her wings beat at his face as his feet left the ledge. He thought she would bring him back down after suspending him above the ground for a while, but instead she flew higher, the cave entrance receding below.

Eleria's grip was strong, but he felt his fingers slipping slightly. With her wings beating furiously, she pulled him up toward her.

"Wrap your legs around me," she said. "It will be easier."

Héctor felt his fingers slipping a little further, so he did as she said. Once his legs were locked, she released hold of his wrists and wrapped her arms around him, pulling him tightly to her chest.

She had full control over him and he began to panic. She could do whatever she wanted and he was powerless to stop her.

She soared further into the night sky, past the highest cliffs that bounded the valley. He clung to her as she increased speed and stars flashed past them. She swooped and arced, swerving rapidly in one direction and then in another.

Héctor could barely breathe. He struggled to accept what was happening. She flew even faster. One moment she climbed to the stars and the next she plummeted to the ground, looping back up just when he thought they were in freefall. He felt light-headed. The stars wheeled around him. He closed his eyes but still sensed the swift changes in direction as the wind buffeted him from different sides.

"Enough!" he cried. "Enough!" But the vastness of the night sky stole the words.

She held him more tightly. He felt the warmth of her body against his, her powerful arms enveloping him and her heart pounding in her chest as the heavens of Nueva Tierra embraced him.

And when tendrils of light crept over the horizon, Eleria finally arced back down toward their cave and landed gently on the ledge.

She barely looked at him as he untwined his legs and she released him.

"I'm leaving now," she said, without meeting his gaze.

***

Eleria returned to the sky as the stars began to pale. Glancing back, she saw that, although Héctor had already disappeared into his cave, a slender figure now stood outside Cristóbal's cave and was beckoning her. She hesitated for a moment and then turned around.

Chapter 70

Corpse Gold

The bloated late-afternoon sun of Nueva Tierra burnt down on Rodrigo and his conquistadors as they picked their way through the bleached ñakaq skeletons that covered the battlefield outside the abandoned Incan village. While the stench of death had long since dissipated, the work was strenuous, the piles of bones made it difficult for the soldiers to negotiate the valley, and the odor of failure permeated the company.

Rodrigo lifted another helmet and, using his knife, pried out the gold inlay and placed it in the sack slung over his shoulder. This time he accidently cut his thumb, swearing as he tried to stop the flow of blood. He knew he needed to take more care, but it was dispiriting labor and he had grown tired of it.

Carlos and Martín, who were working near him, also stopped.

"Is this our great conquest?" asked Carlos in a defiant tone Rodrigo was hearing more often. "Cutting gold pieces from the helmets of corpses?"

Rodrigo needed to crush the complaint before it spread, especially from someone who had always supported him. The soldiers had already shown they could change their leaders. "Gold is gold," he said. "At least we'll have something to show."

"If we ever get home."

Rodrigo wiped his blood-stained thumb on his shirt and picked up another helmet. "So you want to go back to the ñakaq heartlands and keep searching for their gold source?"

"No, Capitán, but why are we letting the duendes treat us like this? They promised us gold. If they're not going to give it to us, we should take it."

"You want us to take the duende gold by force?"

"Why not?" said Carlos. "Our cannons are here in the village where we left them. Why don't we take from them what they won't give us?"

Rodrigo could see other conquistadors had stopped working and were now waiting on what he was going to say. "You want us to attack them in their High Palaces, you *maldito idiota*? How are we going to get the cannons up there? And even if we kill them all, how would we get back down into the valleys?"

"Anything would be better than this!" Carlos threw the helmet he had been holding away and it clattered against the ñakaq armor that littered the valley floor. "You're frightened of them, aren't you, Capitán?"

"The duendes saved us, remember? Why make them our enemy? They treat us well."

"As long as we don't challenge them like Padre Núñez?"

Rodrigo dug his knife into another gold inset. "I don't know what happened to Padre Núñez."

"Or all the children."

"They were still-born."

"You know what I think, Capitán? I think they've taken away your manhood."

Rodrigo forced out several more gold insets, which fell into a jumble of ñakaq skeletons. He pushed them aside with his sword, chinking bone on bone in his search for the pieces. Anger boiled inside him. He knew Carlos was right.

"You killed Luis because Ithilia made you. I saw it. You know what else I think, Capitán?"

Blood rushed to Rodrigo's face. "I don't want to hear what you think, Carlos. Get back to work."

"We should have just stood up to the duendes from the start, the way Capitán de Varga wanted us to."

Rodrigo glared at him. "You want them as an enemy?" His voice shook.

"The way we're going, we could end up as their slaves."

There was a shout from one of the other men, and Rodrigo looked up to see a duende flying toward them. She circled once and then glided onto the ground in front of Rodrigo. Her nostrils flared and a look of disgust crossed her face. "This valley still reeks of ñakaq after all this time." She kicked one of the skeletons away from her feet. "Ithilia wants you all to prepare to return to the High Palaces tomorrow."

"Tomorrow?" said Rodrigo. "We'll be finished here in a few days."

"She said tomorrow."

"Why?"

The duende looked at him as if he had just asked an insane question. "Be ready by mid-morning. She wants all of you to come. Is that clear?"

"Yes, yes, of course."

With that she spread her wings and took to the sky again.

"This could be our chance," said Carlos after she had gone.

"Enough, Carlos."

"Did you hear how she spoke to you? Are you under Ithilia's command?"

"I said enough."

"Then why not show her? We have the advantage here in the valley. Once we're in their High Palaces, we'll be at their mercy again."

"We will do what Ithilia asks," said Rodrigo between gritted teeth.

"Why don't we ask the others?" Carlos raised his voice. "Why don't we hear what the men say about it. Hey, Martín, do we want to kill the duendes when they come for us?"

Martín had no chance to answer, and Carlos had no time to take another breath because Rodrigo had run his sword through his throat. A faint gurgle erupted from his mouth and he sank to the ground, joining the ñakaq skeletons.

"Are you going to answer Carlos's question?" asked Rodrigo.

Martín shook his head. "I don't think I heard it, Capitán."

Chapter 71

The Bargain of Ashes

The tragedy of the burnt valley extended in all directions as Cristóbal and Héctor waited for Ithilia. Cristóbal could barely comprehend that this charred wasteland was once the most verdant valley in Nueva Tierra. Ash drifts swirled along the ground and tree husks creaked and groaned in the wind.

"Do you think Sarpay believed you?" asked Héctor, scanning the sky for approaching duendes.

"Why wouldn't she? As far as she's concerned, you and I have been invited to the ñakaq Great Halls."

"What did you say to her about Eleria?"

"I told Sarpay that the ñakaqs took her because they wanted to question her."

"I think I see something." Héctor squinted into the distance. "You're convinced Sarpay would try to stop you if she knew your plan?"

"She doesn't want any of us to return to New Spain. That's one thing I'm certain of. She knows Huarcay revealed Vilcabamba's true location in the Amazon."

"So where does your plan leave her?"

Before Cristóbal could answer, a gust of wind blew a flurry of ashes into their faces and they both started coughing. Another gray squall struck them before the air cleared and they struggled for breaths.

When the ash finally settled, they could see a large duende host approaching in the distance.

They watched as the duendes drew closer.

"I pray this will work," said Héctor.

Most of the duende host circled above while Ithilia and several others landed in front of Cristóbal and Héctor.

"Capitán Cristóbal de Varga," said Ithilia, folding her wings. "I thought you were dead."

"As Eleria no doubt told you, your rain of fire wasn't quite as successful as you were led to believe."

"It appears we were tricked, something we would not expect from the ñakaqs. I wonder how much was your work."

"Maybe you underestimate them, Ithilia."

"Or perhaps it's you who I shouldn't underestimate. I have to tell you I am not at all pleased to hear that despite everything, the last sixty-three ñakaqs are still alive."

"And having more children."

Ithilia scowled as she glanced across the blackened landscape. "Then who were the ñakaqs whose corpses we found here?"

Cristóbal said, "I'll reveal all the ñakaq secrets I know once we've struck a bargain."

"Eleria tells me you claim to know where the Great Halls are."

"I've seen them."

She nodded in the direction of Héctor. "And you, do you also know where they are?"

"He hasn't seen them," said Cristóbal. "The ñakaqs entrusted only me."

"Can he not speak for himself?"

"My name is Lieutenant Héctor Valiente and, like you, I have no knowledge of the Great Halls."

"I see, so you are unimportant to me."

"But Héctor *is* important to me," said Cristóbal.

"So, Capitán Cristóbal de Varga, how will you prove to me that you know where the Great Halls are?"

"I can't prove it to you without giving away the location. That's why I'll remain behind and take you to them *after* my men have returned to New Spain."

"And why do you need my people to return to your lands?"

"The salida back to our world is high above a lake of molten gold."

"Molten gold?"

"Yes, we call it the Boca D'oro. It's another of the secrets shown to us by the ñakaqs. The source of their gold."

Ithilia eyed Cristóbal up and down. "No one else has ever been told these secrets. I don't understand why the ñakaqs have chosen to reveal these things to you."

"Because they've grown to trust me."

A twisted smile crossed Ithilia's flawless face. "It appears their trust is misplaced."

"I want to finally end my campaign," said Cristóbal, looking Ithilia in the eyes. "I want my men to have their fill of gold and finally go home as we had always planned. They followed my command because that's what I promised them, and that promise is what I want to fulfill."

"You keep talking of your *men*, yet I see only one soldier here."

"Those who Lieutenant Benalcázar claims command over are my men. I brought them here to Nueva Tierra, and they are my responsibility.

"And Rodrigo?"

"I'll strip him of his rank, and he'll return with us to New Spain to stand trial as a prisoner."

Ithilia gave a signal to the circling duendes. "How much easier would it have been, Capitán Cristóbal de Varga, if you had simply done what I asked of you when we first met?"

"Sometimes the tortuous path is the one best taken. If I had done your bidding, I would not have found the gold source or the way home, and you would not have the chance to kill the ñakaq wives and children and sack the Great Halls."

"Then as it turns out, the events have been fortunate to us both."

"It appears that way, Ithilia. Do we have a bargain?"

"Yes, we have a bargain, Capitán Cristóbal de Varga." She stepped toward him, bending down to touch foreheads.

"Will you take us to my men now?"

"You sacrificed the chance for me to carry you when we first met," said Ithilia. "You can't imagine how much pleasure it gives me to do so now."

She wrapped her arms around him and lifted him off the ground.

One of the other duendes stepped toward Héctor as another ash-squall hit them and he started choking.

Chapter 72

The Two Lieutenants

Cristóbal's eyes followed the raging torrent below as he and Ithilia passed over the gorge, and the valley came into view. Past the outskirts of the Incan village lay jumbled piles of bones and armor, gleaming in the sun, while in the village square stood two hundred conquistadors, each holding a sack and looking up at the approaching duendes. As Cristóbal drew closer, he tried to pinpoint the exact moment when the realization dawned on Rodrigo that he and Héctor were with the duende host.

When he landed and Ithilia released him, he saw the shocked looks on the soldier's faces, none of them more stunned than Rodrigo who stared at him in utter disbelief.

"I have returned to renew my command, Lieutenant Benalcázar," said Cristóbal.

"You no longer have a command," said Rodrigo, finding his voice, "and you forget it's now *Capitán* Benalcázar."

"Calling yourself Capitán doesn't make you one."

"And wearing armor doesn't make you a conquistador."

"So, what mighty battles have you fought since you took command from me, Lieutenant Benalcázar? You've chased defenseless Incan villagers along a river. You attempted an assault on a tree-covered valley that was abandoned before it started. And now it appears you're here picking through the bones of long-dead ñakaqs searching for scraps of gold."

Cristóbal addressed the conquistadors. "From the beginning of this campaign, I undertook to bring great fortune to each of you. I'm here now to finally fulfill my promise. You will have all the gold you can carry because I am going to lead you to the ñakaq gold source."

He pointed to the discarded helmets littered across the village. "It looks like you've been scratching gold inlays from ñakaq armor. Don't bother bringing your sacks with blood-stained nuggets when we leave. Where I'm leading you, you will see more pure gold than you've ever dreamed of."

"You lie," said Rodrigo, spitting on the ground.

"We shall see." Cristóbal smiled. "And that isn't all that you'll see. There's no point to being laden with gold if we never see our homes again. I've found a salida back to our world."

Several conquistadors gasped.

"Come with me now and I'll show you. You don't have to accept my word. The duendes will take us to where we can have our fill of gold and then carry us home."

"Don't believe him," said Rodrigo. "He's the one that led us into this trap."

"And now I'm going to be the one who will lead us out."

Rodrigo looked around anxiously as the conquistadors unsheathed their blades. "I'm your leader," he cried. "I'm your capitán."

"Disarm him," said Cristóbal. "He will stand trial in Lima for his crimes."

Rodrigo implored Ithilia. "Why would you believe this *malparido*? Are you going to let him do this?"

"You've been a disappointment to me," she said, looking away.

Several conquistadors now surrounded him.

"What are you doing?" said Rodrigo, brandishing his sword. "Don't let him fool you. He'll only lead you deeper into disaster."

As they drew closer, Rodrigo grew more agitated, his head flicking from one soldier to the other. "Who of you thinks you're a better swordsman than I am?" He looked into the eyes of one of them. "Is it you, Martín?" He laughed, moving on to the next face. "What about you, Hernando? Or you, Juan? Or you, Miguel?"

None of the soldiers moved.

"So no one believes they are a better swordsman than I am?" Rodrigo grimaced. "Maybe if all of you came at me at once, one of you might survive. What do you think? Maybe it will be the one who attacks me from behind." He swung right around to face the soldier who had been at his back. "Who will that be?"

The conquistadors now glanced nervously at each other and started backing away.

"Anyone else?" cried Rodrigo. "Is there anyone here who thinks they can defeat me?"

Cristóbal stepped through the circle of soldiers with his sword drawn. "I'll make sure you face justice for what you've done."

"Ah, the honorable Cristóbal de Varga comes at me without his crossbow." Rodrigo smiled an ugly smile as he raised his sword. "Another foolish decision."

"Wait!" shouted Héctor as he pushed his way through to the front. "You want to know who believes themselves to be a better swordsman than you. Here I am."

"Lieutenant Valiente, this is my battle," said Cristóbal.

"No, Capitán, it's mine." With that he stepped so close to Rodrigo that he was just beyond sword's reach and stared him down. "You gave me no chance to defend myself when you put me in chains."

"You were never free. Once a slave always a slave."

Cristóbal shouted, "Lieutenant Valiente, I order you to step back."

"Go ahead," said Rodrigo, "follow your master."

"Lieutenant Valiente, I said step back."

Héctor clenched the hilt of his sword, his knuckles whitening.

Cristóbal could see in his lieutenant's face he wasn't going to follow his command this time. It was as if all the anger he had buried for so long now came screaming to the surface.

Héctor thrust his sword suddenly at Rodrigo who fell back to avoid the strike. Héctor then moved forward stabbing and slicing as Rodrigo frantically defended from the ground.

"I should have expected you wouldn't fight like a conquistador," cried Rodrigo as he parried. "You know you can't best me in a fair sword fight."

Héctor lowered his sword. "Stand up!"

Rodrigo slowly got to his feet. The sneer had returned to his face.

Héctor beckoned him forward. "Let's see who is the better conquist—"

Before Héctor had finished the word, Rodrigo lunged at him, cutting him in the shoulder with a sudden thrust. Héctor looked down and saw blood welling from a deep gash. Before the pain hit him, he swung his blade furiously in response, forcing the still smiling lieutenant back.

As Héctor pursued him, Rodrigo threw one of the sacks of gold inlays at him, knocking him off balance. Rodrigo then leaped at him with both hands on his sword, but Héctor rolled away and Rodrigo stabbed the ground.

Just as Rodrigo regained his balance, Héctor got to his feet, and they glared at each other.

This time they both swung together and the clash of their swords rang through the air. They fought furiously without either of them gaining ascendency. Héctor's shoulder ached each time the blades jarred, and he knew he was losing strength in his arm. Before long Rodrigo would push through his defenses.

Wincing again as their blades struck, he knew he needed to do something drastic. A battle of attrition wasn't going to end well for him.

Héctor slowed his thrusts to draw Rodrigo in, and he took the bait, moving into position to finish the battle. Héctor seized his chance, grabbed his sword with both hands and swung at the unsuspecting Rodrigo with all his might, knocking his rival's weapon from his hand.

In a single fluid motion Héctor lunged at the disarmed lieutenant and held his blade against his throat. "I may not be a better conquistador, Rodrigo," he said, "but I know I'm a better man."

He kicked the sword out of Rodrigo's reach, then sheathed his own blade. "Someone tie him up quickly. I don't want to look at him any longer."

As Héctor walked away, Martín rushed from the circle of soldiers toward Rodrigo brandishing his knife and crying, "This is for burning Luis." Before he could stab him, Cristóbal grabbed his arm and stopped Martín from plunging his blade into Rodrigo's throat.

"Under my command," said Cristóbal, "no conquistador murders another conquistador. No matter what the crime." He pointed his sword at Rodrigo. "Lieutenant Benalcázar will return to New Spain as a prisoner to stand trial."

He surveyed the faces of his men as Rodrigo was bound. "Those of you who do not want to be under my command, leave now. I don't want to lead anyone who does not want to be led by me. For the rest of you, I want each of you to take a ñakaq helmet. You'll need them at the Boca D'oro. And when the helmets are so heavy with gold you can barely hold them, you're all going home."

Chapter 73

The Salida

Stretching out below, Cristóbal saw the endless sharp-toothed mountain range of Nueva Tierra, while above him the sky bled red across its vast canvas. Instead of the exhilaration he expected, this flight across the crimson heavens evoked a profound sense of calm he had not felt since he had entered this strange world. Soon it would all be over, the striving, the ceaseless struggle. He had set in train a course of action that now couldn't be reversed. All the decisions in his life came down to this moment. Here at the head of the duende host, being carried by Ithilia, he felt perversely comforted that there was nothing else he could do, no more choices he needed to make.

He pointed the way to the mist-veiled peak looming up ahead that concealed the Boca D'oro. Turning his head, he saw hundreds of wings glinting like shards of sunlight, a host of duendes, each carrying a conquistador who in turn held a ñakaq helmet, with the bound Rodrigo at the rear. The duendes flew through the cloud-line and the fiery lake came into view. Although Cristóbal had seen the Boca D'oro before, it hadn't been from above, and he drew in a sharp breath at the sight of it. The molten surface boiled and raged, and countless golden spears traced spectacular curves above the surface.

Cristóbal indicated a safe landing area on the rocky shore some distance away, and two-by-two, duende and conquistador touched ground.

The air was still. As all the conquistadors other than the scowling Rodrigo were released, Cristóbal said, "Welcome to the Boca D'oro."

"You spoke the truth, Capitán Cristóbal de Varga," said Ithilia.

"I'm surprised you doubted me."

A lance of gold shot their way and landed in front of them.

A conquistador walked toward the lake with his fire helmet in position to scoop the molten gold directly but was forced back by the heat.

"Watch!" shouted Cristóbal, and he took the helmet and showed the others how to catch the golden rain. Then he sat down and viewed the scene before him.

With looks of fevered joy on their faces, the conquistadors zigzagged in all directions. They frantically captured the gold, at times crashing into each other and narrowly avoiding being struck by the scorching liquid. Even in the full bloom of their disease, as they struggled for breath, their chests heaving and their arms trembling under the increasing weight of the helmets, the conquistadors continued running for the molten arcs. And when the bliss that shimmered from their eyes dwindled into little more than a glassy grimace of determination, still they staggered on, striving to capture the next spear of gold before it hit the ground.

The duendes were unmoved by what they saw. They stood together far away from the gold's reach and watched the scene impassively, occasionally speaking among themselves in their wind-blown tongue. Did they not understand the value of gold?

When Héctor joined him, Cristóbal saw his lieutenant's helmet was almost empty.

"That's not going to be enough when you get home," said Cristóbal.

"I know."

"Well don't just sit here. The wind's springing up. The salida might appear any moment."

Héctor stared at the scene in front of them. "I'm not going back."

"What? This is the only chance you'll ever have of reaching New Spain."

"I don't know if New Spain was ever my home."

Cristóbal grabbed him by the shoulder and looked him straight in the eyes. "You need to leave."

Héctor pulled away. "Eleria wants me to stay."

"Eleria?" Cristóbal could barely comprehend what he was hearing. "*Eleria?* You've seen enough of these duendes to know you can't take anything they say at face value."

"I think I know her enough to believe her."

"How can you know her, Héctor? She's been your prisoner. How can you trust what she's said to you?"

"You trust Tagón, don't you? He was your prisoner."

"That's different." He grabbed Héctor again. "I've seen enough of these duende to know they are powerful women. What's she done to you?"

"Nothing, Cristóbal, nothing." He pushed him away.

"I shouldn't have let you keep her in the cave with you."

"No, Cristóbal, you're wrong. She was always just my prisoner."

"Then why listen to her."

"She's begged me to stay with her."

"Begged? I don't think duendes beg. If it feels like they're begging, then it's almost certainly something else." Cristóbal gritted his teeth. "I'm ordering you to leave, Lieutenant Valiente."

Héctor shook his head. "No, Cristóbal, I can't accept that order. This is a world where I can make my own decisions. I don't need you to grant my freedom. I'm staying."

Just then a gust of wind cleared the smoke above the Boca D'oro to again reveal a window to a snow-lined slope under a fragile blue sky.

"There it is!" cried Cristóbal, jumping to his feet. "The salida."

Chapter 74

The Final Conquest

The conquistadors stopped running, placing their helmets on the ground and staring dumbstruck at the vision that materialized mid-air, as if someone had torn the sky with a blade to reveal what lay behind it.

"Come, before it disappears," said Cristóbal, gesturing the soldiers in the direction of the duendes. "It's time to go home."

Carrying their helmets, the conquistadors ran toward the duendes, who also stared in awe through the window to a world unlike their own.

Cristóbal and Héctor joined Ithilia.

"These white-capped mountains and blue skies are your world?" she asked.

"Yes, but if this is anything like the entrada we used to come in, once you go through, you won't be able to come back, so your people should take my men just close enough so they can jump through."

Ithilia gave the duendes a series of commands in her wind-blown tongue.

"Héctor says he won't be going," said Cristóbal.

"I know."

Cristóbal watched each of the duendes grasp a soldier carrying a gold-laden helmet, and spreading their giant wings, begin their flight across the lake. Each duende appeared to struggle at first, coping with the extra weight of gold, but they soon climbed high enough to be out of reach of the gilded spears.

It was as if a great weight had been lifted from Cristóbal's heart. The burden of a lifetime seemed to dissipate. He wanted to savor this, his moment of triumph. And in that moment, Diego was with him again.

Finally, cousin. We've finally done it.

Diego opened his mouth to answer him but his words sounded strange, and Cristóbal realized Ithilia was shouting a series of breath-filled commands now that the leading conquistadors had almost reached the salida.

What happened next was the stuff of the most evil nightmare. With conquistador cries echoing across the heavens, Cristóbal and Héctor were disarmed and bound, so that all they could do was watch the horror unfold.

With the window to New Spain in sight, the duendes released their grips on the conquistadors so that they plummeted from the sky. Some of the Spaniards desperately tried to grab hold of the duendes carrying them, while others reached for their swords. But without exception, they all plunged into the seething lake.

One by one they fell, clawing manically for an invisible ladder.

One by one they fell, screaming wordless screams.

And one by one the screams fell into silence.

Rodrigo was the last. Despite his bound hands, he momentarily rose to the surface like the gilded statue of a shrieking man, only to sink again, never to emerge. And just as his final cry was smothered, the smoke gathered and the salida vanished from view once more.

Cristóbal's throat tightened with each death until he was choking, unable to breathe. Impossible. It couldn't be happening. He struggled like a madman against the cords that bound him. What had they done? What had *he* done?

Ithilia smiled as the duendes returned from the lake and landed on the shore. "Your men should be grateful, Capitán de Varga. I have given them the baptism they so desperately desire."

Cristóbal gasped for air. "How...could you do this? I've promised you the greatest ñakaq secret of all."

"You lied," said Ithilia. "You don't know where the Great Halls are. You were going to sacrifice yourself to allow your conquistadors to go home."

"How could you have known?" Cristóbal's legs buckled, a storm raging through his head.

"I knew everything from the beginning, Capitán Cristóbal de Varga."

He looked across at Héctor who had also collapsed. His eyes were blank and haunted, like they had been blinded by the horror they had seen.

"Let Héctor go. He wasn't a part of the plan."

"I don't believe that." She called out, "Eleria!" and the duende flew out of the clouds that clung to the mountainside below. She was carrying someone, and they both landed in front of Cristóbal.

"Sarpay?"

She had tears in her eyes and could barely meet his gaze. "I'm sorry, Cristóbal. I told Eleria about your plans before she left the cave."

"You're sorry?" What was she saying? *"You're sorry?"*

"I...had to tell the duendes."

Cristóbal shook his head to clear confusion. "So you've betrayed me a second time? First, you imprison us all and now you make sure we die?"

"No...no one was supposed to die..." She reached toward Cristóbal, but he shrank back.

"Why didn't you just slit all our throats when we were drugged? It would have been more honest. At least then you couldn't pretend you didn't kill us."

Sarpay was trembling. "You must have known I couldn't let any of you return to New Spain when all of you knew the true location of Vilcabamba. Everything I've done would have been for nothing. You of all people should be able to understand, Cristóbal."

This time Sarpay had truly destroyed his last chance of achieving his life's work.

"You have to understand, Cristóbal. Please. You've seen what's happened to my people here in Nueva Tierra. They're weak. I thought the Incas could build an empire wherever they were because they were superior. I know now that's not true. If Vilcabamba is found, the Spanish will rule us, and our empire will disappear forever. I couldn't let that happen. Not even for love."

Cristóbal barely heard the last word as he slumped slowly to the ground. Now it had all vanished. His command. His ambition. His dream. Even his honor. There was nothing left. It was as if he had passed through the shimmering veil once more, but this time it had twisted and deformed everything inside him.

"Ithilia has promised not to harm you," said Sarpay.

"Does it matter? There's nothing left of me."

"I won't be harming you," said Ithilia. "You will enjoy your time attending to me in our High Palaces."

"I for one won't be attending to anyone," said Héctor, glaring at Eleria who looked away.

"That wasn't our agreement, Ithilia," said Sarpay angrily. "You can't take either of them as servants."

"They will come to no harm," said Ithilia. "That was all I promised."

Sarpay reached out to Cristóbal again, and this time he let her touch him for a moment before he pulled away. "I *am* truly sorry," she said. "I wanted us to be together."

"So did I..." He looked into her eyes. "What I don't understand is how you knew of my plans."

"You taught me to read Spanish, remember? The words were in your diary."

A succession of whistling sounds suddenly pierced the air, and a volley of weighted nets shot toward the duendes from the downslope clouds, pinning everyone to the ground. The duendes hissed in a wild panic, but the more they struggled, the more their wings became entangled in the mesh.

Then several hundred armed ñakaqs, mostly female, emerged from hiding and threatened the trapped duendes with their horcas, so that they stopped thrashing.

With Malín's help, Tagón cut Cristóbal, Héctor and Sarpay loose.

Cristóbal retrieved his sword. "At least one part of our plan worked."

"I wish I could take some credit," said Tagón, "but you know all my instincts were to hide, not attack."

To Cristóbal's surprise Tiso stood with the ñakaqs, brandishing a crossbow. The two nodded to each other.

Eleria tried to reach out for Héctor as they walked past. "Help me," she pleaded, but Héctor couldn't meet her gaze.

"So you finally have us," said Ithilia, glaring at them through the netting.

"Yes," said Tagón, "but there are more in your High Palaces, aren't there?"

"Of course."

"And they'll avenge your deaths."

"With every breath."

"And the war will continue."

"As always."

Sarpay indicated the tangled mass of duendes covering the shore of the deadly lake. "What will be their fate?"

Sala stepped forward and stood next to her husband. "Something different this time. The killing is over."

Turning toward Ithilia, Tagón said, "My wife has convinced me that the wisest course is to end the deaths. We've all sworn an oath never to kill your people again. And you know us well. We'll hold fast to that oath for eternity."

"An oath?" said Ithilia, her eyes wide in surprise. "Then we will swear our own oath in return."

"Ah, but we know your word can't be trusted, so your oaths are meaningless."

"We can change."

"No, you can't change. At least not without help."

"So what will you do? Are you going to release us?"

"No, but we'll leave you to untangle yourselves, by which time we'll be long hidden again." Tagón stepped closer clutching his horca. "But there's something we're going to do first."

Ithilia shifted anxiously under the netting.

Tagón said, "We are not demons, and you are not gods. The Spanish have given me the words to make this clear for both of us."

"What are you going to do?"

"Make certain you can never think of yourself as a god again, Ithilia."

He raised his horca.

"No...not my wings..."

Chapter 75

The Quipu's Tale

Cristóbal sat by his fire in the burnt valley, the swollen sun casting cold light across the open pages on his lap. These days he spent more time reading his diary than writing it, enjoying the silence of its words echoing in his head— a sure sign his greatest deeds were now behind him. He shivered, shifting closer to the fire. Nueva Tierra had surprised him again over the last months, with seasons he didn't expect.

A noise distracted him and he looked up. It was good to hear the birds returning. All around him green was battling the ash-black that dominated the valley. He had no doubt which would be victorious. Eventually a canopy would cover the valley again.

"So you're still happy alone?"

It was Sarpay. She walked toward him holding a quipu. He was a little surprised how good it felt to hear her voice again.

"I often see Tagón," he said. "And Héctor visits, but he has his own life."

Sarpay nodded in the direction of Cristóbal's hut. "You've done well. It could pass for an Inca home."

"It's not perfect. I've never been much of a builder, but I wanted to see what I could do without help."

He offered a spot by the fire and Sarpay sat down next to him.

"I see you're still writing your diary."

"Well, reading about great battles and great regrets, anyway."

"Am I one of the battles or one of the regrets?"

Cristóbal smiled. "You said long ago that our battles were over and we needed each other. Maybe I should have listened to you." He gestured at the quipu. "It looks like you've been busy."

Sarpay held up the mass of colored knots. "I've been trying to tell my story. Like you."

"Your tale must be very different to mine."

"You might be surprised how much they have in common." She looked up at him. "Do you want me to teach you how to read it?"

Cristóbal nodded slowly. "There's something I need to do first." He started riffling through the pages of his diary.

"What are you looking for?" asked Sarpay.

"Ah, here it is." He grabbed the page, tore it from his journal and threw it in the fire.

They both watched it curl to ash in silence.

"Only one page?" asked Sarpay.

"Yes, only one."

"Which regret was it?"

"It was the page where I revealed the true location of Vilcabamba."

The ashes fragmented into pieces and floated away.

Cristóbal and Sarpay leaned into each other.

Chapter 76

El diario de Cristóbal de Varga

The inevitable conclusion that I will never return to New Spain, let alone to Spain itself, has seared my soul, but after so many years, I have become resigned to it. And it is through my resignation that I have celebrated the only true conquest, the conquest over the flaws and obsessions with which you imprison yourself. I take some comfort in my nightly solitude that I never betrayed my friends. As a young man, I had always believed it was the outcomes of battles that determine a conquistador's life. I cannot say that I still hold this to be true. Perhaps the decision not to enter a battle is of greater importance. I have learned many things in Nueva Tierra.

So it is that a man chooses both his demons and his angels, lives by his decisions, and then ultimately dies by them. Nothing will return those whom I commanded to any world that I have ever visited, nothing will right the deaths I have caused through my actions, and nothing will truly ease the pains in my heart. I can only bring my story to a close, as I have done in these, my final years, in the hope that someone may one day read it and take some truth from its pages.

I was once given to consider that which in life I most fervently strove for. In the honesty of my old age, I now accept that the answer does not lie in the command of men, nor in the honor my father held above all else. No, I now understand with the certainty of all my glorious and pitiful experiences that I value above all else that my words are heard. Even if no one saw the condor disappear, it existed.

And so, I long ago made peace with Sarpay who, while being an enemy to my cause, remained an ally to my true conquest, and as proof of the love which bound us, I tore Vilcabamba's truth from these pages. Tomorrow I will, with the aid of those who have ultimately remained loyal to me, Héctor and Tagón, climb the slopes to the Boca D'oro a final time. There I will tie this account I have so painstakingly written to a bolt, using Sarpay's quipu, and when the smoke clears over the golden lake and the salida appears, I will aim Diego's crossbow at the vision. And, if my aim is true, our tales will arc unscathed over the gilded fires and reach the blue skies of New Spain.

Dirk Strasser's epic fantasy trilogy *The Books of Ascension*— *Zenith*, *Equinox* and *Eclipse*—was published in German and English, and his short stories have been translated into several European languages. "The Doppelgänger Effect" appeared in the World Fantasy Award-winning anthology *Dreaming Down Under*. He is the co-editor of Australia's premiere science-fiction and fantasy magazine, *Aurealis*. Dirk was born in Germany but has lived most of his life in Australia. He has written a series of best-selling school textbooks, trekked the Inca trail to Machu Picchu and studied Renaissance history. "Conquist" was first published as a short story in the anthology *Dreaming Again*. The serialized version of *Conquist* was a finalist in the Aurealis Awards Best Fantasy Novel category. Dirk's screenplay version of *Conquist* won the Wildsound Fantasy/Sci-Fi Festival Best Scene Reading Award and was a featured finalist in the Cinequest Film & Creativity Festival and the Creative World Awards.

The Books of Ascension by Dirk Strasser

Zenith: The First Book of Ascension

Imagine
A mountain so great it takes a year to travel from base to summit
A sun so powerful it drives you into madness if you look at it
An ascent so vital it determines the fate of the world
A summit so precious it holds the key to the divine

The world of the great Mountain is unstable. Giant pillars erupt from the surface and yawning chasms form unpredictably underfoot. Since the Maelir first stood on its slopes in the distant past, they have sought to still its anger and control its power. Each year, twin brothers are chosen to make a perilous journey to the summit. If they survive they will be witness to Zenith, and the secrets will be revealed to them.

When Atreu and Teyth embark on their Ascent, their Talismans lead them onto conflicting paths that will ultimately set brother against brother. And this time the Ascent itself is in peril as unknown forces that have long craved the power of Zenith will stop at nothing to make it their own…even if it means destroying the very thing that sustains all life — the Mountain itself.

Equinox: The Second Book of Ascension

Can you see the story breathing?
The Keep
The most beautiful city on the great Mountain
The pinnacle of Maelir culture
The home of the Inner Sanctum
The place where secrets hide

The fate of the Mountain hangs in the balance at the time of Equinox, and even the Keep can no longer remain untouched. The Maelir are desperate to defend it, the Faemir to demolish it, the windriders to claim it. But unknown to them all, a dark force has already emerged from the chaos to seize power.

As Atreu and Verlinden strive to decipher the power of the Talisman that has defined Atreu's Ascent, Teyth and Valkyra are locked in a desperate battle that neither of them can win. At a time when darkness and light are in perfect equilibrium, when Maelir and Faemir must find a way to break the deadlock and avoid annihilation, the world's fate lies in the Book of Ascension.

Eclipse: The Lost Book of Ascension

Can you still see the story breathing?
What happens if after the winter solstice, the days keep getting shorter?
And shorter?
Until there is an eternal night?
What happens as the darkness grows?
And the creatures of dusk take control of the Mountain?
And the quest for the third Book is the only hope?

The Mountain is in its death throes as the Nazir send their wraiths to finish what the dusk-rats and grale had begun. Soon there will be no daylight to protect the Maelir and Faemir, and with each twilight there are fewer places to hide. Will the Mountain finally collapse under its own instability or will Atreu and Verlinden's descent find the words of salvation in the Lost Book of Ascension?

From the Author: Thank you for purchasing *Conquist*. I really hope that you derived as much from reading this book as I have in creating it. If you have a few moments, please feel free to add your review of the book to your favorite online site for feedback. Also, if you would like to connect with other books that I have coming in the near future, please visit my website for news on upcoming works and recent blog posts: http://www. dirkstrasser.com/ and follow me on Twitter: @DirkStrasser. Regards, Dirk Strasser

ROUNDFIRE
BOOKS

FICTION

Put simply, we publish great stories. Whether it's literary or popular, a gentle tale or a pulsating thriller, the connecting theme in all Roundfire fiction titles is that once you pick them up you won't want to put them down.
If you have enjoyed this book, why not tell other readers by posting a review on your preferred book site.

The Cause

Roderick Vincent

The second American Revolution will be a fire lit from
an internal spark.

Paperback: 978-1-78279-763-0 ebook: 978-1-78279-762-3

Don't Drink and Fly

The Story of Bernice O'Hanlon: Part One

Cathie Devitt

Bernice is a witch living in Glasgow. She loses her way in
her life and wanders off the beaten track looking for the garden
of enlightenment.

Paperback: 978-1-78279-016-7 ebook: 978-1-78279-015-0

Gag

Melissa Unger

One rainy afternoon in a Brooklyn diner, Peter Howland punctures
an egg with his fork. Repulsed, Peter pushes the plate away
and never eats again.

Paperback: 978-1-78279-564-3 ebook: 978-1-78279-563-6

The Master Yeshua

The Undiscovered Gospel of Joseph

Joyce Luck

Jesus is not who you think he is. The year is 75 CE. Joseph ben Jude
is frail and ailing, but he has a prophecy to fulfil …

Paperback: 978-1-78279-974-0 ebook: 978-1-78279-975-7

On the Far Side, There's a Boy
Paula Coston
Martine Haslett, a thirty-something 1980s woman, plays hard on the fringes of the London drag club scene until one night which prompts her to sign up to a charity. She writes to a young Sri Lankan boy, with consequences far and long.
Paperback: 978-1-78279-574-2 ebook: 978-1-78279-573-5

Tuareg
Alberto Vazquez-Figueroa
With over 5 million copies sold worldwide, *Tuareg* is a classic adventure story from best-selling author Alberto Vazquez-Figueroa, about honour, revenge and a clash of cultures.
Paperback: 978-1-84694-192-4

Readers of ebooks can buy or view any of these bestsellers by clicking on the live link in the title. Most titles are published in paperback and as an ebook. Paperbacks are available in traditional bookshops. Both print and ebook formats are available online.

Find more titles and sign up to our readers' newsletter at http://www.johnhuntpublishing.com/fiction

Follow us on Facebook at https://www.facebook.com/JHPfiction and Twitter at https://twitter.com/JHPFiction